Slinn.
Little.
CARTER.

TIME PASSES TIME

It is 1941 and the Second World War is in full swing. Young Theresa Crompton is left devastated after giving up her illegitimate child and joins the Special Operations Executive. Her mission is to assist a Resistance group run by the handsome Pierre Reuben and it is not long before they fall in love. In London, 1963, an older Theresa is haunted by her experiences during the war. Meanwhile, her long-lost children are seeking answers. Will Theresa be reunited with them and reconcile herself with the past, before it is too late?

TIME PASSES TIME

TIME PASSES TIME

by

Mary Wood

Magna Large Print Books
Long Preston, North Yorkshire,
BD23 4ND, England.

British Library Cataloguing in Publication Data.

Wood, Mary
    Time passes time.

    A catalogue record of this book is
    available from the British Library

    ISBN   978-0-7505-4014-8

First published in Great Britain by
Pan Macmillan Publishers Limited 2013

Copyright © Mary Wood 2013

Cover illustration © Gordon Crabb by arrangement with
Alison Eldred

The right of Mary Wood to be identified as the author of this work has
been asserted by her in accordance with the Copyright, Designs and
Patents Act, 1988

Published in Large Print 2014 by arrangement with
Pan Macmillan Publishers Limited

Magna Large Print is an imprint of Library Magna Books Ltd.

Printed and bound in Great Britain by
T.J. (International) Ltd., Cornwall, PL28 8RW

Dedicated to my wonderful husband, Roy, for his belief in me and for his encouragement during this long journey to realizing my dream. His love has helped me to reach the top of my mountain. Thank you.

Author's Note

The characters in *Time Passes Time* are fictitious. Their involvement in events that took place during the Second World War is a product of the author's imagination. No likeness to any person is intended. At all times the author had respect and admiration, and many times cried over her research, for those who served as Special Operations Executives (SOEs), especially those who were executed, and for all who fought so valiantly to bring peace to the world.

'Lest we forget'

One

War is a Tangled Memory Linked to the Present

Theresa – London 1963

'Hey, let go, you old hag...'

Theresa staggered. The hooded young men in front of her grabbed at her bag. Fear paralysed her. Unreleased screams filled her head... *My secrets... Oh, God!*

Images flashed into her memory, but faded away into a haze of confusion as she tried to decipher the snippets of information that her brain managed to filter. She struggled to make sense of them and to separate *the now* from *the past*. Her fragile mind had little capacity to give her reality, having never recovered from the mental breakdown she'd suffered after the suicide of Terence, her twin brother, in 1958. And now it took her back in time, compounding her fear as she desperately sought for answers: *What's happening? Are they SS?*

Frail, and old beyond her years, every bone in her body hurt. The sockets of her arms burned as she fought valiantly. *Stay quiet,* she told herself. *Name and number only... Don't give in.*

A sudden thought trembled a deeper dread through her. The training officer of the Special Operations Executive had warned, 'If caught, you may be subjected to torture.' He'd listed several

11

possibilities, but one had stuck in her mind: 'Sometimes they resort to pulling out your fingernails...'

Her terror of this often catapulted her from sleep in the middle of the night. How close she'd come to such a fate! Betrayed and captured, she'd felt the chafing of the irons that had held her and had sweated the cold sweat of terror as she'd thought her fate the same as her fellow SOE officers, Eliane, Yolande, Madeleine and Noor. Just saying their names was an honour, as they were the bravest women she'd ever known. The Germans had captured and executed them. After forcing the women to kneel in pairs, they had shot them in the head.

With these thoughts intensifying her fear, the cloying darkness of the cell the Germans had thrown her into enclosed her once more, as did the desperate feeling of being alone. Alone and about to die.

Was it happening again? Were these Nazis? Had they found her? Would she tell them what she knew? *Please, God, help me not to...*

'For fuck's sake! She's got some strength for an old 'un.'

'What's that she said? Did she call us *Nazi bastards?* The bleedin' old cow...'

Theresa's head flew back with the force of the blow. Her fingers felt the cold pavement slab but could not prevent her fall. A boot hovered over her hand.

'Give us yer bag, you stupid old witch. Let go...'

The boot came down. Bones cracked. '14609, Theresa Laura Crompton, Officer...'

12

'Christ, she's bleedin' mad. She's saying something about being an officer. Ha, she must be ninety-odd. Fucking officer, my arse. This is 1963, you stupid old bat! Get her bag, quick, she's let go of it. Come on, leg it.'

Pain seared her. Jumbled questions frustrated her: *Is this London? Is the war over? Oh, dear God, what year did he say it was?*

No answers came, only the knowledge that she had lost the fight and that her attackers had gone. So too had the spirit that had powered her efforts. In its place lay a pit of despair.

The leg she lay on started to throb. She had to shift position to release the pressure on her hip. As she did, an agony beyond endurance brought vomit to her throat. She swallowed it down. Felt the choking sting it left in its wake. How could Derwent have thought her capable of doing this job? Yes, she spoke French, and yes, she knew the country well. But she wasn't brave enough... She wasn't brave enough...

And what about the mission? *Pierre will be waiting... Oh, Pierre, my love. Please, God, keep him safe from capture. And our son, protect our son.* For hadn't she put them in grave danger? Those Nazis had her bag, her papers and the secrets she was charged with keeping. 'Never write anything down!' they'd told her. She'd disobeyed that golden rule. She'd written everything down. She'd told where her baby son and his grandparents were and that they were Jews. The Germans would... Oh, God! Why had she done it? Why had she compiled a complete record of her life from the day she'd had to give her first child away? Now the Nazis would know everything: the rendezvous point, the codes... *Millions will die...* But, no, that wasn't right. *It was 1953 when I began to write about it all – long after the war. Oh, why do my thoughts swim away from me?*

A voice with a twang of Cockney to it broke into her thoughts, 'Blimey, it's that Miss Crompton. Have you fallen, love? It's alright, don't be afraid...'

It sounds like Rita, but no, Rita wouldn't call me 'Miss Crompton'. Rita loved her and called her nice names. Rita was a Land Girl on her brother's farm. They were having an affair, a liaison. Exciting, different... *Oh, God! Stop it, stop this confusion... That was then. Rita is old now and smells of drink. She can be cruel and demands money. Has Rita sent these people to hurt me?*

'Her nose is bleeding, Mum. She's shaking...'

'Okay, Trace, don't just stand there. Nip across to that phone box and dial 999. Now then, love, help will be here soon. You keep yourself still. Bleedin' 'ell, this is a turn-up, but you're safe now.'

Theresa's trepidation intensified as her yesterdays crowded her brain once more: *These people seem to know me. Are they the ones who will be nice to me and try to gain my confidence?*

'Don't he scared. We ain't going to hurt yer, love.'

Opening her eyes she tried to focus, but the glare of the sun overwhelmed her and she snapped them shut again. Before doing so she'd seen a blue light flashing. She'd never known the Germans to use such a warning sign. Would they take her back to Dachau? Would they shoot her? Or – *no, dear*

14

God, not that... Not burned alive in the oven as they'd done to one poor girl. Oh God, help me!

More voices. How many were there? Men's voices, trying to soothe her and to calm her. *I must stay strong. Sing, that's the thing. Concentrate on a song.* 'There'll be blue birds over... Tomorrow, just you wait and see...'

'That's the spirit, love. My old mum used to tell us to sing when we were afraid or in pain. I'm Marcus, and I'm just going to give you an injection to make you more comfortable, then we need to put a splint on that leg. We think you may have fractured it. Lie still now.'

'No... No...' She tried to push the man's hand away, but couldn't. Her thigh stung; her head swam. *Oh, God, no!* They had warned her about this new method. 'They may inject you,' they'd said. 'It's not lethal, but it relaxes you and you are no longer on your guard. If they do, try to think of something important and concentrate on it. Shut everything else out.'

'Don't like needles, eh? Nearly done. You'll be better for it, love.'

Pierre, oh, Pierre, I have let you down. Please, God, don't let them capture him. He will face certain death! No, I couldn't bear it ... I love you, Pierre. The words he had said to her came into her mind: *'Tu es le souffle de mon corps. Le sang qui coule dans mes veines et la vie dans mon coeur.' That is what I will think of.* She could hear his voice, and drank his words deep into her as she said them in her mind over and over: 'You are the breath in my body. The blood that courses through my veins and the life inside my heart.'

15

Two

A Journey into the Past

Rita, Lizzie and Ken – London 1963

''Ere, sis, you said you wanted a new bleedin' handbag, so I bleedin' got yer one.'

The brown, square-shaped bag landed and this set up a worry in her. Turning it over she noticed, though old-fashioned, it showed hardly any sign of wear. The leather, soft and of good quality, was gathered into a brass trim with a tortoiseshell clasp that she had to twist to undo. As she did, a fusty smell clogged her nose. Sifting through the contents – some papers, a few exercise books rolled up and secured with an elastic band, and several photos, all yellowing with age – she found the bag didn't contain a purse or anything of value. But then, she hadn't expected it to. Ken or his cronies would have removed anything of that nature.

'Look at you, ferreting already. I knew it would suit yer. You're a right old square.'

'I ain't–'

'Well, what's with the Perry Como, then?' A screech set her teeth on edge as Ken shoved the arm of the gramophone, causing the needle to slide across the long-playing record. Perry's 'Can't Help Falling in Love' stretched and distorted on

16

the last line.

'Don't do that! You know it scratches the record! And I ain't a square. Rita put that on before she fell asleep. I just didn't bother to change it, that's all.'

'Huh, in that case yer won't like rummaging through that crappy old stuff, then. No one who's *with it* likes the stuff you like. Who digs history and antiques these days? Accept it, me little skin and blister: you're a square.'

Ken came towards her. A cold feeling of apprehension clenched her stomach muscles. She turned in her wheelchair, but what she saw gave her no hope of help from Rita. Slumped on the settee, dead to the world, Rita's lips flapped on every exhaled breath, filling the room with alcohol fumes. One slack arm rested on the empty gin bottle lying on the floor.

'What's up, darling? You look like a bleedin' caged animal. Don't yer like the present I got for yer?'

His voice soothed some of Lizzie's fear. It didn't hold a hint of what had fuelled her dread. His mood changes had her treading on eggshells. She didn't like how he talked at times, joking in a way she knew wasn't a joke about how, even though she was disabled, she shouldn't be deprived. At these times his body leaned closer than she was comfortable with, and his eyes sent messages she didn't want to read as he made out that one of his mates – the one he nicknamed Loopy Laurence – fancied her.

She kept her voice steady as she answered him. 'Course I do, but it's where you got it from that worries me.'

'Found it.'

She doubted that – more like *half-inched* it, as he called pinching stuff. He always used Cockney rhyming slang. It was as if he thought it added to the tough, bully-boy image he liked to portray. Snatching bags was a bit below his league, though, so he wouldn't have done the deed himself; he'd have got it from someone who owed him. It must have seemed strange to them, him wanting the bag as well as the valuables it contained.

Rita stirred and opened one eye. 'You bleedin' got it, then? How much were in it? The old cow's been a bit tight lately with what she'll give me.'

'Shut your mouth or I'll shut it for yer, you bleedin' drunk.'

'Don't talk to Rita like that, Ken...'

'Don't you bleedin' start or–' The shrill tone of the phone cut his threat short. 'Fuck! That'll be bloody Rednut. He can't do pig-shit on his own.'

Relief slowed Lizzie's breath and released the tension in her as she heard him say he would meet Rednut in ten minutes. From what she picked up of the conversation, something had gone wrong with a collection. She didn't know the extent of Ken's dealings, but he'd talked about some of the known gangs running protection rackets and that kind of thing, but to what extent he was involved and exactly who with she wasn't sure. She knew he wasn't big-time, not in the league of the Krays and gangs like that, but she hated to think of what he did get up to. If she could get real proof, she would go to the police. But then, would she? Always conflict raged inside her where her brother was concerned, one minute wanting him to get caught, and the next praying for his safety.

'Right, I have to go. Will you be alright, love?' His tone surprised her. She'd thought she would bear the brunt of his anger at Rita and Rednut. Still might, but that didn't stop her retorting, 'If you would stop doing whatever it is you are up to, I would be.'

'Not that again. Whinge, whinge, whinge. You don't mind when I get things for you out of the proceeds, do you? Look at that chair. The National Health Service would never have got you one like it. You're such a bleedin' ungrateful sod!'

Taking hold of the handlebars and squeezing the lever set her wheelchair into motion. She needed to get out of his presence. He jumped in front of her. 'Where're you going?'

'To my room.'

'Look, sis, I brought the bag back for you, didn't I?'

His pleading look sickened her, but the softening of his attitude towards her gave her courage to take him to task again. 'Ken, it ain't right what you do, why can't yer see that? I know yer mean well, and think getting me things will make up for everything, but the way yer get them ain't right. I'd rather go without. What happened to the lady this belonged to? Is she hurt?'

'Lady? She ain't no bleedin' lady! I could tell yer tales. Anyway, Ken, where's me cut, then?'

This from Rita shocked her. *Rita knew the owner!* And by the sounds of things she'd helped to set up whatever Ken had done to get the bag.

'You'll get it when I'm good and bleedin'

ready.' Ken had moved towards Lizzie's bedroom, a ground-floor room originally intended as
a front room. A beam of sunlight shone through
the door as he opened it for her. It lit a trail back
to the sofa and glinted off the gin bottle. Ken
stood still. His face held a look of contempt.
'That bag was a payment. I earned it for you, sis.
I hurt no one. What others did, including her,' he
pointed at Rita, 'ain't my fault. Christ, you're a
bleedin' hypocrite, sis. Look how you're clinging
to it, afraid I'll take it back, and yet you're on
your high horse about *my* morals!'

As she passed him, tension and fear tightened
her throat. *Please don't let him follow me in.*

He didn't. The door slammed shut behind her,
giving her a feeling of safety from the threat of
him, but the knowledge of why he did what he
did completed the circle of her inner conflict. He
wanted – no, *needed* – to get things for her to
assuage the constant guilt that nagged at him
over her disability, and it was this need that had
started him down the road of his illegal activities.

Throwing the bag onto her bed, she let her
head drop and screwed up her eyes. The latch to
the part of her she kept locked away had shifted,
letting in unwanted thoughts. She tried to fight
them, but her mind ran back down the years.
Shudders rippled through her as she saw again
the blood – always the blood. Her mum's blood,
spurting from her nose, her lip and her forehead.
And Ken's, seeping through his shirt as their
dad's belt lashed his back. The screams and the
vile threats assaulted her ears afresh. Her dad's
face, ugly with his intent, flashed into her mind,

and she saw again his big, muscle-bound body dripping with sweat as he turned and aimed another blow at their mum as she tried to stop the onslaught on Ken. And into the memory came the moment when something had snapped inside her and had taken away her fear...

Her teeth clenched, as if they remembered independently of her how they had sunk into her dad's leg. The taste of the oil and gunk spilt onto his jeans came back to her. Its tang stretched her mouth and brought her Aunt Alice to her mind. Her dad had been mending Aunt Alice's car. Hate welled up in Lizzie. Alice should be the one to shoulder the guilt. She shouldn't have told their dad about Ken pinching from her purse. She'd have known what would happen. Mum would have sorted it on the quiet.

Lizzie held her ears, trying to block out the memory of her dad's howl of pain. Like the soundtrack to a horror movie, it had stayed with her down the years, filling her head each time she relived the scene. With it came the feeling of her hair being wrenched till she'd been forced to release her bite, and the sensation of hurtling through the air and down the stairwell. *He'd thrown her!* Her own dad had thrown her as if she was nothing. The world encompassing her had changed from the moment she'd hit the bottom step.

She'd never seen her mum again. A brain haemorrhage that night had taken her. Her dad, wanted for her murder, had been missing ever since.

Rita, her mum's youngest sister, had taken her

and Ken on, which couldn't have been an easy thing to do. Rita had come back from Australia after her man had conned her out of everything she had. Knowing what had happened to them hadn't stopped her going, but she'd thought one of the other family members would take care of them. Finding her, a fifteen-year-old, in a children's home and sixteen-year-old Ken in Borstal had enraged her. She'd not given up until she had them both with her, falling out with all of her sisters and brothers in the process and never speaking to them again. Five of them, there were – well, five still alive though there had been ten altogether. There'd also been two aunts on her dad's side, and not one of them had stepped in to help her and her brother. They would have let them rot.

She and Ken hadn't known Rita very well, and their mum hadn't spoken much of her. Their dad had referred to her, for as long as she could remember, as 'that bitch in jail', and as being no better than her mum's brother Alf, but that hadn't meant much at the time. Now it didn't seem possible that Rita coming into their lives was just four short years ago. It had been wonderful at the time, but things deteriorated when Rita took to the drink and Ken's carry-ons caused friction. Ken had no respect for Rita.

These last thoughts held in them the misery of their lives today, but they still couldn't hold a candle to what had gone before, nor stop the quiver of her nerves when she wondered about the future. But dwelling on it didn't help. Physically shaking herself free of the terrible recollections,

22

she felt the pain of her nails digging into her palms. Taking her time, she unfurled each cramped finger from the tight fist they had curled into, took some deep breaths, and wiped the sweat and tears from her face.

The bag came into focus. Leaning forward, she pulled it towards her. Maybe she could get a clue as to the owner by going through it. An address, perhaps, though if she did find that she'd have to post the bag back to whomever it belonged to, as taking it might implicate Ken.

A frayed, faded-green, wartime ID card lay on top of the pile of paperwork that had dropped from the upturned bag. Opening it revealed a black-and-white image of a young woman. Her face, though not smiling, was beautiful. Her hair – old-fashioned in its style: rolled on the top and falling into soft waves – caught the light in its dark colour. Something about the eyes and the expression told of this girl having hidden depths and a strong determination. She read the information: *Theresa Laura Crompton, born: 23.3.1911, York, United Kingdom.*

Looking at the date stamped on the card told her Theresa would have been thirty at the time. That would make her fifty-two now. *Oh, God, please don't let her have been hurt...*

Something had fallen out from inside the ID card: a similar document in French, though smaller and brown in colour and with the same picture inside. And yet, it bore a different name: *Olivia Danchanté, date de naissance: 24.5.1911, Paris, France.* Puzzled and with her interest piqued, Lizzie shuffled through the rest. An envelope tied with ribbon revealed several scribbled notes, again written in French. If only she'd paid more attention to languages in school. But, excelling in history, English and maths, she had given little to anything that bored her, and her education had been cut short after... No, she'd not let those thoughts in again. They had already taken her spirit and shredded it.

Laying the letters down, she picked up the photos. Some of them were in sepia, while others were in black and white. There was one of Theresa or Olivia – confusing with the identity cards showing different names – with a young man of the same height and very similar in looks and age, around twenty to twenty-six-ish at the time. She'd have thought them to be brother and sister, as there was another photo of them with an older couple that had *Terence and me with Mater and Pater* written on the back, but in this picture, their way of leaning close and how he looked at her suggested a lover; turning it over, Lizzie read, *1938, Terence and me at Hensal Grange.*

There were others of Theresa/Olivia with young people in uniform, and in a separate envelope there was one of her in a man's arms. They were holding a baby, one of a few months old, and looking into each other's eyes – clearly lovers. Husband and wife, even? In this one she noted that Theresa/Olivia had pencilled a Margaret Lockwood beauty spot on her cheek, and that she had exaggerated the fullness of her lips with her lipstick. This made Lizzie smile. As a young woman, she must have been a romantic and a

24

follower of the latest fashions. A happier thought from Lizzie's past surfaced, bringing the image of her mum all dressed up and ready to go out with her dad and looking similar to the young woman in the photo. Her dad, looking dapper in his dark suit and white shirt and with his white silk scarf dangling from his neck, had leaned forward and tickled her with the scarf's tassels. The memory cheered her as she looked at a photo taken in a field. Remnants of a picnic could be seen in the background. Theresa/Olivia was bending forward with her arms outstretched. Her skirt clung to her legs at the front and billowed out at the back. It must have been a windy day. A little boy held on to a wooden truck as if he might let go and walk towards her, but he looked only around ten or eleven months old. His face was a picture of joy. On the back it said, *my son, Jacques, August 1944.* And yet another of the man on his own – a foreign-looking man, with floppy hair parted on one side, nice eyes and a handsome face, though his smile, tilted to one side, gave him a rakish look. This connected with Lizzie. She loved a sense of humour in a man. On the back of this photo she read, *Pierre Rueben, October, 1943, the father of my son.* Then in French, and in a different handwriting, *Je t'aime, jamais m'oublier.* With the little she remembered from her French lessons, she could just make out that this said something along the lines of: *I love you, never forget me.*

Putting these to one side, Lizzie picked up the roll of exercise books. The strong elastic band rasped along the cover of the outer book as she forced it to release a bulk that was almost too much for it.

With edges resisting her attempts to straighten them, the books – ten in all – lay curled in front of her. On the top one, written in neat handwriting, she read:

MY WAR – MY LOVE – MY LIFE
Theresa Crompton

With her imagination fired, Lizzie opened the book. On the first page she read how Theresa had begun the memoir in September 1953, to commemorate the tenth birthday of her lost son Jacques, whose whereabouts she did not know. The milestone of his birthday had prompted her to write about her life and her war, as now the world was at peace she felt she could hurt no one by doing so.

Even though she did not know Theresa, it saddened Lizzie to read that as she wrote Theresa was fragile in her mind and body and hoped the writing of everything down would act as a cathartic exercise for her.

The dedication fascinated her and she felt her heart clench with sadness.

This work is dedicated to Pierre Rueben, my love and my life. And to our son, Jacques Rueben, and to my first child, my Olivia, who will probably never know who I am but whom I have never stopped loving. Not a day passes that I do not think of her and of Pierre and of Jacques, and of course Terence, my beloved late twin brother.

To Lizzie, these words held a story in themselves. One of a lonely woman, left without everyone she'd ever loved. But why? So many questions she hoped the books would answer.

King's College Hospital – London 1963

'So, no one has come forward to claim the old girl, then, nurse?'

'No, Officer, and we think her general frailty is giving us the wrong impression of her age. She tells us she is fifty-two, but as you can see, she looks nearer seventy. Who she is, is a mystery. One moment she is Theresa Crompton, and the next she says she is Olivia Danchanté. But then, she is obviously suffering some kind of mental illness or dementia. She seems to be reliving the war years, talking of the Nazis and someone called Pierre. Sometimes she speaks in English, sometimes in French. Poor thing thinks we are the Germans and have captured her. She's terrified.'

'That would explain her house. The whole place is barricaded with old newspapers and cardboard boxes stacked from floor to ceiling. There's just a small gap to get in and out through, and the smell... Well, anyway, as of yet we haven't found her bag or any private papers, but the woman who found her confirmed she is Miss Crompton.'

Theresa lay still, her fear compounded. *What are they saying? They've been in the house? How did they find it? What of Monsieur et Madame de Langlois? Smell...? Have they gassed them? Please, God, no...*

27

But they haven't found my papers. Oh, Pierre, they don't know of you yet. My darling, please wait. I will get to you. How brave you are, my darling.

'Oh dear, she's getting agitated again. It's alright, love. Miss Crompton, come on. You're safe now. You're in hospital. No one can hurt you. Look, I'm sorry, Officer, you can see how distressed she is. I'll have to fetch the doctor. She needs a sedative. There's nothing more I can tell you at the moment anyway, but if she does have a lucid moment and gives us some indication of what happened to her, I'll contact you.'

'I'd like to try to talk to her if I can...'

'Sorry, not until the doctor says so. I won't be a moment.'

Fear once more gripped Theresa as she listened to this conversation. *Oh, God, they want to talk to me. Pierre, take over my thoughts. Help me through this.*

The scent of the meadow on that Sunday afternoon when they'd picnicked filled her nostrils. Was it last week? Her mind gave her the moment she'd said, 'Look, Jacques is sleeping. We have tired him out.' Laughing, Pierre had picked a buttercup and she saw in her mind's eye how the sun had reflected the gold of the flower as she'd held it under his chin. His giggle at her funny British custom tinkled in her ears. *'Ma chérie, how can a reflection tell if I like butter or no?'*

Explaining how the myth amused children in England on sunny picnic outings had brought a happiness into her as she'd thought of her and Terence, but, as always, thinking of him had prickled her conscience. For hadn't they tainted such innocent moments?

Pierre left her no time to let her thoughts drift to those painful parts of her inner self as he'd gently laid her back onto the soft grass and lifted her face to his. 'Let me show you a good French tradition, *ma chérie.*' His kisses had reeled her senses. Her body had yielded to his with a passion that released her very soul from the shackles that held it. But something gave her the truth of the moment and brought her back to now, and she knew it hadn't stayed free for long.

Three

Lizzie Meets the Theresa of the Past

London 1963

Flicking through the books and aching to know more about Theresa's life, Lizzie read a bit here and a bit there. Excitement built in her as the work transported her back in time to Theresa's world...

South-west Scotland – Spring 1941

Theresa knew her innermost core had undergone a transformation. It seemed the dawning of a new season had unfurled the last resistance in her and made her ready to face the challenges ahead. The trees around her burst with buds that swelled with impatience to be allowed to bloom. Daffodils danced in the wind, and the sun, though weak with its warmth, shone down on her as she closed the door and looked around the garden and at the view beyond. None of it helped assuage the pain and guilt she held in her. If anything, the beauty of it all compounded the thought that she did not deserve to be part of it. Not yet, she didn't, but her plans might make a difference. She looked up at the windows of the house where she had spent the last few months sitting out her pregnancy, before shifting her gaze to the little party about to drive away from her, taking with them a love that had attached to her very soul.

Her father stood, uncertain, holding her gaze and ready to change everything if she gave the nod. She almost did, but Terence calling out to her stopped what would have been a foolish act: 'Come along, darling. No point in dwelling on it all.'

She didn't miss the catch in Terence's voice, and knew he shared her grief – a grief that gave a physical sensation as if lead weights had been placed where her heart should be. The cry of her daughter still reverberated in her mind. Now sleeping and peaceful, she was just a bundle swaddled in a blanket and held by the nurse Pater had brought with him.

Watching them get into the car and then hearing the sound of the wheels crunching on the pebbled drive as they pulled away crushed her soul. She wanted to cry out, *'No, no, I can't let her go.'* But she knew she had to. The moment froze. A deep breath released it and steadied her. Her father turned and looked back at her through the car window. He smiled and waved in what seemed like a final gesture, closing the part of her life that included her child. She walked in the opposite direction towards Terence and got into his car.

The driveway sped by tree after tree. A grouse danced into their path. Terence's hooting of the car horn was a rude intrusion into a moment that should have held silence for a lot longer. The stupid grouse scurried towards them. Terence braked hard. The action jolted Theresa forward and brought her out of the daze she'd descended into.

'What did she look like?'

'Darling, we said we wouldn't go into this and I–'

'I have to know.'

'She resembled Billy Armitage's mother, Megan Fellam.'

Hearing Billy's name jarred her, but she didn't say so. Instead she continued to probe. 'Had she the same golden-red hair?'

'She had. Look, old thing, it is best not to talk about it. It won't do any good.'

This reluctance on Terence's part to discuss it all with her, made her realize how deeply her dear brother had been affected by it all.

'I'm glad she looked like her grandmother. Maybe Megan will look down from wherever she is and take care of her.'

'That's a bit religious for you, isn't it? I thought you only gave lip service to all of that mumbo-jumbo?'

31

His stilted reply cut into her, and yet it marked the change that had taken place between them. *My Terence, my love, my sin. All in the past – no longer...* It didn't have to be said. She knew and she knew that he did too. Their incestuous love affair was over.

'Will you marry Louise?'

'Yes.'

'I want you to be happy, my love. We have to carry on.'

'But why should *carrying on* mean you having to go into the bloody Army? For goodness' sake, Theresa, won't you give that ridiculous idea up, please, darling?'

'No. Try to understand. I have a skill that will help in the war effort. Besides, I need to do it. It is the only way I can cope.'

'Cope? Will any of us ever cope again?'

The question shuddered through her, bringing to her the reason for it. It wasn't just the war, which now seemed almost secondary to all that had happened in the last months.

Rita came to her mind. A niggly feeling had never left her where Rita was concerned. She wondered what it felt like to be incarcerated in prison. Did Rita deserve to be? Or was she really a victim of the ambition Terence had ached for and now looked like achieving?

'Has Father consented to you taking the stud farm over?'

Terence shifted uncomfortably in the driving seat. They were so tuned into one another that he would know what had prompted the question – know she suspected him of setting Rita up and that he was guilty of destroying the Fellams' stables, and for what? So that he could manipulate their father into at last funding him to take over the business that poor Jack Fellam could no longer sustain. Not now, he couldn't. And it wasn't just the question of finances, but after the murder of his wife he was a broken man. The fire had compounded that.

'Theresa, are you determined to chew over everything that is upsetting to us both? I know you are hurt. God knows I am too, but we can't do anything about it all. We have to accept that life has changed. Our cosy little existence has been torn away at the roots. But barbed accusations won't help. Rita burned down the stables because she wanted to get into my good books...'

'She was already in them, wasn't she? You were fucking her every time you came across her!'

'And you weren't? For God's sake! Look, old thing, we have to stop this or we'll destroy each other.'

'Hitler has already done that. If it wasn't for his bloody war, none of the Land Girls would have come into our lives. No Rita, no Louise...'

'Is that why you want to join up? You can't fight Hitler alone, you know. And you aren't the right kind anyway. You're like me: a good-time sort of person. We don't take up arms and fight in a physical sense. We fight by manipulation to get what we want, and you can't do that to Hitler, no matter how much you blame him for everything.'

Of course he was right, but she would feel better hitting back even in a small way. Because what had happened in her life, and in all the lives of those of

33

Breckton, could be laid at Hitler's door. Hadn't the country's need for soldiers led to the release of the evil Billy Armitage from the mental institution? Billy Armitage – a murderer who, yes, she had to admit, had fascinated her and appealed to her need for different experiences to satisfy her deep sexual hunger.

Billy, whose actions had been put down to mental illness, had been considered cured when they released him. She'd believed it. They all had. Even Fellam, whose daughter had been Billy's victim, had found forgiveness for Billy and had allowed him to marry his only surviving daughter, Sarah.

But the evil core of the man had been unchanged. She'd seen for herself the depth of it. Seducing him had been easy and exciting, but she hadn't been prepared for his lack of sexual prowess. Teaching him things had added to her enjoyment, as had his rough ways, but when he'd not even had the common decency to pull out of her at the end and she'd berated him angrily, his true colours had shown. Fear still visited her at the memory of how he'd beat her, kicked her and threatened her life.

Theresa shivered. She'd never known the anger of a man, and had never thought to experience a man being violent to her. And yet she knew it was part of everyday life for most of the wives of the pit workers and farm labourers. And, worse, they had to accept their plight, as there was no one to help them escape it. Most even thought of it as a normal part of their lives – herself included, though she felt differently about it now. Maybe the war

34

would change things. After all, women were being empowered, taking on work the men normally did and bringing home a wage. They were making decisions in the absence of their menfolk and gaining positions in life that before were closed to them. She hoped so, for she hated the thought of them living the fear she'd lived after her own experience. The worst of it had been the threats if she'd exposed him. He'd meant every word, and she'd feared for her own and her family's lives. Darling Terence had helped her to cover up the resulting pregnancy, and together they had conjured up a story of her being raped by a stranger whilst out riding. Father had believed it and had taken care of the rest.

Some of her time in Scotland had been spent thinking about her life. She regretted now not staying married to the Hon. Raymond Hawthorn. His confessing his homosexuality to her on their first night together had shocked her. But now, what he'd offered her – a life of being able to do as she wanted and have affairs with whom she pleased whilst under his protection, as long as she allowed him to do the same – would have suited the person she became after their divorce. Always a flirt, and having had many experiences girls of her age shouldn't have had, she wondered now why she even considered the shame she thought would have come down on her from society. She would even have been able to keep her child… Still, that's as it was. Done and dusted.

The rest of her time she'd spent waiting for Terence's visits. The servants thought her husband had died suddenly and that she needed to be away from home to come to terms with things. They didn't know Terence was her brother and may have gossiped at how close they were, but it hadn't affected her or Terence. They had cemented their relationship as lovers as often as they could. They'd become inured to the sin of it, and their love was the most passionate she'd ever known.

Sitting back and relaxing a little as the car whisked her further and further away from all that had gone before, she reflected on how she couldn't remember the exact moment the idea came to her to serve her country. Something had stirred her conscience, and she'd had a time of feeling sick with shame at how she'd behaved in her life so far. It had come to her that she had to do something to assuage that, and so she had contacted Derwent, an old friend who worked in the Foreign Office. He had told her about the Special Operations Executive.

'It's going to be a very big part of our war effort. Winston Churchill and the Economic Warfare Minister, Hugh Dalton ... you've met him, I believe?' he'd said, and she'd told him she had and that she'd also met Mr Churchill on many occasions.

'Cracking Prime Minister. The best man for the job,' Derwent had said, and she had agreed. 'Well, they formed the SOE together. It was Dalton's idea, but Winston took it on and is championing it despite some opposition. It will be British-led. Its members will facilitate espionage and sabotage behind enemy lines. We need the best calibre of men and women, and you have every qualification except...'

He'd skirted around his reservations, but she'd known what he was getting at; did she have the courage and tenacity? Up to now she hadn't been called upon to show any of those things. Derwent had seen her as a flippant, rich, good-time girl, and who could blame him?

'Look, old thing, if you are serious, then join the Army. Go through the training. I will keep an eye on you and have your progress reported to me. If after that you still want to do specific work for the war effort, and you show the guts we are looking for, we'll see what we can do.'

Something in his words had fired her determination. She wanted to prove to him, to the world, that she was worth something. And at that moment she'd made up her mind and looked into enlisting.

'You're quiet, darling.'

'There's a lot to think about.'

'I know.'

His hand reached out for hers. The touch burned like a hot poker searing the memory of everything they had to leave behind. She snatched hers away.

'Sorry...'

'No intimate moments. We agreed!'

Silence that gave her no comfort fell between them, and her thoughts drifted to Billy Armitage's final act. How happy she'd felt when she'd heard the news of his death. Her immediate reaction had been elation at the release from the fear he'd bound her in. But then she'd given her thoughts to how devastated Jack Fellam and Sarah must have been. Billy had brought so much suffering down on them. He had beaten Sarah almost to death and killed Megan, his own mother. In losing Megan, Jack Fellam had lost the love of his life, and Sarah, Jack's daughter, her beloved stepmother, come mother-in-law.

A funny tangle, the relationship between them all. Jack's marriage to Megan had made Billy and Sarah stepbrother and sister. At some point along the way that must have turned to something deeper. Nothing illegal of course as they were not blood related. But surely, Billy's mental state and his murder of Sarah's sister and then his own father, when they were all children, should have prevented any such feelings developing? Unless it all happened through fear? This seemed the most likely scenario. From all she knew of Billy Armitage, he should have remained sectioned for ever, not released to kill again. It appears his killing himself was the only decent thing he'd ever done in his life.

Thinking of Sarah, she remembered Terence had told her she'd given birth on the same day as herself. She'd had a girl too. Funny, that. Two girls born on the same day to the same father, but to different mothers – not that Sarah or anyone else knew anything about her own little girl. They all thought she'd spent these last few months away doing war work – a clever story that even her mother had been told to cover her absence from Breckton and Hensal Grange during her pregnancy.

She should feel sorry for all Sarah had gone through, but she didn't. She envied her. Billy's suicide had released her from the shackles he'd held her in, and she'd been able to go to her true love. It appeared she'd only married Billy out of fear of what he might do if she didn't. Well, that turned out to be a farce – he did it anyway.

Sarah having a love waiting for her wasn't the source of her envy. No, it was the fact that she could keep her baby. *But then, I have to admit, she deserves to and I don't.*

Guilt overrode all of her emotions once more as she thought about her own actions. She knew she couldn't always blame her sexuality or the fact that it seemed to drive her back then. Not now, though, and she would never allow it to rule her again. She would never return to thinking there were no boundaries, no lines that she shouldn't cross. How had she ever considered it her right to have sex with her own brother, and with Billy Armitage – a married man – and with a woman, their Land Girl, Rita? Her only saving grace was that she hadn't used any of them for anything other than pleasure. She couldn't say that of Terence. Sex to him was sometimes a means to an end, as it was when he'd had Rita, she was sure of it.

1963

Lizzie slammed the book shut. *My God, Rita! And ... and with BOTH of them! And those two together. Brother and sister – twins, even...*

A sick feeling took her. She swallowed hard. Her cheeks burned with the embarrassment of it all, and with the feeling she'd delved into some-

39

thing very private. Not the biography, for Theresa wanted that to be read by all those concerned in her life or affected by it – her children, the wife of that Billy, *and yes, me. As the niece of one of her lovers I qualify as someone who should know* – but by the intimate nature of everything Theresa had disclosed.

Was Rita still her lover? It did sound like she was involved in getting the bag, and she'd said she hadn't got much out of *her* lately, which suggested she was still seeing her. The thought had Lizzie shrinking back onto her pillows. Could she read more? Already she'd found out the reason for Rita spending fifteen years in prison. A fire! Rita had set a fire and destroyed someone's life. Or had she? This Theresa seemed to think she'd been set up by her brother, Terence Crompton... Yes, she had to read on. She owed that much to Rita. And this woman, this Theresa, she owed *her* that much too, as reading on would surely unfold the reasons.

A noise from the lounge had Lizzie grabbing the rest of the books. Her heart raced as she pushed them under the mattress. A crash had her manoeuvring her chair frantically towards her door.

Shards of glass lay strewn across the floor and a broken bottle neck swivelled like a spinning top in the doorway. She stared at the red-blotched face of Rita, framed by greasy tendrils of bleached-blonde hair. 'What did you throw that for?'

'It's empty. What's the use of a bleedin' empty gin bottle, eh? Go and get me another, love. I have some money in me purse.'

Anger made her snap, something she rarely did

40

at this woman who'd at first seemed like their saviour and was still, in a way. 'How come yer have money for drink? Has Ken paid yer out for betraying the owner of the bag? That was a foul act, Rita. What if he hurt her?'

'What's it to you? They don't call me *Resourceful Rita* for nothing, yer know.'

Her toothless mouth opened and the room filled with her cackling laughter. The sound repulsed Lizzie, and yet her repulsion mingled with love. Rita had given her reason beyond measure to hate her, but she didn't. In moments during the dark hours she'd spent soothing the sorrow of this woman, she'd heard the story of how she'd tried to better herself. Taking any road to achieve that, she'd seized an opportunity she'd thought might open up a few choices for her and had turned her hand to war work. 'A Land Girl, I was, Lizzie,' she'd said. 'A bleedin' Land Girl. I could tell you some tales about them toffs in the country with their acres of land. You wouldn't credit what they get up to. Manipulative, they were. Took someone like me, naive to their ways and trying to make me life better, and framed me, they did.' She'd gone on to tell of her fifteen years in prison before explaining how she'd come to lose everything. 'I made good when I came out, but I just trusted the wrong one – Vince bleedin' Yarman. I thought he loved me, but he bleedin' took everything I had, he did. Anyway, I still have a goose who lays the golden egg, and so she should.'

Lizzie hadn't taken much notice of this last at the time, but now, even though she knew the answer, she challenged Rita with the question, 'How do you know the lady that Ken got the bag from, Rita? Is she the one you visit?'

'Stop asking bleedin' questions and get down the pub and get me gin.'

Afraid to push things further, Lizzie took Rita's purse from her bag. Once outside she breathed the evening air deep into her lungs. She couldn't call it fresh, clogged as it was with the smog that often hung over London, but just being outside the confines of the home lifted her. It wasn't far to the pub, but some of it was tricky going as her wheels caught in the ruts of the uneven pavement.

A familiar voice shouted, *Evening News,* read all about it!'

The billboard in front of the kiosk caught her eye, and she stared at the headline: POLICE SEEK WITNESSES. WAS 52-YEAR-OLD MISS CROMPTON ATTACKED?

As she came up to the stand, Ray, the paper-seller said, 'Evening, Lizzie. Shocking, ain't it? And in our own back yard, so to speak – or at least not far away. She's from those houses on the edge of Brixton. Most of 'em have been made into flats now, but it used to be a posh area, that did, when I was a boy, but now the gentlefolk still living there have found themselves surrounded by all sorts. What's the world coming to, eh?'

'I know, Ray. Rita says the same. I'll have a paper, thanks.'

'Here you are, luv. I'll tuck it next to you. Where you off to? It'll be dark soon and it ain't safe to be out.'

'Oh, just going to the pub for Rita's gin. I'll be home in no time. See yer.'

Still reeling from the headline, Lizzie didn't want to linger. Ray could keep you talking for ages once he got started.

Back in her room and with Rita content with her bottle, Lizzie laid the paper out on her bed.

The story sickened her, but the picture wrenched at her heart. Blackened, swollen eyes holding a deep fear looked out at her. This Theresa didn't seem at all related to the heroine of the memoirs, and yet her hair still fell into the same style – rolled at the top – although the smooth wave had gone. It fell down round her ears in wiry strands, and the dark lights were now grey streaks. A clip like the one in the ID picture held it in place.

Lizzie traced her finger over it. Tears of anguish ran like a river down her cheeks. This battered and bruised lady, who looked older than her years, had risked her life as a young woman for the liberation of France, and therefore for their own freedom.

A knock on her door stiffened her body. She closed the newspaper and turned it over so the sports page was face up.

'What's that you're reading, darlin'?' The soft strokes on her head made her cringe. She knocked his hand off. 'Don't, Ken. I don't like you doing that.'

'Is that right? So you're no longer me little sis, then, eh?' He turned the paper over. 'Well, well, been doing some detective work, have yer? Where's the bag? What did them papers in it say about her?'

'I... It's over there on me dressing table stool. Is the lady in the newspaper the one it came from? Have you stooped that low? You're vile, Ken. You sicken me. You're no better than Dad... Don't... No!'

Her head stung, and his grip on her long fair hair brought back the stinging tears she'd managed to hide.

'You bitch! Don't you ever compare me with *him!*' The glare in his eyes chilled her bones. Smoke, alcohol fumes and the sweet scent of marijuana made her retch. His fist clenched. He drew it back. It hovered. She waited for it to smash into her face, but after a moment he lowered it and grabbed her arm. Twisting it behind her, he leaned even closer. 'Don't push it with me, sis, I'm warning yer.'

With her free hand she clawed at him. 'Leave me alone, you bastard!' Her nails dug into his cheek, scraping skin and flesh. The ugly wound seeped blood.

The injury triggered one of his episodes. His regression showed in his voice and how he cried like a child. For her own safety, she hoped it played out how it often did, with him losing all sense of time and place. And then, tired beyond anything normal, falling asleep only to wake hours later and not remember a thing.

'Oh, Lizzie... Lizzie, I'm hurt. Look, I'm bleeding...' His tears mixed with his snot, leaving a silvery line on his sleeve as he wiped it across his face. Stumbling towards the door, his expression one of a lost child, he left the room.

Lizzie hugged her slight body, and rocked herself. Sick fear stayed with her. She knew his episodes didn't always last. In her despair lay questions: why did he think he could treat her like he did? When did he lose respect for her, or put her into a different place in his mind to where she belonged? Oh, God, what if one day he really lost it? How would she defend herself? She had to speak to someone, but whom?

'Get out of me way!'

His voice coming from the living room jolted her out of her thoughts. It was no longer child-like. Rita screamed, 'Lizzie, Lizzie... He's got a needle!'

The drumming of her heart against her ribs was as if it demanded freedom from her body. She rocked to its rhythm. Trapped by her useless body, she had no escape.

'You leave her alone, you pervert... Agh!'

The sentence swam into a holler of pain that died into a silence. An agony entered Lizzie at the thought of him hitting Rita. The door flew open. Ken stood in front of her like a smiling demon. 'I've got a treat for you, sis.'

A watery-red trail of blood mingled with his sweat and ran down to his neck. It matched the thread veins in the whites of his staring eyes. She could not look away. The evil inside him bored into her soul.

Shrinking back from the phial he held didn't help. The fluid glistened as he pumped some of it into the air. 'What is it? What're you going to do? Ken... No!'

'It's something to make you shut your mouth and do as I say. You'll like it. You'll like it so much you'll beg me for more, just like *she* does.'

Her shocked mind wouldn't give her the enormity of what he intended. She knew Rita used drugs now and again when the gin wasn't enough, but didn't know she'd got to the stage of begging for it. And she'd heard that more and more young people were becoming addicted to hardened drugs like heroin. *No, please don't let it be that!*

'Please... Please, Ken, don't–'

The jab stung her.

'Little sis is going to be a good girl now.'

The pink walls of her bedroom wobbled like blancmange. Voices mocked her. Her body seemed to float round the room, passed by her school picture, and up to the light dangling down from the ceiling. The lightshade began to dance, the blue dots on it twirling round then jumping off and sticking to the ceiling. She laughed. 'Naughty dots. Get back where you belong.'

'Now! Go on, get her onto the bed.'

Arms held her. Lifted her. A chill shivered through her. 'Don't take my clothes off. I'm cold.'

'This ain't right, Ken. You said she was willing.'

'Just do it, Laurence. She needs it. Who's going to take her on? She needs showing about life and to have experiences. Besides, yer bleedin' fancy her, don't yer?'

'Not like this...'

'Fucking do it! You arsehole, you owe me. Besides, I'm bleedin' doing it for her.'

'Get lost.'

A door slammed, making her jump. Ken's voice, angry, shouting at Laurence, calling him

46

loopy and spineless. But she wasn't afraid, not like normal. Just confused and ... and light-headed. Nothing mattered. There were no cares, no fears, nothing... She could do anything and be anybody. She wanted to close her eyes. Beautiful dreams came when she closed her eyes. Colours. Wonderful colours swirled around her, brushing away all hurt. All pain. Making her feel safe.

Four

Patsy, Theresa Crompton's Long-lost Daughter

Breckton, Yorkshire – 1963

The sun warmed Patsy, and contentment seeped into every part of her as she sat studying papers about the functions of the liver and the diseases it can succumb to – something she had studied early on in her course, but needed to refresh her memory on.

Richard, a doctor and the man she'd called dad for four years now, sat a few feet away reading through some medical notes. His expression was intent.

Glancing to her left, she saw Harri, her half-sister, lying back in her deck chair, her notes casually held in her hand, her eyes dreamily following anything that moved in the garden. They were both studying to be doctors, but Harri never had to give her full attention to any subject. Being Richard's stepdaughter since birth, she'd been around medicine all her life. A little envy entered Patsy at this thought. It wasn't just the knowledge Harri had picked up over the years, but her having had a stable and settled life surrounded by family and love. It seemed so unfair.

'That were a sigh and a half, love. Having problems?'

The cushion she threw just missed Harri. Harri's laughter broke the peace, causing an impatient sigh from Richard. 'Sorry, Dad. It were Patsy's fault. She threw a cushion at me.'

'For two young women who are about to start your final year and enter the hospital to do your internship, you still act like children at times!' This didn't come over as a reprimand; his accompanying smile belied that. 'And you, Harri, deserved it from what I heard, as you were being a little smug. You should help your sister rather than tease her. She has done remarkably well and deserves your support.'

'Aye, Dad, I know. I were only funning. Eeh, Patsy, sorry, love. Look, I'll go through it with you. When we do that, you find you have absorbed more than you thought. I'll do it as a question and answer session.'

'No, thanks. I don't feel ready for that. I need to take a bit more of it in.' Relief entered her as Harri accepted this and got up, saying as she did so, 'Okay, anyone for a cool drink?'

Watching Harri walk towards the house was like watching a mirror image of herself. Born on the same day to the same father but to different mothers, it was uncanny how alike they were with their golden-red hair, hazel, slanting eyes and petite figures. People often mistook them for one another, but inside they were different. They'd been shaped by the very different hands dealt them by life, and they sounded different too: Harri, having been brought up in Yorkshire, spoke with an accent very different to Patsy's own London one.

It was said that they took their looks from their granny Megan, a woman everyone had loved who had met a tragic end at the hands of her own son, Billy Armitage – hers and Harri's dad.

She didn't let her mind dwell on the rest of it. None of it really touched her, and the bit that did hurt too much to think about. The only way she could cope was to detach herself from it. Yes, it was her father and her granny, but it was like a story from a book about other people. The only attachment she had to it was how the likeness they both had to their granny had led her to find Harri and her family. A family she was now a member of.

It wasn't that she had been looking for them, as until four years ago she'd had no idea who she was or if she even had any relatives.

Brought up in one orphanage after another in and around London and rejected by possible adoptive parents, she'd ended up living in a hostel in the city. When she turned sixteen and was shoved out of care to face life on her own, she had tried desperately to continue the education that she'd been privileged, for someone with her background, to have. An unknown benefactor had seen to that for her – the man who had set up a trust for her had stipulated it must provide for her education. This had meant she'd always been given private lessons after school that had enabled her to pass a scholarship into grammar school.

There she had met an excellent tutor who'd drummed into her that she was a *somebody* and not just one of life's misfits. He'd urged her to carry on her education by going to college, but to do so she'd needed to earn money. An advert for a Girl Friday had seemed the answer. She'd thought it would entail dog-walking or sitting with the elderly, maybe reading to them or some such work. It didn't turn out to be that, and she should have known by the line in the ad that had said, 'Girls willing to do anything and earn good money, please apply.' As it had turned out, it didn't matter, as meeting Rita, the woman who had placed the advert, changed her life.

Rita had been astounded on seeing her to learn that she wasn't Harriet Armitage from Breckton, a girl and a place Patsy had never heard of. But then, after learning she didn't know who her parents were, Rita had wanted to know her birthdate. She had then come to a conclusion about who Patsy must be and told her about a woman called Theresa Crompton, whom Rita had witnessed having an affair with Billy Armitage. It appeared that soon after, Theresa had gone away for some time and everyone had thought it was to do with war work.

The shock had been tremendous. Bitterness towards this Theresa, who had callously given her away, had taken root inside her. Rita had nurtured this and had used her for her own ends, with terrible consequences.

A shudder passed through her, chilling her bones at the memory as Rita's voice came back to her. 'I have a score to settle with them bleedin' Cromptons,' she'd told Patsy, and had then gone on to stir up and intensify the feelings she'd recognized in her by goading her to exact her own revenge. She'd told her about the Crompton twins and their despicable ways, and how they had framed her. 'Getting rid of you is typical of them. They'd bleedin' cast you aside and leave you to fend for yerself without giving it a thought. Well, me and you can see as they get their come-uppance.'

Rita hadn't had to persuade her; she'd wanted to do it. Hate had driven her, but she hadn't been prepared for what her action caused. What her appearance in his life had meant to Terence Crompton, Theresa's twin brother, she had no idea. He'd promised to meet her in Leeds, but had never turned up. Instead he'd... No, she wasn't to think about it. She mustn't... But unbidden, the thought came into her mind that only compounded her pain: *It was only a phone call and a mention of Rita's name. Why would he kill himself because of that?*

Tears threatened, but she swallowed hard and dispelled them.

She'd waited for a long time in the cold and then had seen a headline on a newspaper stand that had told her why Terence Crompton, her uncle, hadn't turned up and never ever would. To escape the icy wind she'd wandered into a shop

51

called Hattie's Emporium where Hattie, a friend so embedded in Harri's family that they called her 'aunt', had spotted her and once more she had been mistaken for Harri. The same error being made by someone so close to Harri meant there could be no question that they were related; amazingly, it turned out they'd even been born on the same day!

Meeting a real half-sister, someone who actually belonged to her, was like a miracle. It was as if all her dreams had come true: Harri's mam, Sarah, her stepdad, Richard – both of whom had insisted she call them Mam and Dad – and Harri's half-brothers Ian and David had all opened up their hearts and home to her, and she'd lived as one of them ever since.

She and Harri had become inseparable, and she loved her with a feeling that encompassed many emotions. Jealousy was one of these, and it frightened her at times, as it gave her feelings close to hate when she dwelt on the injustice of how different their lives had been. But there was another side to her jealousy that made her reluctant to share Harri with anyone. She'd even taken up studying to become a doctor on learning that that was Harri's intention, and now they were in their fourth year.

Harri's voice calling out to her dad took her from these thoughts. 'Dad, Mam's upset. There's sommat in the newspaper. She's crying.'

'What? What is it?' The love Richard had for Sarah showed in his voice and in the way he jumped up and ran towards the house. Patsy followed on his heels.

Sarah stood at the table staring down at an open newspaper, tears streaming down her face.

'Darling?'

'Oh, Richard, it's her! After all this time. Oh, Patsy, I – I...'

Patsy stood frozen by the shock of realization that whatever it was Mam was looking at involved her. She felt Harri's arm come around her. Fear gripped her. She couldn't think what could be in the paper that could harm her, and yet instinct told her it would.

As Richard looked down at the paper, Sarah's plaintive plea of, 'Please God, don't let it all begin again,' deepened the dread in her. *What could all begin again?*

'Darling, don't upset yourself. We can deal with this and we can help Patsy to do so. It was always–'

'What? What do you have to help me to deal with?'

Richard left Sarah's side and came over to her and Harri. 'There's an article in the newspaper about your mother, Patsy. It isn't pleasant.'

'Is sh-she dead?'

'No. She's hurt. She's been mugged. The picture is horrific. You need to prepare yourself, dear.'

Prepare myself! My God, how can I do that! She'd never seen a picture of her mother. She'd even got over wanting to find her – she'd had to, as the bitterness in her hadn't left her and nor had her need for revenge.

'I – I'll look later.'

'Come back out into the garden, love. Dad'll

see to Mam. Eeh, that such a thing should happen, just when you're nicely settled. And your
poor mam.'

'She ain't poor. It's no more than she deserves.
She–'

'Patsy! Eeh, come on now. That's no way to
talk. She's hurt. I know as you're bitter towards
her, but you should think on. I mean, you don't
know why she let you go. She might have had
good reason.'

They were back in the garden and had sat down
on the wooden bench near to the lawn. A calmer
feeling had descended on her. 'What reason
could she have, Harri? She were rich. She could
have taken care of me.'

'Well, it was said as our dad ... well ... that he –
he raped her.'

'He didn't! Rita told me they were having an
affair. She saw them!'

'What? You never said... Eeh, I don't believe it.
He and Mam had only just married! Your mam
were local gentry, and besides, our father ... well,
he were mentally unstable. Dad told us. You remember? I don't think your mam would have
given you up had you been born out of a love
affair.'

'So I've been unwanted from the moment I was
conceived.'

'No. You're wanted now – very much so – but
aye, I can see as a lot of women wouldn't want a
daily reminder of such a horrific thing happening
to them. By, I know we haven't spoken much
about how you came to find me, Patsy, but I never
liked the sound of that Rita. I reckon as she would

54

tell you that it were an affair just to get you going. She'd think on how it would be harder to take if you thought your mam had done what brought you into this world willingly but then didn't want the consequences. Don't forget, Rita's sole aim was to hurt your mam and your uncle.'

'Yes, I can see that. I've always seen it, really, so I've never denied the assumption Hattie made about it being rape when she met me. Though deep down I don't think any of them believe it, really. I don't know why. Maybe that's why Mam's afraid that something may all start again, whatever that something is.'

'There's nowt as can start again. She's just afraid of losing you and of it all raking up the terrible things she and Granddad Jack went through, as a lot of that can be put at the door of the Cromptons. She just can't face any more upset. I mean, your family were ... well, there was the fire and, well, you know. Oh God! I know what Mam means. It's all so painful to think about even for us, and we weren't even born!'

They sat in silence for a moment, holding each other's hands as though they would never let go. But Patsy's thoughts weren't silent. They raged at her. They brought back her need for revenge. She didn't want to feel like this, but then, she supposed it was all part of it – the upset to their lives that no one wanted. She wouldn't do anything for now. She wouldn't even look at the article about her mother.

'Hi, you two. Why so glum?'

Oh no, that was all she needed: Ian and David, returning from work. It had surprised her that with their upbringing and education they both preferred to work on their granddad's farm rather than take up a career. Especially Ian, who was exceptionally clever and into anything scientific – besides being a pain, that was. Him and his silly crush on her. It was embarrassing! It wasn't that he wasn't a nice person – he was, and good-looking too, taking after his granddad Jack in looks and manner, and there wasn't a nicer man he could take after – but he was two years younger than her and had an irritating way of hanging on her every word.

'Patsy's had a bit of a shock and needs to be quiet for a while. Dad'll tell you of it.'

She saw Ian about to respond to this by coming over, but for once he showed maturity and carried on into the house, only saying as he passed them that he was sorry to hear it.

'Thanks, Harri. I'm feeling a lot better now.'

'Well, it came a bit out of the blue, didn't it? Like someone smacking you round the face for no reason, but it might turn out for the best. You never know.'

'I don't want our lives to change. I won't go to her. I–'

'Well, that's up to you, love. No one'll try to persuade you one way or the other. How about we go for a walk? We've been sat down here all afternoon and I could do with stretching me legs. I were thinking of cutting some of them chrysanths and taking them to Granny Bridget's grave.'

'I'll do the walk thing, but I'm not up for going to the churchyard. There's too much sadness there.'

'Aye, I know what you mean. But though I put flowers on them all, it's really only Granny Bridget's grave that means anything, because she was always in me life.'

'I know. Though she didn't live long after I came to live with you, I did grow to love her and I miss her. It's just that after this all happening...'

'Okay. We'll walk into the village.'

'No, not that either. It takes us by that Hensal Grange.'

'Reet. The thicket and the beck, then?'

'Yes, okay.'

'I'll tell you what. We'll take a towel and have a paddle. And a jam jar and see if we can catch some tiddlers. Ha! I've not done owt like that since I were a young 'un.'

'Well, I've never done anything like that.'

Harri visibly cringed at this, and for a moment Patsy felt sorry she'd said it. The difference in how they'd been brought up was so great that it was as if they'd lived on another planet from each other instead of being sisters. But then, Harri had been privileged, and it wouldn't hurt her to remember it now and again.

Harri couldn't think of much to say as they walked arm in arm towards the beck. She didn't want to dwell on the bitterness she'd heard in Patsy's voice, so she lost herself in the beautiful scenery she was surrounded by and the silly excitement inside her at going to do something as daft as fishing with jam jars! But then, she and Patsy were soon to enter a life that wouldn't leave a lot of time for fun. They'd finished their theoretical training and had a few weeks' respite before taking up positions as student doctors in Leeds, so it wouldn't hurt to act a bit childish. Besides, they needed something that would give them a laugh.

They were sitting dangling their feet in the cool water before she spoke. 'Eeh, this is grand. Are you okay, now, Patsy, love?'

'As I'll ever be. I've been mulling it all over and I'm still not wanting to do anything. I've been thinking of what Hattie always says: "When in doubt, do nowt."'

'Aye, she's full of wisdom, is Hattie. I bet her and Arthur are nearly in America by now. Eeh, I'd love to travel!'

'Well, I don't think Hattie thought of it like that. She was really nervous. I can hear her now: "Eeh, the thought of not having me feet on solid ground, it frightens the life out of me."'

'Ha, I know, but she wouldn't have missed the chance of going to see Sally and Mark and their lot. Mam misses Sally an' all. They were very close.'

'Well, maybe she and Dad will go out for a holiday. They should have gone with Hattie. By the sounds of things, Sally and Mark have plenty of room – live in a mansion, don't they?'

'Aye, I can't take it in. Mark, wounded so badly in the war and left blinded, becoming a songwriter, and a famous one at that! But I'm glad for him, and wish I had half his courage.'

'There's a lot of that in the family – *courage* – and it's shown itself down the ages by the tales we hear. I hope some of it rubs off on me. I could do with some.'

'I reckon as you've got it in abundance, love. And it'll stand you in good stead in the future an' all. Come on, let's catch a few of them tiddlers swimming over there.'

'Harri Chesterton, you're nothing but a big kid!'

'Aye, I know I am, Patsy Crompton, and I'm even going to tuck me skirt into me knickers. Ha, hope no one comes up here and catches us.'

As she did just that to the sound of Patsy's laughter, Harri thanked God that the moment that had made her feel uncomfortable – when Patsy had compared their lives – had passed, and now it seemed silly to have even given it a thought.

Five

Jacques – Theresa's Long-lost Son

A Need to Know – Florida 1963

'And to Jacques Rueben, a distinguished pass. Well done, Jacques. You are our youngest candidate and our highest achiever.'

The applause deafened Jacques as his fellow students and their parents gave him a standing ovation. With the embarrassment of being the centre of attention his cheeks reddened, but with the feeling came pride. He looked over at his grandfather, Isaac Rueben. The many lines in his face held the pain of loss. At this moment he

59

must be thinking of those who'd gone before. Most of their family had perished in the Holocaust. Jacques's beloved grandmother had died of cancer just two years before, and his father – his grandparents' only son, Pierre – had been executed by the Germans for his sabotage work with the French Resistance in the Second World War. As had, his grandfather had told him, his mother, the love of Pierre's life, Theresa Crompton.

Jacques lifted his head and stood tall. He hoped he had done his grandfather, and all of these people who would have loved him, proud.

At only nineteen – soon to be twenty in the fall – he'd gained a distinction from college, and was planning to go on to study law.

His grandfather nodded his head. The lines telling his story deepened as his smile lit up his face. The smile held everything Jacques wanted to see. Not just pride, but love and hope – a hope for the future generations of Ruebens.

'So, young man, what are your intentions now? An apprenticeship with one of the giant high-flying law firms in the big city? A good way to get your degree, you know. Earning whilst you are learning.' Professor Berry patted his shoulder. A big man, he stood two inches above Jacques's five-eleven height. 'Or are you going to waste all you have gained fighting for lost causes?'

This was a reference to Jacques's known trait of championing the underdog. He laughed as he said, 'No, neither of them, sir. I'm taking a year out. I have a need in me to find my roots.'

Grandfather shifted uneasily from one foot to

the other. He hadn't said he didn't approve of Jacques's forthcoming trip to France and England, but he hadn't been enthusiastic about it. It was as if he feared there were still people there that would persecute him for being a Jew.

'Oh, and where are these roots?'

'France and England. My father and mother were war heroes. I know I have nothing but a grave to visit of my father, as there are no family left, but my mother must have family in England. I want to find them and make myself known to them.'

'That's very interesting. War heroes? Well, well. But then, it fits. You have a good heart and a strong sense of right and wrong, so those that bore you would have been the stuff of heroes. I wish you luck, young man. But don't let those sentimental matters get in the way of what promises to be a glittering future.'

'I won't, sir. Thank you.'

As Professor Berry moved on to the next group, others who had waited for the big man's retreat crowded around Jacques. The next hour or so was spent shaking hands and exchanging plans for the future. The most immediate of these was to celebrate.

'You will come to the beach, won't you, Jacques? It'll be a whole lotta fun. Everyone's going. There's a bonfire waiting to be lit and the parents have supplied the food. We've crates of beer and ice buckets by the dozen.'

Mary-Beth looked up at him with pleading puppy-dog eyes. She had been his sort-of girlfriend for most of his college years, but they'd never got further than kissing and the odd fumble, and even that had fizzled out of late. They were great friends, and their friendship meant more than being lovers did.

'Sorry, Grandfather and I have booked a dinner at Grecko's. We wanted to spend the evening together. A lot comes back to him on any special family occasion, and he needs my company. I might come along later. Y'all have a good time.'

As they made their way to the parking lot, the air came alive with the roar of Cadillac engines, the screeching of tyres, pop music blaring from car stereos and laughter. A pang of envy for the carefree feel of it all entered Jacques. His friends had such uncomplicated lives – no horrific backgrounds, no justice to fight for. Theirs was a blessed life, with nothing more than the latest car or fashion to think about.

'That was a big sigh, son. Look, we can cancel the dinner and have it tomorrow night. I reckon that you'd far rather go with the crowd and have a good time.'

'No, sir, I want to be with you. I want us to talk.'

'I don't know that I'm ready...'

'Please, Grandfather. I need to know. I only have what Grandma told me, and it isn't enough. There must be more. I'm entitled...'

'Yes, some would say that you are, son. But some would say that I'm entitled to keep things locked away.'

An even bigger sigh escaped Jacques before he could check it. His knowledge of his father and mother was scant, to say the least – just their names and how they had died. His grandfather had always clammed up on the mention of them, and had quieted his grandmother whenever she had started to talk in front of him. Sometimes she had opened up when they were alone, but only to talk of her son and how clever he was and how he took after him. '*Mon chéri,*' she would say. 'You have the same floppy black hair, and his hazel eyes. You are not taking after your grandfather with his fair hair. No, it is my family you resemble, as your papa did.' Anything deeper was left unsaid, and questions steered away from.

Grecko's wouldn't be his grandfather's normal choice of diner, with its loud music, shiny steel decor and car parts hanging on the walls instead of pictures. Jacques suspected he'd chosen it under the pretence of bowing to Jacques's younger taste, but more likely it was because of the difficulty it posed to having a conversation. What his grandfather didn't know was that there was a quiet room at the back, and Jacques had popped in during the week and requested a table in there. His grandfather's face changed from a kind of relaxed *I win* expression to one of dismay when the waiter showed them through to it.

'Jacques, I can't...'

'You have to. You have to for me. I deserve to know. They were my parents and my ancestors. I have to find out about them before I can get on with the rest of my life. And, God forbid, what if anything happened to you?'

They sat down in silence and went through the motions of ordering. Steak for both of them, though neither chose the ten-ounce they would

63

normally have done. Jacques had a pang of guilt at this. His grandfather had a big appetite, and ordering a smaller meal was a sign of the ordeal he was putting him through. As much as his heart wanted to give in, he couldn't let it. He couldn't go to Europe without more information. It would be like a blind man going up an unknown alley.

'This will cost me a great deal, son. I'll be letting in ghosts I've kept at bay. Not because I wanted to, because I had to. It was my only way of surviving.'

'I'm sorry, sir... I...'

'No, don't be. You have a right. I can't leave this world with you not knowing, I know that. It would be a betrayal of all those who went before – like saying they didn't exist and meant nothing. Nothing could be further from the truth. They existed. And they meant the world. My brother, his wife, his three kids. My parents. My sister ... my dear little sister and most of all my son, your father...'

'Grandfather, I'm sorry. Stop. It's okay. I – I'm sorry.'

A big white hanky, like the many he'd used to wipe away Jacques's tears with or to clean a scraped knee, now wiped away the tears streaming down his grandfather's face.

Jacques waited.

His grandfather gave a little cough, swallowed hard and started his story. His voice took Jacques into the past.

Isaac, Jacques's Grandfather – Poland 1939

Father looked twenty years older than his sixty-five years as he bent forward, Isaac thought as he sat at his father's feet. He watched his father's eyes scan his family sitting around the room – a room that told of their wealth with its polished furniture and heavy brocade furnishings in colours of rich ruby and blue.

The skin hanging from his father's face wobbled as he shook his head; it resembled the yellow parchment of the papers in their business office. Their family owned the largest jewellery shop in Warsaw, and several others in smaller towns, and were one of the richest families in Poland.

'Listen, everyone.' His father's voice trembled and had lost the strength it used to have. Isaac watched the frail arms gesture in despair. He remembered how those arms had once been strong and held him high in the air as a boy, pretending to be about to drop him to the ground, hanging him upside down by his feet and then tickling his tummy with fingers that were the size of sausages.

'Times are changing. They have changed. We are all in danger.' A cry from the corner had Isaac rising and going to his younger sister Annagrette. At thirty-five she was only five years his junior, but she had the mind of a child. On her knee she nursed the baby of their younger brother Jhona's children, a cute little girl of six months. Jhona had three children: Axya, a fine boy of seven years, Jhani, his second son of four years, and Anya, this adorable little baby. Isaac's own son, Pierre, named by his French mother, was at university in France. He had never felt so grateful for anything in his life. Pierre's mother, Isaac's beloved wife, was away on a visit to her parents and Pierre. He'd contacted her and told her to stay until what looked like the inevitable occupation of Poland ended. He didn't know if she would or not.

'Father, we know, of course we do, but what are your plans? Do you really believe all the rumours?' Jhona stood in the corner where the window curved around two walls. The drapes of rich velvet framed him, and the autumnal sun lit up his silhouette.

'I chose to look as if I didn't for a long time, but I have done and have been planning for our future.'

'But, Father–'

'The evidence is around us, Jhona. Fellow Jews are disappearing. Some are fleeing, but others... Look, the details are too much for the children.' Father rang a bell next to him and summoned the nanny. Silence held them all like statues as they watched her take the children away. As the door closed behind them his father's voice sounded like a death knell: 'The Rabbi has been murdered...'

Their horror showed in their collective gasp.

'How? When? How did you hear of this?'

'Burned.' Again a silence of fear and disbelief. 'Just an hour ago – the telephone call, it was Peter warning us to get out.'

'Are we going? We can't. The shops, our home, everything...'

'Possessions, Jhona, just possessions. I have a great deal of money in an American bank. We will be alright. But we have to take action, and take it tonight.'

'We can't get to America. The airports are all closed, and the boats are not sailing. We're trapped...'

'We will go to France. We can't all go together. Isaac, you will go first. You will leave tonight.'

'But the curfew...'

'There is danger whatever we do. We just have to take the chance. We need to get to France, and from there to America. The journey will be long and hazardous. Isaac is the first to go as he is fluent in German, English and French. Dressed as a farmer he can easily get passage. Besides, his family is in France and his wife's family will have connections. He will pave the way for us. You will have money available to you along the way, Isaac. I have made prior arrangements. Here is where you will call to make the pick-ups.' His father handed him a sheet of paper. 'Learn it by heart and then destroy it. Your first leg is on foot. You will start tonight at three a.m. Go through the garden into the wood. Make your way through there to the main road. Cross over to the railway and follow that in a north-easterly direction to Lithuania–'

'Lithuania! But that's miles in the wrong direction!'

'I know, Jhona, but it is safest. I have his journey mapped out. I have been sending ahead all he will need to where I know the rabbis are trusted. Business associates are taking care of the rest. I have wired money to them. There is no one who will betray you. Along the route through Lithuania and across the Baltic to Sweden, you should not have a problem. Those countries are as yet free. From Sweden you will fly to France. Memorize and follow my instructions to the letter. Find out the best way for us to make the journey – the pitfalls and the best mode of transport for the children. Act quickly and telephone the number on the page, which again you must memorize. They will get a message to me.'

'Father, this is a lot for me to take on. What if I fail?'

'You will not fail. You cannot. All of us must be out of here within the month.'

'If it is that urgent, Father, I want to move my family away now.' Marika, Jhona's lovely, delicate wife, went to his side. Tears trickled down her cheeks and yet no sound came from her. Jhona held her close. No one spoke for a moment. The silence clothing them held an almost tangible fear.

'Very well. You leave tomorrow. It is difficult. Maybe you could visit your mother-in-law in Russia, for a time at least? Thank goodness, Marika, that you had the good sense to teach the children Russian. But though I didn't want this – the separation of us all – it is maybe for the best. Germany, or any other country for that matter, wouldn't dare to invade Russia. But you will face anti-Jewish factions there, and that worries me.'

'What about you and Annagrette? We cannot leave you here.'

'We will hide in an old factory building I bought

just outside Warsaw. I have had men working for weeks now. Trusted men. They have built an undetectable inner wall, and behind it there is room enough for us to live for a short time. There is a labyrinth of rooms, each big enough for a family to occupy. There is access to the cellar, which is huge. Here I have built a communal kitchen and showers. I have stored food. The story will be that we have fled and no one knows where to. When we get Isaac's message, we will be safe to leave, as they will not be looking for us.'

'And you have enough room for me and Marika and the children in this hide-out?'

'Yes, and it is very safe; from the outside it looks derelict. I had seen this coming and had all the material delivered in plenty of time. My planning was in place as soon as the Nazis rose up and that evil Hitler with his anti-Semitic views started to vilify us. The work was carried out during the night. I didn't want you to know it was happening; I didn't want to frighten you. The workers were picked carefully from the Polish peasants whose work on the land had dried up. They are from fifty miles away from here – uneducated, but they have the natural skills of the builder. Their families are near to starving. They were transported here each Monday and taken back home on each Friday. They knew that if they left a trace of their work or any word got out about what they were doing, they would not have their pay. Until it was completed they were paid with food only. They finished the work three months ago and have probably spent their money and forgotten the project by now.'

Isaac wanted to ask why he hadn't got them all out instead of preparing for them to do so later. But then, that would have been futile, as 'what ifs' always were. His father must have had hope that it wouldn't happen. Jhona asked the question he was about to: 'How do you know you can trust these men?'

'They didn't even know where they were coming to. I told you they were illiterate. They had no idea about what was happening in Germany or anywhere outside their own farming community.'

'What of our neighbours, our workers? Can you trust all of them?'

'There is room for them and their families, and enough supplies. None of them will betray us, as this is a means of saving their own skins as much as ours.'

'God! Father, you don't expect us to live with all of our neighbours, do you? How will their absences be explained?'

'Have you noticed any of them missing?'

'No, but ... well, yes ... you mean...'

'Yes, over the last weeks they have gone one by one into the hiding place. Everyone has assumed they have left, as is natural for any forward-thinking Jew to do ... or that they have disappeared, as has been happening. Oh, I wish I had taken the route of leaving, but then, I thought this the best way. The Germans will come, but the British won't allow it. They will intervene...'

'But how will we leave, Father? We cannot live down there for ever, and none of us knows how long this will take. How will our stock of food be

70

replenished? How do we get in and out for fresh air?'

'We don't, Jhona. The rooms are well ventilated. Comings and goings will be noted by someone, so there can be none. Our access is through the lockers in what was the cloakroom. One of them has a false back. It is small, but none of us is very big, and I have had the biggest, Mrs Goldsmith, pass through without problems. It will be sealed once we are all inside, but in such a way that we can open it again when we need to. Each family has made their own arrangements for when they can leave. That is up to them. Through my work on the Jewish Council I am party to information gathered through intelligence. The Nazis have many plans to exterminate all Jews. They have already incarcerated the Jews of Piotrków Trybunalski, and we believe that is where those that are disappearing around us have been taken. Our last piece of information told us that in an area where five to six thousand Jews lived, there are now an estimated twenty-eight thousand people. And, worse, we have heard the area they live in has been sealed... The water and electricity have been cut off... They have no food other than what the Germans allow them ... and that is very little... They are starving... Disease is rife... Oh, God! Though I miss her every waking moment, I thank God for taking your mother before all of this began.'

No one moved. Isaac looked around at his devastated family. It wasn't that they hadn't heard rumours or seen things going on, but they had all been in denial. None had let in the fear of reality. Holding his sister close, Isaac said, 'Father, you

71

should have talked to us. We should have had a say, but you have done well. Your plan, which you shouldered alone, will work, if we can get out soon. It will stop us all being taken while the world sorts out the Germans and stops their invasion. The Polish have formed an army and are fighting back, but they have very few resources and wouldn't allow us Jews to join them. But we should have offered money to help them, as it is us that will suffer the most. Now, I don't think we can wait another moment. We have to go tonight ... now. Let us get you all safely housed in the factory whilst I am here to help you. Have we much that we must take with us?'

'No, there is nothing we need from here. Everything is ready. But, yes, I think you are right. Now that I have told you all and the burden of my knowledge is shared, I feel that urgency too. We will go in stages. Jhona, what is your decision?'

'I will stay with you, Father.'

'Good. I am glad and relieved. Now, my son, you should leave first with Marika and the children. Drive towards your home as you would normally do, but once out of this neighbourhood, detour to the factory. Here are the directions. Marika, I am sorry; I know you must have things in your home you would want to take with you, but now that we have decided everything, it is best we go without any hindrances. I have made adequate provisions for the children.' Marika didn't object.

Isaac held the now whimpering Annagrette a little tighter. What had seemed like something that couldn't happen was now a reality. His father rang the bell once more and the nanny brought the children back. The two boys skipped in, excited to tell about what they had been doing. Marika gathered the swaddled and sleeping baby Anya in her arms, her tears dripping onto the white blanket, but still she did not speak.

'Look, Uncle Isaac!' Axya held a picture towards him. 'It's you! You remember, that day you took me and Jhani to the fair? See, that's the merry-go-round with the horses. Oh, when can we go again? When will the fair come to Warsaw again?'

Isaac felt tears prick the back of his eyes. The awful truth of their situation was crystallized in the child's plea. Something told him that never again would they live that carefree life in this, their own country. *Please God, we all get away safe so we can resume our lives again in America.*

The night air seeped cold into Isaac as he crossed the road. Out of the protection of the wood, he felt vulnerable. A few minutes earlier he'd jumped back into a ditch as a convoy of lorries full of German soldiers had come towards him. His heart had clanged inside him and his body had started sweating. *Had it begun?* Always they came at night, rousing people when they least expected it and were at their most vulnerable. With that many soldiers heading for the city, what were their plans? Oh, God, was the rumoured ghetto to start now? He sent a prayer of thanks up to God for the foresight he'd had in urging his family to leave tonight. At least they were safe. But he must hurry. He must get as far away as possible, and he must not be caught.

After a few minutes he left the ditch, determined not to hide again. His father had cut off his *peyos* the night before. Tears had streaked his face as he had snipped the long plaits from above his son's ears. 'It has to be done, my son. God will understand.' Without any distinguishing features to mark him out as a Jew, Isaac now looked like any other Polish or German man. Even his hair tended to be on the fair side, and this fact would help him in his cover story. If stopped by the Germans, he was to say his name was Hantz Rplenski. He'd been born to a German mother and Polish father. He had decided to take the side of his mother's family and was making his way to Germany, and although he might be too old to join up, he felt he may still be of some help to the war effort.

The Germans might wonder at the route he was taking, but he would say he had an uncle in Lithuania who would help him to get a passage across the sea – a route considered safer than crossing over the border into Germany. His father had even supplied him with the correct papers.

It seemed to Isaac that a whole lifetime had gone by instead of just two weeks. His thoughts went to the legend of Good King Wenceslas as he trundled through the deep snow, and he wished he had the great man's footsteps to tread and his spirit to keep him going. The boat carrying him from Lithuania had landed on the coast of Sweden, not in a port but in a small cove with impassable rocks that had meant he'd had to climb out and wade through the freezing water to the shore. The boatman's family had been waiting for him. They'd taken him to their home and taken care of his every need. His father must have paid them well. Now he was in sight of Stockholm's Bromma Airport, hoping to get a flight out.

Standing at the gates to Passport Control, he prayed that his false papers would appear to be in order. The only flight he'd been able to get was one to Britain. Standing in the queue with him were many fellow refugees, some from Denmark, whose language he understood. All looked afraid. Some looked Jewish, but he dared not identify himself to any of them. He'd ditched his German papers once he'd boarded the boat, and now had fresh ones that had been waiting for him at his last drop-in. They stated his true identity, and he was now an official Jewish refugee. But he'd been told to trust no one. It was rumoured that the Germans took on many guises in their mission to bring escapees to heel. There were even rumours that they tracked people and kept a tab on their whereabouts for the future. If this was true then they had to be doing it by means of undercover refugees.

An announcement by a distant voice that the last British flight of the evening was boarding caused a surge of bodies to thrust forward to get through the gates. Isaac managed it. Sweat stood out on his body as the moments ticked by with his papers under scrutiny. At last they were handed back.

The apartment block where his mother-in-law lived looked no different from those around it. Here on the outskirts of Paris there were no signs of what was tearing Eastern Europe apart. In England, where war had been declared and he had stayed only a couple of days, they were dubbing it 'The phoney war'. Something told him it wouldn't be so for long.

Standing a moment, unsure, his heart pounded his anticipation. A figure appeared at the window then darted away again, leaving the curtain flapping. He waited. A slow creak signalled the opening of the heavy door. 'Marionette...' His voice broke. His arms encircled his darling wife, the sensation thrashing his emotions. His whole being crumbled.

'*Mon chéri, mon amour, non.* You are here now. Hush.' Her hand soothed his brow and wiped away his tears. A peace entered him, only to be shattered at the sight of Pierre running towards him. Clinging to his son – the boy who had become a man in his absence – should have brought comfort, but Pierre's words after kissing him and hugging him back took the last remnants of his world away.

'Father, oh, Father, thank God you are here and safe. The Germans have crushed all resistance in Poland. Our beloved country is now completely under German rule.'

'Oh God, your grandfather... Jhona...'

'Father, why didn't they come with you?'

'Let us go in. Come along, *mes chers.*'

They allowed Marionette to guide them up the steps and into the hall. There, Pierre, impatient as always, stood in front of him. 'Tell me before you go up to Grandmère ... what happened? Why did you come out alone?'

'Grandfather had a plan. It is a good plan. I have put things into place as he has asked, but I didn't realize that total occupation would take place in such a short time. I wanted them out before...'

'What is the plan?'

It didn't take long to tell them, and some confidence came back into him that it could all still work when Pierre said, 'It is a good plan, Father. They will be alright, I am sure of it. I will do what I can to find out how Grandfather is. I can get messages across the country through the many students here who travel back and forth. Some of them are Polish and travel home to visit. So far there has been no mention of any restriction on students. I will ask them to find out what they can.'

'But you don't know that you can trust them, Pierre. We have to be so careful. You must never let anyone know you are a Jew.'

'Don't be afraid, Father; it is different here. No one persecutes the Jews here.'

Grecko's Diner – Florida 1963

Trying to take all of this in and to imagine it was very difficult for Jacques. In the telling of it, his grandfather had seemed in control. And though he'd conveyed fear, he hadn't shown any other emotion. After a pause, he continued, 'Pierre did find out...'

Again a pause, but this time it was charged with emotion. Jacques waited. 'What happened, Grandfather? How did your – our family die?'

His grandfather's body trembled. 'They ... they burned them. Burned them alive.'

'Oh, God! No... No.'

'Yes. This is why I have not been able to tell you. I have never uttered the words. Those words break my heart and fill me with horror.'

'I'm sorry. Oh, Grandfather, I am so sorry.'

'No, don't be, son. You had to know. And there is so much more for you to know.'

'Can you tell me how it happened? Please don't if it will cause you too much distress...'

After a big intake of breath his grandfather said, 'No, in some strange way it is helping me to share what is inside me. They were betrayed. There was a lot of that. In some ways you couldn't blame people who fraternized. The fear must have been horrendous. They were threatened with their children being burned alive, with torture and with their own death. Under these conditions some even sold their own families down the river. Pierre found out that the Germans went to the factory and sealed all the ventilators. Then ... oh, God!' There was a long moment of silence during which his grandfather held his head in his hands. Jacques allowed it, understanding that his grandfather needed time. When he looked up again, it seemed he'd aged. No sobs came from him, but tears trickled down his cheeks.

'They ... they torched the building. No one got

out. My father ... my brother and his wife ... and my sister ... dear Annagrette ... and my nephews and niece ... those dear little children. And the neighbours ... men, women and children I had lived amongst and worked with... All burned to death.'

Horror seeped into every pore of Jacques's body. It was too much to comprehend. His stomach churned. He jumped up and ran for the lavatory.

They left the diner without eating their meal. Once home, Jacques poured them both a bourbon. The evening had faded into a sunset that lit the windows of their house with a red glow. His grandfather put a match to the kindling in the hearth and then, as the flames became stronger, fed a log onto them.

'Shall I make a sandwich?'

'No, I'm not hungry, son. We'll share a drink together and I will try to continue. Now we have come this far we should cover all of the ground.'

Six

Gaining Strength from the Past

Lizzie, Rita and Theresa – London 1963 and Somewhere in Scotland 1942

'Lizzie. Lizzie, love...'

Lizzie's head felt like a block of cement and wouldn't do as she bid it. She tried to open her eyes to respond to Rita's voice, but the room spun round when she did. There was a void inside her. Her body needed something – it was an urge she couldn't deny. She needed that stuff Ken kept injecting into her. She had to have it.

The trembling started again. Her limbs were out of control. She couldn't stand it. 'Rita, where's Ken? I need...'

'Oh God, Lizzie. I'm sorry ... that bleedin' Ken's got you hooked!'

The bed shook as Rita got in beside her. Her cheeks felt the dampness of Rita's tears. Warmth enveloped her as she snuggled into her arms. But it wasn't enough. 'Rita, please...'

'No, Lizzie...'

'You have to, Rita. I can't stand it.'

'No, Lizzie. You'll get over this, love. You will. Ken's only given you a couple or so shots. You can come back from this. It's just the effect of coming down. It'll pass.'

'Oh, Rita, help me ... help me.'

'Alright, love. Blimey, you're not thinking as I wouldn't, are you? I'd even go to the Old Bill if I thought as it'd help, and that's something I never thought I'd bleedin' say!'

'No, don't ... he'll kill us. He said he'd kill you first and make me watch. He said he'd pour petrol over you and set you alight. And then after I'd seen you burn the same would happen to me...'

'What? Nah, he'd not have the guts.'

'*He* might not, but he knows of them as would.'

'Then we will go to the Old Bill – not that I'm a bleedin' grass, but we need protecting. Who are these cronies you're talking of? Yer can't mean Loopy Laurence or Rednut? They're bleedin' short up top.'

'I don't know. I just know as he's mixed up with some of the gangs, some of the big boys who work in these parts. Extortion and all that.'

'Blimey, you don't mean the bleedin' Krays lot?'

The thought of this put a sick dread into Lizzie, but no, Ken was only small fry, surely? 'I don't think he's mixed up in anything that big, but there's others who work the same stuff round 'ere.'

'Christ, they better hadn't let the Krays find out, then. They own the bleedin' East End, and the West if it come to that, and half the bleedin' government are in their pockets, not to mention the film stars. There was a picture of that Diana Dors with them in the paper the other day. They're bleedin' big trouble. They'd see Ken and his lot dead soon as look at 'em.'

'Oh, Rita, what can we do? I feel sick and I want that stuff. You have it, yer know yer do. I've seen him give it to yer. Please, Rita. I can't bear it. I'm scared of what he'll do next. Oh God, Loopy Laurence... Ken brought him here to–'

'Well, he didn't, did he? Loopy has more about him than that bleedin' brother of yours, and he refused, so that ain't anything to worry about. As thick as his friends are, they have morals, it seems. But, no, Lizzie, don't ask me to help yer get drugs. They get to yer. They gets yer so you can't stop taking the bleedin' stuff. I'll do anything for you but that.'

'You bitch! You bleedin' bitch. You wait until Ken comes. I'll ... oh, Rita, I'm sorry. I'm sorry.' Oh, God... *How had she stooped so low as to speak to Rita like that?* But then, desperation attacked her again and she knew how. 'Help me ... help me, Rita...'

'I'm trying to, love. But I know from me own experience, drugs ain't the answer. Please don't go down that road. Not you. Not me Lizzie. You're different to us, love. You're the only good thing in me bleedin' rotten life. We'll get through this. We will. You'll get back from this and everything will be as it was.'

'A drink, then? You have gin; I know you do. I can smell it on you...'

A tear trickled down Rita's prematurely aged face. Remorse once more bit Lizzie. She couldn't express it in words. Rita's unwashed hair brushed her cheek. Lizzie lifted her face towards her and stroked it. 'It's alright, Rita. I'll be okay. I didn't mean–'

'I know, but it's true. I've failed yer, Lizzie. I've failed yer both. Try to get some rest, love. I'll think of something.'

'Tell me about Theresa before you go, Rita. What's happened to her? Did you set it up so she'd have her bag snatched? Were she the one you always talk of when you're feeling down?'

Rita's weary body left the bed. 'Lizzie, I can't tell yer of it. I've done wrong over the years. I've paid for some of it, but them, they never paid. Not her or her bleedin' brother. Her daughter paid, though...'

'Her daughter! You knew her daughter? But–' Lizzie stopped herself, not yet ready to share the books.

'What do you know of her daughter? How did you know she bleedin' had one? What you up to, Lizzie?'

'I – I... You told me. But yer never said yer knew her. I just wondered. I – I mean, the police are asking for anyone as knows of any family...'

'Tell the Old Bill nuffin, Lizzie. I know I said different a moment ago, but that's how it has to be. They don't protect the likes of us. They just pretend to so they can get information that might lead to the big fry. No, we have to keep our mouths shut. It's too dangerous. We'll look out for each other. I'll sort it with Ken.'

Lizzie couldn't answer. Glad she'd been able to stall Rita from probing further and discovering the books, she watched as she walked across the room. It seemed as if desperation bled from every step Rita took. This fuelled the desolation in her own spirit. Her body flopped back on the bed.

Please, God, give me the courage to get through this.

The Theresa of yesteryear came into her mind. Pain shot through her head as she leaned over and forced her hand under the mattress to retrieve the books. Slumping back on the bed, she had to use all her strength to hitch her useless lower body into a sitting position. The mirror opposite reflected someone she didn't know: long golden hair matted and dull, light blue eyes sunk into dark pools of skin. Sweat beads shining on a ghost-like face. Lips sagging and dribbling spittle down her chin. A tear plopped onto her check. She wiped it away. *No more. No more...* Her weary fingers flicked through the pages.

Somewhere in Scotland – Late Summer 1942

The train seemed to be taking for ever. Sometimes Theresa could see out of the windows, but at others the thick smoke spewed out by the engine blocked everything from her view. Apprehension tickled the muscles in her stomach. Her journey into the unknown...

Having completed the six-week Army training, an officer had summoned her. Derwent had been in his office and had greeted her with a condescending comment, 'Theresa, my dear, you have shown a mettle I didn't think you had in you.'

Annoyed at first, she'd said, 'Oh? Well, thank you for that.' But then she had had to agree with him. 'No, I'm only joking. I know what you mean. I didn't know it myself, but I'm very pleased. I feel a sense of achievement. I take it you being here is to do with what we discussed before?'

'Yes. I have booked you into an assessment centre.'

'Oh, so I haven't yet proved my worth?'

She cringed inside and leaned her body further into the uncomfortable wooden bench seat of the train as she remembered how his wink had embarrassed her. Into it she had read that she had more than proved her worth with him in other ways in the past – a short affair they'd had had come to mind. Shaking herself, she half smiled at the very thought of her actually capable of feeling such an emotion as embarrassment! *Changes are definitely afoot, girl!*

For a moment her thoughts quietened, and she contented herself with watching the scenery becoming ever more rustic as the train chugged further north and into the lowlands of Scotland. But then, creeping into this peace, the fear intruded once more. The officers at the assessment centre where she had spent a few months before an extended leave had told their recruits nothing of what would be expected of them or where they would eventually land up. She only had the little Derwent had said about the organization that she was now a member of. Some of their number at the centre hadn't made it through that process – how she did, she had no idea. Not being a brave person, the alternative jobs on offer – that of an interpreter or a code-breaker – had seemed more and more her thing, but here she was and God only knew what was in store for her.

85

Whatever it was, the location where it would begin was top secret – so secret that not even *she* had been told where! All she knew was that someone would come to tell her when to get off the train, and then take her the rest of the way by car.

As the rolling countryside turned to dramatic rugged landscape, part of her filled with trepidation once more. If this was going to be a training course, then the terrain looked more than she could handle. From what she knew of Scotland, they were headed to the east coast – a much more mountainous area than had surrounded her in the south-west in what seemed now like another lifetime ago. For a moment she let herself dwell on her child, wondering where she was and if she was thriving, but the throbbing ache of pain this set up in her heart had her shaking herself out of it and concentrating on what lay ahead.

She had never been a physically active person. Brought up in York, and attending an all-girls boarding school, things like hockey and netball hadn't been her thing, and she'd avoided them whenever she could. Her father had been one of the benefactors of the school, so she had rarely come up against any objections to her reluctance to PE and games. Her only real exercise had come when they visited her Aunt Laura at Hensal Grange, the beautiful house and estate in Breckton that had eventually passed to her mother on Aunt Laura's early and very sad death. There, she and Terence had roamed the acres of fields, playing out their imaginations, and when old enough they had learned to ride the horses. Something she had loved.

Those years had been some of the happiest in her life. She had even coped well during the times when she and Terence were separated by different schools and by her finishing her education in Paris with her friend and her family, and a year in Belgium.

These last two years of her 'growing-up' time now formed the basis of why the SOE were interested in her. She was fluent in French – not just the copy-book type, but everyday conversation. And she had a good knowledge of the country. This, they said, would help her to pass herself off as a local.

A few hours later, feeling less than adequate and, she thought, judged as such by the officer who stood in front of her, Theresa knew what was meant by having your knees knocking together in fear. Whether he could discern this, she didn't know, but he never took his eyes off her as he explained, 'You are here as part of an elite force. You may have heard something about our operation, but over the next few weeks you will live and breathe it. We are the Special Operations Executive. Your training begins today. You will spend six weeks here, and by the time you leave you will be so fit you'll be able to run up Ben Nevis with a forty-pound pack on your back, without stopping for drinks. Don't let us or yourself down. Your country needs you.'

She'd almost smiled at this. It seemed a trite remark taken from the poster used in the First World War that had made everyone want to join up, and was catchphrased again today by many.

The words stayed with her, and she repeated them many times over the next few days. They had lifted her spirits at first, but now, slumped down on the grassed area of a ridge and with sweat seeming to seep from every pore of her, she didn't feel so inclined to be one of them that her country needed. Taking a deep breath, she heard her own voice cry, 'I can't do this...'

A gentle voice answered her, 'You can do it, Theresa. I'll help. Let me have your pack.'

Looking up, she found herself gazing into the beautiful face of one of the handful of women on the course. Her dark hair, swept back from her face, looked as if it had just been styled. Her eyes were kind. Theresa had heard that this girl had only just been married. How she coped with being away from her new husband, Theresa didn't know, but, she thought, *if she can do it, then I can too.* This thought put strength she did not know she had back into her body. Sitting up, she let her gaze travel up to the mountain top that peaked at around fifty feet above them. It swayed against the blue sky. The girl winked. 'It will take guts to get up there, but we can do it.' Theresa set her jaw. She had to make it. Standing up in one determined movement, she mustered all the bravado she could and challenged the girl: 'Beat you to the top!'

Every day held challenges of a similar nature, plus lectures, tests of knowledge and practising the new identities. Night after night, she and the others went over their cover stories: *My name is Olivia Danchanté. I am to live and work in the* bakery of *Monsieur et Madame Ponté* as their niece from Paris. *My mother – Monsieur Ponté's sister – died, and my father left us when I was young.* As Olivia's background was close to the truth of the life her own friend lived in Paris, and which she too lived for that year with her and her grandparents, it posed her no problems.

The real Olivia Danchanté had died along with her mother in a car accident in America three years earlier. Records of this no longer existed. This saddened Theresa, prompting her to make a promise: *I will become you, Olivia, and I will not let you down. For your part, if there is another life and you are out there, then pray to keep me safe.*

1963

As Lizzie turned the page and started to read more about Theresa's intensive training, tiredness ached every part of her. Tucking the book under her pillow, she lay back. Already, though Theresa did not realize it, she had showed guts. Lizzie decided she would take all she could from that and deal with her own situation. She would start by getting back into Ken's good books. Though her body and mind rejected the thought, she knew she had to find the courage to do all it took to achieve that. After that, she would visit Theresa.

This thought had hardly died in her before the door shot open. 'I've got it! We'll leave. Me and you, Lizzie, love. We'll leave and go somewhere as Ken can't touch yer...'

'But where? How?'

'We'll go to Theresa Crompton's place. I've got a key, and the Old Bill ain't snooping around there any more.'

'But—'

'No buts. It's the best solution.'

'There is a "but", Rita. The police are looking for yer. Look. It says it in the article: *Police are seeking a woman who has been seen visiting on a regular basis...*" The description that neighbour gave fits you, Rita.'

'Bleedin' hell, why didn't yer tell me? Christ! She'll know that... I – I mean...'

'Who will know? What have yer been up to? My God, I can't believe this! You set all this in motion. You did that vile thing of plotting with Ken to have that poor woman attacked and robbed!'

'She ain't no "poor woman". Alright, she may be so now, but she weren't always. She—'

'Rita, I know. I know all about it. You and she were lovers.'

'What yer bleedin' saying? You're off your head! That stuff's turned yer. How the bleedin' hell did yer come to that conclusion?'

'I have her memoirs. They were in the bag... No! No, Rita, they are mine. At least until I meet Theresa Crompton and give them back to her.'

'You give them to me, you ungrateful sod!'

Something in Lizzie snapped. Using every ounce of strength she had, she sat upright and snarled at Rita, 'Over my dead body, you whore! You try to take them and I'll scream this place down and tell everything I know!'

Rita stepped back. Her folded body slumped

into Lizzie's wheelchair. 'Oh, God, Lizzie. My Lizzie...' After a moment, she continued, 'I know as I deserve all you scream at me, but I've done me best by yer, Lizzie.'

'I know yer have, but none of that excuses all of this. What did yer mean when yer said, "She'll know"?'

'Her daughter...'

'Theresa's daughter! Why? How do yer know where she is?'

'I've always known where she is. Look, it's a long bleedin' story, but I met her four years back. She...'

The more Lizzie heard, the more flabbergasted she became. It all seemed like the stuff of movies, where coincidences make the story. But this had really happened! Theresa's daughter *had* approached Rita for a job, and Rita'd put two and two together. But it's what she did with the information that sickened Lizzie, not that Rita could see anything wrong with her actions. She didn't seem to care about the heartache she'd caused the young girl – though by the sounds of what Rita had heard of Patsy Crompton-Armitage, she'd fallen on her feet with her dad's family – and she even seemed pleased by Terence Crompton's death.

What to do now she knew about it, Lizzie was at a loss to know.

'Look, I've got an idea: I know me last one weren't worth a light, but what if I put meself forward? Go to the police, and tell them I am her friend, that I've always tried to take care of her, but that I've been under the weather and didn't see the article in the paper until now and had no idea she'd been attacked. I could tell them of her daughter, and other family I know of. Though why none of them has come forward… Still, that wife of Terence's – Louise, she was called – she had a side to her. Too posh for her own good. She was a Land Girl as well, but she thought herself a cut above us. She was, though, I s'pose, what with her being a member of the upper-crust. She'd never have much to do with Theresa, not after her husband did that and Theresa had the breakdown, 'cos it all came out – not in the papers, nor the inquest, which just concluded that Crompton had had a sudden mental breakdown and taken his life whilst his mind was unbalanced – but after. Theresa told me that she'd said terrible things to Louise. She said she couldn't stop herself, and she'd screamed at her that she was Terence's real love. Somewhere in the telling, her mind snapped and she ended up attacking Louise. She was put into an asylum, and Louise moved back to her mother's and has never spoken or contacted Theresa since.'

'What about her mother? Didn't you say Theresa still had a mother alive?'

'She's another that's away with the fairies, or used to be. It seems she changed after her old man died. That's how it is with some women: they make their husbands think they are vulnerable and need special care. I reckon that's what Lady Daphne did. Anyway, I think with her Theresa was to blame. She'd have turns every time her mother visited, till they advised she didn't visit the asylum. And there wasn't much contact after that. Theresa's fault. She'd never answer any letters or even open the door to her mother. She told me she felt ashamed and didn't want any contact, as doing so only churned up the shame inside of her and made her feel unwell.'

The more Lizzie heard, the less this post-war Theresa seemed to have in common with the woman she'd been reading about. Yes, she'd mentioned her waywardness, and being led by strong sexual urges, and her need to experience everything, but what came through was a sense of remorse and trying to atone. Now it seemed she'd caused devastation to so many lives... But then, she was ill – mentally ill, and not only because of her brother's death, because other things must have happened to her during the war. No, she'd keep an open mind about Theresa Crompton until she'd finished reading her memoirs.

'I think you should go to the police, Rita, but only to clear up with them that you're the woman they've been looking for and to give them any information they need. But the using of Theresa has to stop. It ain't right. You've caused her enough trouble. And I can't see why yer think as Ken won't get us if we're with Theresa in her house. Besides, it would just bring more down on Theresa. We have to go to the police.'

'No! Look, I've changed me mind. Hearing you say it 'as put the fear of them back into me. What if they dig deeper? You can't trust the cops. They might get suspicious and you've to remember, I did play me part. I did set her up. If they come sniffing around, Ken'll tell them that. I'm on a life licence, so I'll go straight back inside. I can't,

Lizzie. I can't...'

Sobs wracked Rita's body, and Lizzie knew they were genuine. Driven by fear and despair, they reached through this new exterior the drugs had given her to the soft, kind heart she'd always had. 'Don't, Rita. Come here. Come back on the bed.'

Rita's weight sank into the mattress, unbalancing Lizzie's body. She fell onto her, and they both giggled. Rita helped her to steady herself and then held on to her. 'Lizzie, I know I'm an old cow, always have been, but I love yer, girl, and I'm so sorry I've brought all this down on yer. That brother of yours is a psycho. He takes after me brother – your Uncle Alf as was. He were hung for the murder of a young lad.'

'What? Oh, Rita...'

'I didn't ever want you to find out, but yer would have done eventually. You'll probably find a lot out if that Alice has her way.'

'Alice? Yer mean me dad's sister? What has she got to do with it all? She's not had any contact with me since me accident. And why did Uncle Alf murder a lad? What happened?'

'Your Uncle Alf were ... well, he were with this young lad. He said the lad were willing, but after, the lad said he was going to the police. Alf flipped. They said at the trial that the kid's body was unrecognizable.'

'Oh, my God!'

'Look, don't fret yerself about it. It were a long time ago. You were only a baby. But it does worry me as to what Ken might be capable of. He has a sort of fixation with you. It mucks about with his head. He wants yer all to himself, but he wants yer

94

to have experiences, like when he brought Len here the other day. It's like he wants to control yer. I'm scared, Lizzie.'

It struck Lizzie that Rita was more scared for herself than she was for her. She said she loved her, but was willing to sacrifice her to keep herself out of prison! She suppressed the anger that rose at this thought.

'I'll tell you what, Lizzie. I have another idea. Leave it with me. I'll get us out of here. I promise. There's still them as I can call on.'

The shocking things she'd heard about her uncle and the similarity between him and Ken overrode Lizzie's feelings about what Rita intended. *And what about her Aunt Alice?* Why was she coming back into her life? Ignoring what Rita had said she asked, 'Rita, you mentioned Aunt Alice?'

'Yeah, she's been sniffing around. She waylaid me in the street. Haven't seen her for years – well, not since your mum's funeral, anyway... Look, I didn't want to tell yer this. None of it, but it seems your dad has been in contact with her and wants to see you.'

Seven

Finding the Link

Jacques – Florida 1963

Despite the log fire crackling into life, Jacques noticed his grandfather shivering as he reached for the quilt from the arm of the sofa. 'Let me help you, sir.'

The many-coloured squares of the quilt brought his grandmother to mind as he tucked it around his grandfather. She'd told him she'd taken up the tradition of the American women soon after she'd arrived here. She had stories relating to each square she'd lovingly stitched into it, and there had to be fifty or more. The one with the tiny rosebuds had come from the dress she'd worn to travel over here, and in the centre was a square that she'd cut from the faded brown corduroy college jacket belonging to his father, which she'd insisted on bringing with her. Then, near to the edge, was a square of blue velvet from Jacques's own first little coat. There were many such pieces of material in a trunk upstairs, each marked with the date of a happening in his life and all preserved for the day his own wife would fashion her own quilt. He laughed to himself, as he doubted any such thing would happen. He couldn't imagine any of the girls he knew going in for such occupations as sitting quietly stitching memory quilts, and he even doubted that their mothers had kept up the tradition. You were more likely to see them driving a big truck – that's when they weren't burning their bras!

Sipping his bourbon it traced a warm feeling down his gullet into his stomach, and he began to relax. His need to learn more about his father hadn't lessened, but he worried about the effect on his grandfather of revisiting painful memories, and once again said so. 'Please don't go on, Grandfather. It is too much for you. Maybe another time...'

'No, now is the right time... Those words of your father's – "No one persecutes the Jews here" – often ring in my ears. They were said so innocently, by a boy I thought had changed to a man, but I was to see him become even more of a man. As I said, he did find out about my family, but by that time his life had changed, and so had his views, as things were coming to light that he never believed could happen.'

Isaac – Paris, July 1940

'Father, you have to get out. You have to go into hiding. You are in great danger.'

Listening to his son, Isaac felt his heart tugged in two. 'But what about you? Pierre, your mother and I are very worried. You have to come with us.'

'Father, there are movements – people who are joining forces and forming secret societies. Resistance groups – people who want to fight the Ger-

97

man rule, and will eventually triumph to free France. I have joined one such group, and through them I have found a place for you and Mother. Here, many people know you are Jewish. It is not safe. Grandmère will have to go with you. This way the neighbours will only know that you have all disappeared. They will be thankful to have you out of their midst, and as you are not yet known to the Germans, they will not mention you. They know that the Germans torture anyone they think may have collaborated with a Jew. The neighbours will fear that their friendship with you may be construed as that.'

Isaac did not argue. He knew what the Germans were capable of, and did not want his friends in any danger. 'Where are we to go, my son?'

'To a farm on the border of Vichy country. You will be safe there. The farmer is very old; all he knows is that you are looking to take your family out of Paris during the Occupation. If asked, he will say you are his son who has come to help him run the farm. There are no neighbours for miles around, and he is known to have a son who went off to make his fortune many years ago. The son has never been seen since, so no one will question his story. He and his neighbours know little of each other, and only met at market when he farmed his land. He hasn't done so for a long time, but now it must be done. It will be hard work, but you will be safe as the Germans are not in that area. It is near to the designated free area. But never trust anyone, as the French people there are collaborators, and carry out the Germans' wishes. You will be okay, as you do not look Jewish; Mère and Grandmère do, so they must stay on the farm and never go to market or anywhere. Your name will be Becke – François Becke. Your French is so fluent that nobody will guess that you are not French.'

'But, son, we must get to America. You must come...'

'We can't, Father. I know there are still those making their way to America, but we can't take the risk.'

'And you, my son? Where will you be? How can we contact you?'

'I will contact you when I can, Father.'

Isaac felt for the second time in a few short months that his world was crumbling. His arms encircled his son. 'My Pierre, I cannot bear to lose you. I have lost so many... So many...'

'You won't lose me. I will be safe. I have Grandfather and Uncle Jhona and all of the family looking down on me. I have to fight for them. I have to know a time when the Jews are safe as a people, and to know that I did my best towards that.'

Florida 1963

'I didn't see your father again until he brought you to me. He told me about the love of his life – your mother, Theresa Crompton – a British agent we knew as Olivia Danchanté. He told me how she was the bravest person he'd ever met and that she had kept her pregnancy a secret from her colleagues and her bosses in England. She'd carried out all assignments given to her during the whole nine months, and to the letter. Even her cover family knew nothing of you growing inside her. The birth took place with just Pierre present to help her. He'd had to leave her after to bring the baby to us.'

'D-did my mother never see me again?'

'Yes, in the early summer following your birth. It was June 1944. They said preparations were under way that could see the beginning of the end of the war. And that they had work to do immediately following this. And again in August of that year. Olivia – I mean, Theresa – should have been lifted out, but she chose to stay and see the last of their planned missions through and to come to see you with Pierre. They had a wonderful time. They were so happy. They picnicked; they danced in the moonlight. They tended to you and indulged you all they could. That was the last time your grandmother and I saw them. They had been involved in the sabotaging of the advance of German troops after D-Day, and their work was all but finished. They had such hope that within weeks the war would be over, but until it was, on French soil, anyway, they would fight on. At the end of it your mother would have to return to England for her official discharge, and then, they would come for us all. They never did. We did not know for a long time what had happened, but then we had the news we had dreaded. We went back to Paris, once it was all over, but all we could find out was that someone had betrayed them to save his own skin. We don't know when, but they were captured and... Oh

God, so much pain...'

The silence filled the space between them. Jacques couldn't take all of the pain on to his shoulders, because in his heart was the warm glow of knowledge that his mother and father had loved one another and had loved him, and a pride swelled in him as he thought, *They gave themselves in the ultimate sacrifice to ensure my freedom.* And with this thought a great love for them surged through him.

Going to his grandfather's side, he dropped down on his knees and took this beloved man into his arms. 'Grandfather, I can't make all of that right, but you have given me something to hold on to. My father and mother are real to me at last. To think of their love for one another and for me, and of them having fun together, means so much to me. I have to go to try to find if I have any family on my mother's side, but I will be back and I will make you proud of me.'

'I cannot be more proud of you than I am, son. And I understand. Go with my blessing, but tread with care. You will be a shock to them, and ... well, they are British, and from what I heard, upper-crust at that, so your birth to their un-married relative may be a source of embarrassment that they might want to keep quiet.'

'But this is the sixties! Surely there are no more stuffed-shirt societies, even in Britain!'

'I think there are, son, though there are those who challenge it more and more. I don't know anything of your mother's family. She did say they came from the north of England – Yorkshire – but I don't think finding them will be a problem. I – I have pictures...'

'What? Of my parents? I thought everything had to be left behind!'

'I know. We – we did say that, and it is true about most things, but we did bring some papers and there are some family photos amongst them. None of your great-grandparents – my mother and father – nor any of your great-uncle or great-aunt or their families, as I couldn't carry anything like that with me when I left them behind... But of that first weekend and of the time later in the year, when they came to visit, of Theresa and Pierre and you, I have copies of those and I left some at the farm house just in case. I could never give up hope, not completely. We ... your grandmother and me, we could not look at them. We kept them hidden away, but now I can, and I want to, and I want to share them with you. They are yours. We had no right to keep them from you... I'm sorry.'

'I understand. Please don't worry. Gee, this is a real turn-up. Where are they? I can't wait to look on the faces of my parents.'

Fetching the wooden box he didn't know even existed from under his grandfather's bed set up an ache of anticipation inside Jacques. And an overwhelming love surged through him as he looked at the picture of his father and mother holding him. Both looked down on him with such love in their eyes, and held him with protective arms. Though he lay in his mother's arms, his father had his hand over hers and one of his fingers touched his son's face. Tears prickled his eyes. He blinked and one escaped and trickled down his nose.

'I know you feel sad, son, but look at them with pride. As they posed for this picture, your dad said to your mom, "This is why we do what we do – for our son and for all the children of the next generation. *His* life will be different. The Germans have to be beaten." Your mother replied, "Yes, I know, but I wish it was over and we could stay like this for ever – a family." Your dad had to dry her tears and comfort her before she could recover to smile for the photo.'

'Do you hate the Germans, Grandfather?'

'No, I don't. Not all of them. They didn't want what happened, but were powerless to stop it. Those who tried suffered as much as the Jews did, and there are far more good ones than bad. They had been taken over by a wicked regime, but they didn't realize just how evil until it was too late. I am sorry that they are now suffering as they are. The wall that divides them is just as bad as the walls that divided our people from everything humane. Families are living apart and never allowed to see each other. Those in the East are desperately poor and oppressed. Many millions of innocent Germans lost their lives in the bombing of their country. No, I don't hate them. I feel for them.'

'I hate them. At this moment, I hate them like I've never hated anyone. They took my life from me. And for what? German supremacy? Well, they didn't bloody get it, and yet so many suffered and died whilst they strived for it. God! I can't forgive them. I can't.'

'I don't blame you, son, but don't direct your hate at a nation. Direct it at the regime – the Nazi regime – and hope that they never rise again.'

Jacques tried to see things his grandfather's way, but at that moment, looking into the eyes of his beautiful parents and thinking about the agony of the death suffered by his great-grandfather and great-uncle and great-aunt and his great-uncle's family – those three innocent little children – he couldn't. And then, to think, an estimated six million of his fellow Jews, burned, gassed, shot, starved, tortured, experimented on... God, how could anyone ever forgive them?

'Look to the future, son. Learn from the past, but look to the future.'

He knew his grandfather was right, and he would try. 'Grandfather, do you know where they are buried?'

'I don't know. I heard that your father was taken to Alsace. I have a map of it, there in the bottom of the box. I found it after the war in a little second-hand shop selling war memorabilia. See – Camp du Struthof. I read later that they have put a memorial there. It is located on France's eastern border and on the west bank of the upper Rhine adjacent to Germany and Switzerland. But from what I have researched, it will be distressing to visit it. It was a concentration camp where twenty thousand Jews and dissidents, as they called French Resistance workers, were executed. They say they have kept the conditions realistic. I couldn't bear to see it.'

'I will go there. I have to. My father was forced there, so I will go willingly in his memory. I will try to feel what he felt and I know that is where I will get the closest possible to him, as that is the place where he left this earth. But what about my mother?'

'The stories that filtered through to us were that she was taken to Dachau and shot.'

'Then I will go there, too.'

'And, my dear Jacques, would you do something for me, as I fear I will never go back? Will you visit my home in Poland? Will you go there and erect a memorial?'

Eight

Bitterness Corrodes

Patsy and Harriet – Breckton 1963

Studying old stuff was getting to be a pain, but Dad insisted they spend some of their time each day going over and over the diagnostics of what could go wrong with different parts of the body. 'It will stand you in good stead when you are in that little group of student doctors following the consultant from bed to bed. It may give you an edge over some of the males who will be out to trip you up at every step to make you look foolish. You will be able to turn the tables on them,' he'd said.

Patsy's umpteenth sigh provided Harri with the excuse she needed to put down her papers. On doing so she saw Patsy had the newspaper article open in front of her. She'd first looked at it a couple of days ago and hadn't been right since, though she couldn't blame her. 'Is it all getting to you again, love? Have you made up your mind what to do?'

'I don't know. Nothing in me is stirred by the picture. You know – no emotions or anything like I should feel.'

'Not even your instinct as a potential doctor? Surely that part of you is moved, even if you have no feelings for the woman as your mother?'

'Don't come all of that with me, Harri. You have no idea with your cosy life that's never been disrupted in any way.'

'Stop it! I know you're upset, but none of what happened to you is my fault and I won't keep letting you blame me. And don't start on the other stuff about the family, as all that about you being less than me in their eyes is in the inside of you, not in us. Once you let go of that, you will be a lot happier, though I'm used to you how you are: Grumpy-Knickers carries the world's woes on her shoulders! If you changed, I wouldn't know how to go on, as me life revolves around keeping you happy. By, I'd be able to bake a cake in me spare time between me studies.'

After a moment's silence Patsy laughed. She couldn't help but join her. This released some of the tension between them.

'Sorry, love. Don't know what's got into me. It must be this woman – me supposed mother – turning up, and in such a predicament. I coped with the fact that I had relatives who knew nothing about me, but *she* does know, and chooses not to. Part of me wants to meet her, if only to give her a

106

piece of me mind.'

'Maybe she couldn't cope with having you... Oh, I don't know, we've been over this so many times, but I do know you'll never find out unless you go to her. I know as I'd want to meet her and find out the truth.'

The telephone ringing cut into their conversation, its shrill tone demanding attention. 'I'll go. I think Mam's out the back, and Dad's not in.'

'It'll most likely be one of his patients, so if he's not in there's not much use in answering.'

This shocked Harri. How could Patsy be so offhand about someone who might need a doctor?

A voice with a similar tone to Patsy's came down the line, only this one was broad cockney. 'Is there a Patsy there? Is this the residence of Sarah, Jack Fellam's daughter?'

'Aye, it is, and there is a Patsy here. Who's this calling?'

'Just put Patsy on, will yer.'

'It's for you, Patsy. The woman won't say who she is.'

The voice sent an instant shock through Patsy. *Rita!* She dropped the phone.

'What is it? Patsy?'

The hanging mouthpiece swung to and fro, giving out an increasingly frustrated voice: 'Hello? Are you there? Hello...?' Harri returned it to its stand. 'Patsy?'

Her body trembled so violently she had to sit. 'That was her ... that Rita that caused me to make the call that led to my uncle killing himself!'

'That wasn't your fault, Patsy, love. You were only trying to find your family, and that Rita had used you. Anyroad, you're only surmising that it was your phone call as triggered what he did, you don't know for sure. Whatever he'd done, it had come back to bite him and it must have been pretty bad, but it were his doing, not yours. You couldn't know that he had sommat in him as he couldn't face. That's even if he did. No one knows.'

'But I did know, Harri. I knew all about him and Rita, and well, Rita had said he had used my own mother, and together they had done un-speakable stuff. *Her...*' Her finger hurt as she stabbed it on the picture of the battered, old-looking woman staring out at them.

'It were all a long time ago – she's made up for how she was as a young-un. Look how the village still talks about what she did in the war. Anyroad, how do you know what Rita said is the truth? If she rings again I'll deal with her or get Mam or Dad to.'

'She must be ringing because she's seen the story. Maybe she wants to complete the revenge she started. She ... maybe she even did this to my mother... Oh, God, Harri, what should I do? My mother may need me help...'

'Let's talk to Mam about it. She'll know what to do. One thing, though, Patsy, love: you're not as callous about your mam as you try to make out, and I'm glad about that. I didn't like seeing you like that. It scared me a bit.'

Patsy suppressed a sigh. Harri was too caring at times, to the point where it got on her nerves. Yes, they were training to be doctors, and having that kind of nature was a good trait, but the profession wasn't all about caring. Sometimes some tough decisions had to be faced and taken, and you couldn't let your heart rule your head. Harri was in danger of doing that a bit too often.

A part of her calmed. At least that was one good thing about Harri: she had a good bedside manner, and could make something as massive as this seem everyday and something that could be sorted. Could it, though? And did she want it to be? No, some little part of her would still like to get revenge on her mother and was now wishing she hadn't cut Rita off. This thought triggered another and something she'd pondered for the umpteenth time came to her, prompting her to ask of Harri: 'You know, it's always puzzled me how Rita knew you, or rather what you looked like. She must have been round these parts after she left the prison.'

'I've thought about that. And I can only think that she must have been the woman who came to Granddad Jack and Grandma Dorothy's house. I used to stay over quite a bit in the holidays, as we lived in Market Harborough then and I didn't get to see them often. One afternoon this woman appeared out of the blue in a flash car.'

'That would be Rita. Everything is flash about her. What did she want?'

'Well, she wasn't welcomed – not by Grandma Dorothy, she wasn't. It appeared they had been Land Girls together, or rather this woman had worked on your Uncle Terence's farm and Dorothy on me granddad's. She'd come because she'd wanted Granddad Jack's forgiveness. And he was willing to give it to her, despite Dorothy not wanting him to. You know how lovely Granddad Jack is. Look how he treats you the same as me.'

'I know. I am a bitch at times. Sorry about me mood earlier. All of you have been good to me and accepted me, although it couldn't have been easy for your mam. I mean, she had to come to terms with the fact that her then husband had betrayed her just after they were wed, and by raping another! It must have been humiliating for her to be faced with me, and me looking exactly like her own daughter!'

'Well, we know it was hard for her. Not that she had any love for our dad. She was afraid of him and had married him out of fear.'

'Harri... How do you cope with that? I mean, sometimes I want to wipe out of me mind everything to do with our dad.'

'I know. It's like wearing a sackcloth shirt of shame. Like everyone around here knows who you are, who fathered you, and you wonder if they think you might be like him. But I try to hang on to the fact that he was sick in his mind. I try to keep in me how Dad explained it all – how he told us of the undiagnosed split personality syndrome he thought our dad suffered with, and so he couldn't really be responsible for his actions. That made me feel better. Especially as I've looked up schizophrenia and read quite a bit about it.'

'You said that you wonder if you might be like him... I do that too. I get scared that one of us might be affected. That we might develop that same disorder. I fear the way I have mood changes–'

'That's just your hormones, you daft ha'p'orth. You're like a dog with a sore arse around the time of your monthly!'

'Harri! If your mam could hear you...'

'She'd say what she's said many a time: "Harriet, you might look like your Granny Megan, but, by, you take after your Great Granna Issy. She were a one for crude remarks."'

'Is that before she clips your ear, or after?'

They doubled up with the giggles. Patsy felt better for it, though it didn't dispel the fear she held about herself. It did sometimes feel like she was two different people, and one of those would gladly murder her so-called mother...

'You're serious all of a sudden. Eeh, it takes sommat to keep your chin up, Patsy. Just think on: we come from good stock. There's not just our dad in the equation; there's some brilliant and very strong women in our background an' all. And that includes your mother. 'Cos despite everything she did before, she was amongst them as received a medal for her services during the war, and the King himself presented it to her!'

King's College Hospital, London

'Officer, you can see Miss Crompton now.'

'Oh? You sound very positive. Have things improved with her?'

'Yes, very much so. You won't recognize her. Oh, of course her face is still a mess, poor thing, but

111

one of my young nurses has succeeded in getting through to her. She has managed to get her eating a little, which is helping. She was starving. Hasn't been eating right for a long time, by the looks of things. Anyway, we are supplementing the little she is taking in. My nurse has managed to clean her up and get her hair sorted. They have a real affinity. Nurse Wilson is a kind and caring girl. Miss Crompton is still having moments when she thinks it is another time in her life, and from the snippets we hear it seems that that life could have been the cause of some of her mental illness. Have you any news on her family?'

'Yes, a doctor from the north contacted us. He works in the area Miss Crompton came from. It appears she has an elderly mother still alive. From what he knows from his wife, who has lived in the area all her life, it appears that Miss Crompton did have another life. War hero, no less! He thinks from his wife's calculations that Miss Crompton is about fifty. Her mother lives in York and is in her early eighties. A lady, no less. Lady Daphne Crompton.'

'Good gracious! Have you been in contact with her?'

'Yes. She knew. She'd seen the papers. She told us she and her daughter have been estranged for a long time. She sounded very sad about it and insisted it was to do with her daughter's mental state, as they had been very close when Miss Crompton was young. She said she had been afraid to come forward, as her appearance in her daughter's life always upsets her and sends her into a worse mental state.'

'Oh ... well, that's a difficult one. There must be some history there. A daughter doesn't just fall out with her mother. Any other family?'

'Yes, but none that she has had contact with for many years. She had a brother. There is still his family – his widow and her children. They live down this end of the country: part of the Rothergill family from Surrey. Lord Rothergill is her uncle.'

'None of that means anything to me. I'm not up on who's who. But I wonder why none of them came forward? I don't know. There's some mystery surrounding our Miss Crompton, that's for sure. A war heroine, mentally ill and left to rot on her own. It beggars belief.'

'It does. And there's more. There's still that woman the neighbour reported – the one who has visited Miss Crompton for years. Why hasn't she come forward? Who is she, and why hasn't she done anything about the state the poor woman was in? There is a line of inquiry opened up concerning that. I can't say a lot, but Miss Crompton's bank manager has also been in touch. He has some worries concerning her finances. I'd very much like to find out who this woman is. That's why I'm here.'

'Well, I know I said you can see her, but that doesn't mean you can pester her with a lot of questions. That decision isn't mine. We have a psychiatrist working with her. You will have to contact her.'

'Right, give me her number. I need to move on this and get it sorted. What's going to happen with the old girl? Is she staying here?'

113

'She's not an old girl; she's not much older than you or me. Anyway, yes is the answer, for the time being. Social services are involved now, and they are trying to find a nursing home to take her once her health is stable. Whether we will get her mental health stable or not is another matter, and that will determine the kind of home she goes to, as she will not be allowed to go to her own home. Before you go, give me all the contact numbers of her family and their details. If they do get in touch, at least I will know they are genuine.'

'Right. I think her mother may ring and enquire after her. As I say, her name is Lady Daphne.'

Seeing the uniformed man enter the ward and look towards her, Theresa felt old fears surfacing, but she quelled them. She would tell him nothing. Just like before. Oh, yes, he was British ... but was he really? You couldn't tell these days. Nothing was as it was. Keeping yourself to yourself was the only way.

Breckton 1963

'Rita! Rita has been in contact? Eeh, dear God, will it never end?'

'Sarah, don't take on like that. It's not helpful. We need to sort this out.'

'You're right, darling. Sorry.'

Richard's words were stern, but Patsy noted that he immediately counteracted that by going to Sarah's side and holding her to him. This had the effect of calming Sarah, and she turned to her now

114

and said, 'Patsy, love. You came to us for help, and all I do is think on what happened in the past. You have the now to deal with and you need us all supporting you. I'm sorry. We are all here for you, dear.'

'It's okay. I know there's a lot of pain in you, Mam.' It came so natural to call Sarah mam, even though Patsy had to admit to feeling there was something in Sarah that hadn't fully accepted her. And it wasn't her being paranoid as Harri would say, as she'd often felt that Sarah was watching her. It was as if she was looking for something in her or was on guard against there being something.

Richard stopped this train of thought as he said, 'Patsy, I think Harri may be right. This Rita has seen the story in the paper. This has led her to know of your mother's whereabouts again, and she is after the revenge she sought before. And she wants to involve you. It would have been easy for her to find you. I know she disappeared after Terence Crompton's death, but she must have known that we had taken you in. Finding a doctor's address and telephone number isn't a difficult task. What we have to decide is what to do next. I think we should call the police–'

'No! I – I mean ... well, that would complicate things.' Richard looked shocked at this, but somehow she had to keep a small possibility of further contact with Rita open. 'I – I ... well, I think we should make sure. If she rings again, we should give her a chance to tell of her intentions. They may not be what we think. Perhaps ... well, she did hint at her relationship with me mother. Maybe that has carried on. Maybe she found her a long time ago and has been a companion of hers. We just don't know. I'd prefer us to go along the route of finding out what she wants. Perhaps me mother is asking for me...'

This last sealed the outcome she wanted.

'Of course, darling.' Richard crossed over to her. His arm around her gave her comfort and confidence. 'I hadn't thought about that. Only, don't get your hopes up too high. The article in the paper did say your mother appeared to be suffering with dementia, and it didn't say anything about a companion. Her neighbour said Miss Crompton is a kind of recluse.'

'Yes, but that same neighbour also said she had seen a woman visit on more than a few occasions, and we know the police are appealing for her to come forward. That may be Rita, and she may be afraid to come forward. She will know that I have seen the article. She may have changed over the last couple of years and doesn't want me making trouble for her, or upsetting me mother by turning up. She knows how desperate I was to find me mother.'

'Okay, so what do you want us to do?'

'Speak to her if she rings again. Tell her you're speaking on behalf of me as I want to know what she wants, but don't want to talk to her just yet. If she is above board she will talk to you, and if she isn't she will put the phone down. It's as simple as that.'

Patsy breathed a sigh of relief when Richard and Sarah agreed to this. At least the path of communication was still open with Rita. And even if she did put the phone down, it wouldn't mean that Patsy couldn't find her. She'd find her alright. She needed to. That was something she was certain of.

Patsy hadn't thought her chance would come so soon, but later that day, with just her and Harri in the house once more, Rita rang again. Without having to think about it, a plan formed as she answered, and she had to act out part of it as it occurred.

'Rita! I know why you're ringing. Well, just leave me alone and leave me mother alone as well. I don't want anything to do with you or her. Me life's sorted.'

Banging the phone down, she sank onto the chair next to it and sobbed. Harri was by her side in seconds.

'Oh, Patsy, love. Eeh, come on now. Oh, Patsy...'

'Fetch Mam. I need her. Please, Harri.'

'Aye, okay, but it'll take me a while as she's gone to help with the antenatal and baby clinic in the village hall and there's no phone in there, besides which, she's taken the car. Look, let me–'

'No... no... I want Mam... Help me. Please get Mam.'

'Oh, God! Patsy stop this. I'm not going while you're in this state. I can't... Besides, you know how it upsets Mam that Rita's been in touch.'

'I – I know, but she helps me. I'll be alright while you go. I just need her ... sh-she understands.'

'Okay, but calm down. I'll get you a glass of water.'

Patsy's fingers shook as she dialled 100. The operator answered immediately, 'Number, please.'

Hoping she wasn't too late to be reconnected she said, 'My last caller was cut off. Can you reconnect us, please?'

'The caller rang from a telephone box, Madame.'

'Well, just give it a try. Please. It is very important.' As soon as she said this, she regretted it. The nosy bitch would probably listen in now!

A tense moment passed as the dull sound of the phone rang out, then Rita's voice came down the line.

'Rita, it's me. I couldn't talk before...'

'Well, aren't you the bleedin' lucky cow? I'd only stopped a mo to light a fag and was just about to leave or yer wouldn't have caught me. Fell on yer feet, didn't yer? That Fellam lot were always a soft-hearted lot. Took you in, didn't they?'

'Yes, I'm with Sarah, only she's a Chesterton now. She's married to Richard—'

'I know all that. I told yer, you wouldn't credit what they get up to. All related, that lot, and half of them murderers. It ain't bleedin' safe in the countryside. Gentlefolk, ha! They ain't bleedin' gentle; they're inbred, and half of them are off their bleedin' nut.'

'Look, I haven't got a lot of time. What do you want? Why do you keep ringing me?'

'I wondered if you still want to take revenge on that cow as gave birth to yer? 'Cos I can help you and you can help me.'

'I'll meet you. But that's all. I don't know... I... Anyway, what do you mean, I can help you?'

'I look after me niece. She needs help. I have to get her out of here and I thought your lot'd take her in. She's ill.'

'What's wrong?'

After hearing what Rita said, she felt as though she'd entered a different world. It wasn't that she knew nothing of the culture of drugs – it was seeping into university life, and she'd come across it herself with the types she'd had to mix with when she lived in the hostel, and had even tried some marijuana once. But for the most part she felt far removed from what she was hearing now. It shocked her to the core. 'Look, it's complicated and not a good idea to talk on the telephone. I'll come down to London tomorrow. Meet me at Euston Station. There's only one train from here that connects with one in Leeds, and it arrives in London at around two o'clock. If I'm not on it, it'll be 'cos I couldn't get around them here to let me come on me own, so telephone me again. I do want to meet you, Rita.'

'I'll be there. I need help and I don't know who to turn to. I've got to get my Lizzie away.'

'Christ, they're back! I can't talk any more... Thank you for calling. Goodbye.'

'Patsy, love, are you alright? Eeh, lass, you had us reet worried for you. Who was that?'

'I – I'm a lot better. Sorry, Mam, I didn't mean to worry you. And I don't know who that was. I was upset and forgot to ask. They asked for you, Mam. I just told them you were out and to call back later.'

'Never mind, happen as they will if it's of any importance, but eeh, lass, Harri says as that Rita's

119

been ringing you again?'

'She has. I told her to leave me alone. I panicked and didn't ask her what she wanted.'

'Knowing her, it won't be owt good. She's a bad 'un. Allus has been. Pity she rang when I was out. I reckon as what we thought must be reet and she's seen the article about your mam and thinks she can get sommat out of it for herself.'

Patsy sank down on the sofa and buried her face in her hands. The action would be expected, and would give her time to cover her guilt.

'Look, lass, I know this is a difficult time for you, though I can only imagine your real feelings. But we are here for you, love.' Sarah's arms enveloped Patsy as she said this. The action compounded Patsy's guilt, but did not lessen her resolve.

'Eeh, I'm so sorry, Patsy.' This from Harri, who'd knelt at her knee, had her reaching for her hand.

'Look, sit a minute with Harri while I go and make a pot of tea, then we can all talk it through and see what the best plan is, eh?'

'Thanks, Mam. I just wanted you here.'

Sarah smiled at her with a smile that didn't touch her eyes, and for a moment it was as if Sarah could see through her to the deceitful bit she'd tried to hide. The look was gone in a second, and an extra squeeze given before she rose and Harri took her place next to her.

'By, Patsy, you're trembling.'

'Really, love, I'm okay. I am. I just had the wind knocked out of me sails, but I'm going to see me mam tomorrow. I've made me mind up.'

'Oh? That was sudden, but I think it best. I'll come with you...'

'No. I need to do this on me own. If I change me mind when I get there then it'll be down to me and no one can persuade me one way or the other. I just want it to be my choice. Help me with this, Harri, please.'

'If you're sure...'

'I am. I should go and see her. It will lay it all to rest and decide things.' As she said this, her emotions fought a battle inside her between guilt at her deceit and elation that at last she was going to get to the bottom of everything that held her back. She allowed the elation to win.

Sarah, coming through the door with three steaming mugs on a tray and saying, 'Reet, here we are, a nice pot of tea for us all,' broke the turmoil and put her in a more normal place. Though she'd never got used to how these northerners called a mug of tea *a pot*. It still conjured up her horror when she'd first heard it said and had thought they would make her drink a whole teapot full!

Whilst sipping on this household's cure for all, she told Sarah of her plans. Her reaction was the same as Harri's: she thought it was a good idea, but she wanted Harri to go with her.

'No, Mam. I have to go on me own. Harri understands.' She explained to Sarah why.

'I think she's right, Mam. It'll be a big day for you, Patsy love, but aye, I think it is sommat as you have to do on your own.'

'Well, let's see what Dad says.'

'Oh, please, Mam, please help me sway him.

Now I've made me mind up I have to do it.'

The sound of a car door slamming stopped Sarah answering. She got up and went towards the kitchen.

'That'll be Dad now.' Harri clutched her hand again as she said this. 'Give them a mo. I'll help if there's any argument.'

There wasn't. Richard thought it a good idea and not before time. His only concern was her doing it alone. 'Mam says as the phone call put you in a state, love, so what will meeting up with your mother do?'

'I know, but that was unexpected, not something I wanted. I want this and will prepare for it. It won't be anything to do with Rita. She won't know, so can't do any mischief. And as I know London like the back of me hand – well, I should, I trudged most of it in me childhood – I don't see what can go wrong. I'll ring you, Mam, throughout the day, I promise. And if I'm too late to catch a train back, I'll let you know where I am staying. Really, you have nothing to worry over. I looked after meself for a long time in the big city when I was only a girl.'

'Okay, love. It won't stop us worrying about you, but yes, I can see your point. I hate to think of you doing this massive thing on your own, but if that's the way you want it, then I'm not going to stand in your way, love.'

They all smiled and nodded at this. Patsy stood and put her arms around Sarah and said, 'Thanks, Mam. It was a good day that I came to Breckton, despite everything that it caused.' Sarah hugged her back, a real hug that held no reservations, and as Patsy looked at the others and saw tears in their eyes, she thought: *Yes! Yes! I've pulled it off. None of them suspects a thing.*

Nine

Meetings of Significance

Lizzie – 1963 and Theresa – 1943

With Rita out, the house took on a cloak of unease. Lizzie felt as if there was a time-bomb ticking, and the feeling tightened her throat with fear. It had been several days since they'd seen Ken, and her sixth sense told her something was wrong and that something really bad was about to happen. She shifted her bottom a little as she tried to ease the pain of the sores that had developed, her grubby baby-doll nightie stuck to her body. She hadn't left her bed since Ken had given her that first injection. Her body gave off a stale odour. Her teeth were coated, but she had no energy to do anything about it. The odd time she did sit up and was faced with her reflection in the mirror opposite, her despair deepened at the sight of herself: hair matted and lank, sores pitting her mouth, red, dry eyes, and bones protruding where they never had before.

Rita had tried to encourage her to get up, but she couldn't – even going to the toilet was too much, and she'd resorted to using the bed-pan, which she hated. It was as if putting that stuff into her, then depriving her of it, had killed everything that she was. The only thing she wanted to do was to read about Theresa's life. Sometimes she felt some of Theresa's courage seep into her, and at those times she'd resolve to do something about the state she was in. But the lack of energy and the fight inside her against the need of the injections thwarted any plans she made.

Reaching for Theresa's books, she opened the first one near to the end – there were only a few pages left in this one to read. She'd learned about Theresa's training: armed and unarmed combat skills from former inspectors in the Shanghai Municipal Police; Commando training in Scotland; security and demolition techniques, and then, Morse code telegraphy; and parachute training at RAF Ringway in Cheshire. Throughout all of this, Theresa had gradually become more confident in her own abilities, and less afraid. Soon she would be leaving England's shores and flying to France to begin her mission – something she dreaded less than her forthcoming visit home...

Theresa – January 1943

As the train pulled into the station, Theresa sighed. Nothing in her wanted to alight onto the platform. The small mining town of Breckton, and Hensal Grange, their mansion-like home on the edges of it, now seemed like another world and alien to her. Had she ever been that woman that had taken all that life gave? That selfish creature that had everything and indulged in every pleasure as it occurred to her? Her cheeks reddened at the thought of some of her behaviour, and once again her mind sent cringes through her nerve ends as images came to her of lying with Rita and with Terence. But even though they were now abhorrent to her, these incidents weren't without some tingle of desire for the pleasure they had given her.

A few moments ago the train had passed the woodland where the summerhouse nestled... Oh God, the pain that had stabbed her... Remnants of it still churned her heart. What had occurred in the summerhouse with Billy Armitage would never leave her, though it sometimes felt as though the pregnancy and birth had never happened, and she had been able to put her child out of her mind while her body had taken the onslaught of this or that training. But in the dead of the night she hadn't been able to, and the ache of loss had twisted her soul.

Taking a deep breath, she stood and lifted her rucksack from the overhead luggage rack. It was the only luggage she carried. Through the window she could see Terence, anxious in his movements, his head searching the first-class carriages. Well, she hadn't travelled first-class – another sign of how different she was to the girl who'd left almost immediately after Terence's wedding to Louise fifteen months ago. It had been a long fifteen months. Now she just had the hurdle of this twenty-four-hour leave to get over and she would be on her way to France. What would that be like? Would she cope? Something in her told her she would.

'D-darling!'

'Why the surprised look, little brother?' Older than Terence by only a few minutes, she'd often tease him by calling him this.

'Well, I – I didn't expect to see you dressed like that...'

'We have to. It's the rule. When travelling around we have to wear our uniforms at all times. Besides, the coat is handy. Keeps out the cold.'

'But I didn't think you were in the Army now.'

'Oh, yes I am. An officer, no less... Look, aren't you going to greet me properly?' She hadn't been able to resist saying this. Some of Terence's discomfort was down to being faced with the reality of her going to war, but most she knew wasn't. His life had changed too – drastically. Now running a stud farm as well as the vast arable and dairy farm, and being married with a baby on the way, it was all very different for him, too. And she knew he hated what she represented to him – a past he wished he'd never had.

'Of course. Come here, old girl.'

His arms encircled her. The closeness of him stirred something inside her, and she knew it did in him too when he jumped away from her. 'Right, let's get you home. You don't have long and we mean to make the most of it.'

'We can hardly do that, dear brother...'

'Theresa, don't...'

'I'm sorry. I'm only teasing. I'll be a good girl, I promise. How are Pater and Mater and Louise? Oh, and that Penny. Is she still a Land Girl with you?'

'Pater, Mater and Louise are all fine, as you will see. But it's bad form of you to mention Penny.'

'Sorry. I know. Sometimes I think the bitch in me will never go, no matter what I do.' Poor Terence. His past kept staring him in the face at every turn, but then, some of it he deserved. He had turned to Penny, their other Land Girl, for his pleasure after he'd got rid of Rita.

'Penny isn't any longer with us. She chose to leave. Gone to do factory work, I believe. We have others, though – three new Land Girls – but before you start to speculate, I am not having an affair with any of them. I am a very good boy now. I love my wife and I'm very happy.'

'Oh, I'm glad someone is... No, sorry. Oh dear, I keep putting my foot in it... Sorry again, that was unfair. I can't keep punishing you. I love you too much, and I was as much to blame. We have to put it behind us. I promise I will. Everything will be alright. No barbed comments to embarrass you. You don't deserve that; you've paid your price emotionally if not in any other way. You need to get on with your life as I do mine.'

'*Are* you "getting on" with it, darling ... really getting on with it, or is this all a game you play to cover up?'

'You have no idea, do you, Terence? A game? Bloody hell, I'm parachuting behind enemy lines the day after tomorrow. I've undergone training that would have killed many ... nearly did some ... and you have the audacity to ask if I am playing games! You take the bloody biscuit sometimes, little brother!'

'Sorry, old thing. Just trying to find out how

127

you really are. All that other stuff ... well, don't you think I know? Don't you think I worry every day about you? It is why you are doing it that hurts.'

'Oh, it has long ceased to be a way to forget. I will never forget. Never. I need to do my bit. I want to feel that my rotten existence thus far is vindicated. I want to hold my head up high once more...'

They had reached his car. The top was open, and she threw her rucksack into the small back seat. 'Bloody hell, Terence, it's freezing! Besides, I'd have thought you'll have to get rid of this sporty number, won't you? You will need room for your family.'

'Oh, I already have another car. I just thought you'd enjoy riding home in this. Blow some of the cobwebs away.'

She hadn't realized she had 'cobwebs' clinging to her, not until the train had reached familiar territory. Then she'd felt them all descending and clogging her up with memories.

The drive home helped; they couldn't talk above the rush of air and the noise of the engine. Besides which, her face and lips tingled. An exhilarating feeling.

Places that had been so much a part of her other life whizzed by at such a pace she had no time to dwell. She didn't want any. Instead she tried to prepare herself for the moment she would see Mater and Pater and Frobisher, the old butler. God, he'd been part of their lives for ever... She'd missed them so much, but hadn't realized how much until now. And the rest of the staff: Cook and the maids and the farm-hands. None had meant anything to her when she'd lived here, but in a funny way they did now. Not that she would see many of the farm-hands, as most had gone off to war. One had lost his life – a young chap with a mop of dark hair. She couldn't ever remember speaking to him, but he'd been there, part of life as it used to be. Oh, it was all so unfair! One wretched man had ruined everything they knew. Suddenly she couldn't wait for these twenty-four hours to be over. She needed to fight back. She was ready.

Tears prickled her eyes at the sight of Mater and Pater as they came running down the drive towards them. Terence stopped the car and she got out to greet them. Their embrace warmed her, reaching the coldest part of her and splintering her resolve. Her face dampened, her body racked with sobs.

'You're home now, darling. Oh, my dear, my darling, girl...'

As the sobs subsided, she pushed them away gently, smiling a watery smile. 'Well, I didn't expect to give a show like that... Sorry, old things. I'm meant to have toughened up, and here I am blubbering like a baby. But it's so good to see you both.'

Her father took hold of her and pulled her to him. The feeling was unbearable, as it held so much anguish and so many unspoken questions. He knew. He held guilt too – must do. No! She mustn't think like that... She must not! He'd done what he'd done to help her. He couldn't know how much hurt and pain it would cause. She'd wanted rid. She hadn't known how she would feel afterwards either...

They walked up the drive arm in arm, one parent on either side of her, their feet crunching on the icy pebbles. The house came into view: beautiful Hensal Grange. Could anything ever change it? The First World War hadn't, although it had changed the then occupant, her beloved Aunt Laura, as she'd been left a widow at a young age and after losing her only child. Dear Uncle Jeremy had been killed at the very end of the conflict. Laura had floundered for a while, and had then had the misfortune of falling in love with her groom, Jack Fellam.

Theresa had once felt disgust at Jack Fellam's treatment of her aunt – having an affair with her, then dropping her and ultimately benefiting from her will – but she didn't any more. He'd been through so much before and since, and she now knew that a lot of what happened was caused by her aunt, including the near-death of the woman Jack really loved. He'd gone to prison for a murder he hadn't committed – a murder done by Billy Armitage even though he was only a child at the time. Christ, she mustn't start to think of Billy Armitage either ... not now ... not ever...

Seeing Louise again hadn't been the ordeal she'd thought it would be. Louise, oblivious to all that had happened between herself and Terence, took her at face value and showed admiration for the work she was about to undertake. They chatted amicably and easily. Terence's relief at this had her feeling sorry for him and wanting to try once more to release him from his guilt. The moment they were alone she took his hand. 'Darling, I told you. Let go of the past. A lot has gone on that shouldn't have. We were both to blame. Put it behind you. We can't change the past; we can only make an impact on the future. Carrying it around with us won't help either of us.'

His eyes held hers for a long moment. When he kissed her cheek his breath fanned her face as he whispered, 'I love you, darling.' His sigh spoke volumes. 'Our love isn't a natural feeling, but we couldn't help it. It just happened. But thank you. Knowing you can put it behind you and not hold me to blame helps. I love Louise very much and I know we can be happy. I want you to be happy. And, I want you to be safe. Please take care in whatever it is you are going to do. Please, darling.'

'I will. I don't intend to get myself killed. I am very highly trained, and know that I can do what is going to be asked of me. I will have a network of dedicated people around me. I promise I will be safe and I will contact you whenever it is possible to do so. By the time I come back, you will be a daddy. Louise looks very well. I'm glad she is making you happy. She … she will make a lovely mother.'

'I am sorry for your loss, darling. I feel it too. I'll never forget her.'

'No. Neither will I. I wish there had been a way to keep her, but I left it all too late. I didn't want her until I had her. Well, that's not true. There were moments when she was growing inside me when I felt a surge of love for her, but I denied it.

131

I let things take the course we had planned. I deeply regret that, but there is no going back. She has probably been adopted by now, and I am committed to something I cannot, nor want to, get out of. Come on. Let's go and dress for dinner.'

It had been a long time since she'd 'dressed for dinner', and a silly tingle of anticipation went through her as she climbed the stairs. Her room was as if she'd never left it. A fire flickered and danced up the chimney, warming and sending shadows that enhanced the magic of being back here. She took a moment to run her fingers along the beautiful mahogany dressing table, pick up perfume sprays and flick open the lid of her jewellery box. The light from the low but strong sun caught the diamonds and gold nestling inside, setting up a kaleidoscope of colour glittering out at her and awakening more memories of her *other* life. Opening her wardrobe sent joy tingling through her. How had she lived without her fashionable clothes, smart suits, cashmere scarves and sweaters, tweeds and sensual silk and satin gowns?

The sound of her bath water running reached her ears, followed by a tap on the connecting door and the familiar tones of her mother's maid. 'I've ran your bath, miss. If you choose what you want to wear, I'll lay it all out for you. I've been through and freshened everything up so as you have the choice of everything. And I'll be glad to help with your hair if you need it an' all, miss.'

She was about to refuse all of this pampering, but stopped herself as she caught a glimpse of her

132

profile in the mirror. She would need help to turn this frump of a girl with weathered, coarse skin and unkempt hair back into the glamour girl she used to be. Besides, why not indulge herself? It would be a long time before she could again.

'Thank you; I will wear the grey silk gown. I'll leave you to choose what to go with it for me. Are you good with hair?'

'Aye, I am, miss. It's a talent I have and I like doing it an' all.'

Another joy she didn't know she'd missed: the sound of the Yorkshire accent.

The time went too quickly. Theresa tried to store up as many memories as she could: the walk around the garden, wrapped up against the cold with their breaths dancing like smoke in front of them; cobwebs like delicate lace clinging to the bushes; finding a snowdrop; watching a robin bobbing from the bird table to the hedge; playing poker afterwards, and winning; listening to Louise playing the piano whilst they sipped a nightcap of hot cocoa with a small drop of brandy; and singing daft songs after Mater and Pater had retired to bed. And the happy feeling that Mater had kept well and had seemed a lot stronger. Usually frail in her mind, she hadn't spoilt one moment by dwelling on petty worries, and Theresa was proud of her – proud of the effort she'd made for her sake, and for how her bravery had helped the time pass without too many episodes where they might have all become sentimental.

Saying goodbye wasn't easy. Like all families sending off a loved one to war, there was an underlying feeling of wondering whether they would ever see each other again. But she had to remain positive, and left with a smile, keeping the tears for when the train had left the little party of her family waving in the distance.

All seemed alien to her now as she looked around her. No one spoke – not that you could have made yourself heard without shouting above the roar of the aeroplane engine, though she knew it wasn't the effort it would take to make yourself heard but fear that was holding most of the occupants quiet. To her left and around the floor of the plane sat five of her colleagues – men and women she had trained with. All were being deployed. She was the first to be dropped. Her deployment was to the area of Marseille, where she was to work under-cover in the bakery of a man she was to know as her uncle, Monsieur Ponté, and his wife. She was to join the Carp Resistance group under the leadership of Pierre Rueben, who would meet her when she landed and take her to Monsieur Ponté's house.

When the officer in charge of the operation opened the door of the plane, the inward draught took her breath away. She wanted to shout, 'No, I am not ready!', but she swallowed hard, looked once more at her colleagues, and acknowledged them as one by one they nodded at her and gave her a smile of encouragement. Lifting her body into position, she awaited the command, 'JUMP!'

Her landing was smooth. Rolling over, she clung onto the silk parachute, trying to control it in the strong wind. Two arms came around her and helped haul it in. Looking round, she found herself sinking into the deep, dark eyes of the most handsome man she'd ever seen. Not a moment for such thoughts, but she could not stop the involuntary skip of her heart. He smiled. 'Mademoiselle Crompton? I – I mean, Olivia Danchanté, of course... I am Pierre. Pierre Rueben. Welcome to France. Come, we must hurry, for it is dangerous to hang around. Someone may have spotted or heard the aircraft, and if they did, we will be in peril of capture.'

His accent was lovely. She'd say he was from Eastern Europe, which gave his French a special sound ... or was it just that she was hanging onto his every word?

'Show me the way. I'm here to do everything you command.'

'Ahh, you may live to regret saying that!' His laughter held a mischievousness that tingled through her. Never in her wildest dreams had she thought of a scenario such as this. Something zinged between them. An instant chemistry. In his eyes she read a return of the feeling. He took her hand and led her to the safety of the trees before running back and gathering up her parachute. 'We will hide it in here. Quickly, get your suit off.'

The increased temperature of this part of the world enveloped her in warmth, and she was glad to strip off her flying suit, though her attempts to straighten out the creases from her three-quarter-length flared skirt proved in vain. She'd wrapped it carefully around her legs to fit inside the suit and to keep it from creasing, but to no avail. Her twinset had fared better, but the thought came to her: *Why didn't I choose a blouse, one that I could have undone a couple of buttons of...?*

Pierre busied himself whilst she did this. He removed a boulder next to a tree, opening up a gaping hole, and stuffed her parachute and suit into it. Pushing the boulder back into place set the muscles on his arms rippling. It didn't take much imagination to feel them around her. He turned and saw her gaze on him. It didn't embarrass her. Everything felt natural, as if they had known one another for ever. And not just known – had been intimate with each other – already made love, even. But then, they had: with their eyes and with every sinew of their bodies.

When he took her hand, a tingle went through her. His eyes found hers again. His words were not the ones she knew he wanted to speak. 'Hurry, Olivia. We have time to get to know one another later. Hold my hand and play the part of my girl-friend. For now we must get you to safety, and pretending we are just young lovers out for a stroll is part of that.'

She didn't have to pretend.

Monsieur Ponté's shop was attached to his house, but they took the entrance to the shop. Though empty of customers, a man stood behind the counter. They didn't stop to acknowledge him. Pierre hurried her through a swinging, stable-like door. The aroma of freshly cooked bread teased her nostrils, and the sight of the delicious-looking loaves and baguettes stacked on wooden slatted shelves in the room they emerged into brought saliva to her mouth. It had been hours since she'd eaten.

Passing through this room, they entered the warm bakery with its large cast-iron ovens. The heat from these reddened her cheeks. Everything was cleaned down and shining as though the day's baking had been completed. Through this they came into the kitchen of the house – a room that took her back years to when she'd stayed with her friend in Paris, as the layout and decor were similar.

There was blue gingham everywhere. Fresh and crisp, it hung around the deep pot sinks and draining board, over the table in the centre, and cushions in the material adorned the high-backed wooden chairs. Matching tea towels hung over the brass rail in front of the large black grate, and curtains of the same material, frilled at the edges, draped the three small windows. The effect was pretty, welcoming and cosy. Madame Ponté motioned to her to sit down. 'You are very welcome, Olivia. My husband will be through in a moment. I will make coffee – if you can call it that these days. It is chicory stuff, but the only likeness we can get hold of. I have a secret way of brewing it, though, so it doesn't taste too bad.'

It tasted very good. Attuned now to their different accents, she attempted to make conversation. 'It is very good of you to have me and to provide me with this cover. I need to sit with you very soon to talk about the family so that I am as familiar with the different members of it as a niece should be. I will work hard during my time in the shop. It is necessary that we maintain that

137

cover to the last detail and that I become known as your niece and accepted in the community. Although I am here to help, not all will take that as a code of honour in protecting me, so you must stick religiously to the story of why I am here, even to your closest friends. Pierre, when I landed you used my real name. You should not have known that. It disturbs me that you did.'

'I am sorry. As the leader of this group I have to know everything about you. Madame Ponté, will you leave us with our coffee and tell Monsieur Ponté not to enter until I call him?' Once Madame Ponté had left the room, which she did without question, Pierre said, 'I know more than you know yourself. Your profile came before you. We accepted you on it and on your dedication to your training. We also know you have no need to do this work. You had a comfortable life at home, which your money could have sustained for you. You could have chosen to do a cushy job for your war effort, and the fact that you didn't makes you more authentic to us. I am the only one who knows these intimate details about you. There is nothing written anywhere. They were communicated in person by another agent – a woman who is working not far from here, but whom you must never meet up with. I won't make the mistake again of using your real name. You can trust me on that.'

'Thank you. How will we communicate?'

'I will use different methods. And I have my bread delivered every day. I look forward to your visits when you bring it to me.'

She ignored the look that went with this. She

had so many questions. 'How is it you are able to move around so freely?'

'I can't; I have to take great care. I was a student in my final year when all of this broke.' He went on to tell her about his family and his reason for fighting. 'I am part of the forced labour group who work for the Germans. Because of my academic skills – maths in particular – I work in a bank. It is an assigned position. I have to be very careful at all times. I introduced myself to you as Pierre Rueben, a name that would be very dangerous for me to use.'

'Yes, I was surprised, as it gives your origin away immediately. And Pierre, I am very sorry about what happened to your family.'

His eyes clouded over for a moment. His guard dropped and she saw his body tremble. She so wanted to go to him, to hold him and to comfort his pain.

'Thank you, but we must stay professional.' It was his turn to bring things back onto stable ground. 'I am known as Pierre Becke – that is the name of the family my father and mother and grandmother are with.'

There was so much to learn, and Pierre seemed to want to brief her right now, as he went on to tell her of how he'd moved his family out and then about the other Resistance workers, one by one.

'Look, I'm sorry. I am very tired and I cannot take all of this in at the moment. It has been a long and very stressful day.'

'But of course. I am sorry. I will call Monsieur Ponté through, introduce you, and then you must get some rest. I will be back tonight. Then we must collaborate our stories until we feel as though we have known each other all our lives.'

'Oh, I have... I mean...'

He took her hand. 'I know what you mean, *ma chérie*...' The light kiss he planted on her fingertips sent waves of pleasure through her whole body. She lowered her eyes, somehow feeling shy and unable to react in her usual flirty manner.

She heard his gentle laugh as he went to the door to call in Monsieur Ponté – a man who turned out to be a stereotype of everyone's imagined French baker, complete with a large manicured moustache, pot belly, receding hair, twinkling eyes and an easy charm that made Theresa feel even more at home.

'You are very welcome, *ma chérie*.'

'*Merci, monsieur*. It is good of you to accommodate me. I will try to limit the danger to you and your family as much as I can.'

'I see no problem, mademoiselle. Your accent is good – Parisian and with only a slight hint of the English diction. That's something local people will pick up on, so it is necessary that you have a story to cover that if questioned.'

'I have. My grandmother was an English woman, and had a major part in my upbringing. I have never lost the touch of her accent, which I latched on to at an early age.' *How easy it is to fit into the role!*

Monsieur Ponté smiled. 'Excellent. Already you are getting into character!'

Pierre cut in. 'I must go, but I will see you later. By the way, you can ride a bike? You will get

140

around everywhere on a bike.'

'More used to horses, I'm afraid, but yes, they taught me how to ride a bike.'

'Good. Well, you will find everything you need in your bedroom upstairs. Clothes, et cetera ... though not what you are accustomed to...'

'But *au contraire*. These last fifteen months have already put me into a different world, Pierre. I will be one of you. Forget my roots. *Je suis une fille de la ville, d'une famille ordinaire qui est venue vivre dans cette région.*'

'You will never be an ordinary country girl to me, Mademoiselle Olivia.' His face was tinged with red as Monsieur Ponté let out a knowing laugh – a laugh that soon turned to a warning look.

Pierre didn't react. His leaving the room took something from it. Theresa mentally shook herself. They could not ignore the concern Monsieur Ponté had shown at the flirtation between them. It had been very unprofessional, and she didn't want to dent the confidence these people had in her.

Nothing more was said about it. Instead, the discussion turned to how Monsieur Ponté had registered her as his niece at the town hall, and how all of her papers were in order and would be presented tomorrow. 'There were no awkward questions. Our story gained us sympathy for both you and ourselves, and admiration that we were taking you in. Now, Madame,' he addressed his wife, 'see that our guest is made comfortable and has everything she needs. I will see you at closing time, Olivia. Pierre will be back. He is dining with

141

us, though he will not arrive at the door – we have another entrance that leads from the sheds at the back. Access to them is through a neighbour's garden, and Pierre lodges with that neighbour, so no one sees him come to the house as a friend of the family. He uses the shop entrance just to drop off any messages he has. Poor man has to buy many buns he doesn't want!'

His laughter lightened the moment, and Theresa felt easy again. She chided herself for the lapse, and determined not to let her feelings interfere with her work from now on – a resolve she hoped she could keep. She was already missing Pierre's presence.

London – 1963

Lizzie closed the book. She'd reached the end of the first one. So now Theresa was in France. She wondered what she would read next, but as always after going back into Theresa's life she questioned her own. A glance in the mirror strengthened her determination to make changes. She had to if Theresa's sacrifices were to mean anything to her – if she was to get anything from the experience of that brave woman. Without allowing herself time to think, and stopping only to hide the books, she swung herself onto the side of the bed. Weakness prevented her from sliding easily into her chair, but she managed it eventually. Feeling exhausted, she guided her wheelchair into the bathroom.

She had to admit her life would be much more

difficult without the many aids Ken had put into the house for her. Getting into a hot bath would have been impossible without the help of others, which she wouldn't have liked. Now, through a mist of steam, she looked at the bath filling up and the inviting bubbles forming from her foam bath essence, happy that they weren't out of her reach. Turning the tap off, she slipped off her dressing gown and grabbed the sides of the hoist. Again it took a lot more effort than it used to take to shift herself onto its seat, but once there she pushed the lever that raised the hoist into the air. The man-oeuvre was easy now and soon she was lowered into the bliss of the comforting warmth.

Lying back onto the non-slip pillow, she felt her whole body let go. Her eyes closed. A sudden draught shot them open. 'Ken...!' Her body trembled; her mouth dried. The moment held fear as he stared down at her, but a relief frag-mented the terror as she recognized the absence of threat in his demeanour. Instead, he had the look of a frightened animal about him. 'Ken, what's wrong?'

'They're after me, sis. The big boys...' His voice shook. A tear trickled from his eye and mingled with the liquid trail running from his nose. He wiped his hand across his face. 'I – I'm in big trouble. I did a deal right under their noses and they found out. I'm dead meat...'

'Oh, God, Ken. I warned yer. Rita warned yer... What're yer going to do?'

'We have to go. And go now.'

'We? They won't hurt me and Rita, will they?'

'They will. They'll stop at nothing. I ain't

bothered about that old cow Rita. They can fry her for all I care, but not you, sis. I can't leave yer behind.'

'I ain't going, Ken. And yer can't make me.'

'Please, sis, please...' A sob caught his voice in his throat. His fear transferred to her. She could feel her world falling around her. Where would they go? She couldn't give her mind to it now, as she had to concentrate on stopping his regression, otherwise they wouldn't be able to deal with anything. 'Pull yourself together, Ken. You won't be able to think right if you get into a state. I'll be alright. Rita's trying to get me away from here anyway–'

'What? What's that old cow up to? Trying to get yer away from me, that's what... Well, she bleedin' ain't going to!'

'Ken... Ken...'

Anger had reddened his face and shot him back to reality. He turned and left the bathroom. Terror once more seeped into her. Why, oh why had she told him?

Grabbing the hoist, she desperately hauled herself onto it and wrapped the towel she'd laid over it around her. She swung towards her chair and dropped into it with a thud. Releasing the hoist, she started to turn it around, but a noise froze any further action. The door opened. The phial glinted in the light from the small window. 'No ... no, Ken. Not that... Not that. I'll come with yer. I will. But please, no more of that...'

Warding him off with every ounce of her strength, she managed to hold his hand inches from her thigh. 'Don't, Ken, please. I'll do any-

144

thing, but don't do that... I can't take it. I don't want to be hooked on it.' His eyes glazed over. Spittle dribbled from his mouth. His body slumped back onto the toilet.

'Ken? Oh, Ken... Why?' The words came through her sobs – weakening, wretched sobs. They joined his.

'I'm done for, sis.'

There was no 'sorry' for hurting her, or for what he'd put her through these last weeks. He was just wallowing in his own fear, but at least he was easier to deal with when he was like this. 'Look, how far will yer get with having to see to me all the time, eh? If yer go on your own, you'll be across the Channel by nightfall. Your passport is still in date from that school trip yer went on. There's still two years on it.'

'Shuddup and let me think.' His tone held aggression, but she didn't take heed. 'I'm not going with yer, Ken, I'm not. I'll scream the place down.'

His head lifted. Evil pierced his eyes. 'You'll do as I say. If yer don't, I'll give yer this.' He held the needle up and pointed it at her.

The fight left her. She hadn't enough strength to ward him off a second time if he came at her. Her body shivered.

''Ere, sis, you're getting cold. Come on, I'll carry yer through and help yer to dress.'

'You can carry me through, but I'll dress meself.'

'You just don't need me any more, do yer? I did all of this for yer. All of it. I chased big money to see as everything were set up right for yer and you've not an ounce of thanks in yer for it. All it's done has taken yer further away from me. You're an ungrateful bitch!'

Fear trickled back into her. He still held the phial. He stared at her, his lip trembling as he spat out, 'It's all your fault that I'm in this fix. You bleedin' set me dad into one of his fits by biting him. I were coping with the beating he were giving me. Mum shouldn't have interfered... Fucking women... I hate the lot of yer!'

He lunged forward, but as he did the bathroom door flew open. 'Leave her be, you bleedin' animal!' Rita stood in the doorway. Her small frame seemed to have grown, and in her hand she held a rolling pin. It crashed down on Ken's back. 'Gerrout! Gerrout of here! Go on.'

Ken's scream filled the space around them as another crushing blow hit his arm. The sickening sound of breaking bone brought the bile to Lizzie's throat, stopping her calling out, but someone else did...

'Stop it, Rita! Stop now!'

The unfamiliar voice took command. Lizzie looked up from where she cowered and saw a young woman of a similar age to herself standing in the doorway. Her beautiful face was coloured with anger, and was nearly as red as her hair. Shock held Lizzie from saying anything. The only noise now came from Ken. His pitiful sobs and cries of pain reverberated off the walls.

'Get out of the way, Rita. Let me see to him. Sit on the toilet, you. Rita, get me something I can use as a splint. I saw you had some sticks in the bucket next to the fire ... get me two of the longest of them and some bandages, or rip some sheeting up if you haven't any bandages. Go on, hurry yourself!'

Whoever this was, she was a commanding figure. Her London accent had posh tones mixed in with it. Ken did as she told him.

'What's in the phial, eh? What were you going to put into your sister?'

'Mind yer own fucking business! Who the fuck are yer, anyway?'

'Right now, I'm someone who'll get you out of pain, mate, and save your arm. Not that you're deserving of it. So shut up with your language. It's not called for.'

Ken didn't protest.

'So, come on. Tell me, is it a sedative of some sort?'

'It's heroin.'

'Heroin! You vile creature. Rita told me you'd been at that, but I didn't believe her. Right, mate, I'm fixing your arm then I'm calling the police.'

'Oh no, you ain't. Don't even think of it, 'cos if yer do, I'll tell them why you're here. I reckon as they'll be interested to know, missy. So button it and get on with bleedin' shutting him up from hollering like the animal he is.'

The girl froze at this from Rita. Her eyes darted between Rita and Ken, and at that moment Lizzie realized who she was. A sick feeling entered her. What was Rita up to, and had this ... this *Patsy* – yes, that was her name. Patsy. Had she come to do harm to Theresa Crompton? *Oh God...* The walls of the bathroom closed in on her. Everything around her blurred. *What next? God, what next...?*

Ten

The Return of Evil Unites Patsy and Lizzie

1963

'Come on, Lizzie. You'll be okay. God, Rita, look at the state of her! Not to mention the filthy state of her bed. You should be locked up for neglect.' Patsy tucked the large towel back around Lizzie's skeletal frame in an effort to stop her shivering. 'Get some clean bedding, *now!* And hot-water bottles, and hurry!'

Rita didn't protest, she just followed all the orders Patsy gave. 'Now, help me to lift her.' Together they managed to get Lizzie onto what was meant to be a clean sheet. Bobbled to the point of having a rough texture, it had long since ceased to be white, and smelt fusty as if it had taken a long time to dry.

When they turned her over, Lizzie's back made them both gasp. Large areas of skin had rubbed off, and blisters covered her bottom, some broken and some full of liquid. Patsy set about gently cleaning her with the cotton wool and the iodine Rita had fetched from the chemist up the road. Throughout, all she could do was say how sorry she was as Lizzie writhed and protested at what must have been stinging pain. 'I have no choice but to do this, Lizzie, love. I have to get you

148

cleaned or you will get infections. One or two are infected already. I can't believe you, Rita! How could you treat an invalid in this way?'

'It weren't all my doing. He's to blame, giving her that stuff. She wanted more of it and got violent with me if I got near to her. It's only been this last couple of days that she's come round a bit, but then she refused to let me do anything. She just wanted to read them damn boo– I mean, sleep and that.'

'Oh? What books? That was what you were going to say weren't it? Do you mean those exercise books we shifted from under her pillow? What are they? Are you studying something, Lizzie?'

'N-No... They're nothing. Just scribblings, that's all.'

Patsy didn't miss the look of fear Lizzie shot in Rita's direction. It seemed to convey a message, as Rita grabbed the books and shoved them into a drawer of the dressing table. She decided to leave it. She wanted to get Lizzie's confidence, and forcing her to show her something she didn't want to, wasn't going to help with that. She could pursue the matter later; at the moment Lizzie's welfare was her main concern. 'Rita, I think you're right. Lizzie needs to be got away from here–'

'She ain't going nowhere without me!' Ken's voice held aggression. It froze the moment. The doorway framed his body. His stance threatened. In his unbandaged hand he held the rolling pin Rita had discarded. Instinct had Patsy throwing the cover over Lizzie's naked body, and as she did so, a defiance rippled through her, bringing with it an anger that made her want to stand up to this bully. 'Don't think for one moment you can stop me, you bastard! Lizzie needs caring for. Now, I know that a lot of questions will be asked wherever she is taken, and that is why I'm gonna take her home with me. And like I said, you ain't stopping me. The bloke as I call me dad is a doctor, and me, and me half-sister, are training to be doctors, so we can look after her and I can fix it so as nothing is said to anyone about how she got like this. Otherwise, I don't care about the consequences to me and I *will* call the police!'

'You're a smartarse bitch! And you, yer cow...' Rita cowered away from him as he lifted the rolling pin above her head. 'What're yer doing bringing the likes of her in here, eh?'

It all happened as if in a film: one minute Patsy saw the rolling pin descending, the next she'd dived and pushed Ken over with every ounce of strength she had. Panting for breath, she lifted herself off him. He didn't move. Blood seeped from a wound on his head and trickled from his mouth. His lips hung slack, his skin relaxed into a waxy mould. 'Oh God! I – I've killed him! But ... how ... what...'

'Noooo... Ken! No! Oh God, please, no...' Lizzie's voice – a hollow sound from a long way away.

'I – It was an accident... I – he hit his head on the corner of the dresser... Oh God, help me...'

'Look, pull yourself together. He had it coming. He was going to kill me. You had to do what you did. You saved me life.'

Some comfort seeped into her at Rita's words.

150

'Yes, I did… He was… I – If the blow had landed it would have killed you. I had to stop him. Ring the police and an ambulance, Rita. I'll see to Lizzie.'

'No. There'll be no coppers. I've told yer. Look, everyone knew he were going to do a runner. It's been on the grapevine for days as he'd stepped too far out of line and had a contract on him.'

'You knew?'

'Yes, Lizzie, I did. Well, I'd heard. Anyway, all we have to do is get rid of his body and say nothing.'

'I can't do that. I told you, I am training to be a doctor. I can't do anything unethical!'

'Since when did you have ethics, girl?'

Something about Rita put a terror deep into the pit of Patsy's stomach. It nudged the knotted fear already there and rendered her unable to move. She watched her pick up the rolling pin. The thought came to her that Rita intended to hit her with it, but still she couldn't move.

''Ere, take this. Ha! I ain't going to hit you with it, or hurt you in any way, as long as yer do as I say. Take it!'

'W-Why?'

'Just do it.'

Compelled to do as Rita said, she took the rolling pin from her. Control came back to her with the feel of it. 'I could overpower you with this, Rita and–'

'You've no need to do that. Just do as I say and we can have an end to this mess and can all come out of it without any problem. But think on, missy: if yer don't, I'll say as you did this deliberate. That yer came here trying to force me to take yer to yer mam's house as yer felt entitled to have stuff from it, and when our Ken tried to stop you yer threatened him and then yer hit him with the rolling pin.'

Her movement took Patsy by surprise when she jumped forward and snatched the rolling pin. 'Christ, Rita! What ... what are you doing?'

Rita didn't answer. Her body bent, and taking hold of the knob on the end of the pin she wiped the end Patsy hadn't touched in Ken's blood. Nothing came to Patsy to give her an idea of what the implications of this were. Rita turned to go out of the room, saying as she did, 'Right, I'll be back in a moment. Don't even think of doing anything while I'm gone, 'cos I'm telling yer, it'll be worse for you if yer do.'

Lizzie's whimper turning to a full-blown howl brought Patsy out of the shocked stupor that had gripped her. 'Oh, Lizzie, I – I'm sorry. I didn't mean to... Please stop, please, you'll be ill and ... and a neighbour might hear you. I promise I will go to the police. There'll be no more–'

'That's what you think! Shuddup, Lizzie, for Christ's sake. Hit her or something. She's hysterical.'

'No. Leave her. Lizzie, Lizzie, it will be alright. I have folk who will help us. Everything will be alright. Just quieten down, love. I can't think.'

'You have no thinking to do, girl.' Rita's shove unbalanced Patsy. She fell back into Lizzie's wheelchair. 'Now, shut yer face, Lizzie, or I'll bleedin' well shut it for yer.'

Patsy could do nothing about the cutting blow

152

that Rita landed on Lizzie's cheek. Her heart cringed against it, but it did the trick and Lizzie's wails lowered to whimpering sobs.

'Right. No more talk of the police. I have evidence to back up me story that you killed him – one rolling pin with your fingerprints on and *his* blood. And I'll use it if yer do anything. Now. We all have to calm down and sort out a plan. We have to get rid of him.'

'Rita, please... We can't. It's criminal. We have to report the death, tell them how it happened. Everything will be okay. No one is to blame except himself. He was going to attack you.'

'Listen, girl. Are you deaf or something? WE ARE NOT GOING TO THE POLICE! I'm on a life licence. They'll delve, they'll find out things, and I'll be recalled. That ain't going to happen, but if it does, I'll make sure as you go down with me.'

'But Lizzie saw what happened. She can tell them the truth... What things? What have you done?'

'That's for me to know. And Lizzie won't do anything that would put me back in prison. Not to save your bacon, she wouldn't. Not when I tell her who yer are and why you're here.'

'But–'

'That's enough talking.'

'No, it's not, Rita.' Lizzie sat up. Patsy was amazed at the strength she showed to help herself. 'I know who this is. I've guessed. I reckon as her being here is part of some scheme you've thought up, but I'm not going to be part of anything, whether it's to save you or not. Christ!

153

My brother lies... What is the matter with yer! How can yer be so cold as to try to sort that out to save your own skin? You disgust me... You both disgust me. You! The only reason that you can be here is to help her in some scheme that will hurt your mother... Well, I won't have it, and Theresa doesn't deserve–'

'What do you know about my mother? How do you know she's called Theresa? What's going on here? It's a nightmare. I feel like I'm going mad!'

'I told her.'

'No, she didn't. Not exactly, anyway. When she was down she'd talk of her, but I – I have her memoirs...'

'What ... how? My God, this is all incredible... My mother wrote a memoir?'

'Just leave it, Lizzie.'

''Ere, what's going on 'ere, then?'

The rough-sounding male voice seemed like it had come from another world. Patsy couldn't sort out in her head where the man standing in the doorway had come from. Lizzie's scream pierced her ears. Rita fell back against the wall, her face deathly pale. The silence that followed the scream held a tangible terror. The man stepped into the room and walked over to the body. 'Ken? Christ! He's dead! What's going on here, Rita?'

Rita shook her head. Her mouth still hung open, and her eyes stared out at the man. As he moved towards her, she shrank even further back. 'I asked what the fuck is going on here...' His hand shot out and grabbed Rita's blouse, bringing her face close to his. Lizzie's scream turned to a pitiful plea, 'Don't, Dad. Don't hurt her...'

Her father ignored her. With one swift movement he had hold of Rita's arm and twisted it behind her back. 'Tell. Me. What's happening? Who did this? And who's this...?' His head nodded in Patsy's direction.

'I – I'm Patsy Crompton. I – I live in Yorkshire, but Rita knows me mam, whom I've never met. Sh-she's helping me to find her. This was an accident. He–'

'It weren't no bleedin' accident. *She* did it! She did it deliberately.'

Patsy held her breath, willing Lizzie to speak up, to deny what Rita had said, but Lizzie just sat there staring, her eyes bulging in their sockets and her mouth wide. Dribble ran down her chin.

'You what? Why? Why would she kill me bleedin' son? None of this is making any sense.' He let go of Rita and walked towards Patsy. 'You say you're here to find your mam? How does Rita know her, and how come you, a girl from Yorkshire, knows Rita? Fucking hell, I come back after all these years to see me daughter and I find this lot!'

'Never mind all that for now, Jim. What're we going to do? You've gotta help us. We gotta get rid...' Rita's voice quivered, and her body took on the stance of a helpless woman. A sick fear curled around Patsy's already churned insides. It was like she'd been catapulted into an alien world a million miles from the safe world she'd left this morning. *God, help me, help me, please...*

'Shuddup, Rita, and let me think.'

'We should call the police. Rita isn't telling the truth. It–'

'And you shut your mouth, missy. There's going to be no coppers involved in this.' His face held a threat like none Patsy had ever seen in her life. Her body trembled; tears prickled her eyes. For one moment she thought he'd grab her, but he turned back to Rita. 'This is a bleedin' mess, Rita. I reckon as this one ain't to be trusted, and what about '*er*?' His finger pointed at Lizzie. Lizzie's face paled even further, until it looked almost like a mask of death. Her mouth quivered, but still it hung slack and spittle ran from it. Her body trembled as though someone had taken hold of her and was shaking her.

Patsy's medical instincts penetrated the armour of terror that had held her back from seeing what was happening before her very eyes. Lizzie was going into extreme shock. She needed help. She moved towards her, took hold of her body and laid her flat. 'Rita, quick, put these under her feet.' The pillows flew through the air as she chucked them towards Rita. 'Hurry, she's in shock. Oh, that's not high enough. Jim, pass that cushion from Lizzie's wheelchair. Hurry, for God's sake.'

Neither of them questioned her. Jim had a look of astonishment on his face, but Rita had returned to being a caring aunty. 'Oh, Lizzie, Lizzie, love, come on. It'll be alright. Come on, m'darlin'.'

'Throw those blankets over her, Rita. And Jim, grab that hot-water bottle and refill it. It must have gone cold by now.' Still they obeyed her without question, the Ken problem forgotten for a moment as they worked in unison to bring Lizzie back.

With the first measures taken, Patsy took stock.

Lizzie had a bit more colour in her cheeks, but her pulse was very erratic and her breathing was shallow. 'She needs to go to hospital.'

'No!'

'Rita, for Christ's sake, shock is a very serious condition. She needs oxygen. She could die!'

'You're a doctor, ain't yer?'

'No, I'm not. I've done four years' initial training, and I have a long way to go yet, but I do know that Lizzie needs help. And it's help I can't give her. Please, Rita...'

'Fucking hell! I've stepped into a bleedin' disaster pit. There's going to be no hospital and no coppers. Right? Now, do what yer can for her. And it'd better be enough to save her life, 'cos you're already on me death wish-list, and if yer lose me daughter, yer own death'll be a fact. Now bleedin' get her right.'

Desperation entered Patsy at his words. What more could she do? Taking Lizzie's pulse again set a panic in her. The beat was hardly discernible. Her breathing was even shallower, and her lips had turned blue. Patsy sought frantically for knowledge of the right thing to do in this situation, then remembered Harri telling her about something she had read: something about a man called James Elam. Funny she should remember his name. This Elam had been advocating a new procedure of chest compressions and blowing air into the mouth to bring up the oxygen level in a near-death patient. If only I'd read it... But there was no time for 'if only'... *Which to do first? Oh God, help me!*

Lowering her head, she tilted Lizzie's, holding

157

her nose and covering her mouth with her own. She took a deep breath and then, praying like she'd never prayed before, she began to blow gently into Lizzie. Trying not to panic, she kept the rhythm steady, deep breath in, then gentle exhale into Lizzie. Stopping after a couple of sets to do checks, relief flooded into her as she saw Lizzie's lips had turned pink again and she was breathing normally.

Everything went out of Patsy at the sight of this. Her body slumped down onto the bed. Sobs racked her. Through this release of emotion she felt a hand touch her hair. Lifting her head, she looked into Lizzie's face. Lizzie's expression held a message – an unspoken hope. Nodding her head, she pulled herself up. 'She'll be alright now.'

'Oh, thank God! Lizzie, love, yer gave us a fright there.'

'Stay back, Rita. Let me get near. Hey, girl, don't you worry. Your dad's here now. I'll sort this lot out. You just have to do as I say. I won't let anything happen to yer.' His hand went towards Lizzie's hair but she shrank away from it. 'Don't ... touch me!' Hate rasped her voice. The swift raising of Jim's hand didn't affect her. Defiance showed in the way she stared back at him from eyes sunk deep into darkened sockets.

Fear that if he landed the blow it would kill Lizzie had Patsy throwing herself at him. His reaction was quicker than hers. His body turned. His hand sliced through the air, catching her cheek and sending her reeling backwards. There was nothing to stop her fall. Her nightmare was compounded when she stared into Ken's unseeing gaze. Twisting her body, she got up and scrambled towards the door. Something hit the back of her head, jarring her teeth together on her tongue. The door swayed towards her, her vision distorted then faded into ever decreasing circles. Her ears zinged with a high-pitched sound that went into the distance as she sank into a dark, deep pit of oblivion.

'Patsy, Patsy.' The voice came through the fog in her brain, bringing with it a searing pain that stabbed her temple. There was a note of desperation in its tone, and this compelled her to open her eyes. Peering through the darkness, she could just make out a figure lying beside her.

'Patsy, are you okay?'

She tried to speak but couldn't. Her mouth wouldn't move, and she growled deep in her throat. Fingers felt around her mouth and then a ripping, stinging sensation removed the tape that had held her mute. 'Ouch! Lizzie?'

'Yes. Oh, Patsy. Are you alright?'

'Yes ... well, no, but don't worry. Where are we?'

'We're on a boat on the Thames. They brought us here in a van. Me dad wrapped a blanket so tightly around me that I couldn't move, and then he put me in me wheelchair and told me that if I made a sound he'd kill you. He wheeled me out to his van. He didn't care about being seen, but then, even if anyone did see anything, none of them would do anything. No one interferes round our neighbourhood, nor would they call the police – they'd be scared of what would happen to them if they did.'

This rambling in a trembling, terrified voice

159

helped Patsy to gather her own fear and think in a logical way. She had to, as Lizzie sounded on the verge of hysteria. In reality she could have screamed till the breath left her, but instead she kept things matter-of-fact. 'Was it dark?'

'No. I reckon it was about five-ish.'

'So how did he get me out, and did he move Ken's body?'

'Yes, they did it the same way as I heard the wheels of me chair. Th-they laid yer in the middle next to...'

'Don't think about it, love. Do you know how long I've been unconscious?'

'Yer came round in a sort of way, moaning and that, a few minutes after Rita hit yer with that lady ornament I have on me dresser. It's a brass one. Then they forced some pills Rita had down yer throat. Yer still moaned for a while, but not for long. I screamed at them to stop, but... Oh, Patsy, I'm scared...'

'I know. Where are Rita and your dad now?'

'I heard them planning to dump Ken's body in the river...' A sob accompanied this.

'Try to keep it together, Lizzie. I know it ain't easy, love, but the more I know the more I can think if there's anything we can do. How long have we been here?' Patsy's eyes tried to penetrate the dimness. The dank stench permeating her nostrils and the sensation that her body was rocking confirmed they were on a boat.

'I don't know, but not long. Oh, Patsy, what're we going to do?'

'Try not to get upset again. You're not well. Are you warm enough? We seem to be on a bed of sorts. Can you move much?'

'Yes, I'm warm, but I can only move one arm. I can't get any leverage. We're too close together. They've tied us to the bed.'

Patsy tried to move, but couldn't against the restricting ropes. Every part of her cramped with pain. 'It's no use, I can't budge. Look, we won't help ourselves by panicking. Better that we lie still and wait. They can't leave us here.' She wished she felt as confident as she sounded, but she had to help Lizzie. If Lizzie went into shock again, she'd be powerless to do anything. 'Tell me what you know of me mother, Lizzie. It'll help to pass the time.'

Lizzie's voice grew in strength as she talked. 'She was an amazing woman in her younger days. She loved yer, yer know. She just didn't feel like she had any choice... I mean, to us she could have, but she were living in a different time and in a different social class. It wasn't easy for her, but she never stopped thinking about yer and it hurt her so much to give yer up.'

A tangible pain grasped Patsy's heart. *Me mother loved me!* Had she got all of this wrong? 'Did she write all of that, or are you surmising it from what you've read?'

'Yes, she wrote it. It made me cry. You're not going to hurt her, are yer, Patsy? Is that why yer came?'

'No. Well, I did want some sort of settling of scores, something to help me live with it all, but I'd never physically hurt her. I can't say as I won't have me say. I want answers, but I'm not out for revenge.' And she knew she wasn't, not now – not after hearing that her mother had written that she'd loved her. 'Anyway, that was only part of why I came, and part of the bait Rita used to get me here. She said she needed help, and she told me about you. She wanted me to take you out of there back to me family and to take care of you where you would be safe.'

'You mean yer were really thinking of doing that? Or was it just an excuse to get Rita's help with yer other plans?'

'Look, it ... well, it's not simple. You must feel some of what I feel towards me mam. You must feel like you'd like to get back at your dad...'

'No, I don't. It hurts – it hurts a lot that he could do this to me, and I've cried buckets with the pain of it, but I never thought to get revenge and hurt him back.'

This shocked Patsy and woke in her the secret fear she held about herself. To her it seemed natural to hurt back and to make that hurt deeper than the one inflicted on herself. Not wanting to give thought to it, she turned the conversation back to her mother. 'Maybe I'll feel like that when I know more about me mam. You knew your dad before this happened. You probably had as many good times with him as you had bad ones. I had nothing and know very little about me mam. What I do know isn't good. You have a different picture of her. Tell me some more.'

She drank in every word about how her mother had wanted to atone for everything and set out to do that by doing what she could in the war. She was enraptured by her mother's courage during her training and her determination to see it

162

through, and as she listened, some of the coldness seeped out of her heart. But nothing prepared her for what came after her mother landed in France.

'This man met her – the head of the Resistance. His name was Pierre Rueben. They fell in love... You ... you have a brother.'

'What? A – a brother!'

'Well, a half-brother...'

'Where? God this is madness! I thought my mother was a lesbian. Rita told me...'

'It sounds to me like Rita, and all of the people you've come in contact with, have only told yer the bad bits about your mum, and there were plenty of them up until you were on the way. She's very honest in her memoirs; she don't skip over anything. But what happened to her at yer dad's hands, and having you, changed her. She seemed to wake up, and all she ever wanted to do was to make up for everything. I could tell yer it all, but it won't be easy for yer to hear.'

'Oh, never mind that. I've long known my mother is not your ordinary, run-of-the-mill kind of woman. And it won't hurt me. Nothing can hurt me more than I am already. And it's not that I love her or anything – in fact, I hate her – so don't worry about my feelings. Just tell me.'

A tear seeped out of the corner of Patsy's eye as Lizzie came to the end of her telling. So, it was true, her dad hadn't raped her mam, then, but had beaten her – and her a posh girl who'd never known such treatment. She had seduced him, though, and then turned on him. *But she hadn't wanted to give me up!* Somehow the knowledge of

163

this ground a pain into her.

They lay in silence. Lizzie broke it. 'I know I haven't got to the part where she actually does anything heroic, but I have skimmed a few pages and read some at the end and in the middle. From what I have gathered, she paid – and I mean *really* paid – for her wayward ways, and that's what she set out to do.'

'Would you like her for your mam?'

'Yes, I'd be proud to have her. She has inspired me. She's shown me that just because yer take one path, yer don't have to keep going down it. Everyone can change things...'

'But she still has a relationship with your aunt Rita...'

'We don't know that. I don't believe anything that Rita says any more. If yer want to hate anyone, she's a good candidate. She's evil, I know that now.' A shiver rippled through Lizzie's body. 'Yer know, despite me brother being what he was, I loved him. I can't believe he's dead...'

'I'm sorry, love. Look, let's get off these gloomy subjects. We need to think what we're going to do. Don't be afraid, Lizzie. You have a lot of courage – you must have to have coped with what you've been through. Rita told me what happened to you. Dig into that courage now, and into some of what my mother gave you, if you can, and let's face our situation and see what can be done.'

'I will, Patsy.'

'Right. For one thing, if it's as late as it feels and I haven't rung home, then they are going to be alarmed and will do something – ring the hospital for one, which will tell them I haven't been there. That will set up alarm bells and they will call the police. They know I have been contacted by Rita and they may think I was foolish enough to get in touch with her despite saying I wouldn't. So that will–'

'No! Oh God, Patsy, that can't happen. If Rita and me dad get an inkling that it might, they'll kill us! They're both on the run – me dad for murdering me mum, and Rita ... well, she's done a few things. The police don't know of them yet, but they will connect her to them once they have her in the frame for this and they make the link to yer mum. She told yer: she's a lifer and she's desperate not to go back inside.'

A chill went to the very bones of Patsy as all the bravado she'd mustered ebbed away.

Eleven

Jacques's Research Pays Off

London 1963

London was all he thought it would be – the excitement of it, and the feeling that everyone had somewhere they should be right now. He even enjoyed the noise of it all: traffic, hooters blowing, bells ringing and street vendors calling out their wares. All of it added to Jacques's experience. Even the oppressive heat of August, which was very different to the humidity he was used to, added to the atmosphere. Listening in to people's conversations, he found most discussed the weather and all had the foreboding that they were in for a bad storm later.

He had never known anything like it. Even his one visit to New York – which had been a cultural shock to him, someone who had spent their life in the Deep South – couldn't compare to this. In New York the streets had a different feel. There wasn't this sense of past mixing with, and steering, the present – no traditions that had to be followed, and everything had a glass or plastic appearance. Here, the buildings, the street names and even the people were steeped in history.

Standing outside Buckingham Palace that morning had made him feel he belonged somehow. The young Queen Elizabeth was *his* queen. After all, he was half British. That thought gave him a nice feeling, and it was this half that he hoped to find as he trawled through records in the family history section of Guildhall Library, a magnificent building that seemed to dwarf him.

The fact that his family were from the upper classes made researching them easier. A funny term that, 'upper class'... They didn't have a class system in America... Well, he had to admit, that wasn't quite right, especially in his own state. The need for Martin Luther King to have to fight for the rights of the black man belied the notion that his was a society of equals. This thought shamed him. Why should a man have to fight to see his people free to roam where they liked, to vote, and to enjoy what all white people enjoyed, in this day and age and in the United States! He'd seen nothing of this inequality here in England. So maybe their class system wasn't so bad.

Taking his attention back to the family line of the Cromptons, he found that a Lord Crompton had lived in Breckton until his death a few years ago. He had been survived by a son, who had since also passed away, and by his wife, Lady Daphne Crompton and ... oh, my God! His daughter, Theresa Crompton... *My mother!*

Swallowing hard, he peered again at the words. Nothing indicated that Theresa Crompton was dead. But how could that be? Grandfather had said she was shot at Dachau.

He peered at the words on the page, trying to read into them something that wasn't there. He checked how up to date the record was. Everything was as it should be, the assistant assured him. Records were updated as events happened.

He read the piece about his mother, and found that she had married before the war, to the Hon. Raymond Hawthorn. *Umm, didn't last long!* They were divorced within a year, and she had taken her maiden name back by deed poll. There had been no issue from the marriage. What did that mean? Again he sought the help of the assistant, and then felt silly when he was told it meant there had been no offspring. But then, why not say so? *Issue... Ha, a silly word!* But this word meant he had no siblings – part of him felt sorry about this, while another part of him struggled to come to terms with the fact that she was still alive! *My mother is still alive!*

Happiness at this revelation chased his shock

away. And, to add to his joy, it seemed his grandmother was still living, too – though of course she may not know of his existence.

There was no mention of where they now lived, but surely that wouldn't be difficult to find out? Maybe they lived together ... yes, he'd try to find out where Lady Daphne lived, and visit her. He would most likely find his mother there. No, better that he sent a letter to his mother. He had no doubt she would welcome it. Even if she hadn't told her mother about him, as his grandfather cautioned was possible, it wouldn't matter. Whether she introduced him to her or not would be up to her. But she wouldn't reject him, he was certain of that. She had loved him; she would still love him.

A warm feeling filled him. He couldn't believe it. She was alive... Alive!

York – 1963

Lady Daphne looked at the post on the silver platter. It had been a long time since a letter had come to her house addressed to her daughter Theresa. Curious, she turned it over, to check the postmark again. London – strange, you would think anyone who knew her in London would know that she lived there, and yet this was a handwritten envelope, not a typed, business one. Should she open it?

Her mind went to the plight of her daughter, and as always she was attacked by the physical pain of the thought, and her heart seemed to fill with molten lead – burning, agonizing and heavy. How had it come to this? Her alone, and her daughter alone. Terence ... darling Terence, no longer with them, and Charles, a husband in a million whom she'd adored, and ... and her divine sister, Laura. Oh, how she mourned them all.

How often she had tried to get through to the traumatized Theresa, but her very presence seemed to take her further over the line of insanity. *Why, why?*

They had been so close when she was younger, before the war... God, the bloody war took away so much from everyone. But then, things weren't that bad, not when she first came home, a fragile creature needing support. No, the real breakdown for Theresa came when Terence took his own life. Even thinking the words still hurt her, cutting deep into her like a razor, slashing her and inflicting wounds with jagged edges. *Why ... why did Terence do it? And what did it have to do with Theresa? Why did Theresa think herself responsible?* Would she ever know? Was Theresa anything to do with it?

The envelope seemed to call to her. *What would it matter if I opened it? Theresa would never know.* She could reseal it and send it on.

Her fingers shook as she took the paper knife and carefully lifted the flap of the envelope. Never had she done anything like this – opening one of her children's private letters. Though abhorrent to her, the thought didn't deter her. The crisp, hotel-headed paper crackled as she eased it out. For a moment she hesitated, wondering what secret might be revealed. Then she laughed. *Secret, in-*

deed! Don't be so stupid!

The words of the address, *Dear Mother,* shot her backwards. Her body sank onto the chair behind her. Good God! Someone had addressed Theresa as *Dear Mother!*

Her eyes travelled over the words again, and then further:

Dear Mother,

Yes, I feel I can take the liberty of calling you that, because I know that you loved me and were forced to give me up – that you had no choice but to do so. Yes, I am Jacques, the one you called 'your precious son'.

My grandfather told me everything he can remember. He took me to America, which is what you and Father wanted, and I grew up there. I always thought you were dead, as does my grandfather, but I came to England and I have done some research and find that you are alive.

I cannot believe it that after all these years of thinking you are dead, you are not. I have only recently learned about your life and of my father's and his family.

Now I find we are in the same country – we may even meet. I want that so much, and hope that you do.

Please telephone the hotel address as soon as you can. I intend to go to my father's memorial in France soon. Maybe we can go together. Have you ever been?

I so want the days to speed by until I hear from you.

Your loving son, Jacques x

After a moment of sitting quietly, trying to calm her inner self, Lady Daphne took a deep breath and reached for the bell sitting on the table next

170

to her. Davidson appeared immediately. 'Davidson, will you bring the telephone over here to me,
please?'

'Yes, m'lady. Are you feeling alright? Do you
want me to send your maid through?'

'No, I'm fine. I have had a shock. Yes, another
one concerning Miss Theresa. I didn't think my
legs would carry me across the room to the
telephone. Thank you, Davidson.'

'Is there anything you require me to do?'

'You can organize me a cup of tea. I know it isn't
my usual time, but I think I need one. Or will,
once I have made my call. Will you leave me in
private until I have?'

'Of course, m'lady.'

As he brought the telephone over, Davidson
picked up her rug from the sofa. 'I'll leave this
near to you. You're shivering, m'lady.'

Impatient for him to go before she lost her nerve,
her voice held a sharp tone, 'Don't fuss, Davidson.
I am perfectly alright. I just didn't want to stand
and try to walk for a moment.'

Bowing his most condescending bow, he
turned and left the room. *Annoying little man!*
No, that wasn't fair. He cared about her and was
a jolly good servant, especially in these days when
such people were extremely hard to come by.

Impatience stayed with her as the operator took
a moment to connect her. Her heart fluttered
alarmingly when the hotel answered. This was
incredible. This young man must be mistaken...
Theresa couldn't have given birth without her
knowing, surely?

The American accent took her aback. 'Jacques

171

Rueben speaking.'

'This is Lady Crompton.'

'My grandmother? Gee, I can't believe this! Hi. I'm Jacques... Oh, but do you know about me?'

'I didn't, young man. And I am sure you have the wrong people.'

'No, I haven't. You *are* Theresa Crompton's mother? The lady who worked as a Special Agent in France during the war?'

'Yes...'

By the time he'd finished telling her how he came into being, her emotions had changed. She liked him. He had that open, honest quality that the Americans often showed – a bit too forward, perhaps, but then life was different to her younger days. People were different, and she had to accept that. 'Well, you have taken the wind out of my sails. I don't know what to say...'

'You could tell me where and how my mother is?'

'It is very difficult. Life isn't that simple that you can just walk into our lives. You will cause a lot of disruption, be an embarrassment to our family.'

'I promise I won't be that. I know it isn't every day that a grandson you knew nothing of turns up. But this is 1963, ma'am, and no one bothers about such things now.'

'The people you mix with may not, but my society does. I'm not saying we won't meet, but I have to be sure you are who you say you are. I have to protect my daughter. She ... she's ill.'

'Ill? How ill? Will she die? You can't keep me from her. She loved me. I have photos and... Look, can I come up there to see you? No one need know who I am. I could show you stuff and tell you my story.'

Daphne didn't answer for a moment. A big part of her wanted to say yes, but suppose she was letting in a conman? Or Theresa didn't want to know him. And what of her other grandchildren and Louise? Oh, what the hell. 'I will come down to London.'

'Won't that be too much for you? Can we meet halfway?'

'No. I have a driver...'

As she replaced the receiver she had an attack of *What have I done?* and nearly picked it up again, but stopped herself. It was all incredible, but she believed it, and maybe, just maybe, this was what had been ailing her daughter for years: a terrible secret. A secret she couldn't share. Had she shared it with Terence? But even if she had, that wouldn't have made him do what he did. There *must* be something else that involved the two of them. Still, the first thing was to meet this young man and see how that went, then she would get in touch with Theresa's psychiatrist to see what she thought. Oh, but the scandal... And how did it all happen?

Her head hurt. Her heart hurt. There seemed a lot to face in the near future, but if only it could bring about a reconciliation with her darling daughter. She'd face anything for that to happen.

Twelve

Doubts Cling but Hurt Unites

Breckton and London – 1963

'Mam, what're we going to do? Patsy would have rung if she was alright, you know she would.' Ian's voice held all the anguish Harri could feel inside herself, but for different reasons.

'There isn't owt we can do, love. We just have to wait. Maybe she couldn't find a telephone box.'

'In London? I know I haven't been there, but I can't imagine there ain't a telephone box on every corner. I just feel there's sommat wrong, Mam.'

Harri saw the anguish on her mam's face as she fell silent and knew it wasn't all due to them not hearing from Patsy. Like herself, her mam didn't like how Ian felt about Patsy. They hadn't spoken of it, but she wondered if their concerns were the same.

'Mam...?'

At this plea from Ian, Sarah looked over at her and sighed heavily, in a 'help me out' kind of way.

'Look, Ian, let's wait until Dad comes home. There's nothing Mam can do. Dad said he'll ring the sergeant he spoke to in London when he gave information about Theresa Crompton. He'll ask him if he can find out if Patsy made it to the hospital or if they had any enquiry from her. Now, for goodness' sake stop acting so daft. You make yourself look foolish, the way you hang around Patsy–'

'Harri!'

'Well, it's embarrassing, Mam. He should treat her like a sister, not–'

The door slamming behind Ian cut Harri off and put a regret into her at the way she'd spoken. Ian was a gentle soul, and very loving, just like their Granddad Jack. 'Oh dear, Mam, that makes me feel bad. I'm sorry for him, I am, but he has to realize, Patsy doesn't think of him in that way.'

'Well, I can't say I am sorry about that. I wouldn't want them... Oh, I don't know...'

'What is it, Mam? Is there something about Patsy, or is it the family thing?'

'Nothing, dear, I'm just being silly. My past often visits me and gives me the colly-wobbles, that's all.'

Impatience welled up in Harri, but she said nothing. Her mam had a right to keep things to herself if she wanted to, but sometimes she wished she would talk and not keep everything inside. 'I'll go after him. I shouldn't have snapped at him. He's worried, that's all. I am meself, to be honest. I'm scared that Patsy not contacting us is sommat to do with that Rita woman.'

'But I thought Patsy hadn't spoken to her.'

Harri bit her tongue. She wanted to say that what they all *thought* about Patsy wasn't what Patsy was really like – that she wouldn't be a bit surprised if Patsy had been in touch with Rita. Patsy had a devious side to her at times – not that she took her to task over it very often, as she had

175

a nasty tongue if she thought you were getting at her. But for all that, she had a lot of good points and she wouldn't be without her. She was her sister and she loved her 'warts an' all', as they say. So instead she just said, 'I know, but I'm wondering if she was tempted to, but didn't like to say... I mean, Rita was a link to her mam without there being any pressure. Not that we meant to put pressure on her, but she must have felt the worry we all had in us.'

'Aye, especially in me. I didn't want her to ever have contact with that lot again, and for me own selfish reasons. I tried not to show it, but it weren't easy. But then, why go to Rita? I still don't understand or think she would.'

'I'm just saying it is a possibility we should consider. And one as worries me, as I think that woman has motives that Patsy may not have thought of. Anyroad, it does no good to speculate. While we're doing so, Patsy's probably sitting with her mam and all the past is forgotten. Oh, I didn't mean...'

'I know, love. But that is how it should be, 'cos the past in this family holds a lot of pain and that should be locked away so it can't come into our lives again. Anyroad, you go out to your brother and sort him. I'll be alright, I'll not dwell on stuff. I'll get meself busy.'

Before going after Ian, Harri went over to her mam and gave her a hug.

'Eeh, you daft ha'p'orth, get on with you.'

Seeing Ian standing by the fence gazing out over the countryside, Harri walked up to him and linked her arm through his. He looked down at her and smiled. 'Can't help meself, I'm afraid, sis.'

'I know, love. I'm a pig. I shouldn't tease you. It's ... well, I want you to be happy.'

'I am, and I'd be even happier if I thought Patsy returned me feelings. But...'

'I know, but she looks on you as a brother, though I think she's aware of how you feel.'

'Has she said owt?'

'Not really. But I do see her handling you well when you're doing your flirting bit.'

'Aye, she does. She don't lead me on. Eeh, Harri, am I making a fool of meself?'

'A bit...'

'Ha, say it how it is, why not! But I'm not daft, though I can't help but hope.'

'As long as you don't hold on to false hope too long, love. There's someone out there for you. You're only twenty-one, and I don't think Patsy is the right one. Anyroad, it don't feel right. She's me sister! It's weird, like you have a sister fixation, or sommat.'

'Ha, well, she does look like you! Maybe you're reet...'

'Ugh, Ian!'

'I'm only funning. Eeh, lass, you should be glad I took it that way as it wasn't a nice thing to have said to me. But though Patsy does look like you, I see her differently. It's like I'm tuned into her. I want to be in the same room... Well, thou knows.'

'I don't, actually. It hasn't happened for me. I've had a few attractions, but nothing more. Nor has Patsy – well, not really. Like me she's had a few dates, but I haven't known her to go out with anyone for more than a week. Not that we get much time. It ain't easy being a woman trying to prove yourself in a man's world. We have to fight for every bit of respect we get.'

Privately, she didn't think this was the real reason why Patsy hadn't made many friends of either sex. It was her attitude – her lack of feeling and empathy ... no, that wasn't fair. She didn't have a total lack of feeling for others, but she was just more calculated with it – a worrying trait.

'It makes you feel better just looking out over them hills, doesn't it?'

She followed Ian's gaze, glad of the change of subject. The light was fading and the remnants of the sun had spread a reddish glow over the western side of the landscape, giving it a magical feel. The hills in the distance had turned black, but still looked majestic. Turning her back to the fence, she looked towards their home. Big by the usual standards, Hartington House was a typical Victorian country house. Surrounded by land-scape gardens, it represented all that was good in her life: family and comfort and love. Though she knew it hadn't been untouched by all that had gone before.

There were many tragic stories linking the folk who used to own Hensal Grange – the Harveys and the Cromptons – to her own family, and some of them involved this house in that it had once belonged to an ancestor of theirs. And now one of that family was linked to her in a way that could never be broken. A shudder went through her at this thought.

'Are you cold, love?'

'No, just thinking. We come from a chequered history on our mam's side, don't we?'

'Well, I haven't given much thought to the tales meself. Granddad never talks of them, and if you bring them up he changes the subject. Anyroad, it's in the past now. There's nowt as can affect us. Them as caused it all have long since died or moved away.'

'Patsy's a Crompton...'

'Eeh, Harri, don't be daft. By, look, there's a full moon coming up. No doubt we'll see a wolf howling in front of it any minute. Ha ha... Come here, you daft ha'p'orth.'

His arm felt heavy on her shoulder, but it soothed the feeling that had taken hold of her. She looked up at him and told him, 'I *am* worried about Patsy, you know. I just didn't want to show it in front of Mam. That's why I took it out on you. It was just a diversion, really. Why hasn't Patsy rung? It's not like her.' And, she thought, if Patsy did have an agenda, then surely part of her plan would be to not rouse any suspicion at home.

'Well, what d'yer reckon has happened, then?'

'Ian, if I say, promise you won't do owt. For one thing, Patsy'd kill me if I set up a fuss about nowt, and for another, I'll look silly if Mam and Dad make a big to-do and then Patsy turns up.'

'I can't promise. Don't ask me to, Harri. If there's a possibility that Patsy might be in trouble or owt...'

'But that's it. That's why I feel daft about feeling apprehensive. I mean, why should she be in trouble? She's gone to London to see her mam, and she knows the city like the back of her hand. It could be something simple that's keeping her from contacting, like she might have lost her purse or had it stolen.'

'If that was the case, she'd phone reversing the charges. Look, Harri, what are you not saying?'

'Well, you know this woman that kept ringing, Rita? Well … no, it's daft.'

Ian's hands clamped her shoulders. His face came close to hers. 'Harri, please, love. I feel in me bones as sommat is up. Tell me what's bothering you. At least give me a chance to make me mind up if it might be important. Who is this woman, and what's the worry over her?'

Telling what she knew of Rita and the anxiety her mam showed over the woman turning up only increased her fear.

In the end she decided it best to share her real concerns. 'But that's not all. I – I think that Patsy may have contacted her...'

As Ian listened to Harri's theory about Patsy's reaction to the phone call she'd had yesterday, from this Rita person they all seemed worried about, it all sounded a bit far-fetched to him.

Harri told him she felt sure that Patsy wouldn't hesitate to do something on the sly if she needed to. And the reasons she gave for thinking she may have done this time, Patsy's hatred of her mother, did give her theory some merit. In the end he decided to make a joke of Harri's suspicions. 'Ha, you're a funny one. You were for reading too many of them Enid Blyton books when you were young... *The Famous Five.* You were always making us act out them adventures. I reckon as you still think of yourself as George, the tomboy sleuth.'

'Oh well, you did ask. I was only giving you what I thought might have happened.'

'Yes, but you seem to be saying that Patsy had a plan, like she's plotting a murder or sommat. Come on, Harri... Anyroad, you may as well get it all out. Why should we be worried?'

'Well, if I'm right and she did contact Rita, I just think that she didn't think it through. Like I told you, that Rita hurt her before and all for her own ends. If she got her claws into her again, she may go further. She wanted revenge on the Cromptons, and Patsy is a Crompton. Patsy is the daughter of the woman this Rita wants revenge on...'

'Eeh, Harri, none of it sounds right to me, I'm sure you're reading sommat into nowt. Look, we'll run it by Mam and Dad, and if they think like you, well then, Dad'll do what should be done.'

Sarah greeted them as they walked back into the house. 'Dad's home. Are you alright now, Ian, love?'

'Aye, sorry, Mam. I'll be reet. Harri tells me I have a crush and it'll pass. She thinks it's a sister fixation thing or sommat daft like that, 'cos Patsy looks like her! Have you ever heard the like? That's what too much education does for you: sends you bonkers analysing everyone.'

His mam laughed at this, taking away the

181

embarrassment he felt at having laid his feelings bare earlier. But those feelings wouldn't go away, he knew that. Patsy was under his skin and she would stay there.

'Who's been analysing who?' his dad asked as he came through the door.

'Harri has, Dad, me big-sister-cum-next-amazing-doctor-in-the-world, covering medicine and personality traits and everything else under the sun.'

He dodged the slap Harri playfully aimed at him, but could see she was still upset. She seemed to really think Patsy might have done something to land herself in trouble, but the Patsy *that* painted didn't sit right with how he saw her.

Talking to his dad relaxed his mind.

His dad didn't think there was anything to worry over, so then there probably wasn't. Though as they talked it all through and his mam agreed with Harri about Patsy having another side to her, some of his concerns came back into him.

London

Rita's bones ached as she put the mop into the bucket and twisted it to squeeze it for the umpteenth time. The smell of the stale blood and the sight of it congealing as it mixed with the soapy water bought the bile to her throat. Her heart lay like a piece of lead in her. She didn't care about Ken; she was glad he'd gone. And she hadn't much feeling one way or the other for that Patsy. She'd become like a thorn in her side, though it worried her that she'd have to be got rid of. Still she'd have to leave that to Jim. But Lizzie ... how all this was going to pan out for her, she didn't know. Jim's plan wasn't a bad one: he wanted to take Lizzie and her with him – said he had a nice mooring up north somewhere. It took a couple of weeks to get there, but he said he felt safe travelling the waters once he got into the rural areas. No one bothered you there, or cared who you were.

She'd always fancied Jim, so going with him wasn't a problem to her, although he was a nasty bit of work, she knew that. And she hadn't forgiven him for killing her sister. Violet had been a good girl. She'd never given anyone any trouble and had never refused her anything when she was younger. It still hurt to think of her being beaten to death. And then, look at what Jim had done to Lizzie. But for all that, it was a long time ago. He said he'd changed since then, though she hadn't seen evidence of it. From what she'd seen, he still had the same aggressive 'I must be obeyed' attitude.

Catching sight of herself in the mirror, she had to admit they'd all changed. Look at the state of her! She used to be a good-looker – still could be if she took some interest in herself. She shouldn't have taken to the gin – thinking of which, though, one would go down a treat at this moment.

Surveying the area she'd been cleaning, she decided that one more bucketful of clean water would wipe away all traces of what had happened here. Which was how she wanted it, as when it was realized they'd gone and the landlord came snooping around to find they'd done a moonlight, she didn't want anything left that would arouse suspicion.

That done, and the bucket swilled, she left the tap running for a good five minutes to send all traces of blood down the sewer, before retrieving the bloodied rolling pin from where she'd hidden it. She doubted she'd need evidence to blackmail Patsy with now.

Pulling the only case she owned from under Lizzie's bed, she began to fill it with what she thought she and Lizzie would need. Opening the small drawer at the top of Lizzie's dresser revealed the exercise books. 'Bleedin' hell... Well, I suppose I'd better take 'em, as they seem to keep her happy.' Anyway, she wouldn't mind reading some of it herself – see what Theresa had put about their relationship. She hadn't read any of that when she'd peeped at it all those years ago. She'd only read ... no, she'd not think of that. It was unbearable and incredible that Theresa went through so much, and she'd often wondered what happened to that son of hers. That would be a shock for Patsy.

'Are you done yet? I ain't hanging around here for much longer. Someone might spot me.'

The aggression in Jim's voice made her freeze for a moment. She hadn't heard him come in, and thought she had longer to sort things.

'Come on. It's dark now and the streets are quiet... What's that?'

'It was me insurance to stop that Patsy going to the police. I just need to get rid of it. I'll throw it over the side of the boat when we get going.'

Shoving the books into the case and grabbing a few more items from the drawer, she ran back into her own room and checked to see if there was anything else she'd need. Her teeth sat in a glass on the side of the bed; she hadn't had them in for ages. Dipping her fingers into the cold water, she fished them out and placed them in her mouth. They felt as though they didn't fit, and chafed her gums. Still, if she wanted to attract Jim, she'd better persevere. To that end, she grabbed the brush from her dresser and tried to do something with what looked like a haystack on the top of her head. In her hurry she tugged at the knots, bringing tears to her eyes as great chunks of it came out.

'Christ, you're not going to improve on yourself, you stupid old bag! Just get what you need and let's get out of here.'

'You get the case, then.'

The night air chilled Rita – a chill that not even the heater in the van could keep at bay. Jim hadn't spoken, which had left her to her thoughts as they travelled. They hadn't far to go, as he'd moored just the other side of Teddington Lock in a rural area. He'd 'borrowed' the van from a farmyard nearby, so she assumed they would dump that somewhere soon. Her thoughts returned to Patsy. Part of her didn't care what happened to the girl, but a small part felt responsible for her. 'What're yer going to do about that Patsy, then?'

'The same as you're going to do with your "insurance" that you no longer need: dump her in the river. Should've done it at the same time as I

185

did Ken, the bleedin' murderer.'

Rita's blood ran cold. Her earlier thoughts on Patsy dissolved. Now that it seemed a real possibility, she didn't want the girl dead. She racked her brains for a way to save Patsy, but then another thought occurred: if she did, what of the consequences to herself?

Lizzie heard the noise above, and fear clutched at her heart. Patsy, still under the influence of whatever Rita had given her, had fallen asleep again. She'd told her that her brain felt like it was clogged with spider's webs. She knew that feeling and knew it wasn't easy to fight through it, so hadn't tried to wake her.

Now she snuggled into her, not just for warmth, but for comfort, and stopped the desperate attempt she had been making to free them both.

Another bang came from up above. She had to wake Patsy now... In response to her shaking her, Patsy stirred. 'They're back, Patsy.'

'What? Oh God, Lizzie. What now? I'm scared...'

This show of fear helped Lizzie. Strength she didn't know she had surged through her as she felt an urge to help Patsy. 'We'll find a way. While yer slept I've been picking away at the knot in the rope holding yer. I think I've loosened it a bit.'

'Oh God, if only you could undo it. Keep at it, love, keep at it.'

Sweat ran off her body and pain seared her as she wriggled her arm between them again. Finding the knot, she could feel it had slackened a little. Digging her fingers into the space she'd made, she prised and prised until she could get her whole hand in the gap. Now it all depended on how long the ends were. She daren't tell Patsy to try to wriggle free – not yet, as that might tighten the knot again. Her fingers chafed as she worked. The soreness of them burned against the rough cord, but now she had enough loose to grip hold of. 'Right, try to move, Patsy. I think I can stop the knot tightening again.' Patsy eased her arms out.

'I'm free... Oh, Lizzie, I have me arms free!'

'Quick, try to get the rope off your legs. I think it must be round mine too. I wouldn't know as I have no feeling in them, but the only way they could secure yer is by passing it under me and then under the bed.'

'Yes, I can feel that's what they've done.'

'Can yer pull it up to the top half of me body?'

'Yes, it's coming. Oh, why didn't we do this before? How stupid!'

'I don't know, but we're doing it now. That's it, now if I roll a bit yer can push it further under me, then I'll roll back and yer can put your arm over and release it.'

They had just accomplished this when they heard steps descending towards them.

'Stay still, Lizzie. Just pretend we're not free. We'll wait–'

The door crashed open, flooding the cabin with light.

'Lizzie, are yer alright, Lizzie, love?'

'Rita, how could you?'

'I'm sorry, love. It had to be done. Yer going to be alright now. We both are, and we're going to continue to be, as your dad's taking us with him.'

'I don't want to go with him.'

'You've got no choice. I'm taking yer.' Her dad's voice cut through her. She hated the sound of it. Her body stiffened as he approached and said, 'Right, Rita, help me to get this one out.'

The vicious swipe that Patsy unleashed caught Jim unawares. His body reeled backwards. Losing his balance, he landed flat on his back. Patsy jumped off the bed and looked around for a weapon. As she turned to grab a brass replica of an anchor secured to the beam by iron hooks, a hand grabbed her ankle. Kicking out didn't help: the force of the tug pulled her over. An arm grabbed her neck. It tightened until she couldn't breathe. Lizzie's screams took over the space, blocking out her thoughts.

'Get Lizzie out of here, Rita! Get her up on top and stop her fucking racket.'

Rita jumped to do Jim's bidding. It seemed like she'd become a puppet, ready to dance when he pulled her strings, even if it meant hurting Lizzie! The sickening, full-blown punch that she landed on Lizzie's jaw catapulted her body backwards, her gasp of pain fading into a moan that went into oblivion. But Patsy's own desperate attempts to get air into her lungs took away her anguish at Lizzie's plight, as did the only sure knowledge her brain could interpret: *I am going to die!*

Through the red mist that clouded her vision she saw Rita drag Lizzie's unconscious body off the bed and registered it rubbing against her legs as it passed her. From a long way away she could hear Rita's cusses as she struggled. 'You'll have to give me a bleedin' hand. I can't get her up the steps.'

The pressure released from her throat. Painful gasps didn't help. Her body didn't respond or obey her. She wanted to fight, to stop them lifting Lizzie out as if she were nothing more than an animal, but her head could only process the part of her that wanted to survive.

The door at the top of the steps banged, shutting out the light. Jim's footsteps coming back towards her filled her with dread. She had no strength left in her to help her to combat whatever he planned to do. She didn't pray often, but now she begged that there was a God, and if there was then He would have mercy upon her and save her life.

Hot, fetid air rasped painfully in through her swollen throat, bringing her some relief from the bursting, burning pain in her head. Trying not to over-breathe, she slowed her panic.

He was above her now. She could feel the rough material of his trousers against her leg and hear a rattling noise. In seconds the grating of a match lit up the cabin. Looking up, she saw him put the ignited end into the window of a lamp. The wick jumped into life and flooded the cabin with light – an eerie light that swung shadows across the space around her as the lamp creaked and swayed to the rhythm of the boat rolling gently in the water.

Why isn't he doing anything? The uncertainty of his next action held her tense with fear. She stared up at him, then saw his hand go to his fly. She watched in horror as he slid down his zip. The rasping noise of it reverberated around her. *No, not that... Not that.*

The weight of him crushed her. His tobacco breath and the stench of his stale body turned her stomach. Fear gave her new strength. She writhed to one side, unbalancing him. He grabbed her hair, yanked her head back and once more restricted her breathing.

'You're fucking having this...'

His penis touched her face. Fluid secreted from it onto her cheek. He rubbed it round. She could feel the bulbous end spreading the sticky substance down towards her mouth. She couldn't move her twisted body. Horror grew inside her. She willed him to put it in her mouth, because then she could bite down on it with all her rage. But he didn't. Instead, his free hand shot down and grabbed her leg, pulling it under his knee. Unbearable pain shot through her. Pushing him felt like trying to push down a brick wall, but it did hinder him as he tried to lift her skirt. A stinging blow sent her head back to the floor. He pulled aside her knickers. His penis entered her. It didn't physically hurt, as she'd long since lost her virginity to a lad at the orphanage and had had other experiences since, but the sick disgust of it tore at her soul. His movements chafed her thighs. His guttural moans assaulted her ears as he pounded her body, stopping only to rip open her blouse and release her breasts.

Taking advantage of this respite, she slammed her fists into his face. His clouded sexual expression changed. Grabbing her arms, he spread them wide. His head came towards her. His mouth cupped her nipple, his teeth digging into her flesh. The searing pain had her howling like an animal.

'What's going on in there? Stop it, Jim! Leave her alone. What're yer doing?'

'Fuck off, Rita. I'm giving her something she's familiar with. I'll fucking tame her...'

'Rita, help me... Help me!'

The silence told her no help was coming.

Pulling from her and using all of his brute force, he twisted her body until her face scraped on the wooden floor. The wetness from his penis slid a trail around her thigh. Now it was near to her rectum. *No... No... Please, God!*

The noise that came from her as he forced his entry matched what she now thought of herself: an animal. Blistering pain splintered everything that she was. His struggle to thrust with no lubrication stopped him. 'Christ, talk about a fucking duck's arse...' She almost laughed, but the only sound gurgling from her were agonizing gulps of pain as he pulled from her again, turned her over and re-entered her vagina, thrusting deep. The action did him. His holler, right next to her ear, assaulted her eardrums and reached her soul, fragmenting it and her as his hot semen pumped into her. But the thought came to her: *It's over... over. Thank God!*

She couldn't open her eyes. She didn't want to look on her tormentor. The sound of his zip closing cemented the end of her ordeal. Her body crumpled, cold tears trickled down her cheek and ran into her ears. Painful racking sobs shook the very fibre of her.

'Right, that's the last of that as you'll ever have.'

His hand grabbed her hair. Excruciating pain ripped her scalp as he lifted her head towards him, then his fist smashed into her face. The jolt rocked her backwards and took her spinning down into darkness.

Thirteen

A Watery Grave

London 1963

Coming to, and not knowing where she hurt the most, a suffocating sensation took Patsy. Sweat poured from her. She tried to move, but couldn't. When she breathed in, hessian sucked against her lips, she could taste and smell it. My God, I'm in a sack! Terror gripped her as her feet hit against what felt like rocks. *No! God, no! He's going to throw me over the side!* The slow chug of the engine told her that the barge-like boat was on the move. Her mind filled with the horror of her fate. *Try to think!* Lizzie had said the journey to the boat hadn't taken long. *Think of the Thames ... where does it go on its way out of London? Teddington!* Yes, that could be it, that wasn't far by road. Where did the river stop being tidal? He'd have to drop her before that, so that she was washed out to sea. *Oh, it's no use! I can't calculate where I am or how long I have left...* Nor could she discern whether she was still below deck or not. Listen-

192

ing carefully told her nothing. Should she try to call out to Rita? Beg her to help her? This thought had hardly died when someone touched her. Her breath drew in on a moan as she tried to cringe away.

'Shush...'

Rita! Oh, thank God! 'Rita, help me, *please...*'

'I'm bleedin' trying to. Keep quiet. I've plied him with drink and he's nodded off. I've sat Lizzie at the wheel. She's okay and she's steering us. There's no obstacles ahead and I've tied her so she won't slip. I'm going to undo the sack and give yer a knife so yer can cut yerself free the minute yer hit the water. Then I'll tie the sack again so he don't suspect anything. But before I do, promise me yer won't give any information about me whereabouts. Promise.'

'I won't say anything, I swear to God. But, Rita, use the knife to kill him, then we'll all be safe.'

'No, I can't do that. He ... well, he's going to give me a new life, and it's a life I want for me and Lizzie. He loves her, and he's always fancied me, and me him.'

'Rita, he raped me! He raped me while you weren't many feet away!'

'Shuddup! That's of no account. Men have these urges – stuff turns them on. Now, do yer want this knife or not?'

'I do. If that's all you're offering me, it ain't much of a chance, but at least it's something. Oh, God, Rita, I don't want to die...'

'Yer won't. Anyway, the knife will give yer a chance not to. When I open the sack I'll cut the ropes on yer hands first, but if you try anything,

I'll stick the knife through yer as soon as look at yer. And, I've another one here with me, so if yer attack me when yer have this knife, I'll not only fight yer, but I'll scream out for him, and he'll not show yer any mercy.'

'I promise. But, please, please, Rita, think about it. You're giving me a chance, but it ain't much of one. Please, Rita.'

'Shut yer mouth. He could wake at any moment.'

At the despair this put into her, Patsy's body seemed to ricochet off the floor and back again with violent trembles. Terror seeped into every part of her. The rush of cold night air as Rita pulled down the sack from her face took her breath away, giving her the knowledge that she was already on the deck. He'd got everything ready. She moved her neck, and a pain shot through her head. 'Where are we?'

'We're headed back to London. Bleedin' daft if you ask me. There's river police everywhere up there, but he reckons as he knows what he's doing. Said as he needs to be in the tidal bit. Right, am I to give yer this knife or what?'

'Let me go now, Rita. Let me swim to the shore. Lizzie can steer nearer to the bank. *Please, please…*'

'And where will that leave me and Lizzie, eh? He's likely to kill me, and Lizzie will be at his mercy. No, this is the only way I'm going to do it. Yer have to stay in the bag, play it as though you're unconscious when we lift yer, and then once yer hit the water it's up to you. Any tricks before then and I'll scream blue murder and

194

confess to him what I've done. Nuffin' will save yer then, girl.'

Defeated, she gave in. She couldn't put Lizzie in further danger. 'Okay, thanks, Rita. I promise; I'll play dead for yours and Lizzie's sake.' They were brave words, but they belied the sheer horror that burned into her soul – a horror that vomited from her in billows of vile-tasting, stinking sick as Rita tied the sack.

'There, that's it. Good luck, girl, and I'm sorry. I mean it. I'm bleedin' sorry, I am, but there's nuffin' I can do.'

Panicked into lifting her hand, her only thought was to slash the sack open right away and take whatever consequences that brought, but a voice stopped her.

''Ere, what's goin' on? Get away from her, you old bag.'

'Leave her alone, Dad. She were only checking that Patsy was still breathing. Get up, Rita. Get up, love. Dad, please, please don't kill Patsy. Let her come with us. She won't tell. She wouldn't put me in that danger. Please, Dad.'

Patsy held her breath. She didn't think for a moment that Jim would take any notice of Lizzie's plea, but she hoped with all that was in her that he'd come over to check what Rita had been up to. That would at least give her a chance, because no matter how abhorrent it was to her, if she got the chance, she'd stick the knife into his heart.

'Lizzie? What're you doing up there? Christ, Rita, what're yer up to? Yer fucking messing about with me head.'

195

'She's alright. She's secure. I thought it best she steered, to give us two free hands. I were just getting stuff ready, that's all. That cow's still out for the count, and as we've entered tidals I thought now were the best time to do it. Once I had everything ready, I were going to wake yer.'

'We ain't where I want to be yet. I need to be sure she'll go out with the next tide.'

'But it's getting rough, and the river police'll be patrolling. We've got to do it now, Jim.'

Patsy's heart raced. Her fingers tightened around the knife. Fear gripped her. Her soul begged of God to give her a chance of escape, but then her mind turned to the horror of what would happen if she failed. Supposing she couldn't make a big enough hole to get out? What if the water was so cold that it stunned her?

'Yeah, I think you might be right. Help me get her to the side.'

This is it! Help me... Help me.

Lizzie started up with a moan. The eerie sound further chilled Patsy, and she hoped with all her heart that Lizzie was faking. The noise was one of great distress. How much more could Lizzie take? Already fragile, she'd taken one shock after the other in the last twenty-four hours. *Oh, why did I ever want revenge? What's the matter with me? Why can't I be normal and do what Lizzie or Harri would have done?* They'd have gone to see their mother and forgiven her... Thinking of Harri put a fresh ache in her heart. Would she ever see her again? But these thoughts swam away in a new tide of horror as she felt Rita and Jim take hold of the sack and roll her over. Gritting her teeth, she tightened her grip on the knife and lifted her hand, willing herself not to make a sound as the bricks hit her ankles. The boat swayed. Something heavy dug into her side. A foot. He was ready to push her, but he didn't. The pain of the pressure of his heel in her ribs brought a moan from her. 'She's bleedin' coming round. Quick, shove her. Hey, let go of me... Jim... No! Aghhh!'

Lizzie's scream intensified Patsy's anguish as it mingled with Rita's and elongated her name. 'Ri-i-i-t-aaaa! Noooooooooo. No–'

Both screams died at the same moment. A split second elapsed, and then came the sound of something heavy hitting the water... *No... God, no! He's thrown Rita over!*

Within seconds the foot increased its pressure. Her body moved. Resisting as best she could, she once more lifted the knife and aimed it in the direction of where his foot was, but as she did he moved it and his hands came onto her back. She could not resist the power of the shove. The edge of the boat left her. Her body dropped ... dropped...

Gasping as much air as she could into her lungs, she clamped her mouth to hold her breath in an effort to be ready. But the icy-cold smack of the water made her release some as the shock trembled through her.

The sack became a cloying net trapping her arms. Her lungs burned. She writhed and wriggled as she sank deeper and deeper with the weight of the bricks ... *help me... GOD HELP ME!*

Breckton

The strain of not knowing had caused a tension between them during the long hours of waiting. Speculation of this possibility, and then that one, had given Harri a headache, but that came nowhere near to the pain in her heart at the thought that something might have happened to her sister.

Everyone had gathered: Mam and Dad; Grand-dad Jack and Grandma Dorothy and David; and, a few paces from her, Ian, whose stance showed his despair as he held his head in his hands. Her heart went out to him. Her granddad's voice breaking into his heartache seemed like an intrusion, 'Ian, lad. Let's go for a walk, eh? I've not seen owt of this garden and the hills beyond for a long time with how busy we've been around the farm. Get your gun and we'll do a bit of shooting, what d'yer think?'

'I'll come too, Granddad. Eeh, it's been ages since we just messed around. It'll pass the time.'

'Aye, that'll be grand, David. And what about you, Harri? The fresh air will do you good. Come on, lass, there's nowt we can do and we ain't achieving owt by sitting around here going around the houses with what we think has happened.'

Ian didn't move. She knew how he felt. It seemed like a betrayal to leave the house and not be in when the phone rang. As it must do soon. *It must...* 'I just want to be here, ta, Granddad. I just want to wait for news.'

'Alright, lass. Come on then, me lads. Let's away and do something to take our minds off of everything.'

Ian stood up as if driven by an outside force. Never one to assert what he wanted, he would go along and do as his granddad said. Not that she thought he shouldn't, as Granddad was being sensible and trying to help the situation, but she wanted Ian for once to do as *he* wanted to do, not what others suggested. It was this pliability that didn't appeal to the strong-willed Patsy, who clearly thought of him as a bit of a wimp. This saddened Harri, because she knew he wasn't. She'd found more of an understanding for his feelings since they'd had that little talk in the garden and knew that this trait of his was misunderstood, and was more because he was loving and kind and thought what others wanted was more important than his own needs.

As the door shut on the little party, her mother asked, 'Did the police say owt about how Theresa Crompton was, Richard? I forgot to ask you with everything that's happened.'

More distracting conversation. This was driving her mad! She didn't care about Theresa Crompton or anyone else. She just wanted to know that Patsy was safe.

'Yes, I asked after her. He said she was doing well. Some of her confusion is lifting, which will be down to the care she is having. She was near starving, apparently. And when I told him of Rita, he said that Miss Crompton has already mentioned that lady.'

'In the context of now, or in the past?'

'They think Rita may have been the woman who has been visiting.'

'Oh? Well, that could be good. If she were still

looking out for Theresa and she thought as she were hurt and going to die, then she'd think on about her daughter and that could be a reason for her contacting Patsy.'

'Stop this! I – I mean... Oh, I'm sorry. I...' The tears that had threatened tumbled from her.

'Harri, darling?'

'I'm sorry, Dad. Sorry, Mam, I didn't mean to shut you up. I – I just can't take any more speculation. I just want Patsy back.'

'We know, love. It's been a long night and I doubt that you slept any of it. Here, dry your eyes. Come on, lass. Getting yourself in a state won't help matters.'

'No, it won't, dear. Your mam is right.' Grandma Dorothy had come over to her. 'Patsy *will* be alright. We have to think like that. Hope is our best weapon, and if we let go of that we'll have no defences. Talking through things gives us hope. Coming up with outcomes that are good gives us hope.'

'I know. I just feel so helpless. I should have gone with her.'

'She wouldn't let you. Now, come on, love. Help me make a cuppa for everyone. I'm parched, or as me granna used to say, me throat's like it's filled with the sand at the bottom of a bird cage.'

As they went towards the kitchen her mam leaned towards her and whispered, 'Actually that were a bit tame for me granna. She were more likely to compare stuff with the more private parts of her body. I remember her once saying as her throat were as dry as her fanny–'

'Eeh, Mam!'

A silence followed this for a moment. Into it Harri felt a giggle bubbling inside her. *Eeh, I wish I'd have met me Great Granna Issy! I reckon her and me are two peas in a pod. Dry as her fanny, ha!* The thought broke the strain in her and the giggle won. Her mam looked like she were bursting to laugh out loud too.

Dorothy followed them in. 'What's so funny, then? Come on, I could do with a laugh.'

'I were telling Harri about me granna. Eeh, me granna. She were a one. You dreaded to think what would come out of her next. You hadn't to be a prude. Not where she was. By, I miss her. I miss all of them...' As her mam said this she picked up the kettle off the hob and walked over to the sink. Harri watched her as she stopped and looked heavenwards and said, 'Come on you lot, work your magic and make things reet–'

As if all them that had gone before were answering her, the phone rang. No one moved for a moment. Two rings, then a third...

They all dashed into the hall. Her dad stood staring at the phone. Then his eyes found hers. Fear gave them a staring, pleading expression. 'Answer it, Dad.'

Her heart seemed to stop as the ringing sound cut off. She stood close straining to hear. Her dad asked few questions; whoever was on the line was giving him all the information. As they did so his face drained of colour. 'We'll come straight away, thank you.' Replacing the receiver he turned and said, 'They've found her...'

No one reacted. Her dad's voice shook. 'She ... she's ... very seriously injured. A man pulled her

201

from the Thames. We have to go. There isn't ... she doesn't have much time...'

The moan started in her bowels and racked her body as it travelled to her throat. 'No... No...'

'Don't, Harri, don't.'

Her mam's face held an anguish she'd never seen in it before as she whispered these words. Dorothy's arms came around her. Together they supported her as it seemed she had nothing left in her. *Patsy... Oh God, Patsy. I can't lose you ... I can't.*

Fourteen

Spiral Downwards and Theresa's Encounter

London 1963 and France 1943

The wetness Lizzie lay in chilled her body. The stench of her own urine sickened and shamed her, and stung the sores on her buttocks. She'd held on for as long as she could, but her screams and then her desperate pleas for help had gone unanswered. Her wretched sobs of grief had exhausted her. Her mind couldn't take in all that had happened. The thought of Patsy and Rita sinking down into the black, murky depths of the river was too much for her. *Please, God, let Patsy have escaped the sack and swum to safety. And Rita... Oh, I can't bear it!*

Curling the top half of her body, she managed

to shift her legs with her hands and turn them more towards the wall, which meant she could get some of herself off the stinking, soaked sheet beneath her.

What was her dad capable of? Murder, yes, but would he do that to her? Would he really leave her without help to freeze or starve to death? And where was he? After he'd thrown Patsy over the side of the boat, he'd dragged her from the wheel and carried her back down here into the dark cabin. She'd told him then that she needed the lavatory, but he'd taken no notice of her. He'd thrown something onto the bed and left.

The boat had come to a halt soon after. Maybe that was his way of saving her? Maybe he'd gone, and in the morning she could call out for help again, or perhaps he'd alert someone.

Shivering with fear of the eerie silence, broken only by the hoot of an owl and the splish-splash sound of the water rocking the boat, she tugged at the blanket he'd thrown over her and pulled it further around the top half of her. This exposed her legs, but that would be the least uncomfortable for her, as she couldn't feel them anyway. Something knocked against the wall. Feeling for it, her hand clasped what felt like a torch. That must be what her dad had thrown. *Oh, thank God!*

Its beam lit the cabin, illuminating the case Rita had brought with her. Could she reach it without falling off the bunk?

Sweat mingled with tears of frustration as every effort proved futile. Only the tips of her fingers reached the top of the case. She had to do something! She would freeze if she didn't, as the balmy August evening had turned into a cold night.

Deciding she would be better off on the floor with access to dry clothes, she rolled the blanket and threw it down. It would cushion her fall. It wasn't that far to the ground anyway.

Thank God. Rita had put in one of her warm jumpers and some underwear, and yes, the thick slacks she wore in her wheelchair. The relief these items brought had her crying again, only this time not from despair. Practised at dressing herself, it didn't take long before some warmth began to creep back into her.

She remembered there were some steps to the right of her, which she assumed went down to the galley. For a moment she considered pulling herself along on her hands, to see if she could get down there and find a drink. But she decided against it, as she'd never get back up again and no one would hear her from down there. There was just a chance Rita had put the bottle of Coca-Cola from her bedside cabinet into the case. Her search proved fruitless, but then, if she had found it how would she have opened it? Rita wouldn't have thought to put a bottle opener in.

Just as she was about to take her hand out of the case she stopped, as it brushed against what had to be Theresa's books. The joy of this discovery took away her thirst and all her needs. Pulling them out lifted her spirits further. She could roll herself in the blanket and read about Theresa. She always lost all sense of herself when she did this. *Please let that happen now...*

Theresa – Late January 1943

The German officer stood by the counter, eyeing her up and down. In other circumstances she would have found him attractive: very tall, fair hair, striking blue eyes and a square, determined chin. 'Hired new help, Monsieur Ponté? See, I told you we Germans would bring prosperity to your village. Ha, it will be good to have new blood around here. What is your name, mademoiselle?'

'She is my niece from Paris. My sister died. We are taking care of her.'

'Has she no tongue? What is your name, mademoiselle?'

'Olivia, monsieur. Olivia Danchanté.'

'Olivia. I like that. Olivia Danchanté. Well, Olivia, you will deliver our bread order to us and you will ask for me. I would like to have a conversation with you away from your uncle.'

'But I have done nothing wrong, monsieur.'

'No, you haven't, but there is something you can do right...'

'Monsieur, you should not speak to her like that. It is an insult to her and to me.'

Theresa jumped as the German's cane rapped on the counter, his anger bringing forth more German words than French ones. 'You have taken my remark in the wrong way. I meant no insult. You will send her with our order! Good day, Monsieur Ponté. It is lucky for you that you are the only baker in the area.'

As he turned on his heel and left, Monsieur

Ponté looked over at her. 'That is not good, Olivia. We have to contact Pierre. He will be at work now. There is an order for the bank canteen. I will take that and get word to him. Madame Ponté, you will have to hold the fort here. Get the German's order out quickly, and Olivia, don't do anything to upset Herr Gunter.'

His eyes held a message. Was she to prostitute herself, then? Because the intention of the officer had been clear in his expression. Fear trickled into her. How was she to handle this? Her refusal of him could bring trouble, if not harm, to the Pontés.

Her fear was compounded by watching Monsieur Ponté hurrying across to the bank. If she was compromised, the whole operation could collapse!

'Here is the order for the officers, Olivia. Hurry... And, Olivia, be careful. Herr Gunter can be a pleasant man, but if crossed he is evil and swift in his revenge. The younger women around here have all had to fraternize with him. He threatens ... no, he carries out atrocities on their families if they do not.'

'Why didn't anyone think of this scenario? I could have worked in the backroom, or perhaps disguised myself, padded my body so I looked overweight... Anything...' She could hear her own voice rising in panic. She had to stop this. She'd just have to use all her ingenuity. And if she had to ... well, a shag was a shag, wasn't it? Except it wasn't, not any more. At this moment she knew that her old self had truly gone, and the only person she ever wanted to sh– No, that word didn't fit what she wanted to do with Pierre. She wanted to love him, to make love to him, to give her body and soul to him. These were already tainted, but how much more spoiled they would be if she had to lie with Herr Gunter...

'We did think, but there was nothing we could do.'

She wanted to scream at the woman, to tell her she had betrayed the Resistance. They could have made sure Derwent knew the danger for a young woman in this area, but the thought occurred: if they knew, then so did Pierre. Had he been willing to sacrifice whichever young woman had come here?

'Besides, you will get vital information if you are cunning.'

'You mean all of this is part of the plan?' But no, it couldn't be. Otherwise, why would Monsieur Ponté have run to Pierre? Wait a minute... Was he expecting her to be willing? Was the reason he had to be told because she showed signs of not cooperating? Had Derwent sent *her* in particular, knowing of her loose morals? Was this an unspoken part of the assignment? Derwent's face came to her, his leering at her as he praised her 'many talents'. *I've been bloody stupid! I really thought I had been chosen because I had shown courage, tenacity and that I could master the needed skills. Now I think I was chosen because of my past... Sold like a piece of meat... Well, I'll show them they can't do that to me.*

'Ahh, Mademoiselle Danchanté. Come in.'

As soon as she'd arrived at the German garrison, she had been shown into Herr Gunter's office. He'd stood as she entered and proffered her a bow accompanied by a clip of his heels. 'Our mystery woman, eh? Coming out of the blue into our lives, from Paris, no less. *Oh là là,* as they say. Tell me, what was the weather like when you left?' His French was good, but his German inflection meant she had to listen very hard to what he said. His question caught her off-guard. No one had prepared her for this!

'But, monsieur, it is well known that summer in Paris is always warm, is it not?'

'A cunning and evasive answer, but not one that fits this time of year.'

'I know, but I left a few months ago. I travelled to my aunt's first.'

'Oh? Well, we haven't been able to trace when you left, so that would account for it.'

He seemed convinced, but she wasn't sure. Her heart pounded with an unsteady rhythm. She willed herself to keep calm.

'Tell me, why have you an English accent to your French?'

This shot a shock through her.

'Herr Brugen is a language expert. He is the one who asked you to wait in the hall a moment. I believe he held you in conversation for a moment or two?'

Lifting her head, she answered with all the conviction she could. 'My grandmother was English, and I spent a lot of time with her as a young child learning to talk. I copied her pronunciation. Much of it has left me over the years, but people do still say I have a trace of it.'

The silence and the scrutiny that followed this unnerved her. Was she compromised? Would he arrest her, even? *Oh, God!*

'So, we have a young woman suddenly in our midst. She has an English accent to her French, oh, but yes, there is also a great deal of the Paris slant to it, I am told. What am I to believe?'

'You can check my credentials and my papers. Everything is in order. You can check the fact that my mother died.'

'Oh, yes, I have all of these things, but these can be arranged. Heaven and earth can be moved in a war. So, let us talk about London, it is suffering for its stubborn stance, but we will win it over – we will bring it to its knees, but not by negotiation. Don't you blame them for the plight of France?'

She was nearly tripped by the sudden switch in his conversation, and by the fact that he'd spoken in English. For a moment she'd been ready with an angry retort – a retort that had shot into her mind also in *English,* but just in time she had swallowed the words and switched her mindset to French. 'I am sorry, Herr Gunter, but I did not understand all that you said in English. I have very little of that language. Grandmother did try to teach me, but...'

'Very clever.'

She froze. *He doesn't believe me!*

A knock on the door and an officer entering gave her a moment's respite from the uncomfortable glare of his scrutiny. His voice rose angrily as he addressed the officer, *'Ich sagte, ich war nicht gestört warden!'* From the way he spoke, she guessed he'd said he had given orders not to be disturbed. The officer apologizing and handing him a note further seemed to anger him. '*Schweine!*'

That, she did understand. Someone had done something to really provoke him. He'd called them 'pigs!'

'Something has happened that takes my attention away from you, but you remain a mystery to me, mademoiselle. We will dine together this evening and you will tell me more about yourself. We will meet at eight in the only restaurant this town possesses, La Cuisine des Romarins, but it is good. Cooking is the only thing I can credit the French with. Till tonight, then?'

Again he clipped his heels. The relief in her was so strong that she trembled. He didn't miss it.

'You seem nervous. Is the prospect of dining with me abhorrent to you?'

Not sure what made her do so she answered him with defiance: 'Do I have a choice? No, and it is that that makes me nervous. If I had a choice I would choose to dine with you, so then I would anticipate the evening.'

'Ah, refreshing indeed, or once more a very clever ploy. I do not know as yet, but I will find out, Mademoiselle Danchanté. I will find out.'

Going through the door with her back to him and him close behind her, she had a sense of having lost ground. It wasn't often she couldn't get the measure of a man, and it had never occurred before that she hadn't won them over. She'd thought her remark would have gone some way towards that, but it clearly hadn't. The sinking feeling in the pit of her stomach increased.

Outside, chaos had descended. An ambulance raced out of the gates, orders were barked, and soldiers ran in all directions. When she arrived back at the bakery, she found out the reason.

'Pierre organized a distraction. There is a farm on the perimeter, from which the old farmer can see miles along the road. Pierre telephoned him and asked him if anything was happening. He said he could see three motorbikes approaching in the distance. Pierre arranged for the riders to be shot at by a sniper. One dead, the other two injured. But one of them not so badly that he could not get back to the garrison to raise the alarm. He did it to help you.'

'After having set me up in the first place! What is this, monsieur? What is the real plan for me here? My remit is to work with Pierre in facilitating messages via a code to England, and to arrange for the needs of the group – supplies and ammunition. And to do anything else that is asked of me that would further... That's it, isn't it? The "anything else" includes fraternizing, doesn't it?'

'No, it does not, but we knew it was possible you would come to the attention of Herr Gunter if you were attractive. He cannot resist. He is more French in that way than I am! But we thought we could handle that. We thought...'

'Did Command in England agree to this?'

'They said you would do what was asked of you.'

Fuck Derwent!

'I won't do it! Contact Pierre again. I must get out of here, now. I will send a distress code. They will arrange to pick me up.'

'But Mademoiselle Olivia, we will be in grave danger.'

'No, you won't. Tell them you sent me to an aunt.'

'They won't believe it. They will kill us...' Tears of distress ran down Madame Ponté's face. 'Please...'

The atmosphere held a tension that was fraught with emotion. Pierre stood away from her, and yet it seemed he held her. 'I do not want this for you. We did know it could happen, and as soon as I saw you I knew it would.'

They were in her room. The door at the bottom of the stairs led into the garden. Pierre had crossed the garden from his lodgings and come straight up to her on his return from work.

'I – I didn't realize how much it would matter to me. I don't want you to go.'

'Oh, Pierre. This puts me in grave danger. Herr Gunter is crafty. He talks in smooth tones and then comes out with a question you least expect.' She told him how the interview had gone. 'If I go to dinner, I'll have to go further...'

'*Non! Je ne peux pas le supporter!*'

'I cannot bear it either, but what choice do I have? Command at home knowing about this possibility sickens me. The danger to our operation and to myself has increased to disastrous proportions.' Her body sank down onto the bed. Pierre was by her side in an instant. His arm came round her. She leaned into him. Her senses drank in the smell of him, the feel of his strong body, the brushing of his breath on her hair. His lips found her forehead, touched lightly on her closed eyes, then drew everything that was her into his kiss. They swayed backwards. The bed took them like a welcoming lover. Her pulse throbbed feelings around her that she'd never experienced. This was love – not uncomplicated, but good, clean, sensational love. Clean of sin, clean of predatory lust and clean of all that was unnatural – a love like none she'd ever known. And she wanted it. Needed it. The feel of his hands caressing every part of her fed her very soul with that need. Nothing before had touched the depths of her as this kiss did. She thirsted for it, consumed it ... wanted more. She arched her body towards his, meeting the urgent need in him that pressed the hardness of him against her.

The peeling off of her knickers didn't distract them. Pierre did this as if they were a veil draped over her, making the sensation of them passing over the heart of her sexuality like the caress of a lover's hand. She did the same for him, sliding his trousers down in a gentle, loving way and stroking him as soon as he was released. His eyes held love as he gently laid her down. His entering of her sealed everything she was – the Theresa of now, the Theresa who had nothing to do with the woman she'd been. The Theresa ready to love the love of a million generations with passion, with adoration and with commitment. Together they rode to the height this love can give. Together they hollered out this love until the room filled with the reverberated echoes of it. Together they sealed this love with the searing ecstasy of reaching the pinnacle of sensation. And together they lay still, their bodies aching with this love. Binding them for ever to each other.

After a long moment, he released her and pulled from her. His body stayed close. His kisses tingled on every part of her face. *'Ma chérie. Je t'ai trouvée, mon autre moitié.'*

'Yes, I am found. You have found me and I have found you. The other half of my soul.'

His eyes glistened with tears. They matched hers. He held her gaze. After a moment the touch of his nose on hers in a gesture of finality had him turning away and reaching for his cigarettes. The second held a moment of loss for her, but every moment had to end. This one ended with the promise of a lifetime together to come.

Smoke curled up into the space above them that had held their cries of joy as they both exhaled at the same time. The taste of the rasping of the tobacco on her throat tingled a satisfying sensation for her. She'd inhaled deeply. As she did, it came to her that no words had been uttered of love until after, when he'd simply said, 'My darling, the other half of myself, I have found you.' But somehow they spoke more deeply to her than if he had said 'I love you'.

It took another moment or two for them to descend to a place where they could talk. They did so without having to go over how they felt. In a quiet tone, Pierre said, 'How can we get you out of this mess we have got you into? I am mortified. I cannot bear you to be in danger and I cannot think of him... NO! It will not happen!'

'What are you thinking?'

'I will kill him.'

'Oh, God! Pierre, no. No, the reprisal will be too much to take. The town will suffer, everyone...'

'Then we must get you and the Pontés away from here. We have to act fast. It must look like they have fled with you. Everyone will say how devastated Monsieur Ponté was at bringing you here to look after you as a father would, only to have brought you to where you may be forced to fraternize. Come, get dressed and gather your things. I will tell the Pontés. It is our only hope.'

'Will we go far away? What about our work?'

'I have an uncle who lives up in the mountains – my mother's brother. He lives in a remote place that the Germans probably don't know exists, and have no need to, as it's of no use to them strategically. The road to it goes nowhere, but because it is on a mountainside, we often use it to send messages from. It always has a good signal and one that cannot be detected down here. He has goats, herds and herds of goats, and is always away with them, travelling as a shepherd. His wife is no longer with us and they have no children. We have access to his place. I will move you all in there. You will be safe. I will visit you and you will be able to carry out the work you came here to do.'

'What if the Pontés don't agree? What if Command don't agree? And I don't think they will somehow. The more I think of it the more I am sure they wanted me to prostitute myself.'

'They did not indicate that. They said you would be able to handle the situation. It is a situation all

215

over France, which most of the female agents will come across. They said you would handle it how you saw fit. Anyway, why would they think you would?'

'I–I have...'

'Don't, not now. I know that you were married for a brief time. I know you were not a virgin. If you have had affairs, it is something for only you to know. I just know you as you are now, and that is how it will stay. And as for Command, they will see this move as us limiting the danger for you. The Pontés ... well, they will be sad to leave here, but they know they will be in grave danger if they don't.'

Thank God for Frenchmen! The thought felt a little trite, but she hadn't meant it to. It was a difference that could be defined between a Frenchman and an English one, this acceptance of the body, male or female, needing to have sex. That was it in its simplicity. They accepted it without question. The English did it, but caused scandal and heartbreak, and ruined reputations. *Yes, thank God for the French way of thinking.* She wouldn't be called upon to account for her actions in the past, or even to confess them. They could stay in the part of her where she held her secrets. For a moment those secrets prickled as if demanding release, but she closed them down and got on with the practicalities of their move.

They left soon after. Monsieur Ponté left first with the van. Inside he had trays of bread for delivery to the restaurant and the local school – deliveries he always did in the evening. Everything had to appear normal. Madame Ponté and

Theresa left soon after with Pierre.

After passing through Pierre's lodgings, where they left some of the things for him and others to bring up at a later date, they cycled for two hours. Madame Ponté cried the whole time, and would not be consoled. Theresa understood this. It wasn't every day that you fled what had been your whole and only way of life. Madame's father had owned the bakery, and she had been born in the house. Her husband had come as an apprentice and stayed, married her and taken the business over on the death of her parents. What was happening now was devastating for her. 'I'm sorry, Madame Ponté. I feel terrible that I have brought this down on you.'

Pierre stopped any answer she may have given, 'It isn't you, Olivia. It is the war, and the bloody Germans. Everybody's lives have changed. Life as we knew it is being eroded. My own parents have had to move. My country is occupied and no longer open to us. We are refugees, all of us. All we can do is fight back – to help the British in their stance. And we have to win. We have to.'

'How often do you usually come up here, Pierre? Will your comings and goings not be noticed?'

'I hope not. I have to break the curfew to get up here, but I will get messages to you. Once you make contact with Command and give them your new location, I will need you to make calls to them. But you will need to travel around too. There are people we need to make contact with. I cannot travel easily in the day, but you can. There are only a handful of Germans who know your face. There is a factory that is involved in making parts for U-boats. The next project we have to undertake is to disable it. We will have to blow it up. The man I need you to contact is an expert. You will have to travel to Paris to meet him. He will tell you what you need to ask for from Command, and how and where to place it. You will have to make all arrangements for the drop.'

As they sat on the side of the road waiting for Monsieur Ponté to arrive to take them the rest of the way in his van, Pierre outlined more of the mission. 'There is a portable radio for you to take with you. It is an ingenious device. It looks like a make-up bag, but each lipstick, powder puff, cream jar, et cetera, is made of papier mâché and contains pieces of a radio. You will learn how to put it together so that you can make contact wherever you are. The aerial is disguised in a belt.'

'I am familiar with the technique. When will I leave?'

'The day after tomorrow. I want you to contact Command the moment we get into my uncle's house, then we will go through everything. Your route, your cover – everything.'

'Pierre, how were you going to get me out of the bakery to do this kind of mission?'

'The story would have been that you were taken ill suddenly and your uncle had taken you to the hospital and they had kept you in. It would not have worked now that you were spotted and taken note of so soon. The Germans are already suspicious of you. I wouldn't be surprised if one of the people you came into contact with at the garrison today wasn't an artist and has by now made an impression of you to circulate if need be. You must proceed with the utmost care. Tonight we will bleach your hair.'

This shocked her, even though it had been part of their training to effect disguises. Using peroxide on your hair was only one of the techniques. Appearance in general was vital. The small details were very important, as the Gestapo were trained to spot giveaway signs. If you were meant to be a factory worker, you had to make sure every bit of you fitted with that, even down to grime under your nails and ground into your hands.

'Pierre, how long can you stay?'

'Tonight I will stay all night, *ma chérie*. Tonight we will make love under the stars.'

This to a background of Madame Ponté's sobs seemed wrong, but was still exciting and wondrous.

Sated beyond anything she'd ever known, she lay in Pierre's arms. The moon shone through the window and lit their bed. His beautiful body glistened with sweat as his chest rose and fell in a breathless way. 'You're beautiful, Olivia ... *"Tu es le souffle de mon corps. Le sang qui coule dans mes veines et la vie dans mon coeur."* You are the breath in my body. The blood that courses through my veins and the life inside my heart.'

'That is beautiful. I will remember it for ever.'

'We will get out of this, Olivia. And maybe I will always call you that, as that is who you are to me.'

She liked this. It gave her a clean slate. A new beginning.

1963

Despite extreme tiredness, and at times having to fight to keep her eyes open, when Lizzie finally closed the book, light poured through the one porthole above her. Warming rays of the sun touched her face. Her stiff limbs protested when she tried to manoeuvre them into a sitting position. Each intake of breath rasped the soreness in her parched throat, and once more she needed the bathroom with an urgency that set a pain in her stomach. Her attempt to call out resulted in a croaked whisper. Despair entered her. She tried to combat it by thinking about what she'd just read. The love between Theresa and Pierre ... oh, how she longed for such a love for herself. But this time thinking of Theresa's bravery, and now her love, didn't help. Lying back down caused a tear to trickle into her ear. *Please, God, let someone find me soon.* But then, was there anyone looking?

Fifteen

Harri's Heart is Rocked

1963

It didn't seem real, looking at Patsy. Vibrant, vivacious Patsy, lying so still. So pale. Her ugly, blue-black bruising stark against her pallor, her skin torn and her eyelids swollen and bulging.

Harri stood like a statue. If she moved, if she touched Patsy, she would have to accept that it was her. Her dad's voice, whispering and anxious, came to her, asking questions of Patsy's doctor. He was using medical terms she wished she didn't understand. Patsy had a fragile hold on a frayed cord to life. It could snap at any moment and she would be gone. They could do nothing more than they had done for her. It was up to God and Patsy's will to live they said.

How could God have had a hand in this? To her mind he'd turned his face away and left Patsy alone to face the horror. Someone walking his dog along the towpath had heard a splash – well, two splashes, and then agonized screams. He'd seen a boat. Shining his torch on the water, the ominous ripples told of something alive writhing about under the surface. Diving in, he'd thrashed about, searching in desperation around him. Someone had grabbed his feet. The weight of them had pulled him under. In the blackness he'd touched what felt like a sack. Wrestling with the grasp of the arms, something slashed his face, then he'd felt the solid steel of what could only be a knife. Grasping it, he'd slashed at the sacking. The body had been freed and they'd floated to the top. The man lay in a cubicle a few feet away. She wanted to go to him, to thank him, but her legs wouldn't take her anywhere.

Ian stepped forward. She wanted to stop him. It seemed like an intrusion. He bent over Patsy. A tear plopped from him and landed on Patsy's face. A trickle of clear fluid hung from his nose. He wiped it. Then bent nearer to Patsy. 'Don't go. Patsy, don't go, please...'

Mam moved for the first time from the cocoon of the frozen scene and put her arm over Ian's shoulder. Her face was hard to read. She held it like stone, not letting in the hurt.

The others had been in, but were now in the family room – the room in which she knew you waited for news. Rarely good news. She wasn't going in there to wait. If she stood here she could know, not wait.

The police had found the cause of the first splash the man who had saved Patsy had heard: the body of a woman. They'd identified it as Rita... *Why, Patsy? Why did you go to her?*

Her eyes travelled down Patsy's body. The revulsion of the other part of the story shuddered through her. Patsy had been raped. *Oh, God!*

It all beggared belief. Again her mind screamed the question, *Why, Patsy? Why? What did you think you were doing?* Anger shot through her.

'Patsy! Bloody well wake up now. Are you listening? Eeh, lass, if you think you can lay there and drift away, you've another think coming. Wake up!'

Shock at her own words jolted her. She hadn't meant to utter them; she hadn't meant to sound so cold-hearted. Mam looked up, as did Ian. The astonishment of their expressions nearly made her laugh, but she daren't, as she'd never stop. Mam opened her mouth to speak, but a movement from the bed stopped her. The tension as they stared at Patsy enclosed them like a vice. Patsy's swollen eyes flickered. There was no way she could open them, but the movement told them she was there. 'Eeh, Patsy, it ain't often you do as I say, lass, but I'm so glad as you did this time.' Now she could touch her.

She stepped forward, and Mam and Ian moved aside. A gentle brushing of Patsy's hand was all she would allow herself. The doctor, who had moved to the other side of the bed, took charge to make checks – checks she knew were for all the vital signs. An arm came round her. A dry-sounding voice said, 'Not your conventional bedside manner, young lady...'

She smiled up into her dad's face. 'The best one for this stubborn miss, though.' He nodded and his smile held relief. 'You girls will be the death of me.'

The man looked ordinary – well, if you could say having a gash down your face and looking like death was how you should look. 'She's conscious, my sister. The one you saved.'

223

His smile took some of his stunned look away. He must be wondering what had happened to him, how he'd come to go through such an ordeal. He hadn't anyone with him. Harri stepped closer. 'Thank you. Eeh, that don't sound much like what I have inside me, but I can't express it different.'

'She's going to be alright, then?'

'Aye, physically. How she'll get over this ordeal, though, is sommat else. We don't know what happened or why she was where she was, but the main thing is she's going to be alright.'

'Thanks for telling me. I'm Greg King...'

'Harri Chesterton. Patsy is me half-sister. Are you badly hurt?'

'Well, your sister did a good job on my face, but otherwise no. I just feel as though everything didn't happen to me – that I watched it happening to someone else, and yet the way my limbs are trembling I know it did happen.'

'That's a coping mechanism – part of the body's defences. You'll have to take care when the reality hits you. It was a brave thing you did.'

'It didn't feel like it. I thought I was an idiot and cursed myself for not ignoring it and carrying on. My dog drowned.'

This statement pierced Harri's armour. Her eyes blurred, and the wetness soothed the prickly dryness of them before it brimmed over and ran down her cheeks. Her throat constricted. 'I – I'm sorry.'

Greg didn't speak. His hand stretched out. Taking it made him real to her. A man... A hero, yes; her saviour, yes – but just a man, hurting from loss like she was. The tightening of his grip took this thought away, and she knew he wasn't just a man. He was special. His eyes held all that she needed in the depth of them: a kindness, an understanding, a kindred spirit.

'Ah, you're awake?' Her dad's entrance broke the moment. She withdrew her hand, but hadn't wanted to. Whilst her dad and then her mam and Ian thanked him, her mind took in more details of him. Though he was lying down, she could see he was tall. His face looked squared off, with the straight line to his chin – a chin that held a dimple. His eyes, blue, but not at their best with their blood-filled appearance, held a twinkle. A good-looking man and a nice one. No, more than nice... *God! What am I thinking? It must be the shock.*

'Well, thank you again, Greg. An inadequate word for what you did for us ... for Patsy.'

Greg nodded at her dad. She had the feeling that it was all too much for him. The others sensed it and withdrew. She smiled and went to follow them, but his plea stopped her, 'Don't go... I mean. Well...'

Nothing about the moment felt awkward to her, and she didn't want it to for him. 'I won't, but I warn you, you don't know who you're asking to be your bedside companion. I've a reputation, you know!'

This brought the colour to her cheeks. As usual her feet had stepped in with a clip that could be taken two ways and made her sound very forward. But he laughed – a painful sound. 'Oh? Well, you haven't heard about mine yet!'

This stopped her blush. She sat down. 'Tell me about your dog.'

Though tired to the bones of her, Harri would not have chosen to spend the night any differently. Patsy had been moved to the intensive care unit from the resuscitation ward, and Greg had been put into a quiet room in a side ward. Going from one to the other, making sure they were both alright and letting them know she was there for them, had meant her legs ached with all the walking, but her heart was at ease.

She'd learned a lot about Greg. A bachelor in his thirties – something that had pleased her more than it should – he ran the London branch of his father's chain of jewellery shops. His parents had retired to Cornwall and he'd spoken to them on the phone. They were travelling up tomorrow. He had a sister, a lecturer at the university in Bristol, but she was abroad as the long summer break was in progress. A friend had been in to see him and had contacted one of his senior staff to make arrangements for the next day's trading and that had put his mind at rest. He'd be allowed home tomorrow. Home was an apartment above the shop.

He'd held her hand often, sometimes for reassurance, and at times just because he'd wanted to. Even the trauma that they were going through didn't stop her heart singing at this.

A good moment came when the tube that had passed into Patsy's stomach through her throat had been removed and she'd managed a few words. Though what she said set up more concerns and fears.

In between saying that she was sorry, again and again, she became very agitated about a girl called Lizzie. 'She needs help, Harri...' Her distress worried Harri into talking to the officer sitting outside the ward.

'We are looking for her and her brother,' he told her. 'They're not at the house, and there's no sign of them. The girl's in a wheelchair, so she must have been taken somewhere. If she's on that boat they probably have her by now, but I'll see if the doctor will allow me to talk to your sister: any information she has is vital to us. The girl could be in danger.'

This hadn't been comfortable to hear. *It wasn't all over, then?* But why she had thought it was, with another body and what had happened to Patsy, she didn't know. No. More like it had just begun, and they had more to face...

Sixteen

A Love Across the Generations

Jacques and His Grandmother, Lady Daphne Crompton

Lady Daphne sat upright in her chair. The waiter had been very attentive, and she had all she needed: tea served in beautiful bone china, with biscuits of the finest, and all the possible choices for how she might like to take her tea: fresh lemon slices, white cubed sugar, a jug of hot water, milk and a tea infuser. Perfect. Peeling her gloves off, she began to relax. She was to meet Jacques at three-thirty, but had arrived three hours early to make sure she was ready. Davidson was seeing to checking her into her room. Once she'd had her tea, she would go up and rest for a while before freshening up. Carmen, her Spanish maid, would see to laying out her clothes and running her a bath. Plenty of time. No rush, no harassment.

The journey had tired her, though the comfort of her Rolls-Royce had cushioned that, as had being able to do sections of her journey on the parts of the new motorway that were open – a marvellous road, and one long overdue for this country.

The surroundings were familiar to her. Did anything ever change at the Ritz? *Oh, the shopping trips she and her dear sister Laura had made to London in the old days!* And staying here had been part of them. Sometimes Lady Gladwyn, her friend and confidante, had accompanied them, and when she had, the evenings had been full of parties of the grandest kind. Lady Gladwyn had been very well connected.

Life was very different now. It wasn't just old age. The dowagers of her past had still lived a grand existence, and it was this 'grand existence' itself that had gone, and she put it all down to the rising up of the lower classes. Working classes, they called them now. They had too much, in her view, and were always striving for more. They lived far above their station, and one found oneself often sitting next to them in places they would not have been allowed to set foot in in her younger days. It would all end in tears, she was sure of it. At least having Alec Douglas-Home as their Prime Minister meant they had one of their own still at the helm, but for how much longer? That wretched Harold Wilson was gaining ground and popular support for the Labour Party. Oh dear, sometimes she longed to go back in time.

Jacques whistled under his breath as he entered the Ritz, the sumptuousness and grandeur of the place was more than he was used to. Standing at the reception, he looked up into the never-ending spiral of a beautiful ornate staircase.

'Lady Crompton has a table reserved in the hall for tea. Come this way, sir.'

As they walked through to the hall, the thick tread of the carpets and the splendour of the decor made him relieved that he'd chosen his suit rather than his casual denims for this meeting. The Ritz being the venue had given him a little insight, but even so, for a man who liked the casual look and rarely chose the formal, it had been a toss-up which to wear.

His first look at his grandmother gave him a feeling he didn't expect. Love? Yes, he would say that was it. The serene lady was sophisticated in her manner and dress, wearing what he had heard termed a 'costume' – a sage-green satin-look jacket trimmed with black and a matching skirt. She sat bolt upright, trying to look unaffected by everything that was happening, but she came across as frail and vulnerable, yet with her past beauty still evident in every part of her elegant appearance. Her precise, dainty features defied age, showing only traces of lines, and her hair was a shining blue-grey, swept off her face in a soft way and gathered into a bun.

She stayed still as he approached, feeling uncertain, he suspected, and that would be an uncomfortable state for one used to being confident in her surroundings. 'Lady Crompton?' As she glanced up at him he found himself looking into knowing, wise, dark eyes, lightened by age on the perimeter but still sharp and keen.

He took the tiny, blue-veined hand she offered to him gently in his and proffered a bow, something he'd never done in his life. Her tinkling laugh held a mockery of his action, but when he looked up he saw it was an amused gesture tinged with a little pride.

'Sit down, dear. You are very handsome, and yes, I do see something of my daughter in you, though I can see you have inherited more of the French look you assign half of your parentage to.'

'A quarter French. The other quarter is Polish. Have you come to believe I am, or may be, your grandson?'

'A little of me believes it. You would be part of why things are like they are. Shame can do strange things to people's minds.'

'Are you talking about my mother? Has she problems?'

'Shall we establish you are who you say you are first? Then I will talk about my daughter to you.'

Her hand went up and a waiter attended immediately, 'Madame?'

Without conferring, she ordered afternoon tea, then stopped and said, 'Wait a minute. Don't you Americans drink coffee no matter what the hour? Or maybe you would prefer something else?'

'What I feel like is champagne! This is a great occasion for me...'

Her 'tut' amused him. He already loved her beyond measure, and to think she was what they had been led to believe most *English* ladies were: refined, prudish, stiff-upper-lipped and... But no, he couldn't say emotionless. That didn't describe how he'd seen her shake a little as she'd fought for control on first seeing him, but she was full of propriety, yes. Wonderful!

'Coffee will be great, thank you. Erm, strong and black, please.'

'The way they serve it, you will be able to determine its strength yourself, Jacques.'

Another barbed reprimand, but he didn't mind. It was what he would expect from a grandmother if her grandson stepped out of line. Even if she was unsure that's what their relationship was, she was taking on the role like a natural.

'Shall I show you what I have now?'

'Yes. But please remember, Jacques, this isn't easy for me...'

'I know. I understand. I am a shock to you, but you are doing very well. Best get it over with, eh?'

'Your "getting it over with" will be just a beginning for me and my daughter...'

'I'm sorry. I've been insensitive. I didn't mean to be, Gran– Lady Crompton.'

'A lot has happened since the war. Oh, a lot

happened during it that changed our lives and our relationships drastically too. I have lost a son ... well, and a daughter, really... Oh dear, why am I talking to you like this? I intended to keep this very business-like, but...'

'It is hard to do that with your own, ma'am. And we are family, I know that. You only have to let me prove it to you and you will know it, too.'

'I think I do, Jacques.'

What this had cost her to say he didn't know, but the saying of it sent a warm glow surging through him, so much so that he forgot himself again and leaned towards her. 'That means a lot to me. To have you recognize in me something of yourself ... of your family, without proof...'

'Stop that! I don't go in for all of this sentimental nonsense...'

The pretty lace hanky she brought out of her bag and touched her nose and the corner of her eye with told him a different story. Time to show her what proof he had.

He laid the photos out in front of her and waited.

Though he knew she wouldn't want it to happen, a little tear did escape her as she turned each photo over and looked at the inscription of who was who. Still she didn't speak, until she lifted his passport and checked his name. 'So, it did happen. A wartime love affair and here you are...'

'Yes, Grandmother, here I am!'

'Well, I suppose we had better deal with the situation.'

This wasn't the reply he would have liked, but

he could see her inner turmoil.

'I won't embarrass you or ask anything of you, Grandmother. I–'

'Grandmama, please! As in "mam" and "ma".' This came with a little smile. 'And of course you will cause me embarrassment, but I am prepared for that and it isn't your fault. But I hope too that you will bring my daughter back to me.'

He sat listening to her quiet, dignified tones with shock and a churning of his emotions as she told him of her estrangement from his mother. 'We never quarrelled, but for some unknown reason your mother refused to see me. It broke my heart, but in the end I had to accept that by persisting in trying I was only making things worse for her. Now I am wondering if she held a deep shame in her at having had you out of wedlock. This, mixed with the pain of losing her lover and her son, might account for Theresa's rejection of me. Maybe somehow I made her relive her shame over and over and therefore the pain. Poor darling, she must be living a private hell and I can't help her.'

At this point his own eyes prickled with unshed tears. He reached out and gently took her hand. She didn't resist. They stayed still just looking at each other. Someone dropping and breaking a piece of china splintered the moment, but not before they had sealed the deep feeling they shared.

'Oh, this is such a public place, and we are embarrassing ourselves. I am booked into a suite. Let us go up. My staff will take care of us.'

'Are you sure, Grandmama? I don't want to tire

you. Would you like me to come back later?'

'No, Jacques, I don't want you to go anywhere. I want you to stay with me for ever. You may be my little family embarrassment, but now that I have found you I intend to hold my head up high and never lose you. Help me to get up, dear.'

His heart sang. He'd found the other half of him ... well, not the whole half, but a big part of it.

Exhaustion hazed her eyes at times, but she insisted on carrying on. They covered a lot of ground. He told her of his Polish family and his grandfather, his French grandmother, and what he knew of his mother and father's love for each other and of his life now, and he listened to her telling of his late Uncle Terence and the family Terence had left behind – his cousins! *My God, so many people to get to know!* And then she went on to tell of his late grandfather, someone she had loved dearly and missed to this day. This prompted another regretful moment in him – something he hadn't had when she'd spoken of his Uncle Terence and his suicide, although he didn't know why.

Finally she told him about Hensal Grange, now no longer in the family, which was the grand country home left to her by her sister, whom she'd adored and who had been involved in a little scandal. When she finished, she sat back. She looked ... happy. Yes, that's how he would describe the look that had settled on her face and the aura that surrounded her.

He couldn't help himself. He stood up, pulled

her to her feet, and hugged her, taking care not to hurt her. She allowed it for a moment then slapped him gently. 'You Americans, all sentiment and flattery...' He laughed out loud. Her tinkling laughter joined his. It was as if the years of not knowing each other had slipped away. They were family, and he knew they had a great, unforced love between them.

As she sat down, she said, 'You must come and stay with me in York. I haven't a huge, grand place now, but there is plenty of room and I still retain some staff: my butler who you have met, and maids, and...'

Staff! That sounded alien to his ears. *Staff, in a house?* When she'd initially said about her staff, and a gentleman had been in attendance to their needs when they first came up here, he had just thought it was a service supplied by the hotel. But she was talking as if she had a rook of them at home! Oh, he was used to hired help, as most of his friends' families had them, but only because both mom and dad had high-flying jobs. His grandmother was talking of a butler, a personal maid, a cook and household maids, not to mention a gardener and chauffeur – and all just for her! It was as if he had stepped back in time.

'But, you know, I still own a house in the country. Tarrington House. Again, not large. It is in Breckton, near to Hensal Grange, but it has been shut up for many years now. My daughter-in-law couldn't bear to go back to the area after she lost Terence, and Theresa would never visit. I went to York to stay with friends after Terence died, and there just didn't seem any reason to go back, so I

235

bought a place there of my own and where at least my grandchildren would be brought to see me. I'm sorry, I haven't said, but my daughter-in-law Louise – a lovely person – is also estranged from your mother. I don't know the reason. I do know they did have a terrible screaming row not long after Terence died, but what was said that was so bad they cannot be friends, I don't know. But whatever it was, I have to accept that Louise will never forgive your mother.'

'Never is a long time; things can change. But what you haven't told me is where my mother is.'

'No.' She leaned back.

'You're tired, Grandmama. I'll go now. I have waited a long, long time to find out about my parents. Now I have, and have had the amazing discovery that one of them is alive, and I have met you, I can wait for anything further. You rest now and I will come back later. We'll have dinner together.'

'No. I should tell you now. Let us get everything over with. This isn't going to be easy for you.'

Not easy! If ever there had been a way to describe how he felt, he would not have used those two inadequate words. The news of what had recently happened to his mother, and her present state, had devastated him.

'I'm sorry, dear. It is breaking my heart, and yet I cannot go to her. I – I only seem to make matters worse for her. In *her* head, I am someone to be avoided. Like I said, I think your existence may have something to do with that.'

'But why? Oh I know she couldn't have told you back then, but when attitudes changed over

236

such things and, well, the war produced more than a few of us illegitimate children.'

'Not in our class, dear. We didn't behave in that manner. Well, we did, I suppose, but we were very discreet about it.'

He almost laughed. Discreet! His mother had been discreet, keeping him a secret for all of her life, and look where it had got *her*. But then, there must be something more. He couldn't accept that his birth, coming as it did from a deep love, could be the full cause. He could see that what she had been through and not knowing where he was would contribute to her mental condition, but not to want to see or be with her own mother! For a moment these thoughts caused him to doubt this lady, who he'd come to love deeply in such a short time. Was she telling him everything? Yes, she was. One look at her distress and he knew that. She loved her daughter, and she was mystified and very, very hurt as to why she was shut out of her life. 'I know you don't like shows of affection, Grandmama, but I need a hug.'

'So do I, my darling grandson, so do I.'

This sealed his love for her, but more than that, it cemented his faith in her and his sorrow for what she had been through.

'Now, darling,' the endearment as she sat down again warmed him, 'you coming into our lives will have to be handled with care. I know you want to rush over to the hospital, declare who you are and your undying love to your mother, but you can't. There are channels you must go through. Her psychiatrist, for one – well, the most important one, of course – but what I am saying is, you have to handle this with care. You said in your letter you want to visit your father's memorial?'

'Yes. He was shot in a prison camp. There is a memorial erected to him in France – well, not just to him, but to all those who perished. I will feel more at peace when I visit, I am sure. But first I want to go to Poland. I want to see if I can get to know my father more – what he was like, where he lived, played and went to school. I want him to be real, not just a dead father. I want to talk to people who knew him – that is, if there are any still alive.'

'Then that would be the best thing for you to do right now, to get on with your plans, and I do hope they meet your expectations, dear. In the meantime, leave me to pave the way for you with your mother – and, of course, your aunt Louise and your cousins. I think Louise will be very happy to meet you, and won't hold anything against you that she has inside her where your mother is concerned, and though a shock to your cousins, I know they are going to like you. But everything needs preparing so that it all goes smoothly. We can't just impose you on them. You understand, don't you?'

Being someone that everyone had to *prepare* for wasn't a comfortable place for him, but he had to let her handle the situation how she felt best. 'Yes, it hurts that my turning up to claim my rightful place in my family and to be by my mother's side is something that needs the way paving for, but I do understand, Grandmama.'

'I know, darling, but that's the way it is. I'll take

238

that rest now, and then later we will enjoy dinner. I will have it served in the dining room through there,' she pointed to a closed door on the right of her. 'That way we can continue to enjoy our privacy and we can exchange stories with each other – stories that are not clouded by the facts of who everyone is and what their present situation is, but ones of our lives so that we get to know each other, really know each other, and how we tick.'

'Ha – that was an Americanism, "tick". I'm educating you already! Tick, indeed! I would have expected you to say: "how we have conducted our lives".'

Again they laughed, and it lightened the heavy feeling that had threatened to descend in him.

'Go on with you! You have your Uncle Terence's cheek.'

This didn't sit right in him, and it worried him. He knew nothing about Terence, yet he had a feeling he wouldn't have liked him and that he was responsible for a lot of what was wrong in the family. Maybe it was just the fact that he'd taken his own life with seemingly no reason to do so that made him think this way. Because there must have been a reason, and whatever it was, he felt sure that it was somehow connected to his mother. Otherwise, why the row between her and Terence's wife, which had never healed, even after all this time? This family of his was turning out to be very complicated. But it didn't matter; they were *his* family, and he had found them. That was all that mattered.

Dinner further cemented their relationship,

and it saddened him to learn all that he had missed. On parting, they left their next meeting open, with him promising to ring her often. This wasn't an empty promise, but one he'd find hard not to keep, because now he'd found her he didn't want to ever lose her.

And now, he thought, he felt ready to go to Poland – to do as he'd said to his grandmama: to trace his father's life before he traced his death. To see if there was anything left of the factory his family had died in, and see if there was a possibility of having something erected on the spot, so that everyone would know what had happened there. This is what his grandfather had asked him to do, and if that wasn't allowed, he had to find the local Jewish cemetery and to buy a plot. He'd promised to take some of the dust from the factory site and bury it there, and then to sort out having it landscaped and a stone erected with all the names on it. At first, he was just to have his own family names engraved, with their ages, dates of birth, and approximate date of death. His grandfather had given him a list. Once that was done, he was to advertise it in the local paper with the full story and ask any relative of anyone who had perished in the same fire and who wanted their names on the memorial to contact his grandfather by letter with the details.

Although this was an important mission for himself as well as for his grandfather, more than this, he wanted to walk the streets where his father had played, visit the school he'd attended and, if it was still there, the synagogue in which he had prayed. Maybe he'd even find some surviving friends of his father's – after all, his father hadn't left Poland until he was a young man of eighteen. That would make any of his peers who were still alive around forty or forty-one. It would be good to meet them. Yes, that's what he'd do: build a picture of his father, his nature, his likes and dislikes, make him real. Then he would go to France and mourn his death.

Seventeen

Love is a Promise

Patsy 1963

Ian leaned over Patsy. Everyone had left now, but he'd stayed on a while, just sitting watching her chest rise and fall, gaining reassurance with every breath she took. 'Patsy. Can you hear me, love?' A small flicker under the swollen lids told him she could. 'They've found Lizzie, and she's safe. They will be bringing her here.'

The dry cracked lips formed a little smile and mouthed the word 'good'. Just like he'd seen Harri do, he took some cotton wool, dipped it in the small bowl of cold water, and gently dabbed her lips. She was trying to speak again. Leaning closer, he could just hear her saying, 'Thank you ... love.' He dared not hope that she meant anything by the endearment. 'There's more news, if you're ready to hear it.'

241

Her nod told him she was. 'They have confirmed the woman's body was that of that Rita whom you had phone calls from.' There was no reaction to this. 'And they have the man–' at this, she gasped, 'Th-they have him? Oh, th-thank God.'

His heart hurt at how relieved she was. This man must have been the one to rape her before throwing her overboard. How was she going to come to terms with everything? 'It'll be alright lass, I'll make it alright, I promise.'

'Ian ... I – I'm sorry. I ... know how you feel. I...'

He didn't want to ask what she was sorry for. He had a good idea she meant she couldn't return his feelings. 'Don't be, love. There's none of us as can help how we feel. Stop worrying and there's no need for guilt. I'm no catch, anyroad. Ha, you were cut out for better things than me, lass!'

One unbandaged finger moved. He took hold of it. If only he could take hold of the whole of her and love away her pain and hurt.

'Harri?'

'She'll be back in a little while. We're staying in a hotel nearby, and Mam took her back there to rest, so don't worry. Everything will–'

A knock on the door interrupted him. On answering it, he'd thought to see one of the medical staff, but Greg King stood there, unsteady on his feet.

'Hope you don't mind. They've discharged me and I wanted to come and say goodbye. Is Harri not here?'

'No, but she wouldn't have wanted to miss you.'

'May I?'

'Aye, of course. Patsy, the man who saved you is here. Greg King.'

A tear fell down Patsy's cheek. Greg took hold of the finger Ian had just released. 'Hello, you. I've come to see who it was that slashed my face.' His voice held laughter, and Patsy smiled.

'Th-thank you... S-sorry...'

'Seeing you is all the thanks I need. They tell me you are going to make a full recovery, though it may take time. I don't live far from here, so I'll pop in and out when I can to keep a check on you. And, if that sister of yours will let me, I'd like to take her out to dinner.'

Patsy seemed to wince at this, and Greg looked over at Ian, a worried look on his face. Ian shrugged. He knew with how close they were that Patsy did sometimes show a bit of jealousy if anyone took Harri's attention from her, but decided to make a joke of it. 'Everyone Harri goes out with has to be vetted by Patsy first.'

'Ian!'

Patsy's voice came out quite strong.

'Uh-oh, I'm in trouble now! Sorry, Patsy, but it's true and they're both the same. They watch out for one another.'

Patsy shivered. 'Don't take ... n-notice.'

'Ha, I may if you were able to do anything about it. And I gathered how close you are by what Harri said, so don't worry. You look cold...'

Greg pulled the blanket up further round her. He touched her hair. 'You have the same colour hair. It's beautiful.'

It was Ian's turn to feel a pang of jealousy. This

243

man had an easy way with him that he himself didn't possess. He brushed the thought away and told Greg, 'Not only that: though you can't see it at the moment, they're almost identical at times. It's uncanny. And they were born on the same day an' all.'

'I know. Harri told me. Well, I'd better go. My mum and dad have come up to stay for a few days. They're waiting outside. I'll pop in tomorrow, Patsy.'

'Yes ... please do. And thank you. Th-thank you.'

'You don't have to keep saying it. I'm just glad I was where I was, though at the time I wished myself a thousand miles away. But we're safe, and that's the main thing. Is there news on the other girl and the body?'

Ian told him what he knew.

'That's good about the girl. I feel bad about the woman, but there was nothing I could have done. Still, apart from that, I have a good feeling that all this will sort itself, and I'm really glad I've met you all. See you tomorrow.'

When he'd gone, the silence seemed to hang uncomfortably between them. Patsy said something he didn't catch. When he leaned over her, she said, 'Shouldn't tell him ... th-that.'

'It was only a joke – sommat and nowt. Don't fret yourself. He took it as it were meant. Anyroad, it seems Harri has told him everything. They've really hit it off.'

'Not funny.'

'Oh, Patsy, I'm sorry. Don't get upset with me. I'll not be able to take that.'

'I – I'm tired. Le-leave me now.'

His heart dropped. She wanted him to leave. Why had he been so stupid as to even comment? But, no, he'd done nothing wrong. 'Well, you can just sleep, then. I'm not going anywhere. I'm not leaving you on your own, and I'm not fighting with you either.'

She made a noise that sounded like, 'Oooooooh!'

He laughed. 'Yes, I am getting out me pram. So there, Miss Likes-Everything-Her-Own-Way!'

She smiled at this, and the moment had passed. Perhaps he should be more forceful with her in the future. Maybe that's how she liked it. As he watched her relax, something in him settled in a good place. The sight of the state of her and the thought of what had been done to her cut him in two, but it didn't take away from the lift in spirits and hope that had sparked up inside him at this moment.

Harri met Ian standing outside Patsy's room when she came back an hour later. 'What's to do, are the nurses with her?'

'No, they've just brought that girl Lizzie to see her. It seems that she wouldn't take no for an answer, so I thought I'd take the opportunity to go and get a pot of tea and leave them to it.'

'Oh, I'll just pop me head round and say hello. Mam and Dad are here. They're in the waiting room. I said I'd come along first and then give them a turn. If Patsy and Lizzie want to be alone, I'll come along and join you all in a mo.'

The scene that met her as she opened the door

tugged at her heart. A frail girl, who didn't look much younger than she and Patsy, sat in a wheelchair. She had long, blonde unkempt hair, her face and body looked skeletal, and her eyes were huge in the bony structure of her high cheekbones. Her look held surprise. The way she twisted her head back and forth to look at Patsy and then back at her, told of why. 'Hello, I'm Patsy's sister. Me name's Harri. And aye, me and Patsy are alike. You're Lizzie, I take it? How are you feeling?'

'I'm doing okay, thanks. That is ... well...'

Harri's heart went out to the girl. She moved into the room and took her hand. Kneeling down, she said, 'You're safe now. I'm sorry to hear of your losses. Your brother and Rita...'

'It hurts.'

Taking Lizzie in her arms as best she could, she held her while painful sobs racked the girl's pitifully thin body. 'Lizzie, love, it's good to cry, to get it out, but I'm worried for you. Let's get you back to your bed and ask for sommat to help you sleep, eh?'

'I want to be with Patsy. She's the only one in the world that I know now, well ... want to know. She helped me. It turned out bad, but she was only trying to help me and Rita.'

There was a plea in Lizzie's voice, as if she was trying to convince herself as well.

Patsy stirred. 'Lizzie?'

'Yes, I'm here, Patsy. I – I thought yer were dead. Rita's...'

'I know. I'm sorry.'

Patsy looked from Lizzie to her and said, 'Harri,

246

I did a daft thing. I wanted revenge. I couldn't shake that feeling from me.' Then to Lizzie, 'I'm sorry, Lizzie, love. I'm so sorry.'

Lizzie put her head down.

For a moment Harri felt an anger surge through her. Patsy wanting revenge had triggered a series of events that had left so many devastated, but then Lizzie lifted her head again and surprised her by putting another perspective on it.

'Things would have been worse for me if yer hadn't come. Ken were going to take me away with him. He would have carried on giving me that stuff, and Rita wouldn't have been a match for him to stop him. He ... he would have killed her, I'm sure of it. But you saved me, Patsy. Anyway Rita didn't help. She should have let yer call the police, but instead she thought to save her own skin and frame yer. None of us could know that me dad would turn up... It's me that is sorry, Patsy. Sorry yer walked into that.'

The breath caught in Patsy's throat. 'I – I know, but I killed your brother... Oh God, Lizzie, I didn't mean to.'

'What! What are you saying, Patsy?'

'Harri, don't... I didn't mean to...'

Patsy's sobs were too much for her, and her breathing became laboured. Harri ran out of the room to fetch help.

As the medical staff stabilized Patsy, Harri's heart began to steady itself. Sitting next to Patsy, she took hold of her bandaged hand. Patsy looked over at Lizzie and with more strength than she'd shown before she asked, 'Did you tell the police?'

'No, they came to me but I couldn't tell them. I choked up and the nurses said they'd have to wait a bit to talk to me.'

'We have to tell them. Harri, will you help me? I need to tell everything, but I can't go through it all twice. Will you fetch the police for me, and the others? I want you all here.'

'Are you sure, love? Shall I get Mam and Dad in? They're in the waiting room.'

'Yes, everyone who is here. I need to tell everyone in one go.'

'Right, Miss Crompton, I understand you have further information?'

'Yes, I do. It's about the death of Lizzie's brother, Ken.'

'He's dead, then? We thought it a possibility. Who else knows this? Did you know, Miss Railbury?'

Lizzie's 'yes' was hardly audible.

'Were you present when it happened?'

Again, a whispered 'yes'.

'Well then, I will need you to go with my colleague. We cannot take a statement from one of you whilst the other is present. We need separate accounts.'

Harri saw a look of fear in Patsy's eyes. She went to her and held her hand once more.

Lizzie turned as they wheeled her out and said, 'I'll tell them the truth, Patsy. I'll tell them how it was. But ... but I – I don't want to be on me own when I do.'

The policeman answered her, 'You don't have to be. No one is accused here – as of yet. But we have to do things by the book.'

'Can't Lizzie make her statement afterwards so that we can be with her, too?' This from her dad warmed Harri, and she could see it helped Lizzie too.

'Yes, but none of you must react in any way to what you hear from either of them. I don't want them holding back from revealing everything for fear of upsetting any of you. At this stage all we know is that a man is dead, and that he didn't die of natural causes. We haven't got his body, and have no idea where it is or who moved it or why. Verbal evidence that is the same from both of them and given independently is very important at this stage of our investigation. So you are present to support them, and that is all.'

'We understand, Officer. Patsy, you won't be judged by any of us. We promise, dear. So tell everything as it happened.'

'Thanks, Dad, I will. I have to. I didn't do anything wrong – not intentionally, anyway. It was my need of revenge on my … on Theresa Crompton that drove me and caused it all. I don't have that need now, and I'm worried about her. Does anyone know how she is?'

'Aye, love. Dad telephoned and they say she is still making good progress. Soon as you're better we'll go and see her, eh?' Harri's anger had left her, but now she held in her a worry that what Patsy might not think of as wrong would be looked upon as such by the police.

At the end of Patsy's telling, Harri could feel the silence and the shock. Such things seemed to be played out on the telly, but not in their lives. Well, not in hers, anyway. Her mam had been through that mill, but she never thought as her Patsy would.

The policeman shut his notebook. He'd remained silent throughout, but now he began to probe, asking questions that made Harri want to shout out at him to stop and to believe what Patsy had told him. Patsy did well. Nothing he asked tripped her, but Harri was left wondering, God! Who was this Rita? Oh, she knew *who* she was, or rather who she had been, as of course she was dead now, but what had driven her and why had she ever come into Patsy's life? Still, she had to admit that if she hadn't, then she would probably never have known of Patsy's existence, and she couldn't imagine that. She didn't want to.

'Right, young lady. You seem to have got yourself caught up in a world you're not used to. Now, we will see if Miss Railbury's story matches your version.'

'I'll stay with Patsy. She needs someone with her.'

Harri held her breath at this from Ian, but then knew her heart to sing as Patsy said, 'Thanks, love. I need someone to, and you'll do.' There was a little smile to accompany this. It held relief and ... well, she'd to stop romanticizing...

'I'll stay if you like.'

'No, Harri. I think Lizzie would like you there above any of you. She's met you, and I'd feel better if you was with her.'

Turning as they left the room, Harri saw Ian gently take hold of Patsy's hand. Patsy didn't re-

250

sist his touch. Harri crossed her fingers and went out.

The sense of relief for Harri was overwhelming. Everything Lizzie said matched what Patsy had said. *Why did I worry that it wouldn't?*

The police seemed satisfied, though they did say that there could be more questions as the investigation progressed. They needed to find the body, as that was the key to substantiating how the death occurred, and if that happened and all was as it should be, then that would be an end to the matter. Patsy and Lizzie still had a lot to face with the trial of Lizzie's dad. That would be difficult for both of them – for Patsy because she would be forced to go over the details of the rape, and for Lizzie because she would have to revisit the death of her mother.

Once again, everyone had left her with Patsy and Lizzie. Both seemed exhausted, and she wished they would rest and go over things they needed to at a later time, but Lizzie didn't want that and Patsy said she didn't mind her staying.

'Harri, does anyone know about me, yet? Anyone connected with me mam, I mean?'

'Yes, Dad told them – well, the police, anyway. He and Mam thought it best as ... well, when they thought you had gone to see her and didn't know about...'

'It's alright. Have they told me mam?'

'No. Dad told them not to. He said that he didn't know your wishes as you hadn't turned up there.'

'I know a bit more about me mam now, Harri,

251

as Lizzie has me mam's memoirs.'

'Memoirs? How...?'

'It was the mugging, Lizzie's brother was involved and he gave the bag to Lizzie, it was inside. You still have them, don't you, Lizzie? Oh God, Rita put them in a drawer...'

'They're safe; I have them. Don't worry. Rita packed them in that case she brought back with her. I read some more of them last night, kept me going. I read about her first days in France ... and her and Pierre... She really loved him. Sh-she had a love with him that ... well, like we'd all like to have.'

'I'm glad for her.' There was a moment when no one spoke, and then Patsy said, 'Harri, you don't know about that yet. I – it seems I've got a half-brother.'

'Eeh, Patsy! What? By, lass, you don't have to do everything by halves, you know.'

Again a moment of silence, but then the penny dropped and Patsy giggled. 'Oh, don't make me laugh, don't...'

Lizzie's giggle started as a pitiful sound, but the joke hadn't missed her. She was a nice lass; she looked neglected and hurt – like an injured animal, really – but it was nothing they couldn't put right. They would. They'd take her in and look after her, she'd no doubt of that. 'Lizzie, you're going to be alright, you know. You can come home with us and stay as long as you like. We're a bit mad – well, me and Patsy are, but Mam's lovely. She'll take to you; I think she has already. Our brothers are a pain like anyone el– I mean, well, you'll like them, and like us you'll wish they'd grow up at times! Dad's a doctor, and he's grand as you saw. Well, he ain't our real dad – no, that ain't right, as we couldn't have a more real dad than him. Me and Patsy share the same biological dad. He's dead now, but we're in the same boat as you in that our dad were a bad 'un an' all. We're better for not having him in our lives, love, and you are without having yours, I reckon.'

Lizzie didn't say anything. She just smiled a teary smile.

'D'yer need some time on your own with Patsy, love? I don't mind. I can go and be with me family and get a pot of tea. The WRVS have a trolley on the corridor. They make a good pot.'

'Yes, if that's alright. I – I mean, well, I don't want to be rude.'

'No, you ain't, love. I talk too much. I'm known for it. Anyroad...'

'Before you go you have some explaining to do.'

This from Patsy surprised her. 'Oh?'

'Nabbing me man when me back was turned. He saved me, not you! And before I could get me head round things you have him hooked.'

'Greg?'

'Yes. Don't play Miss Innocent with me.'

'Eeh, I know. Have you seen him, then?'

'Yes, he came in before he left.'

'Oh?' Why did she feel fearful?

'Unfair advantage. I must look like a freak, and you saw your chance and took it.'

'No, it wasn't like that!'

'Only kidding. He's coming tomorrow. He wants to take you for dinner, no less.'

Her heart did a flip without her bidding. Her face reddened. All she could do was laugh and walk out of the door casually enough that she didn't give her feelings away.

Standing for a moment on the other side of the door, Harri held the deep breath she'd taken. Something in her felt unnerved. No. She was being silly. Patsy was very poorly. She was trying to tease her, and it was only coming across as one of her jealous moments. Why should she be anything but pleased for her? *Stop being daft. She'll be glad about it once she feels better – has to be, 'cos Greg is in the very fibre of me and that is where he is staying! Eeh, Harri, you're a fast one!* This last thought made her smile and settled whatever had been disturbed inside her.

Patsy's head ached. Challenging Harri about Greg had made her cross. If they took up together, where would that leave her? She needed Harri. Harri was everything in her life that was good. And she was *hers!*

At this moment, she'd do anything to have Lizzie – needy Lizzie – just go away and leave her alone. She couldn't cope with the reminders of all that had happened, or the constant niggle over her mother. This girl had been through so much, but so had she. She had told her story, but she hadn't really given her mind to the revulsion of that vile man raping her body, or of her killing someone, or to the dark depths of that water... *Oh God!* Once more her heart cried out with the horror of it all. *Will I ever be the same again?*

'Patsy, if yer like I can just sit here. I just wanted

to be with yer and reassure meself that you're okay.'

'Yes, that's what I'd like. I'm not ready. It has been...'

'I know. But we came through, that's what's important. And if your mam – I mean, Harri's mam – will have me for a bit till I sort meself out, then we've plenty of time to talk about anything we want to.'

This wasn't what Patsy had expected, and although she was grateful, it wasn't what she wanted. Facing what had happened at Rita's house and afterwards had taken its toll, but she did want to hear about her mother. 'Just tell me about my mother. What you read last night. Just tell me while I rest. Has she become a hero yet?'

'No, but she has a mission and she is going to be in danger and she has had a narrow escape from being captured...'

Lying there listening to her mother's life story, some comfort seeped into her. She would go and see her, and once she had all the facts of how things happened and how her mother came to be how she was, she'd be able to cope. Then after that, she would look for her brother.

Eighteen

Jacques – A Father by Proxy

Poland 1963

Warsaw, though vibrant, still showed many more signs of the war that had ravaged it than London did. While London had rebuilt itself in the eighteen years since the end of the war, Warsaw's buildings, once proud and ornate, showed a weary face to the world. Some were dilapidated and crumbling.

Jacques had a sense of being where part of him belonged, and this feeling intensified when he found himself standing in the street of his grandfather's family home. The house still had an air of grandeur about it, but now it was divided into four apartments – not upmarket, but uncared-for and poverty-stricken.

Feeling silly but unable to control himself, he had to wipe his face with his handkerchief. An old lady said something to him in Polish, and uncertain what had been said, he just nodded. His grasp of the language wasn't good. His grandfather had always tried to teach him, but he had mastered the language of his grandmother much more easily and could converse in French very well.

Persisting in her quest to find out what ailed

him, the old lady came up to him and in an almost cross voice said something along the lines of, 'Why the sadness? You are young; you are free.'

'My family used to live here.' This was a simple phrase that he had been practising. 'My great-grandparents, my grandfather, his brothers and sister ... my father too, as a child and as a young man.'

'Aah, the fire...'

'You know of them? Of the fire in the factory? The Germans burned them alive...' His tears flowed freely. He fought for control, but lost the battle.

Spittle hit the ground next to him. 'Curse on the Germans! Come. I live in there. First floor. Though it is no longer the grand place it used to be. I have coffee.'

'Oh, no, I couldn't.' This came out in English, but she understood. Her 'yes, yes' reply surprised him, as did what she said next: 'I speak English. Come.'

The huge door creaked a cold welcome – a ghostly, unearthly sound that echoed around the high walls and tiled floor of the hallway. A once-magnificent staircase spiralled up from the hall, every stair, now bereft of carpet, was worn in the centre and showing splintered wood.

The woman turned towards the first door leading off the hall, but he couldn't follow her straight away. She seemed to understand and allowed him his moment. He tried to imagine his family in here: kicking off outdoor shoes, discarding coats – maybe to a butler? – then ascending the stairs, up

257

and up and up, the young ones perhaps sliding down the banister. The banister still shone as if polished by a hundred bottoms clad in the traditional soft-leather shorts of Eastern European boys. Maybe the kids of today still came zooming down?

Ornate carvings decorated the ceilings and a gargoyle looked down at him from each corner, though pieces were broken off the faces. One was missing a nose. And where a magnificent chandelier had perhaps presided over the space, a single wire hung, holding a bare bulb.

The emotions that had racked him gathered force again. *Why, why? What did my people do that was so wrong? What did my great-grandfather do, other than work hard for his family? How could it have happened?*

The whistling of a kettle coming from the open door took his attention. He entered the room – a shabby but tidy room with no curtains, just a blind at the window. The sun shone through, making a pattern of slats across the floor.

'Sit down. I have some good strong coffee. It will help. I am Verkona Romanski.'

'Jacques. Jacques Rueben.'

The steam tickled his nose to an awareness of the delicious aroma, the best since he'd left America. The British did not understand coffee, serving wishy-washy coffee essence – Camp Coffee, the bottle proudly proclaimed – that to him tasted like he imagined dishwater would taste. Why had his thoughts gone to such things when he was sitting in what was probably once the hub of his family's household staff? The sight of a row of bells high up on the wall had indicated this to him, and as if reading his thoughts Verkona said, 'Yes, this was once the kitchen. I am lucky to have it as it still has the range through there – a huge one and far too big for me, but when lit it heats all the rooms I occupy.'

Looking around for the first time, Jacques saw that the space had been divided up by partition-type walls. It must once have been huge, he thought, with a very big table for the staff to eat their meals around. How happy it must have been in those days, for he was sure his family would have treated their staff well.

The woman's voice broke into his thoughts. 'My mother worked here. We had a room at the top of the house. My father worked at the factory before it was closed and became derelict. Our room was large and I slept behind a screen. Father worked nights, so I would creep into my mother's bed. Your great-grandfather had me educated with his own children, as he did all of the servants' children, but I was particularly bright. Your grandfather must have been Isaac, as he was the only one to escape...?'

'Y-yes.' His voice had deserted him. He just wanted to listen.

'I was in love with Isaac, but a French cousin of the Potinskis along the street came to stay with them and Isaac fell in love with her. I was devastated and never found another to take his place. Oh, I am not saying he let me down. He did not know how I felt and wouldn't have looked at me anyway.'

'I – I'm sorry. I am sure he would like to know

you are alive and well. He—'

'He is alive? But I thought...'

'Yes. We live in Florida. He and Grandmother got out of France and took me there. My grandmother has since passed on.'

'Oh, but this is wonderful... Sorry, not your grandmother dying, of course, but you must forgive an old lady a short sojourn into her past.'

Her cheeks flushed and her eyes... Yes, as he looked at her properly for the first time, he saw that she had pretty, soft blue eyes, and her delicate skin rippled over high cheekbones. Tiny lines led to thin lips that still had a firmness to them and a pretty shape.

After a moment she continued, 'My father was taken. He was caught up in a raid one night and we never saw him again. Mother would not go with your great-grandfather. I was an interpreter in the war for the Germans. I had to listen into the messages sent, and decipher the coding. It is what saved me from the gas chamber, though not ... not my mother. But it didn't save me from the horrors of living in the concentration camp at Auschwitz, which was my home. I was taken out once a week at different times to work in what is now the council office, but was then the headquarters of the Gestapo. Once, because I changed the code, I was taken to the doors of the gas chamber with all those unfortunates, and I thought I was going in. Fear made me sick, but at the door they turned me round. They beat me and told me if I did anything like it again I *would* go in. When the liberators came, the Germans began to shoot us. A man in front of me fell on me, knocking me to the ground. He lay over me, suffocating me, but the delay this caused saved me. The Germans surrendered, but I couldn't shift the man off me. Though emaciated, his dead weight was too much for me.'

Jacques waited, wanting to give her time to process her painful memories.

'A Russian soldier heard my cry. We were saved, but not many of us, and some died anyway, too sick to recover. But it is all so long ago now.' Without warning she changed the subject: 'Your great-grandfather was a good man. So you must be Pierre's son? How is he?'

To his telling her all he knew of his father and his quest to know more about him, she shook her head. 'A brave man. You must be proud of him. I do know someone who you could talk to: Gustov. Gustov is still alive. Gustov and your father played as boys and grew up together. When your father went to university in France, Gustov went to work in your great-grandfather's factory. I will take you to meet him. You can talk to him and I will interpret for you. Gustov escaped the fire...'

'But ... but I thought no one got out!'

'Only Gustov. He was a thin young man, and he is double-jointed. He could get through the bars of a gate by dislocating his arms and then his legs. He worked in a circus for many years after the war. When the fire started, he got through bars that your great-grandfather had erected over the waste outlet in the basement and swam out along the sewer. He lived down there until the end of the war. It is a remarkable story. At night he came out and stole food and water. It is a miracle he was never caught.'

Sitting across from the strange-looking wiry man, Jacques suddenly felt unsure. What should he ask? Would his questions stir up painful memories for this man? Gustov and Verkona chatted for a while. He caught a few of words: 'son of Pierre … wants to know about him...'

When Gustov looked over at him, it was with a fierce, penetrating gaze. 'Yes, I can see the likeness. Pierre was the boy's age when he left. He is dead, you say? Executed? Yes, I can imagine that would be the fate of Pierre. He was a young man with principles and the courage to see them through. I am sorry. What do you want to know?'

It was difficult speaking through Verkona, but somehow they managed it and Jacques learned that his father liked to play jokes on others. 'I remember he called over to me once. He looked strange – bald... He told me that we all had to have our hair cut and shaved like his because there was an epidemic of lice. Even our *peyos* – his *peyos* were gone! I was astonished, as this couldn't be possible. I ran to my mother and she told me Pierre was lying. When I came out again, Pierre was laughing his head off and his hair was restored and his *peyos* hung where they should in front of his ears. Then he showed me the cap. It was rubber and fitted over your head to make it look as though you were bald. It had come from the theatre where his aunty Annagrette used to work.'

Jacques smiled at this. The thought of this mischief trickled some knowledge of his father into him – a man who, not unlike himself, enjoyed catching his friends out in a joke.

Gustov was quiet for a moment, and Jacques didn't want to hurry him. Anxious as he was to ask questions, he respected the man's right to sift his memories according to how he wanted to present them. Nothing prepared him for what came next. Verkona paled as she translated, often hesitating and asking if he was sure he wanted to hear it as Gustov went into details of the fire. Mesmerized, Jacques nodded.

'The fear was the worst thing. You could smell and taste the fear more strongly than you could the acrid smoke, and the wails of despair from the adults and the high-pitched agonized screams of the children rang in your ears. I can hear them today. I ran. Down into the basement, clambering over others in my haste to escape. I couldn't save anyone. It wasn't possible. Not even a child could get through the bars I knew I could get through. I can fold my body.' In a moment of silence a tear trickled down Gustov's face. 'The smoke choked me and stung my eyes. Once through the grid, the stench of the sewer was almost a relief. Standing in the pipe with all manner of stuff running around my feet, I stayed still, trembling, vomiting, not knowing what my next move should be. I held my ears closed against the onslaught of the cries of pain. My nose clogged with the smell of burning flesh. I could do nothing. It took about half an hour for the last whimper to silence. When it did, there was a relief in me. It was so strong, I wept with it. But then began a nightmare of a different kind, as I had nowhere to go and it dawned on me that the sewer had to be my home.'

From lips that had dried to parchment, Jacques managed to say that he was sorry. But the images and the thought of his family dying in such a way had taken everything from him.

'But you are here to hear about your father, Pierre. I am sorry. I shouldn't have gone over all of that...'

By the time they left Gustov, Jacques felt as though his father had come alive to him. He'd learned so much about him, and all of it good. A good scholar, footballer and runner, he'd been a loyal friend, and though studious, always had time for Gustov who had struggled with his academic studies.

He'd listened to an idyllic childhood: camping in the summer, hunting in the winter, trips to the horse racing, and shooting parties. And he felt glad, for history had shown that the boys' lives were to be short-lived – stolen from them just because they were Jews.

He made the trip to the site of the factory with Verkona and Gustov. Standing looking at the waste ground, it was hard to imagine such an atrocity taking place there, although the hush that descended on the place had an eerie feel. He felt himself connecting to his family once more.

Outlining his grandfather's plans to have a memorial stone here or in the Jewish cemetery, he was pleased that they thought it a wonderful idea and that Gustov would like to take on the project, on behalf of Isaac and Pierre. Gustov didn't think the Communist regime would object. They were trying to appease the people, who were ready to revolt, so they wanted to look as though they were going along with the people's wishes. 'This is something I know the people of Warsaw will get behind, and it can be no more fitting than if it is organized by me – the one and only survivor.'

'I am sure my grandfather would be honoured if you would take the project up. I am telephoning him tonight, and I will see what he says.'

'And will you give my regards to your grandfather, along with those of Gustov?' Verkona asked.

'I will. I am sure he will be thrilled that you are both alive and well. It will seem impossible to him, but he will be thrilled.'

Over dinner that night, they talked of happier memories – Verkona's of Isaac and Gustov's of Pierre. Lots of little anecdotes came out and were laughed over. There were no more tears. These people had, over the years, shed more tears than should have been allocated to them for a lifetime, and although they had come through it all, they hadn't come through it very well. Both were extremely poor. Jacques made his mind up to do something about this, and asked them if they would ever consider leaving Poland. Both shook their heads. 'Not even to come to America?'

'I would love to come for a visit, but that is all. Poland is where my heart is and I will die here.'

Gustov agreed with this from Verkona.

'Well, then, I will have to try to get you a visit, and very soon. It is easy now. I know I came from

England to here, but I had no problem as an American citizen getting here. Travel restrictions are easing all the time and many Americans have been able to welcome Polish friends and relatives to our country. I'm sure we can add another two to the numbers!'

'But ... well, we cannot afford...'

'It will all be taken care of, I promise you. My great-grandfather was very astute and had large amounts of money deposited in an American bank. My grandparents carried on the tradition of the family and ran a chain of jewellery shops until they retired, when, knowing I did not want to go along that route for my career, they sold them. Grandfather is very rich. It will be an honour to get you there and to see to all your needs. As to whether you stay in Poland, leave that an open question until your visit. I will of course book return travel for you.'

'That would be wonderful!'

Again a flush prettied Verkona's face. This amused Jacques as he thought of his grandfather. *I hope she isn't expecting the dashing young man he used to be!* But then, maybe that was what she would see, as he'd heard that in the eyes of someone in love, the person they loved never changed. He hoped so, though it would feel very strange indeed if his grandfather and... No. He couldn't even think of it.

His lovely late grandmother came into his mind, with her twinkly smile and kind eyes. No, Grandfather could never love another... Anyway, they were too old!

Later, when he put the phone down after

speaking to his grandfather, he was no longer so sure. Grandfather had seemed over the moon that Verkona was still alive and well. His voice had taken on a soft tone when he spoke her name, and his excitement at her coming over for a visit was evident. Grandfather also remembered Gustov, and was amazed he'd escaped the fire, saying, 'That is wonderful news! I feel a small victory was won over the Germans, and they didn't even know. We should have his story published so that any of them left alive can know they did not succeed in wiping all of the Jews out who had hidden in the factory. And please tell Gustov I would be honoured to have him arrange the memorial. Tell him to go to a solicitor and to have it all drawn up in an agreement, and to open a bank account so that I can put the funds in that he will need. Well done, Jacques! You have lifted my spirits. At last my dear father, my brother and his family and my sister will have a place that acknowledges their lives.'

There had been a catch in his voice at this last and something else he couldn't define. Jacques didn't let him know he'd heard it, chatting instead about general things and telling of his plans to move on to France in a couple of weeks – after returning to England to visit his grandmama again.

His grandfather had been pleased with this development in Jacques's quest to find his mother's family, but saddened to hear of the plight he'd found his mother in. He'd urged him: 'Go to see her, son. Go to see her as soon as her mother has made the way clear for you.'

Yes, he would do that. He would ring his grandmama tonight to see what progress she had made, then tomorrow he would sort out Verkona and Gustov getting visas...

Nineteen

*Life Changes for Lizzie and
Theresa is Captured*

London 1963 and France 1943

Lizzie lay between the snow-white sheets of the hospital bed, their crispness chafing rather than comforting. 'Observation,' they'd said, but they hadn't been near her for hours.

Unsure of her future she had a dread in her as to what might happen and most of that concerned her dad. Now behind bars, he could face the death penalty. What if that was his fate? How would it feel when it was happening? A shudder took her. *Please, God, NO. I know he deserves it, but I don't think I could bear it.*

Other emotions assailed her as she lay alone. Ken ... and Rita ... her whole family gone. A sob caught in her throat. She'd loved them both despite their faults, and she would miss them. Tears broke through. She allowed them. Sobbing into her pillow gave her a little release, but more worries came with thinking of them both. She had their funerals to arrange, but how? She had no money, and no idea how to go about it all – that was, if they ever found Ken.

The lady in the next bed called out to her from the other side of the curtain. 'You alright, love?'

Will I ever be alright again?

'Anything I can do?'

'I – I lost some of me family yesterday.'

'Oh, you poor love. Here, I'll come and talk to you, if you like?'

'N-No. I – I mean, thank you, but I need to be on me own. I don't want to be rude...'

'No, that's alright, love. Don't worry. You let it all out and don't mind me.'

Relief settled over her for a moment. Talking with a stranger was the last thing she needed.

Picking up the second book of Theresa's memoirs, she determined to lose herself in it to help her to cope.

The Fateful Mission – 1943

The stuffy atmosphere of the carriage was un-bearable, and it being full of German soldiers added to Theresa's anxiety. The officer in the corner smoked incessantly, his eyes hardly leaving her through the haze that hung around him. Maybe she was being paranoid. Even if there was a poster circulating with her picture on it, no one would recognize her now. Her hair, now bleached blonde, had been styled onto her face. Her usually thick eyebrows were plucked to a thin line. Glasses, annoying ones as they hadn't been able to get hold of any with clear glass, and the slight mag-nifying effect of the reading specs impaired her vision slightly, sat on her nose.

Looking out of the window, she could see the landscape changing. Countryside gave way to buildings, scattered at first, but now they had taken all the space. Most of them were houses, but some were factories and warehouse-type structures. *Thank God, we are entering Paris at last!*

A movement drew her attention back into the carriage. The man sitting next to her stood up. Her stomach muscles clenched as she saw the staring officer in the corner rise too. The hem of his grey coat chafed her shin as he took the place the soldier had vacated.

'Mademoiselle, I have been watching you. You appear nervous. Is anything wrong?'

'No, monsieur. It is hot in here and I need some air. Excuse me. I think I will stand out in the corridor for a while.'

'A good idea. I will come too. Cigarette?'

'No ... no, thank you.'

'You don't smoke?'

'No. I do smoke, but I am more in need of air at the moment.'

'Where are you from?'

They were standing in the corridor, where the air was cooler. Not answering him but taking the opportunity to slide open a window, she tried to put space between them. The stench of stale tobacco coming from him made her feel sick.

'Parisian?'

'Yes.'

'You don't give much away.' His latest mouthful of smoke billowed out towards her. 'What is the purpose of your journey?'

'I have been visiting family.'

He looked away from her. His cheeks sucked into his teeth, and his lips protruded. He was considering her answer. Turning, she went as if to walk away, but his hand grabbed her arm. 'Where are you going?' His words held a command. His eyes narrowed.

'To the bathroom. We are nearly at my stop.'

'Oh, you are getting off earlier than you thought? I heard you tell the ticket master you were going into the area of Rue Saint David.'

'I – I thought we were approaching there. Yes, look, the next stop after this one is Saint David. I am only going to the outskirts.'

His hand gripped her tighter. Fear chilled her blood. Her mouth dried. 'Have you a problem with me, monsieur? I have not done anything wrong.'

'No, but you intrigue me. There is something… I'm not sure what. Give me your papers and your bag.' His head turned and he directed a command into the carriage, *'Gefreiter!'*

'Sir.' The younger man who had sat next to him stood, clipped his heels, and came out into the corridor.

'Search her bag.'

The strap of her bag wrenched at her shoulder as he snatched it from her. 'Now, your papers?'

Prayers clogged her brain as she pulled her wallet from her pocket.

'Name?'

'Lydia Francome.' The new name they had given her for this assignment rolled easily off her tongue. Rehearsing it constantly had paid off.

A draught of air wafted her face as he flicked her ID card close to her cheek. 'Francome... Not Smith? Or Brown?'

'I – I don't understand.' *Crying would be the thing to do here. I need to show less courage, less defiance.* She thought of Mater and how much she would like to be held by her at this moment. The thoughts brought on the emotion she needed, and a tear tripped from her eye. 'I – I'm Lydia Francome. I've been on a visit to my aunt. I just want to go home...' The floodgates opened. He looked disconcerted. His corporal said something in German. She tried to sort out the words, but the nearest she could get was that he hadn't found anything untoward. Thinking of her papier-mâché make-up, she felt relieved that he hadn't been suspicious of it.

'Very well. You may go.'

Grabbing her bag and papers, she turned and fled, stumbling into other passengers and tripping over bags. *Damn these bloody glasses!*

The laughter of the Germans didn't sting her as they probably expected it would, but was music to her ears. They had believed her...

Paris in springtime – everyone's dream, but this Paris was not how she remembered it from her visit as a young girl. Everything then had had an eager anticipation about it – the people, the art, the pavement cafés, the flowers. Even the birds had given off a joy. Now, the streets held sandbags and men in uniform holding guns. A tank churned its chains into the soft tarmac, and heads were down in fear. Clothes were no longer fashionable and vibrant, but tatty and grey. Eyes looked hungry as they stared out of gaunt faces. No wonder she had come to the attention of the officer. Someone should have researched this. Her coat, though not new, stood out amongst what others had. Her freshly styled hair marked her out as someone who hadn't suffered the shortages. No grime had sunk into her skin.

A tug on her arm heightened her fear. Looking round, she had to lower her head – it was a child, clutching at her sleeve with pleading eyes. Taking her purse out of her bag, she gave him the coins she had. A tear plopped onto his cheek. No words came from his dry lips as he turned and scurried away.

At her hostel, she enquired of Madame Joules. The girl looked at her with suspicion but fetched Madame to her. 'Madame, it is a cold day today.'

'Yes, but soon it will be warmer.'

This was the contact code, word for word. Now she could relax. 'Madame, before we go any further I need your help.'

'I can see that. You were not followed?'

'No. I did have a problem on the train, but I have taken every care.'

'I am not surprised, as looking like you do you are a target. Are you sure you were not followed?'

'Certain.'

'Okay. Come to my apartment and I will make you blend in better. Philippe is to meet you in La Cage de Perroquet Café on L'avenue de la Bourdonnais in one hour.'

Philippe would not be the contact's real name,

but his code name. This matched what Pierre had told her. *Oh, Pierre, if only these were better times...* But no, she must stay focused. Thoughts like these could undermine an agent's resolve.

Emerging a few minutes later in an ill-fitting brown coat tied with string, a headscarf and well-worn boots, her perception of her surroundings changed. Now she could feel the atmosphere, and merge into it.

The café told a story of days gone. Its cast-iron window frames, arched and ornate, still showed traces of the gold-leaf paint. The curtain covering half of the window, though worn in places, had the look of expensive lace as it hung in symmetric folds, thick and luscious with a woven-in palm-tree design.

Opening the door brought back a host of memories as the aroma of good coffee tinged her nostrils. How, she wondered, had they managed to obtain such fine beans? The reason became obvious as she went through into the salon. Germans! The place was full of them, and they had clearly made sure that their favourite haunt had supplies. *But why did Philippe want to meet here?*

A dozen pairs of eyes turned on her. Her legs tingled with the trembling that had set up in them. The women in here looked as she had done: prosperous and fashionable. Thinking quickly, she went up to the counter. *'Monsieur, avez-vous du pain rassis? J'ai faim.'*

'Sortez! Pas de mendiants!'

The group of Germans nearest to her laughed. One of them threw her a coin. 'Here, go to a downmarket café and ask for bread. You can pay for it with this.'

She caught the coin and went to leave, but one of them rising froze her with fear. But he only said, 'Or this...' And made a motion as if to undo his fly, pushing his hips forward in a thrusting movement.

'Ha, Hans, she looks like she is familiar with that, but I would not fuck it. She is unclean. Get out of here, vagabond.'

Their French was good. They must have been here a while, but then they were young. The young picked up languages easily.

The laughter of the soldiers and the women gave her peace as she left as it meant they were not curious about her. But what was the point of Philippe sending her there?

Before she had time to mull this over her arm was once more in the grip of another, but this time it was a firm, bruising grasp that made her cry out.

'Quiet! Here, mademoiselle, follow me.'

Shadows darkened the alleyway as the low sun cast the elongated shapes of the chimneys across it. A smell of urine permeated the air, telling of many a glass of wine pissed up the wall. Rubbish was trodden underfoot, squelching in putrid piles that she could not avoid. Ahead, she could see the light of the end of the alley, but before she reached it she was turned into an open gate. The yard she stood in had to be the backyard to a café, with its empty food boxes and pig-swill bin. The kitchen they went through had that steamed-cabbage smell mixed with garlic. Maybe they never really cooked cabbage, but somehow such places always smelt as if they did.

Entering the eating area, with its wooden table covered in grubby-looking gingham cloths, she saw a man sitting in the corner. His beret was pulled forward, hiding his eyes, and smoke curled up from a stub of a cigarette in his mouth. His dark coat had the collar upturned.

The man holding her pushed her towards the table. A low voice said, 'The coffee in here is good.'

Relief flooded her. 'I have heard so, monsieur.'

A face, unexpectedly handsome and grinning, looked up at her. 'Lydia? I am Philippe. Please sit down. We have much to discuss.'

They were in an upstairs room of the café now. The coffee they had shared had indeed been good, making their contact code a truth. She could still taste the lingering flavour of it. She did not ask how they got it, but had savoured the warmth of it and allowed it to soothe her. His ploy at sending her to the previous café had been his way of testing her ability to handle unexpected situations. He was pleased with her, and listening to him she knew she was with friends – well-organized friends who were on the same side.

Assembling the radio didn't take long, and the signal was good. It worried her that they thought it okay to transmit from here, just around the corner from La Cage de Perroquet Café, but she trusted them.

Broadcasting her poem first and receiving recognition, she went on to tell of the supplies they would need. Philippe had approved the drop arrangements she had made, and had dispatched a messenger to the area to gather men to be ready to meet the plane when they received word of the delivery. 'Now, we must go ourselves. I am the only one who can set the charges. Come, we will beat the curfew if we hurry. We will go our separate ways. We will rendezvous eight kilometres from the port of Lorient.'

'Lorient! But that is in Brittany!'

'Yes. The bunker there is the largest and is our target.'

'But, I thought...'

'Many things are told as red herrings. Lorient has U-boats in the harbour at this moment. They are to be destroyed.'

U-boats meant Germans – hundreds of them! *Then why the drop only fifty kilometres from Paris?*

'Monsieur, you have kept me out of the loop. I am very angry. I have given false information to my command!'

'*C'était nécessaire!* We have to dupe even those who work with us to remain safe. Those that matter know the truth.'

'But does Pierre know?'

'He will know.'

'How will you transport...?'

'Farmers. Farmers will hide it in bales. They are ready. It will go from farm to farm. The details are of no use to you. Just make sure you are in Lorient in five days' time.'

Theresa had thought the cold of Paris biting, but it was nothing to the Brittany coast. Standing outside a baker's shop facing the sea, she huddled up against the wall trying to glean some warmth from it. The family she was to stay with hadn't answered her knock on their door, and this worried her. They knew of her impending arrival, so where were they? Neither had she been contacted by any of the group.

Worry churned her gut. Something was wrong. The darkness clawed at her. Curfew approached, but where could she go? A lorry came up the road towards her. Her body stiffened. She pulled herself even closer to the wall, squirming her body along to try and reach the alley between this building and the one next door. She groped with her hands behind her back to guide her. The lorry kept coming, its lights dim and its windscreen impenetrable in the darkness.

Fear skimmed her heart, stopping its rhythm as a sudden dazzling light held her illuminated in its glow. *'Einhalt zu gebieten. Hände in die Luft!'*

Before she could raise her hands as the command had asked of her, soldiers surrounded her. A kick to her stomach bent her double. Vomit projected from her mouth. Her legs gave way. *Oh God... No... No!*

The rough pebbles scraped the skin off her knees, cutting and tearing the flesh as they dragged her to the lorry. Throwing her inside she landed on feet – feet clad in German-soldier boots, and feet clad in peasant sandals. These last were clamped in irons. Looking up, she saw Philippe and two of the others sitting on the bench. These two looked at her but showed no sign of recognizing her. One of them spat on her.

Did he think her the traitor, or was he trying to disassociate himself from her? Philippe still didn't look at her. The lorry started to move. *They are going to leave me here on the floor!* One of the Germans lifted his boot and slammed it down on her back. The breath left her again. She gasped under its weight, trying to draw in air, but couldn't.

'*Wir wollen sie lebend!*'

The soldier removed his foot. Theresa wasn't sure she should be glad that he had been told they wanted her alive, but her relief at taking a breath gave her those feelings. But then, *alive for what? Torture? Oh, please God, no.*

1963

'You alright, love?'

Lizzie slammed the book shut. The voice and the face seemed alien, an intrusion catapulting her from the horror and fear that had gripped her. Her mind wouldn't process where she was.

'Lizzie? Are you alright? It's me, Harri. You haven't forgotten me already, have you?'

'Oh, Harri.' Without her knowing they would, tears tumbled from her eyes and her breath caught in her lungs in a sob that wrenched her very soul.

'Lizzie, love. Eeh, lass, cry it out. Me mam always says as that is best. We keep forgetting that what is a relief to us is a loss to you. Rita and Ken were your family – and your dad...'

'You must think me a baby. I seem to have done nothing but cry since you met me, but I am quite

279

strong really. I have come through a lot, and...'

'Even the strongest of us have a point that is one too far for us to cope with, love. And, no, I don't think of you as a babby. You're a very brave person. You just need a little more support at the moment, but we'll give it. I've come to help you to dress. I've brought some stuff for you. It's mine, so it should fit, and some toiletries – shampoo and stuff. Come on, you'll feel better after, and then Mam and Dad are taking you home with them. Me and Ian are staying another day while Dad arranges to have Patsy moved to the hospital in Leeds.'

'Oh, Harri, can't I wait for you and Patsy? I wouldn't be any trouble.'

'No, love. It will be best if you go. Mam will take care of you. I can't, not in a hotel room, I can't. Everything will be made right for you at home. We have a room on the corner of the house, next to the downstairs cloakroom, which has a toilet and hand basin in. There's a French door as opens onto the patio at the back. It's lovely and just right for you. Dad has arranged for me brother David as you haven't met yet to get a bed in there for you. You'll have an easy chair and a television. But, of course, you'll not stay in there all the time. You'll live with us as part of our family. Your room will just be a place you can retreat to, sleep in, and get to without assistance. So you have your independence.'

'Thanks, Harri. I – I'll get meself sorted. Yer won't have to put up with me for long.'

'Eeh, you daft ha'p'orth! You can stay as long as you need to, and I reckon it will be a while afore

280

you won't need our support. You've a lot to face, love.'

'Harri, I'm worried over Rita's funeral, and Ken's, if they find him... I – I have no money to see to them.'

'Me dad'll sort it, though it's unlikely as they'll release Rita's body for a while. They said they need to do further autopsies. And as soon as they allow anyone in your flat, he'll see to it that everything you want is brought to you and the rest is disposed of. So, are you ready? If you get into your chair, I'll take you to the bathroom.'

It was the kindness that got to her. She'd never known a family like this. It seemed they'd taken Patsy in without question when she'd come into their lives, and now they were ready to do the same for her. But at least Patsy was related to them – well, to Harri, anyway. But her? A disabled girl from London who they knew nothing of? It was hard to believe there were such people left in the world.

Twenty

Jacques – A Sadness Beyond Measure

1963

The application for the passports and visas for Verkona and Gustov were proving to be anything but straightforward. Jacques had taken them along to the municipal office, thinking it a matter of filling in a few forms and the officials making some checks, and that would be that. But he found that the regime was rife with corruption, and a lot depended on whether you were willing to grease a few palms to get what you wanted. None of this sat well with Jacques. With his ambition to take up a career in the law, it was alien to him to work on the other side of it.

'It is how it is, and why only those in favour or who have the means to pay can achieve anything here. *Communism!* Uh! I spit on it. It is meant to be an ideal that is one for all and all for everyone, but it is far from that. Look how we live, and yet in this quarter where we are now, the standard of living is one hundred times better. It is oppression of the worst kind. The people work for the good of the state while having very little for themselves.'

After listening to Verkona interpreting this speech of Gustov's, Jacques asked, 'So, you think

282

the only way we are going to get the necessary papers and permission is to pay over sums of money other than the normal cost of what we want?'

'Yes. It is as Gustov says: one rule for the officials and one for us. They have all the power. No one will listen to us. If we speak out, we are classed as dissidents. Anything could happen to us. And now that we have put in the application, we are trapped. Unless we go ahead and follow the unwritten rule, we will be under scrutiny and our every move monitored. One foot wrong, or what they could interpret as wrong, and we will be thrown into jail.'

'My God, I didn't realize...'

Again Verkona told him Gustov's reply to this: 'I know, son. Those of you who live in the free world do not have an idea of what it is like. The real basis of Communism, the written ideal, is not a bad thing, but in order to have it work in reality? That can only be done by oppression and fear. That is what is happening here. There is no freedom of speech or religion. Everyone has to follow the party line.'

'Then, Gustov, why not apply for political asylum when you get to America? I know you love Poland, but this is not the Poland you want and are in love with. Especially you, Verkona, as you are not of an age to do anything about it. You should stay in America until things change.'

'We shall see. But first we have to get there.'

This he understood. 'I'll telephone Grandfather. He'll advise us.'

'Please make him see how it is. Our lives will

283

change after this application if it does not go smoothly.'

Jacques looked around him at this from Verkona. The evidence of the inequality of a society and an ideal that was set up for total 'equality' was all around him. In this government officials' quarter, the apartments were of a high standard. The air of prosperity could be felt in everything from the appearance of the housing to the cleanliness and general upkeep of the streets, and in the cars parked on the side of the road. Even though these were not luxury class, they were far newer and better than the scant few seen in Verkona's street.

'I will, Verkona. Come on, let us go for lunch. I'm starving, and don't worry. I will get everything sorted.'

Getting through to his grandfather was proving difficult. On some of his attempts there was no connection available to the United States. On others, the phone rang but wasn't picked up. By the evening of his second day of trying, worry was eating away at Jacques. Where could his grandfather be? He rarely went out these days. With no business to see to and not having many interests outside the home, he could usually either be found at home or down at the Polish club playing cards with his friends, but that only occurred once a week on a Thursday. Today was Wednesday.

At last in the evening when he tried for the umpteenth time he heard his grandfather's voice. His 'Hello, son' held in it the difference of tone that he had heard last time they had spoken. A niggle of trepidation entered Jacques. 'Is everything alright, Grandfather?'

There was a silence. It didn't last long, but the hesitation deepened Jacques's fear. 'Grandfather?'

'I'm okay, son. Just tired. How are things over there? I didn't expect you to ring so quickly.'

After explaining, his grandfather had no hesitation. 'Pay what you have to, son. Get them out of there now you have set the ball rolling. Has anything been done about the memorial?'

'Yes. Permission has been granted. But again, there are people that Gustov has to pay...'

'Whatever it takes. Is there an account I can pay into?'

'Things are not done like that. Everything is cash. If you are in agreement I will draw the funds and make sure the right people are paid. The work will be done very quickly once those who sign on the dotted line are happy.'

'That is what is important. Not the money, or who has it. But I want to know that it is done.'

'Grandfather, is everything alright?' Again the long silence. 'Grandfather, are you there?'

'Yes, son. Jacques, I need you to come home.'

'What? Why? Grandfather, what's happened?'

'How soon can Verkona's visa be ready?'

'Once the bribes are paid, almost at once. It is just the printing of them. Probably about a week. Grandfather, there is something. Please tell me. We may lose our connection.'

'Son. Last week I had a very strange thing happen. When I went to the toilet, it ... well, what I passed was white in colour.'

'But what does that mean? How could that

285

happen? You never said when we spoke.'

'I didn't know what it was and I didn't want to worry you if it was nothing. I went to my doctor yesterday. He arranged immediate tests. I – I have cancer of the liver.'

'Oh, God!'

'Jacques, there is no easy way to say this, but I only have a ... a month at most.'

'NO! No, no!'

'Oh, Jacques, I don't know what to say. I'm scared. I want you with me.'

Hearing this fear in his grandfather, something he'd never heard before, etched a strength into Jacques as he took on the role of protector. 'Don't worry. I'll fly back as soon as I can. We will do something, Grandfather. You won't die. I'm coming.'

'Jacques, there is nothing that can be done. The disease is not detectable until this symptom shows itself, and by then it is too late. There is no substitute for the liver, and no one can live without one. Mine will cease to function very quickly. Come home, son, just come home.'

Tears ran down his face as he came out of the booth. This time, despite her own worry at realizing something bad was happening to his grandfather, Verkona treated him with more gentleness than she had the first time she'd come across him in tears. Then, she'd seen him as a young man with the world at his fingertips who'd not suffered in his life. In that she hadn't been wrong, but since his grandfather first told him about his family, and even more now, he knew what suffering was.

'What is it, dear? Is Isaac alright? What has happened?'

They helped him to a bench. 'Tell us. Tell us what is wrong.'

Looking up into Gustov's face, he had a moment when he thought, *If only this was my father bending over me with concern in his face. What must that feel like? How much easier to bear everything with a father to turn to.* The thought hadn't meant to be derogatory to Gustov, only that, being the same age and knowing his father, his action had prompted the deep longing.

But then he saw more than concern in the face of this man, for though they hadn't known each other more than a couple of days, he read a deep love in him. Putting out his hand, he took Gustov's, then looked from him to Verkona. 'My grandfather, Isaac Rueben, is... I – I'm so sorry, Verkona, he is dying.'

Her intake of breath cut through him and rasped the sore pain that lay in his heart. He told them what had happened. Verkona, in a voice that held her shock, said, 'But surely, in America they can do something? Why so quick? Why...?'

Her last 'why?' seemed to be asking 'why now?', rather than referring to his grandfather's illness, and this compounded the sadness inside him. Verkona had had a dream, and he'd just shattered it. But he could still make a small part of it happen. 'We must pay whatever it costs to get your travel papers in order. Tomorrow, we will go back to the municipal building, and if I have to pay someone a million zloty, I will! We will go to America together. And that must be in the next few days.'

Verkona brightened a little at this, but he knew that nothing could completely lift her now. She was a woman whose hopes had been dashed.

Verkona and Gustov's joy and amazement at every little thing helped to make the trip exciting despite the reason he was going home sooner than he'd intended.

His heart pounded when he drove the hired car into the drive of their house. Part of him didn't want to see his grandfather and be faced with the reality, and when he did, the shock of his appearance nearly undid him. Holding him in his arms and feeling the bones of him did.

'Oh, Grandfather...' They clung on to each other. He could feel his grandfather's hand gently patting his back. Until she spoke, he'd forgotten about Verkona.

'Isaac, dearest.'

Grandfather released him. His gaunt face lit up as he looked at Verkona. 'You haven't changed a bit, my dear.'

'Go away with you...'

'And Gustov...'

The little strength his grandfather had tapped into to greet them, left him. His hand clasped Jacques's shoulder.

The chat that now took place, with Grandfather lying on the sofa covered with Grandmother's quilt, was conducted in Polish. He didn't mind. It was good for Grandfather to use his native tongue, as he knew he loved to on his visits to his club. At times he was animated, at others he laughed, but

288

through it all it was as if most of him had already left this earth.

By the time Jacques came back into the lounge from making a call to his grandmother in England, he realized that was what was happening. Grandfather lay with his eyes closed, clinging on to Verkona's hand. His breathing was shallow, his face was more sunken onto the bones beneath, and his eye sockets were now deep pits.

'Call his doctor, Jacques. Isaac is in pain.'

'N-No... Come ... come here, my boy.'

Jacques took Verkona's place sitting on the edge of the sofa. Fingers of fear clutched at his heart.

'I – I haven't got ... time.'

Somehow his grandfather told him that he loved him and that he wanted his own name on the memorial. It seemed that Verkona and Gustov had told him about how they had managed between them to have a stone erected on the site of the old factory. It was a temporary one for now, and its inscription just said: 'On this waste-ground stood a factory. In August 1939 sixty-six Jews took refuge inside it. They perished by fire at the hands of the Germans.' Grandfather was pleased at this step, and asked about what plans there were for the permanent one.

'Well, that is the best bit, Grandfather. We have commissioned a stonemason to make a beautiful statue of your father. Verkona remembered seeing a clipping her mother had taken from a local paper. She'd been so proud of her boss, so she kept it for a long time and showed it to everyone. That was lost a long time ago, but in the local museum we found historic copies of the newspaper and the archives of the articles and pictures. Amongst them we found the picture. It had been taken outside the factory to commemorate an honour the mayor had bestowed, and the curator allowed us to borrow it to make copies. We gave one of these to the sculptor.'

'Here, dearest Isaac. While you have been talking to Jacques I have searched my luggage and have found the picture. Look, dear, it is your father.'

His grandfather opened his eyes. 'Magnifying ... glass.'

Holding his magnifying glass in his shaky hand, Grandfather looked at the picture. A tear seeped out of the corner of his eye, but the sadness of this was belied by the smile that creased his face.

'Thank ... you...'

The glass dropped from his hand. His head lolled to one side. 'No ... no, Grandfather.'

Despite his grief, the funeral made him proud. The Polish community attended in large numbers, and many had stories to tell – some funny, and some about the bad things they and his grandfather had been through. One stood and told of his grandfather's heroism in escaping and of his son's heroic, if short, life. This shocked him. He had not known that his grandfather had shared so much with others.

Speaking to the man afterwards, he learned that they had only heard of these things recently and had been shocked themselves to hear that Isaac had been through so much. It seemed that after opening up to Jacques, Grandfather was able to talk to others, and listening to their testimony it was apparent that he had spoken with pride rather than sadness. This pleased him. It was as if by forcing his grandfather to speak of it to him, he had helped him to open up and accept it all, and to do so with pride that he had such a son and was the son of such a great man himself.

The eulogy had gone on to say how Isaac was now more than proud of his grandson and of what joy he had brought to his late wife and himself, filling a gap he'd never thought could be filled. At this, Jacques had found the tears wetting his cheeks as they flowed unhindered. But in some strange way, they were not just tears of sadness, but ones of joy at the knowledge that his grandfather had found peace, and that he had helped him to find it.

Two days later, a time when there had been a quietness about the house as each of them had lived in their own thoughts, Verkona came out to sit with him on the porch. Looking out over fields and with the Gulf of Mexico in the distance, the scene was a peaceful one. He'd so often sat here with his grandfather. Sometimes in the daytime, but the best times had been in the evening when to the tune of a thousand crickets the lights had glowed a hazy pattern in the distance and the stars had formed a twinkling blanket of silver above them. These were the times they had talked about everything and anything, except the one subject he'd wanted to hear about and had been afraid to ask about for fear of upsetting his beloved grandfather. Now he felt so glad that he had pushed the issue in the end.

'May I sit with you and have a chat, Jacques? I don't want to intrude, but there are things to sort out.'

'Yes, of course. I'm sorry, I didn't mean to leave you worrying. It has all been such a shock.'

'I know. And we understand. It is just that–'

'Look, I don't want you feeling obliged, but would it be too much for me to ask of you if you would consider staying on here and take care of things – the house and the garden – for me whilst I continue with my European trip? I have so much that I have left undone. My mother...'

'We would be glad to. Neither of us is ready to go back so soon, and we have many invitations from the community that we would like to take up, and Gustov has said he wants to learn the language, and... Well, apart from the deep sadness we feel, we love it here. The freedom, the warmth, the people ... well, everything, really.'

'That's great. You don't know what a relief that is to me. I'll be happier travelling knowing you two are safe and well.'

'It is nice to know you are thinking about us when you have so much on your plate. You are a fine young man, Jacques, and very mature for your age. Your grandparents did a good job raising you.'

'Thank you. It has always been that way. Sometimes it has given me difficulties being much more mature than my friends. Things they have wanted to do haven't always sounded fun to me, but silly. I suppose being around older people made me take on their view of the world. But I didn't miss out on fun. They always arranged great birthdays for me, and took me to Disneyland and all the other things kids do. It was just ... well, I can't explain it, really.'

'Whatever it was, it has turned out to be a good thing, as you have a lot on your shoulders and you are alone in the world to face it all.'

'No, that's not true. I have found a beautiful grandmother in England, and am soon to meet my mother, just as soon as she is well enough to be told I have come back into her life.'

'Of course. And you must go back as soon as you can. We will be fine, only ... we haven't much money.'

He reached out and took her hand, wanting to lessen her embarrassment at this, but unsure how to put what he had to say. On the one hand he didn't want them to feel like his employees, as they were much more than that to him, and on the other, he didn't want them to feel obliged to him. 'I'll take care of you. You too are my family, and family take care of their own. You won't have anything to worry about. Look, we have to go to see the family solicitor tomorrow. There's the will and other stuff to see to, and he rang earlier and asked that you two attend. That may mean more than just the memorial fund to sort out. Maybe Grandfather made sure you will be okay. And if he didn't, it would have been because he didn't have time to and would want me to do it on his behalf.'

'Thank you, Jacques.' With her free hand she used her fingers to wipe away a tear. 'It was a good day when I met you. To me it is as if you are the good thing to come out of all of the horror.'

All he could do was to squeeze her hand, as he felt his own throat constrict.

Twenty-one

Harri in Love

1963

Plans had changed slightly for Harri. Patsy had shown signs of developing pneumonia. Mam and Dad and Ian had stayed with her, which meant Harri had had to bring Lizzie back to their hotel. Settling her into her room and having ordered dinner to be sent up for her, she said for the umpteenth time, 'Are you sure you'll be okay, Lizzie?'

'I'm sure. Look, you've been looking forward to going out to dinner with Greg. I can look after meself. I have me chair so I can take meself to the toilet. There won't be a problem. I want yer to go.'

'Eeh, thanks, love. I were that excited, then it seemed as I'd have to cancel. Mam and Dad will be back later. If anyone has to stay with Patsy, Ian will. Mam even said they might take you back to Breckton tonight. Dad's eager to get home. His partner is running the surgery and all the visits on his own and that's a big thing.'

'I hope not, I'm very tired. I'll probably sleep once I've eaten. Not that I'm very hungry.'

'But, what about, well, I mean, being on your own and that, are you ready for that? I'd cancel in a flash if you need me here.'

'No, I'll be okay. I'm used to being on me own. And, even if yer weren't going out I'd want yer to leave me.'

This relieved Harri's mind. She couldn't think of cancelling with Greg.

With Lizzie's assurance that she had everything she'd need to hand, and with those exercise books Lizzie put so much store by tucked under her pillow, Harri left the hotel. What those books contained fascinated her. To think they held all of Patsy's history ... well on her mother's side, at any rate, but they must mention hers and Patsy's dad.

It was strange that Patsy hadn't taken them off Lizzie, but then it wasn't as if she could read them yet with her sore and bloodshot eyes. But to allow an almost complete stranger to read all about the most private life of your mother ... well, it just didn't seem like Patsy. And what of this half-brother Lizzie had found out that Patsy had! That was a turn-up. Eeh, life could get very complicated in the future.

Still, she had other things to occupy her thoughts: Greg! By, in less than an hour he'd be calling for her. She couldn't wait. But first she had to run along to that shop she'd passed every day on her way to and from the hospital. She'd checked it out tonight as they had passed, and the blue dress was still in the window. Its tight bodice, cut low in a rounded neckline, fitted into the waist then gracefully flowed into a sort of lampshade-shaped skirt. A bow sat at the waistline, and the hem was cut to at least three inches above the knee – not too short, but enough to show off the one asset she would admit to having: her nice, shapely legs. Oh, she knew the old adage that girls with red hair should wear green, but she didn't always stick to that. Anyway, blue suited her, and this one was a lovely subtle shade.

Anticipation shortened her breath as she waited in the foyer later. When he finally came through the door, she stood up and ran towards him. His look held surprised pleasure. Taking her in his arms, he kissed her cheek. 'You look beautiful.' His husky voice told her that his feelings matched hers. They were like a collision of souls. Once their paths had met, she'd known their lives were entwined for ever. There was no questioning it; there were no boundaries to surmount. There wasn't even a life to tell of as nothing that had gone before meant anything. Nothing at all.

Dinner had been a magical sealing of them as two people with a lot in common: the music they liked, the films, the kind of books they had read and wanted to read. The only differences were in their upbringing. Greg being a city man and her from the country; his coming from the south and her from the north – it all meant they had different outlooks on some things, but both knew these would be new horizons to discover rather than fences to climb.

As they travelled back to her hotel, she realized she couldn't bear to part from him. She'd never been with a man – not properly, she hadn't. She'd had her chances, but she'd felt differently about it than Patsy, and had preferred to keep herself for the right man. Mind, something in her was glad that Patsy was experienced, as she worried that the rape – oh God, she felt sick at the very word – could have damaged her more otherwise. Not just mentally, but physically too. Maybe even to the point that she'd never want to do it again – still may have done, in fact. Her heart went out to Patsy. She could think of nothing worse, but at this moment she didn't want to give her mind to anything other than how her blood seemed to have warmed inside her, and with its flowing it tingled places that had never been touched by another. The sensation gave her urges she didn't want to deny. It lowered her resistance to a point where she knew she couldn't think of doing so. 'I wish I could ask you in...'

'I know. I feel we should always stay together now we have found one another. Would you think bad of me if I asked you back to mine?'

'No, I would say, what took you so long...'

His grin held a magic that she wanted to bottle and keep for ever. His pulling her closer intensified the feelings in her to a point where she wanted release for them right now. Her conscience stopped her, and she pulled away from him. 'I just need to check on Lizzie – make sure Mam and Dad came back from the hospital and everything is okay.'

'Let's hope it is. I don't know if I can cope if I have to leave you now.' His voice, already low so as the taxi driver couldn't hear, dropped to a whisper, 'Harri, I know we haven't known each other long, but I love you. You are the other half of me.'

'I know, because I feel the same. If you asked

me to marry you right now me answer would be: aye, let's run off to Gretna Green... Eeh, I've never been so forward in all me life! You're doing things to me that's changing me.'

'Our meeting changed us both, as that is how I feel too. And I'd do it, but we would upset so many who don't deserve it. But for all that, I *am* asking you to marry me. It's not the most romantic place to ask, and I haven't a ring to give you tonight, but with your help I will design one and have it made for you and ready for when I can get your father's consent.'

'Eeh, Greg.' She wiped away the tears that had filled her eyes. 'Me answer is yes. Yes, yes, yes.'

The kiss took them to another world. The driver tapping on the dividing window brought them out of it. 'We're here, mate, and you may have nothing better to do, but I have a living to make, so if you don't mind, that'll be six bob.'

Shocked for a moment, they pulled apart and stared at one another before the humour of the situation hit them and they burst out laughing.

'Right, I'll pay the taxi off and come in with you. We can get another one once you are happy all is well.'

As they walked into the reception, the duty manager called her over. 'There is a message for you, Miss Chesterton.' Taking the envelope from him and slitting it open, she read the note from her mother.

Sorry we couldn't wait for you to come in, love. Patsy turned a corner and is a lot better. So much so that her doctor agreed to transfer her to the Leeds hospital. Not

*that Patsy was too pleased by that, though she saw the
sense in it for the rest of us. She fears that those she will
be working with will see far more of her than she would
like, but Dad laughed at this and told her she should
learn from the experience and take heed of how it feels
to be a patient. That didn't go down too well!*

*Ian has stayed over and Patsy was glad of that. They
are getting along much better, which is nice for Ian.
Though Patsy was a bit grumpy that you hadn't been
back tonight. Don't worry about that, though. I think
she was feeling a bit jealous. For our part we hope you
and Greg had a lovely evening, love, and you deserved
the break.*

*We are taking Lizzie back with us. She is very
happy about that and felt up to making the journey,
as she had slept since you had left her. We will stop for
a few hours at a hotel somewhere en route, as that is
better than making the journey all in one go. Dad
managed to get the wheelchair to the station and it
will be delivered by rail.*

*If you can get up to the hospital by ten in the morn-
ing, love, that will be a help, as Patsy will need a hand
and then you can follow the ambulance with Ian in
his car. See you tomorrow sometime. Let us know
when you arrive at Leeds hospital.*

Love, Mam. X

Harri stared at the note. In it she saw the end
of her time with Greg for goodness knew how
long, and that she couldn't bear.

'Is it bad news, Harri?'

'No, not really, but yet it is in a way. I have to
return up north tomorrow.'

He didn't speak. His face told how he felt. After

299

a moment he said, 'Come on, then, darling. Let's not waste a moment.'

Lying in Greg's arms, all fear of the stories she'd heard about the pain of a first time left her, and with it disappeared all the cold medical terminology that she'd learned about the process. This feeling that had taken her was a million miles from all of that, as Greg's gentle foreplay heightened her desire to the point where she could have begged him to enter her. When he did, there was no more than a momentary resistance, but no pain. And when he finally fully immersed himself inside her, there was a feeling of being stretched, but it didn't hurt and it quickly gave way to sensations that gripped the heart of her.

Her whole being came alive and responded to his every thrust in a way that shocked her. Gone was any shyness or ignorance of what she should do or how she should react. Making love to Greg came as naturally as if they had been doing it for ever. Their bodies were one. They entwined one another. They drank in deep and beautiful kisses. They explored each other's bodies with their hands and their lips, giving all of themselves in a frenzy of hungry love that enhanced all that she was.

When feelings began to build on feelings, she knew she was ready to ride the crest of her first orgasm – to be taken to a place she couldn't imagine. She gasped out her plea for him not to stop. She could feel the grip she had on him as she clung on with her arms and her legs, and the almost painful deep, plunging breaths as her body took the onslaught of sensations that had her arching her back to help them to build more and more. Then the moment came. The power of the first wave shocked her to her core, rocking her very being, but her hold on it seemed fragile as if it would slip away from her. She stiffened, holding herself rigid and begging Greg to be still. She heard her own voice holler out before drowning in a moan from Greg that seemed as if it came from his soul.

Together they slumped into a place that held their release – a release that had drained them, and which left them exhausted. Relief mingled their heartbeats and coated them in the dampness of each other's sweat.

'Harri... Oh, Harri!'

Her name sounded like a song set to the sweetest music. All she could do by way of answering him was to stroke his hair and look into his eyes, which she saw glistened with tears. One trickled over and ran down his cheek. She caught it with her thumb and licked the saltiness of it. 'I love you, Greg.'

His nose rubbed hers. She wanted to take hold of the promises his look held as he eased himself from her. Keeping her eyes on him, she knew she would never be the same again. Greg now owned the most vital part of her, and she had given him possession of it. In return she knew he was hers for ever, and nothing could ever part them.

Twenty-two

Escape

Lizzie 1963 and Theresa 1943

Lizzie's sigh was one of contentment. Despite what had happened in the last week, her mind and body were at peace. She'd rested well at the hotel they'd stopped at, and they'd made good progress this morning. The journey had given them time to get to know one another, and had taken away any apprehension she'd had over the arrangement for her immediate future. She liked Sarah and Richard – they were easy to like. And best of all, they were always sensitive to what others were thinking. She hadn't detected any feelings of resentment in them at having been put in a position of having to take her into their home. This had gone a long way to relax her, though she did still have some nerves as to how this new life would pan out for her.

As they drove along a leafy lane, Richard said, 'Nearly there. We live at the end of this road.'

They were in the middle of nowhere with only trees and fields surrounding them. It would be strange to live in such a place, she thought, with no houses near, no flats, no noise or smog, and no shops! But something told her she'd get used to not being around those things. She'd more than landed on her feet. Rita'd said these were good people, and she hadn't been wrong. Poor Rita. It seemed funny to think of her working around here. It didn't suit her somehow. A city person through and through, she must have been a shock to the folk who lived around here. An embarrassment took her at this thought as she remembered what Rita had done to Sarah and her dad. 'Sarah, I ... well, I were just thinking about Rita, and I wanted to say I'm sorry about what she did. I'm not like her. I sometimes think it strange that we were born into the same family, though Ken took after her.'

'You have nothing to be sorry about, love. Eeh, it were a bad time for us, but we're healed – well, as healed as it is possible to be, so don't you go worrying yourself. None of that will be held against you, and no one round here need know who you are. We'll just say you were a friend of Patsy's when she lived in London and you've come to have a break from the city.'

'Life around here is a million miles from what you're used to, Lizzie.' Richard looked through the mirror at her as he said this. 'Everyone will be curious and there will be gossip. In London everyone is a stranger to you, so I don't expect you even think about them. To us, everyone is known, and those we don't know are of great interest.'

'Eeh, there'll be some tongues wagging as to who you are and where you come from and how you fit in with our family... By, the place'll be on fire with talk!'

This banter helped to calm the unsettled feeling that had come with her thinking of Rita. But in another way it enhanced her nerves. Country folk were so different to any she'd ever known, and this gave her a trickle of trepidation as to whether she would fit in with them, or whether they would take to her. Being the subject of their gossip wasn't a comfortable place to be.

'Here we are, then. Eeh, home at last!'

As Sarah said this, Richard swung the car into a drive and before her Lizzie saw the most beautiful house. The sight of it deepened her concerns. It was grander than anything she'd ever seen.

It hadn't just been the outside of the house that had been beautiful. Everything about it was like nothing Lizzie had ever seen. It wasn't posh, but homely with soft colours everywhere, and though she could tell the furniture was expensive, it had that lived-in look about it. Here and there were signs of wear that only added to the whole feel of it being a family home. The kitchen was like she would imagine a farmhouse kitchen to be: a place where wellies could be kicked off and yet lovely baking was done on the range, which took up almost the whole of one wall, and family meals were eaten around the huge oak table in the centre. Oak beams were hung with pans of all sizes, and a string of onions draped down one beam that stood the length of the ceiling to the floor. The Welsh dresser, laden with pretty china, and the lovely yellow curtains dressing the window both enhanced the feeling that this was a home – a real country home. It welcomed her as if it had wrapped its arms around her, taking away her doubts and settling a happiness inside her that threatened to make her cry.

Now she was in the room they had put aside for her. Between them they had lifted her, crossing their arms and holding each other's hands to make a sort of chair lift for her. Their way of making this a giggle took any embarrassment from her, and they'd said that David, their other son, would be bringing her chair from the station later for her. He had done so not ten minutes later, and he'd made her laugh with his antics as he'd tried to unfold it. She liked him. He was easy to talk to, and again she didn't get any vibes that he resented her intruding on his family. Then they'd all left her alone for a while, telling her to settle herself in and come out when she was ready.

This room was everything Harri had said it was, with a wonderful view she could sit and gaze at for ever. After putting the few things away that she had from the case Rita had brought to the boat for her, she did just that.

The beauty of it and all the kindness she'd been shown suddenly overwhelmed her as she looked out. Tears spilled from her. Her whole body cried in a way she'd never known. Her heart emptied itself of all the hurts, all the fears and the losses in painful sobs that shook her very roots.

A knock on the door slowed the outpouring. 'Eeh, love, I thought I heard you. Come on. It's all going to be reet, I promise. I'll fetch you a pot of tea, eh?'

All she could do was nod.

The tea helped. Sipping the hot liquid calmed her.

'Look, why don't you get into bed for an hour or so, love? You look done in, and there's nowt spoiling. We haven't heard yet from Harri and Ian, so we don't know if they've arrived in Leeds or not.'

Again, all she could do was nod. At this moment she could think of nothing better than getting between the sheets on the deep divan bed in the corner of the room.

'I'll fetch Richard to help.'

'No, I can manage. I can get from my chair into bed on me own.'

Sarah stayed while she did, helping her with her clothes and fetching a warm flannel for her to wipe her face. Although she didn't like any fuss usually, it was all very welcome at this moment.

'I can't thank you enough, Sarah, for taking me in. I promise I won't be a lot of trouble. I can do most things for meself. But I don't know what would have happened to me if you hadn't offered me this, as the social wouldn't have let me carry on on me own. Not that I could manage altogether, but the alternative scares me. The homes where they put people like me are not what I'd want.'

'Well, you have no need to worry on that score, Lizzie. You are welcome here for as long as you need, you know that, love. Is there owt else that you want?'

'I have some exercise books on the coffee table...'

'Oh, yes. There you go.' Sarah's hand shook as she handed them over. 'Does she ... well, is there a mention... I mean, has Theresa Crompton told it all as it was?'

'I think she has. She's very honest about her life

before the war, about her waywardness and stuff she did, but after Patsy was born she wanted to make up for it all. She loved Patsy, and had she had another way she wouldn't have given her away.'

'There's allus another way. Did she say whether ... still, there's nowt to be gained by us going over it all. I'll pop in in a little while and see if you're okay.'

'I know what you're referring to. She does say. I'm sorry about all the hurt, Sarah. Yer didn't deserve it.'

'No, none of us did. Look, tell me. I can take it. I think I know, but it's better to have the truth of it than to think on it.'

'If you're sure. I mean...'

'Aye, I'm sure.'

The bed sank as Sarah sat on the edge. Her face had paled. Lizzie had a feeling that she wasn't really ready, even though she said she was.

'I – I ... well, it weren't rape. Theresa made that up, and she told her dad that it was rape by a stranger while she was out riding. Your... I mean... Billy, well, he did hurt her. He punched and kicked–'

Sarah's gasp held pain.

'I'm sorry. I shouldn't have said.'

'Why? Why if it wasn't rape did he hurt her?'

'It ... it were to do with her not wanting him to... Well, at the end...'

'Oh, I see. She didn't want any consequences of her actions. Eeh, poor lass... By, what am I saying? She asked for... No, that ain't reet. No one asks for such treatment. I shouldn't have said

307

that. He were not right. Billy. He had a mental illness.'

A tear ran down Sarah's face. This shocked Lizzie. Surely she couldn't still have any feeling for him?

'I'm being silly. It's the memory of it all. It was horrific, and in some ways I was to blame. I should have spoken out about his threats. They wouldn't have let him free if I had, but I was so afraid.'

She couldn't say anything, as she didn't know what Sarah was referring to. She knew Billy Armitage had been let out of a mental institution because of the war, and that Theresa had said in her memoirs that he must have duped those responsible for letting him out, but to think Sarah could have stopped his release was shocking. Surely she couldn't mean that?

'Anyroad, like I say, it's no use going over it all now. It's all done and dusted... Well, it's done. But I doubt it will ever leave me.'

With this she got up to leave, giving a nervous smile as she reached the door and saying, 'Don't worry about it all, love. I'll cope. Even if them Cromptons come back into our lives, I'll not let it affect me. I can't. For Patsy's sake, I can't.'

Once she'd gone, Lizzie let out a sigh. There was a lot of hurt in Sarah and she wondered if it would ever heal. She hoped so, because she didn't like to think of her suffering like that. She didn't deserve it.

Snuggling back into the umpteen soft pillows, she felt tired, but overriding this was her need to find out how Theresa had escaped, as she surely must have done. As she opened the book she prayed, *Please, God, don't let her have been tortured.*

Theresa Takes her Chance – 1943

The lorry rumbled on. Each bump or rut in the road increased Theresa's discomfort, and yet the side-to-side motion lulled her a little. She closed her eyes. Marvelling at how her fear had levelled to a point where she could cope, she began to think of ways she could escape.

From the count of feet it seemed there were only two Germans, and she'd already noted that the other prisoners numbered three. Why they were allowed on the bench while she was kept on the floor she didn't know, but though her hands were tied, the position had some advantages.

No one had spoken for a little while. At first the Germans had kept up a conversation and during it she'd heard mention of Camp du Struthof. This had intensified her fear as the camp was known as one that no one came out of. There were stories of gassing and the stories were that all dissidents taken there were tortured and then put to death. One of the soldiers had kicked her as they'd had this conversation and had laughed out loud at doing so, saying something she thought meant, 'just the place for the likes of you, whore'. The only thing the camp had in their favour was that it was miles away to the east of France, and would take many hours to get there. Hours when there might just be a chance...

The silence around her now and the fact the

soldiers hadn't kicked her for a while and their feet were still, suggested they may have nodded off. To test this, she wriggled her body. Nothing happened.

A light from the vehicle following filtered through the canvas curtain that was pulled down over the back of the truck. Turning her head, she confirmed that both soldiers had their heads leaning forward. Looking the other way and craning her neck, she saw the same appeared to have happened with two of the prisoners, but not Philippe. He nodded his head towards his shoe.

Another rut shook the lorry, rattling its sides. The noise gave her fear that the soldiers would wake, but they didn't stir. The light danced from the floor to the roof of the vehicle and back. As it did, it glinted off the buckle of Philippe's sandal. He moved his foot very slightly but enough for her to see something protruding from the leather strap and stretching in a taut line to the buckle. Wire! The thin strong wire they often used to lay traps with, but its thinness and strength also made it very sharp.

Rolling on her side, she edged backwards towards Philippe. Her movements, slow and difficult, sweated her body and increased the depth and sound of her breathing. Feeling his sandal on her hands, she waited. His foot moved up and down against her hands. Tension held her almost suspended from life itself as he worked. Her eyes never left the two sleeping soldiers. Fear pumped her heart faster and faster until she could feel its beat against her ribs. Then her hands fell apart. She was free!

Lying still for a moment, she watched the soldiers. Neither showed any signs of moving. Sitting up, she wriggled towards them. Stretching out her hand, her fingers touched the cold steel of the barrel of a rifle. The weight of the soldier's hands held it upright. Grabbing it dislodged him. Turning in a movement that only took a split-second, she blasted the astonished face of its bearer, sending him out of this life. The other soldier jumped up. Making an apology, she pulled the trigger again. The place she hit, if it didn't kill him, would render him unable to function as a man ever again. He hit the ground, landing on her legs. Shoving him off she shot him in the head.

The lorry swerved, unbalancing her. German anger exploded in the form of voices coming through the window of the cab, swearing and demanding to know what was going on. Philippe answered in a perfect imitation of one of the Germans' voices: 'It is under control. One of the prisoners of no consequence managed to free his hands and lunged at us. He is dead. Pull over when you can. Contact the convoy and tell them you will re-join on the back when we have dealt with his body. The others, including the girl, are still alive.'

Whispering to her, he said, 'Be ready to shoot the irons off your feet as soon as they stop. Then you have to deal with them before you release us.'

Terror gripped her. Their liberation was down to her, and so were their lives, as certain death would follow this attempt to escape.

Twisting her body round so that her legs were

311

facing the back of vehicle, she parted them as far as possible. Pointing the gun as near to the centre of the irons around her ankles as she could, she braced herself for what would be excruciating burns. She had to be able to ignore them and react as fast as she could, as the releasing of her feet had to coincide with them opening the flap. *What if they hadn't believed Philippe and held their own guns at the ready?* She couldn't let this thought in as she knew she wouldn't stand a chance.

'Philippe, I need to release you and give you a gun. I may not be able to overpower both of them. We cannot take the chance.' A movement stopped Philippe answering her. The man next to him had difficulty keeping his body still. 'What's wrong with him?'

'He is an epileptic. He does not work with us, only shelters us. I am sorry I have caused him to be caught. His fear must have triggered a fit. There is nothing we can do but pray the truck stops soon.'

Getting Philippe's hands free proved almost impossible. The positions of them and the movement of the truck hindered her from reaching the binds. As the lorry made a sudden turn to the right she stepped up her efforts. They must have found a place to stop!

At last his hands were free! Grabbing the other gun she thrust it towards him just as the truck came to halt.

Holding her breath, she listened. Other trucks rumbled past. Both she and Philippe had their guns aimed at the irons on their feet. The man having the fit spat froth into the air, and his body juddered against Philippe's. Would he impair his aim? *Christ! We'll have to shoot him! Please don't let that happen.*

The last truck passed. Darkness fell as no more headlights shone into the truck. A door slammed and then another. Footsteps crunched on gravel. Sweat ran down her face. The glow of a torch swung in then out of any open places around the canvas covering the back of the truck. A voice shouted a man's name. Philippe answered.

'*Öffnen Sie die Kiappe.*'

She understood something about opening something – *they are asking for the flap to be opened!* She looked at Philippe.

'*Ich kann nicht von innen.*'

Not understanding this, she waited. A grunt signalled the soldier's annoyance at whatever the answer was – probably a refusal to open the flap. Another noise came, and this time she knew the flap was being released. Her finger tightened on the trigger. Her hand shook. She must ignore any pain that was coming, no matter how bad.

Air hit her face. The combined shots from hers and Philippe's guns deafened her. Agonizing pain caught the breath in her lungs. For a second it took her attention, but the gunshots had surprised the Germans. They dropped their torch and fled. Jumping from the wagon, she quickly retrieved the torch, flashing it towards the trees. She saw the backs of the fleeing Germans and fired quick successive rounds. Philippe picked up the torch and highlighted two bodies on the ground at around twenty feet away. He handed her the torch and fired a couple more rounds. The bodies jumped and collapsed again. Satisfied they were dead, Philippe ran over to them and took their guns. 'Right. Help me out with the other two bodies.'

Climbing back into the truck, they saw the fitter had fallen asleep. His body doubled over away from the third man's. This man cringed away from them. Her mind questioned this, but there was no time to ask why as Philippe grabbed her and pushed her out of the truck. 'Get into the cab. Let's get out of here.'

They drove for miles, but passed no other vehicle. Their journey soon took a mountain path, but with the safe feeling this gave came other feelings. Now her body shook. Now her ankles smarted, but neither the fear nor the burns could take away the sense of relief.

'Where are we going?'

'There's a place up here where we will be safe. There is a radio. You need to abort the mission. It is too dangerous. I will get the explosives moved at a later date. Security will be tightened. The mission is compromised.'

'What happened? How did they find out about it? That man, the one in the corner. He spat on me. Does he think I betrayed you?'

'No. He is the traitor. He will be shot once we reach the safe place.'

This shocked her. 'But why is he tied up?'

'They do that to informers and keep them until they are sure. Or they may torture them to find out more, but whatever, they usually end up killing them. Our way lets him off as it will be a clean kill without the pain of torture.'

There was nothing to argue against. If called

upon to pull the trigger, she would do so. Traitors were a curse. As well as putting hers, Philippe's and the epileptic man's lives in danger, this traitor had stopped an operation that had been months in the planning, and that would have saved countless lives and brought forward the end of the war. She hoped he would rot in hell!

Disguised as a factory worker and with her ankles healing, Theresa journeyed back without incident. It seemed the trains going north were the most occupied with German troops, as were the roads she saw through the window. This was a worrying trend, as it indicated they were nervous of what the future held from that quarter. She knew it held something big, but knew nothing more than that. The sick feeling in her stomach and the realization she hadn't seen her period took her mind off everything other than the fact that she might be pregnant. How would she handle that? If she told HQ, they would lift her out of France. No. That must not happen. There was much to do. She had proved how useful she was. Besides, she could not leave Pierre.

He stood a little away from the station. Cigarette smoke curled up from his mouth into a cloud above him. He did not look in her direction nor acknowledge her as she walked past him. Now dressed in her usual clothing, but still with her blonde hair, her nerves jangled in her stomach. She still had to negotiate the village without being stopped by a German. Deciding she couldn't, she turned into a lane that she knew led to Monsieur Langlois's house. The Langloises were in the

Resistance, so she could cut through their garden. Managing to get to their gate without being seen, she dodged the house and made for the thicket at the bottom of their land. Once in the shelter of the trees, she stopped and leaned against one. Taking off her scarf, she shook out her hair.

'*Ma chérie!*'

His voice brushed every part of her as if a feather had been passed over her. 'Pierre, oh, Pierre–' His arms grasped her, stopping her from sinking to the ground.

'What is it, Olivia? My darling, I have missed you. I have stood by for every train that arrived – whenever I could, that is. I couldn't believe it when you alighted today. How did the mission go?'

'Oh, Pierre, we were betrayed...'

'No! How did you avoid capture? *Mais, ça ne fait rien.* It does not matter. You are here, my darling. That is all that matters. I will arrange a car to take you up to our hiding place. It is still safe. The Germans suspect nothing. I have to return to work, but I will be with you in a couple of hours. Get some rest.'

For a moment she clung to him. All that was Olivia had gone; only Theresa was left – and a vulnerable Theresa at that.

'Go, my darling. Wait at the edge of the wood, but don't show yourself. Watch out for a van. A black van with "Vassel's Plumbers" on the side. Wait, as it will go past your hiding place first then will return. It is then you can show yourself. I love you, my darling, and want to hold you and kiss you, but I dare not.'

She knew what he meant, as she had the same feelings inside her. To give in to the urge to kiss would be their undoing. Better to get to the safe house and await his visit later. Savouring the anticipation of this, she moved with stealth further towards the road.

Monsieur Ponté greeted her. His face held pain.

'Has something happened?'

'Our bakery was burned to the ground...'

With relief, mixed with a little contempt for this couple who still held so much store by the old life they had lost when others had suffered far worst fates, she said, 'But buildings can be rebuilt, as can businesses. You must not fret so.'

'Not lives, though. Four of our neighbours were forced inside. They were burned to death...'

'No! Why? Oh, God...'

'These *bâtards,* they do not have to have a reason, but this one is a reprisal. They suspected my closest neighbours must have known where I had gone to, and that my disappearance was because of you. You are in grave danger and you increase the danger to us.'

'I am sorry. I will contact Command. But first I will wait until Pierre comes so he can tell me what he wants me to do.'

At this moment all she wanted to do was sleep. A bath would have been a bonus, but the bathing process here was a long, drawn-out affair of collecting the water into the boiler, stoking the boiler and then transferring the hot water to the tin bath. Privacy was also an issue, so she chose to swill her face and take to her bed. Not even a bowl of soup offered by the still tearful Madame Ponté could tempt her to do otherwise.

1963

Knowing Theresa was safe, Lizzie gave in to the tiredness and lay back on her pillows. The last few days had drained her. But, making the effort, she threw back the covers and edged her way out of the bed onto her wheelchair. Sarah had laid a dressing gown over it. She pulled this on and steered over to the window. What she'd just read shuddered through her. The evil acts done under the guise of war were difficult to understand. People were people, weren't they? How come that some could burn others alive in such a callous way? But then, Ken had been like that. She had to admit that. He could have shoved those innocent people into the flames without even thinking about it.

Twenty-three

Harri's Shock Decision – Patsy's Shock Reaction

1963

'What do you mean, Harri hasn't come back with you? Why?'

'One word: Greg.'

'But...?'

'There are no buts, Mam. Harri said to tell you that she is in love with Greg, that she cannot leave him and that she has moved into his flat with him.'

'My God! Our Harri? Our sensible Harri? I can't take it in. I've never heard the like. Being in love, yes, but to give up everything and her not knowing him more than a couple of weeks? It's...'

'She's in love with Greg, Mam. That's all there is to it.'

'And she couldn't telephone me and tell me herself?'

'She gave me Greg's number where you can reach her. She felt that with settling Lizzie in you had enough on your plate and could talk to her in your own time, when you've had time to absorb it.'

'That's considerate! I'm very cross with her.'

'Not as cross as Patsy. She's furious – that's when she could stop coughing long enough to express her feelings. She reckons as Harri has shown no consideration for her at all! Don't see it meself.

Why does Harri have to consider Patsy all the time? Anyroad, Harri hasn't given up everything. She wants Dad to help her to transfer to a London-based teaching hospital so she can continue her medical studies.'

'Well, we'll see what Dad has to say about it. Harri... My God, I can't believe it, but if I think about it, she's like me and me mam and me granna in that, we all knew our man once we spotted him. Let's hope this Greg is all he seems. Mind, she'll get a name for herself and that won't help matters. Not in the medical world, it won't.'

'Mam, they're getting married!'

'What? She wouldn't! She...'

Ian watched his mam's body slump into a chair. She'd coped well with the news of Harri not coming home, but Harri getting married without even telling her seemed a step too far. But he'd no option but to tell her. 'They are driving to Gretna tomorrow.'

'No... Why?'

'Because Harri didn't want to live in sin. But she told me to tell you that they plan to come here in a couple of weeks and will arrange a blessing in the church and a family do. She wanted you to understand, but knew it would be difficult. She just cannot leave Greg's side.'

Though he knew this to be true, he also knew Harri didn't want to give Patsy a chance to spoil things for her. Why she imagined she would, he didn't know. Well, maybe he did, if he was honest. Patsy did feel that she owned Harri, and her fury at the news had shown him she was capable of making mischief if she got the chance.

'I suppose we have to accept it. There isn't anything else we can do. But whether as a married woman she'd be allowed to continue her studies is another matter. Oh, Harri, Harri.'

'What is it, dear? Is anything wrong with Harri?'

It was a relief to Ian that his dad came in at that moment. His mam had come over all emotional and he wasn't one that could handle that.

Listening to her telling his dad, he knew she'd accepted it and taken it quite well. She even went to the trouble of giving little excuses such as 'when the heart is smitten, there's nothing we can do about it'.

'Not when the smitten heart belongs to a twenty-two-year-old, I'm afraid not, dear. I am shocked though. Harri? Never dreamt it of her. I wanted to give her away at her wedding, and now ... well, what am I to do with her wedding fund?'

'Spend some on the day she does plan on sharing with us and the rest, well, let her have it to do what she likes with. Oh, Richard...'

'I know.'

'Do you? I feel like I have lost her. It was bad enough when she went to university, but I knew she'd come back, but now... She's gone, Richard, really gone to another.'

'Come on, dear.'

Time to leave. Ian made for the door without saying anything. Looking back, he saw his dad take his mam in his arms. Could anyone wish for a more solid person for a dad than he had? Folk often said that he himself was like his Granddad Jack in nature, but he hoped there was a lot of his dad in him too. He'd need it to win over and keep

321

Patsy for himself. By, she was a hard nut to crack!

Being like his granddad didn't come into it where the ladies were concerned, as Granddad Jack had had no problem in that department. Nor did his brother David. He'd been with his lass since his school days, but then, David was a plodder: happy with the farm work and with his lass from the village. Whereas he had to go and aim for a lass like Patsy – a complicated lass with stuff from the past that guided her actions, and a lass that looked down on him as some kind of simpleton.

The thing was that he wasn't really a plodder. He enjoyed the farm work and so he'd just allowed that side to happen. He hadn't strived for anything more. He had it in him to, he knew that. And of late he had thought about it all a great deal, and had come to the conclusion that he wished he had taken up medicine. He had enough qualifications to get a place in uni; he just hadn't bothered. He regretted that now. He'd speak to his dad later... If it was a possibility it might cheer his parents up after this business with Harri. And it might just impress Patsy.

Patsy's face sweated under the oxygen mask, but her anger made her body sweat too. *How could Harri have done this to her?*

The voice that had spoken to her many times since the deep, dark, watery depths of the river had engulfed her, spoke again: *'Don't allow it! Get out of here and get back to London!'* All her life she'd wondered if she was like her father. Did this prove that she was, this hearing a voice? Many times she'd tried to find out if Harri had fears in that direction. She'd questioned her about it. But Harri had always convinced her it couldn't happen. Now, in her own weakest moment, what she'd fought against since hearing about her father had beaten her.

Her father, or so Sarah told her, was dictated to by what he called *a redness* in his brain. Would this voice dictate to her what she should do? No, she wouldn't let it.

But that thought had hardly died in her when she found herself planning to go through with going back to London.

She knew there wasn't a train now from Leeds, and it had to be today as Ian had said Harri and Greg were going to Gretna tomorrow! She'd have to get to her bank and get enough money out so she could get a taxi to the nearest place where she could catch a train. She'd go and see her mother if she arrived at a decent hour. She'd feel better once she'd done that. Then she'd find this Greg, whoever the hell he thought *he* was, and make sure he regretted ever setting his eyes on Harri!

At last she was on the last leg of her journey. No train from anywhere nearer than Crewe had gone straight through, so it had been a long taxi drive and cost her just about every penny she'd taken from her account.

Getting out of the hospital had been easy. Slipping into the kitchen where the nurses made drinks and snacks for the ward, she'd found a doctor's housecoat hanging on the back of the door. Why it was there, she hadn't thought to question, but she knew that in the hospital in London the junior doctors often went into the ward kitchen during the night to half-inch a biscuit or make a quick cuppa, so maybe one had left it the night before. But whatever, it had fitted and had concealed her clothes, which she'd managed to put on under the bed covers.

Waiting for a time when no one was about had been the worst. With her being a new arrival, they seemed in constant attendance on her. But there had been a moment when there was only one nurse on duty – during what they called the rest period when all good patients were meant to sleep – and she had been called into the sister's office.

Moving had been painful, but she'd managed it and had taken her toilet bag to the washroom used by visitors. As there were no visitors at this hour, she hadn't been disturbed. Here she'd had a shock at the state of herself, as her bloodshot eyes, sunk into a puffy, almost unrecognizable face, had stared back at her from the mirror. Her hair resembled that of a rag doll: as if it had been knitted and stuck on her head. Washing and towel-drying it had taken all her energy, and she'd had to sit on the toilet for a moment, gasping for breath. Fear of discovery had urged her on. They may have been looking for her by then! But the effort had been worth it: she looked at least half-human with her hair restored to its usual glossy, bouncy self. Make-up helped with the rest.

Her health had caused her some problems, with pain being the least of them. Her breathlessness was the main culprit, rendering her almost useless at times as she'd struggled to get oxygen into her lungs. She'd soon realized she needed medication.

Stealing the medication hadn't proved as difficult as she'd thought. Dressed in the doctor's coat and now sporting a stethoscope – this she'd pick-pocketed from a passing doctor who'd had it hanging out of his flowing white coat as he'd hurried along the corridor past her – it had been easy to walk on to a ward and pick up a prescription pad from the charge-nurse's desk. Writing the script, she'd had to rack her brains as to the spelling of the medication they had been giving her in London, and was now glad she'd taken enough interest to ask what it was.

Somehow she'd kept her breathing steady enough for her to walk out of the building. The only security guard she passed was on the maternity ward, as across the country in the last couple of months there had been a couple of instances of women walking into these types of wards and stealing a baby. The guard showed a little interest in her, but didn't question her once he saw she paid no attention to his ward.

Stepping off the train to the half-light of evening with lights beginning to flicker into life all around gave her a feeling of elation. London! She loved it. But where to go first? She knew where Greg's jeweller's shop was: King's, it was called, and their slogan was 'Jewellery Fit for Royalty'. And she knew it was a popular store with the middle classes, selling mid-priced jewellery that could increase in value but didn't start off at extortionate prices. She'd often passed the shop. It took up the whole of the corner of Greendale Street in the west of the city.

Tiredness ached in every part of her, and her legs didn't seem to have anything in them. Opening her bag, she took out the two bottles containing the pills she'd got from the chemist. She'd taken some, but when was that? She couldn't think. She'd find somewhere to sit and decide if she could take some more. Shoving them in her pocket, she made her way through the station to the underground. Crowds jostled her; her breathing became laboured.

'Ere, love, are yer alright?'

For a moment the voice froze her as Rita came to mind. Looking round she saw a bag lady, her toothless face creased with concern.

'Yes, I just ... need to ... sit a moment.'

'Over there, love, there's a bench. Sit down and I'll get Rufus to get yer a drink. You'll like Rufus.'

Whoever Rufus was she was certain she wouldn't put him in the category of people she liked! But she could do nothing to escape him or the bag lady, as her body wouldn't take her any further.

A tear ran down her face at the realization a few minutes later that she'd been fleeced. As she'd opened her handbag to get money to give to Rufus, he'd snatched it. All her money and her savings book had gone, and the bag lady and her companion, who'd turned out to be just as toothless as his partner in crime, unshaven and with his coat tied around him with string, were hurrying away. *Stupid idiot, what was I thinking of?*

She could still see them ambling along at the top of the tunnel. Shouting, if you could call the croaks she made shouting, after them, made no difference. Dozens of folk were milling about, but none of them even looked at her, let alone tried to stop the thieves. If only she wasn't so ill she could catch them in an instant.

Swallowing some more penicillin and respiratory drugs without thinking about whether she should and without the aid of a drink nearly choked her. She gagged on the bulk as she tried to get it down, but a few moments later she began to feel better. With her mind clearing, she remembered she'd put the change from the five-pound note she'd purchased her ticket with into the pocket of her jacket, and feeling for it now she found her underground ticket, a ten-bob note, and two one-pound notes. *Thank God.*

That would be more than enough to get her a drink and a taxi to King's Cross Hospital from the station, and then the underground to Greg's shop. She also had her return ticket to Leeds, as she'd bought one to go straight back there rather than just to Crewe. This prompted the thought: *That's if I ever go back. After what I'm planning, I doubt they'll ever want to see me again!*

This thought upset her. Could she live without the folk she'd come to think of as family? Her resolve began to waver, but the voice urged her on: *'It has to be done, no matter what the consequences!'*

The corridor seemed to go on for ever. Richard had found out which ward her mother was on when she'd first said she was coming to London to visit her. How often she'd wished that was all she'd done rather than meet up with Rita!

Following the signs to the ward, it seemed they were directing her to the end of the world as she turned endless corridors. Her body began to shake, and sweat stood out on her forehead and trickled down her face. Her vision blurred. She had to sit down. Stretching out her hand, she felt the smooth surface of the gloss-painted brick wall, and pressing against it steadied her. Damn feeling like this, it is a bloody hindrance!

'Do you need some help, miss?'

'I – I... No, I'll be alright. I've had a long journey and haven't eaten.'

The young woman persisted: 'There's a WRVS counter just around the corner. They have seats and you can get a hot drink and biscuits. I'll help you round there, shall I?'

Not wanting any attention, this irritated her, but she let the woman take her arm. How she got to the seat she'd never know, but the relief at sitting down and sipping the tea overwhelmed her and tears ran unbidden down her cheeks.

'Well, you are in a state. And you don't look well. Can I get someone to look at you? I could ask one of the nurses that pass by?'

'No, I'll be alright. I – I had an accident and I'm just recovering. I'll sit here a while, thanks.'

The woman apologized, but said she had to leave as she had an appointment. Patsy had never felt more glad of anything in her life. Well-meaning, interfering busybodies were the last thing she needed right now. She just needed to get to her mother! What she would do when she did, or how she would react at the sight of her mother, she didn't know, but there was no going back now.

Setting off again, this time with the knowledge from one of the volunteers that the ward she needed was just around the next corner, she found to her relief a door that proclaimed, 'Ward 34'.

Pushing it open gave her a confusing sight of two long rows of beds, all occupied and all with very elderly women in them. Her mother wasn't that old, surely! But then, the picture in the paper did show her looking almost as old and frail as these women.

'Can I help you?'

'I – I'm looking for Mrs Crompton.'

'Discharged this morning. Are you Miss Crompton? There was a phone call from– Hey!'

Crashing back through the swing door, she stumbled as fast as she could. The nurse had looked to be on her own so couldn't follow, but she might telephone someone.

Dodging round the corner, she stood a moment. Her mind went through the possibilities. It had been hours now since she'd escaped from the hospital. The family would have been told. Places she may go would have been discussed. In the mood she'd been in before Ian had left her she'd talked of hating everyone and everything... They would be afraid for her, but they might also be afraid of what she intended to do. *Yes, it must be that. Why else would that nurse know who I am? Damn!* She'd have to get out of here... Disappointment swelled her tears once more. *So near, so near!*

Anger turned her tears to ones of frustration.

Her life was her own! Why should other people determine what she should do or who she should see? *They can all fuck off!* But even so, now she didn't even know where her mother was, and if she asked she might alert them to call her family. They may even have her detained here until her family came, and then they would take her back, and that would stop her carrying out her plan. But what plan? What was it I was going to do? Her hands went to her head. Everything seemed confused. The clear voice she'd heard giving her precise instructions wasn't there any more... *It's left me. I'm on me own!*

People and the walls of the corridor merged into a blur as she ran. The walls kept hitting her, bruising her sides. The glass doors at the end seemed to get further away. She had to get out!

Something hard dug into her side. 'Hey, watch where you're going! This is a hospital, you know!'

The man looked as though he was under water. The trolley he pushed took on gigantic proportions, and the sick person lying on it stared at her with black hollow eyes. Stumbling away from them, she at last felt the cool air on her face. Her eyes cleared, and to her left she saw an ambulance with its doors open. The person she'd knocked into must have been brought in from it. This logic calmed her a little. If she was capable of making deductions, she couldn't be completely insane.

Sitting on a low wall, she tried to analyse why she was here. What had prompted her to take the actions she'd taken and to even think of coming to her mother in this state, let alone to plan such a revenge on Greg? Putting her hands in her pocket, she felt the cold tin of the lighter fuel she'd bought. *My God! I really did intend to burn Greg's shop! But then, why shouldn't I? He stole my Harri from me...*

Twenty-four

A Fragile Mind and A Family Disrupted

Theresa and Lizzie – 1963

Theresa looked around her room. Nothing about it was familiar to her, and yet it was like she'd lived here before. The furniture, square and plain and of a light colour, and made of a material she suspected wasn't real wood, was put together solely for its functionality: a bed, a dresser and a wardrobe. All very similar to the furniture in the institution she'd spent months in a few years ago. A fear clutched her. But no, she mustn't think like that. This was different. This was a convalescent home. Carleton House – a sort of halfway stopping-off place before she would be allowed to go all the way to her own front doorstep. That was, if she continued to make the progress she had been making.

Looking into the wardrobe, she saw that there were one or two items in there from her home. The social worker must have been and chosen them. Most were suits she'd had cleaned and hadn't worn for a long time. These still had the zipped covers from the dry cleaner's on them. And there was a coat and two dresses she'd forgotten she had. They looked fresh and clean. Someone must have seen to that for her.

Walking to the window gave her a view of the garden: neatly trimmed lawns and precisely cut flower beds made a pleasant enough outlook for her.

There had been a lot for her to take in. Most of it didn't make any sense. Her doctor – well, psychiatrist, Dr Stinstone, a doctor of the mind, and it seemed from what they had told her that she was in sore need of one – had informed her of the state they had found her house in. *How did it get like that?* And she'd helped her to rid herself of some of the nightmare. The revisiting of the past. *Oh, the wonders of medication and therapy!*

She would never forget. But that was okay; nobody wanted her to. It was the jumbling of it all up that terrified her, and that needed fixing. Revisiting wasn't the right word. It was the constant reliving of it all. The thinking she was still there, that Pierre was still alive when... Oh God, they'd shot him! In front of her. They'd shot him. *Stop it, Theresa, stop it... Don't go back. Not to all the fear and the heartbreak. Hold on. Hold on!*

Sitting down on the chair next to the window, she concentrated on steadying herself: taking deep breaths; telling herself everything would be alright. She just needed to get well.

Her thoughts went to her memoirs. The lads that had attacked her had never been identified, and her handbag with all her memories and memoirs in it had never been found. Again, she had to stop herself dwelling on this. They were probably rotting away in some hedge or taken away by the dustbin men and burned on some huge pyre that turned all the waste that humans discarded into ashes. *Dust to dust...* A shiver went through her. And yet, she hoped that had been their fate, which was better than the alternative of someone finding them and making a mockery of them. That possibility made her feel sick. *What possessed me to write it all down so graphically and, worse than that, to carry it around with me?*

Who knew where her mind had been these last years, but she hoped to God she was coming out of it. She'd managed it once – well, she'd fooled everyone that she had, just to get her release, but that had been silly. She needed healing, and healing properly, but would that ever take place?

The doctor had said for that to happen she'd have to be open about her life – about every aspect of it. Well, she had certainly been that in her memoir. Now that it was gone, could she be that open with anyone else? *My mother, even?* That lovely, fragile lady who would be hurt so badly by the truth? *Oh, God. If only...* But then, didn't Dr Stinstone say she had been speaking with her mother? That her mother knew about Jacques and had forgiven her? But how? How could she know unless Dr Stinstone had told her? She'd promised to keep her patient confidentiality. Had Rita told her mother? Oh, dear, she hoped Rita hadn't made mischief. Somehow, she needed to get away from Rita. She wished she'd never to see her again, in fact. Her head began to ache. She had so much to face, so much to put right. Could she? But then, if she wanted to get better and that's what it would take, she'd do it. She'd have to... Her limbs began to tremble again at this. Her mind began to let go... *No. Please, no.*

Lizzie – 1963

Lizzie had a feeling that nothing would ever be right again. All of the family was distraught at the news that Patsy had left the hospital. Ian was beside himself and had set off to go to Harri's. It would take him hours, but he didn't care, as he felt certain that was where Patsy would go. 'Perhaps,' he'd said, 'she's gone there to persuade Harri to come home and to do this whole wedding thing sensibly.'

Her own thoughts were not as kind towards Patsy. She'd seen something in her – something she knew well. A kind of madness ... no, she couldn't call it that. Patsy wasn't mad, but there was something that was like Ken. One minute they were fine, the next ranting about this or that, and they both dealt with things in a violent way. Look how Patsy had lunged at Ken, whereas shouting in her commanding voice could have been enough. And the vicious swipe she'd given her dad, when maybe if she'd taken the cunning way she could have persuaded him she was on his side and taken her chance later, once she had his confidence. And at times her way of thinking had been irrational; her thoughts over her mother showed this. No. *If Patsy has gone to Harri's, it isn't to persuade her one way or the other, but more likely to force the issue to go the way she wants it. She may*

334

even cause harm. A shiver passed through her at this thought and she felt glad she had escaped into her room.

No one needed her for anything. Sarah was lying down for a while, as the whole thing had taken its toll on her and Lizzie wasn't surprised! They'd only arrived here this morning, leaving everything reasonably sorted, then Ian had come home without Harri and with shocking, unexpected news, and by midday they'd heard Patsy had left the hospital! Sarah had calmed down now, but was exhausted.

Richard had rung to forewarn the hospital where Theresa was that Patsy could turn up there, but had found out Theresa had been moved. This had given them all a relief. None of them said why.

Richard and Sarah had also spoken to Harri and Greg. They had assured them that they would be fine and would be able to deal with Patsy if she turned up. Richard had tried to persuade them to come home in the circumstances, but Harri had wanted to go ahead with her plans. At least she was forewarned, thank God. And with Ian on the way, surely everything would be alright there?

With Richard now out at his surgery and David still at work, Lizzie had told Sarah she would be fine sitting in her room reading. Still feeling no stronger than she had earlier, she was glad of the chance to think through something Richard and Sarah had spoken to her about before the telephone had rung with the news over Patsy, and after they had explained to her about Harri.

It seemed Richard and his partner were trying to turn part of the rambling old building that housed the surgery into a cottage hospital, where they could deal with minor emergencies and look after any patients needing round-the-clock care, but not essentially in the hospital in Leeds, which was an hour away. Richard had put the idea forward and his partner agreed; he then discussed it with Sarah before approaching her. The idea was that she could be the practice receptionist, and she could start as soon as she felt fit! There was a lot of organizing of the medical records that had to be moved to where the new surgery would be, and the move had generated far more paperwork than the present part-time receptionist could cope with. The idea had excited Lizzie and lifted her, giving her life a purpose and lessening the burden she thought she might have been to Sarah and Richard. But then, with the news about Patsy, all that had dimmed into the new worry they all had to cope with.

Losing herself in Theresa's story always helped. Picking up the books, she wondered how Theresa, now almost nine months pregnant, would cope with childbirth and what they would do with the baby. From what she'd read earlier, when Richard and Sarah were tied up with everything, no one but Theresa and Pierre had known she was pregnant. Theresa had managed to conceal her condition from everyone, even the Pontés! She hadn't gained a lot of weight, and what she had gained she'd passed off as being due to the delicious bread Monsieur Ponté baked on a daily basis. Wearing a corset, which often caused her agony, had helped to keep the area most expanding from showing too much. And yet her missions had intensified.

She and Pierre were still passionate lovers. Some of Theresa's accounts of their love-making had set up longings inside Lizzie, and she wondered if there would ever be a man that wanted to love her in that way. She doubted it, and that made her sad. She may be confined to a wheelchair, but she wanted just the same things as other girls wanted. But even if it was a possibility, her chances of meeting anyone had now diminished. At least in London she could take herself out and meet people in the cafés she was able to get into. Here, she wondered if she'd be able to get out on her own. Even though the surface of the lane was smooth enough, some of the bends were very dangerous. If a car came round at speed, she could be killed. These thoughts set a sadness in her as she realized that in some ways she was more trapped now than she'd ever been. Opening the book, she decided to tackle her own problems later. For now she needed escape from them.

A Battlefield Baby – September 1943

Theresa could see the Germans over the ridge. The local intelligence had passed information to Pierre that Herr Gunter had ordered that his men go through a refresher course in battle-training. He'd been heard shouting that they were all getting soft and that they must be ready to fight in combat if called upon. His battle cry of *'Unser Führer könnte auf uns an rufen an jedem Tag!'* had been heard and interpreted as 'Our Leader could call us to arms any day' by Randolph – not the young man's real name, but she didn't know what that was.

Randolph, a German-born Jew, had been sent by his parents to live with a distant French relative who owned the flour mill in the area. When news came through that his parents had been taken to Auschwitz, his relatives adopted him. Randolph didn't look like a Jew and, in fact, attended the local Catholic Church with his adoptive parents, but in his heart he was one, and he hated his native countrymen.

Joining the Resistance at fourteen years old, and accepted because of his language skills, Randolph worked in a café, which was popular with the Germans. He was sixteen, but looked younger. The Germans took no heed of him when he waited on them. They discussed things they would not have done had they known he spoke their language fluently. The intelligence he picked up was delivered to his father at the mill and given to Pierre. This used to happen through Monsieur Ponté, delivered in notes hidden in the flour sacks, but now it came through various sources. It never came direct from Randolph.

In this instance, Randolph had learned when and where the training was to take place. The *where* had posed them problems, as it was close to their safe house and they had had to minimize their comings and goings. Pierre had not been able to visit during the last week, and had sent messages through various means about how they should prepare and where they should all be at a given time. They in their turn had dispatched the messages through a complex system to each of the men they would need to help them with this ambush.

Randolph had told them that from what he'd heard, it appeared Herr Gunter was disenchanted with his role of running the affairs of the occupation and security force and wanted to be on the front line. He had said what they had all been thinking: that he could see a day coming when the Allied troops made a big push to end the war. Very foolish and, Theresa thought, dangerous talk for a German. It could put him in deep trouble with his Führer, but it also showed a foresight that in her experience the Germans didn't usually possess. They seemed capable only of seeing their own victory and supremacy – at least, this was what they put over to the masses.

Out here on the edge of the wood, the German soldiers, complacent from their years of controlling and riding roughshod over the town and village people, were putty in their hands. Pierre had masterminded a plan to attack and kill as many as they could, steal weapons and ammunition, and generally disrupt Gunter's plans for his men being ready to take up arms to fight.

So near now to her time, lying face down on the damp grass sent excruciating pains through Theresa's stomach, which a couple of times had had her rolling over and drawing up her knees. Terrified as to the reason for them, she silently begged, *Not now, God, not now!* She couldn't go into labour tonight!

Though she couldn't see the others through the blanket of darkness, she knew they hadn't heard her movement. If they had, one of them would have come to her ready to shoot her if they thought she was signalling the Germans – their nerves were on edge to the point that it was difficult to stop them shooting anything that moved when it shouldn't during an operation. Fear of this had her clenching her teeth when the next pain gripped her. Sweat soaked her body. If only she knew where Pierre was…

In the camp below, men were drinking and laughing, giving the impression that they weren't taking their task seriously. For a moment she felt sorry for them, as they knew not what awaited them, but as they became more and more drunk, and began to sing, her mind cursed them. *Smug bastards!* They thought themselves invincible. This thought had hardly died before she heard women's laughter. *Collaborators!* Again, she felt sorry. Women often felt they had no choice but to provide pleasure for the soldiers. Often their own husbands forced them to do it for the money and protection it brought, and many lived in fear of reprisals if they didn't. However, no one saw this as an excuse, and the women lived a life of outcasts from their own society and under threat from both sides. The unattractive women were the worst condemners, braying for blood whenever they could and revelling in exposing the girls who succumbed. Well, these ones tonight would end up dead. They were too dangerous to leave alive. If they recognized any of the Resistance, they might betray them.

If only the soldiers would settle down and fall asleep. She didn't know how long she could last. Not crying out when a pain began to build had her biting her knuckles until she could taste her own blood.

A movement next to her had her turning, mid-contraction, gun at the ready. A wood pigeon's coo sounded, signalling that this was Pierre. Her fear for him at breaking the rule of the mission had her held in terror. She dared not acknowledge him.

They waited. Nothing happened. Pierre had got away with moving his position. How, she did not know, as she'd known a scared youngster amongst them to open fire on a rabbit once, compromising them all and ending the mission in disaster with two of their number dead.

Pierre squeezed her hand. Her response was a grip of iron as another pain took her. As it passed, she could feel the tension in his body and almost taste his fear. He touched her stomach and then her face, and she nodded her head as she interpreted his action as a question. His tap on her cheek told her he understood. He held her hands and lifted them to his mouth, putting hers on the outside so that she could feel him preparing to cup his mouth and send out the signal to abort the mission. She snatched his hands away.

What happened to her was of no consequence, as they would never get a chance like this again. On rare occasions they had killed the odd German in the village, but never did they have them all together and with their guard down, as they did now. They *couldn't* miss this chance. Besides, they were badly in need of the ammunition. The last drop from England had gone wrong and had had to be aborted. There wouldn't be another one for weeks.

Somehow, through two more very strong contractions, she managed to keep quiet. She didn't know how; she only knew that it was imperative she did as at last the Germans were beginning to settle.

When Pierre gave the signal it made her jump. His wood pigeon coo this time was loud and repetitive, cutting through the silence of the night. A couple of Germans stopped what they were doing and looked towards the trees. She held her breath, then released it as she saw them go about their business within seconds.

Unable to follow Pierre, Theresa watched as the figures of fifty or so men moving forward were silhouetted against the lights of the camp. Prayers for the success of the mission vied with those willing God to keep Pierre safe.

The first shot cracked the air and saw a soldier crumple to the ground. Caught unawares, more followed him as they dropped like skittles. Then return fire began, and she saw one of their own fall. Her heart thumped with fear. Watching it was far worse than taking part. Suddenly she saw a contingent that she hadn't seen before. More than a dozen Germans appeared from the back of the camp. They were setting up machine guns... *Oh no!* The Resistance, now engaged in heavy fire, hadn't noticed!

Another pain had her screwing up her eyes. It built and built and scrunched her into a ball. *Oh God!* This was madness. Her child couldn't be born here in this muddy field, miles from anywhere and in the middle of a battle. *Help me...*

God, help me!

As the pain subsided, her leg touched something. Her belt! She'd had to remove it earlier. Strapped into it were two hand grenades. She could disable the machine gun contingent! Turning round, she saw that they had the guns on tripods and were beginning to feed the strips of shot. The kneeling Resistance-fighters were a sitting target.

Grabbing her belt, she jumped up and ran the fifty yards that got her within throwing distance. Unclipping the grenades, she lay one on the ground and tugged at the pin of the other.

A splitting pain doubled her. *No! No!*

She had seconds. If she didn't throw it, she would die, blown to pieces – along with her child. Making an extreme effort, she straightened, and with everything that was in her threw the grenade, hitting the ground and covering her head as it left her hands. The explosion deafened her. Debris slapped her body. For one moment it seemed everything had stopped. The silence clawed at her, but then from a long way off noise began to filter through to her. Gunfire ... automatic gunfire. Had she missed?

Lifting her head, she saw the shots were coming her way! *Oh God!* Lying as flat as she could, she could feel the rush of air as bullet after bullet went over her head. Then it stopped. Looking up, she saw she hadn't missed: one gun and several men lay in a carnage of bodies and metal, but another had not been hit and was being re-fed with shot and made ready to fire again. Grabbing the second grenade, she pulled the pin. Her hands shook, and sweat ran into her eyes. She had to take the chance and stand up; she couldn't aim unless she did. *Don't let me miss. Please don't let me miss.* The grenade left her hand. She waited. The gun released a round, but it went into the air as the grenade landed and the men began to run. They were too late, and the explosion sent their bodies flying in all directions. An arm blown off one of their bodies came hurtling towards her and landed at her feet. Vomit billowed from her mouth as she sank down. Through her tears she saw the few German soldiers who were left alive running away in the direction of the town.

A pain more intense than any she'd felt before brought a scream from her that stopped the cheers of the men. The pain had hardly died before it built again. This time she screamed, 'Pierre... Pierre!'

His arms were around her.

'It's coming. The baby is coming... Help me!'

Holding her son close, tears of relief ran down Theresa's face as several men lifted her onto a makeshift stretcher. Once she was in Pierre's van, Pierre gave the men orders to drive the ammunition lorry as quickly as they could to one of their bunkers – safe, undetected dug-outs and caves. Here the lorry could be unloaded and then driven away and pushed over a cliff or set alight. The men would change into clean clothes and boots and leave their dirty clothes hidden away. The soldiers who had run away would take around four hours to get back to the town. Everyone should be back in their homes by then with no trace of having

344

been out, and the dead would be buried and their families moved to safe houses, as would the injured and their families.

The men had been chosen from outlying villages and towns scattered over miles and miles, so it would be very difficult to track them down. All had means of returning home within a couple of hours. None from the town had taken part, so any men living there – in the same town as the German headquarters and garrison – who were challenged would show obvious signs of the truth: that they hadn't been out of their beds.

Arriving back at their own safe house in the mountains, Pierre roused Madame Ponté. 'Take care of Olivia. She has given birth to our child.'

'*Quoi? Ce n'est pas possible!*'

'It is possible, and it has happened. Sorry, Madame, we could not tell you. We had to keep it a secret, but now the child is born and Olivia needs your help.'

Snuggled up in Pierre's arms, the baby asleep in a drawer made into a makeshift cot, the reality of their situation hit Theresa. 'What are we going to do, Pierre? How can we keep him safe?'

'I will have to take him to my parents'. There he will be safe. *Ma mère,* she will take care of him and rear him for us until we can go to him.'

Her heart screamed against this. She couldn't go through that again. She couldn't ... and yet, she knew she had to. No more words were spoken, not by her and not by Pierre. Her sobs and his silent tears said all they needed to say.

The low, early-morning autumnal sun woke her. She stretched out her hand, and the void of Pierre not being there opened up a chasm of pain. Her fingers touched the folded note on his pillow, where it lay in the indent left by his head. She didn't want to read it, knowing it would compound the physical pain she could already feel in her lead-weight heart. Compelled to do so, she unfolded it.

My darling, I am leaving early as goodbyes would be too painful. The journey will take me many days. I have a network of farms I can call at along the way. All will take us in and will care for us and give me clothes for our child. Those women who are breast-feeding children will not see our child go hungry. And those who are not will know someone nearby who is, so he will be fine. I have named him Jacques after my French grandfather, as he prospered and was a happy and good man. Luck and love followed him all of his life. I want that for our son.

My absence from the bank will implicate me, so that now I will have to go into hiding. They may think me one of the unfortunates who were killed. Whether it is safe for me to be at the house, I don't know, but we will talk about this when I return.

Stay strong, my Olivia. That will be difficult for you with your son torn from you and me not by your side, but please try. One day this will all be over and we can be a family. Remember, you are the breath to my body. The blood that courses through my veins, and the life inside of my heart. I need you. Be there, be your whole self for when I return.

Pierre xxx

Her body folded. She couldn't breathe. *Be my*

whole self. How can I be that when my very soul has been torn from me for a second time? My children! I ... WANT ... MY ... CHILDREN! Her screams came from the depths of her bowels. They scratched her throat and assaulted her own ears, but she couldn't stop them.

'What is it? *Ma chérie,* no. You must stop...'

The sight of Monsieur and Madame Ponté in their long, white nightdresses and with Monsieur missing his teeth and Madame's curlers sticking out of her mobcap turned her screams to laughter – a painful laughter that she could not control. It stretched her stomach muscles and bruised her ribs and went on and on. A stinging slap to her face halted it.

'Forgive me, *ma chérie,* I am sorry. You were hysterical.'

Through her sobs she reassured Madame that she was alright and that she had done the right thing, for if she hadn't the madness that was pulling her towards it would have won, and she didn't want that.

Once more her body wept, scrunching into her body, into her sobs, soaking her in tears, and draining her of all feeling, leaving an empty shell.

'When you reach the bottom, you can only come up, *ma chérie.* But it is you that must work hard to do so.'

She nodded. She knew Monsieur Ponté was right.

Sitting up sipping the hot coffee Madame had brought in for her a few minutes later, Theresa composed herself and began to work out a way of coping. The birth of her son had brought her daughter into vivid focus. For them she had to make it through this. For them she had to survive. She would write to her father and ask him to forbid whichever convent he had taken her daughter to from letting her out for adoption. Then she would collect her when she returned. This plan helped her. It gave her hope and a promise that one day she and Pierre and her daughter and their son would be a family. Pierre did not yet know of her daughter, but she knew he would understand and become a father to her. They would live in France, away from the stuffy English atmosphere with its social restrictions, and her children would be cocooned in love. Lying back, she thought: *I will call my daughter Olivia. Yes, to me she is Olivia, and she will honour the real Olivia with the life that she has, and the Olivia that her mother became in order to help save the world and keep it as it should be and as she and her brother should know it...*

1963

Lizzie let the book drop out of her hand. Theresa's description of her heart being as heavy as lead exactly matched what her own felt like. But she couldn't spill the tears it held for Rita and Ken, for Sarah and Richard and Ian and Harri. And, yes, for Patsy – poor lost Patsy, who should have had such a very different life. Because if she let one tear escape, like Theresa had, it would open a floodgate and she doubted she'd be able to stop.

Twenty-five

Jacques – A Shocking Revelation Back in England

Jacques had a silly excitement nudge the part of him that held all his sadness as he put the telephone down. He was settled in his mind that everything back home was okay and still feeling pleased with the legacies his grandfather had left for Verkona and for Gustov – enough to keep them in comfort for the rest of their days, a fitting tribute to them both, and a kind of compensation for all they had suffered.

Though he'd had it in his mind to do something by way of a gift if his grandfather hadn't managed to do it, it felt so much better that it had come directly from him. His grandfather's wording had been touching, saying how guilty he'd felt at not having tried to find out if anyone he'd known was still living and if they were okay, but he hoped they understood the reasons that had held him back from doing so.

Verkona had not wanted to take it at first, but he had seen that change when he'd insisted they go on a shopping trip. She'd soon got into shopping, which most of the women he knew took for granted, and had shopped to her heart's content, buying a whole wardrobe of new clothes for herself and for Gustov. It had been touching to watch her glee as she'd tried different outfits on, just as it

349

had been to see how her manner with Gustov had settled into that of a mother figure. Motherhood was something she had missed out on in life, and Gustov hadn't had a mother since he was a young man before the war. By the time he'd left, they had settled into the American way of life, and even though both were still unsure what they wanted to do, his solicitor was looking into getting them permanent residence – just in case.

And now, with all of that leaving him with a warm feeling, his grandmama had just told him she'd opened Tarrington House and wanted him to go there to be with her for this second visit! He couldn't understand why it made him feel like it did: as if he'd been given the best gift ever. Maybe it was that her asking him there meant he was really accepted, though he had to allow himself a wry smile as he realized his grandmother was still hiding him away in a sense – well, she hadn't asked him to York, which would put him where her friends would see him. And she hadn't yet put anything into motion about introducing him to the rest of the family. Still, it would all take time. She'd already done very well.

As he understood it from her description of Breckton, it was a small mining town. She'd told him that her sister, his great aunt, had owned the mine and most of the town, but they'd had to sell it all on her death to pay death duties and a large legacy she'd made to a local man. Something to do with the scandal she'd touched on of this aunt having an affair.

They had still run a sizeable farm and had reared race horses – at least his uncle Terence had, at ...

what was the place called? Something Grange? Oh, he couldn't remember. Anyway, that was gone too, but that didn't mean there wouldn't be people around Breckton who would still know her. Her household staff, for instance. She'd said she'd retained them, and people who'd lived there for a long time. These thoughts warmed him as they showed a willingness on his grandmother's behalf for some folk to know of him. Yes, it was a definite step in the right direction.

But what about his mother? He made his mind up that on this visit he would really press for access to her. It was his right. And now, more than ever, he *needed* to be with her.

The train journey had taken him through many places. Most of them had blurred into one another, as he'd nodded off every now and again after eating a large breakfast in the buffet car. Travelling on a night flight from America to London and then catching the train to Leeds, without stopping for a rest, had taken it out of him.

Now he was thankful that he'd arrived in Leeds and was getting into his grandmother's Rolls-Royce – a beautiful, sleek grey-and-black number that must have been twenty years old but still gave off an air of grandeur. The deep leather seats seemed to hug him, which was just what he needed after the hell of the last leg of his journey. The railway carriage had been full throughout, and the seats hadn't been the most comfortable. Not being a smoker, he'd not enjoyed breathing in his travelling companions' second-hand smoke either, but opening the window had prompted an

351

aggravated 'tut' from an elderly lady, so he'd closed it pretty quickly.

What he'd seen of England so far gave him an impression of everything being cramped together, but this changed as they left the outskirts of Leeds. Mile after mile of stunning scenery greeted him. Hills – some rugged, some sloping and some almost mountains as they reached majestic heights – were a backdrop to a patchwork quilt of farmland, broken only by quaint villages with their stone cottages and old churches. This is real England, he thought, and relaxed back to enjoy it.

It didn't seem long before the wheels of the car crunched on the pebbles of the drive up to the house, and as they emerged from the trees lining the drive and Tarrington House came into view, he didn't agree with his grandmother's description of it not being big! Even by American standards it was big, and back home in his own area there were some large colonial houses, their own included.

As soon as they pulled up in front of the steps leading up to the solid-looking oak door, it opened and the man who had been in attendance on his grandmother in the Ritz hotel came out and hurried down to open the car door for him. 'Nice to see you again, sir.'

'And you, Mr Davidson.' He wondered if the old chap knew who he really was, or if any of the staff did. He hoped so, as it could be awkward for both him and them. These speculations left him when shown into the lovely room off the grand hall and his grandmother opened her arms to him. 'Darling, it is good to see you!' Her face lit up and, he thought, looked younger, which brought home to

352

him what a strain he must have put her under when he'd first turned up with his shocking claims. Her silver hair, styled in a softer sweep into a bun in the nape of her neck, suited her, and her frailty had gone. Now she appeared a strong, relaxed lady, and this gladdened him. As he came out of her hug, he saw her look of concern for him and braced himself for her condolences.

'Sit down, darling. I'm so sorry about your grandfather. He sounded a lovely man and I had visions of one day meeting him.'

'You would have loved him, Grandmama, and he you. Oh, excuse me, sorry.' He'd thought he had himself together, but the tears that had threatened at the sight of her spilled over.

'Don't be, darling. I understand. And it is measure of how you look on me, as you should, as your grandmother, someone you can turn to. It is amazing how close to you I feel after such a short time. Look, this will cheer you up. I have some real coffee for you!' Her joy at this and how she thought it would cure all made him laugh.

'Is that what you think of us Americans? That coffee is the most important thing to us and will lift us, no matter what? Well, you obviously haven't heard, then, that most of the young prefer Coke!'

'Coke?'

Her look of astonishment had him laughing out loud. 'Not the stuff you have to sniff, Grandmama, the drink! Coca-Cola. Ice-cold and refreshing, though I think it does have some real cocaine in it.'

'Oh, well, we haven't got any. Sorry, darling.'

'I'm only kidding. Coffee is very welcome, and

especially this. It's delicious.' He felt sorry he'd made the joke now, as she'd obviously gone to a lot of trouble for him.

'One of my maids is from South America, and she told me you make your coffee from real coffee beans. I had some delivered from Selfridges of London. I have even tried it myself and enjoyed it, though I didn't have it as strong as you have it.'

After a few minutes of this chit-chat, she began to relax, and he felt able to ask her a few questions. 'Grandmama, have you made progress with my mother? I want to see her before I go to France. It seems important that I do, and especially now. Besides, I want her to know that I am going. She may need me to do something for her, but ... well, mostly I just can't wait any longer to meet her, to tell the truth.'

'Yes, I have, dear, and I am glad that you are continuing with your plans. They will help you to cope. And yes, it is good news where your mother is concerned. You can go to visit her...'

Listening to how his mother had been moved to a convalescent home and the progress she had made warmed him and soothed some of the hurt inside him. 'Gee, that's great. I wish I'd known. I would have spent a couple of days in London and gone to see her then.'

'I didn't want that, Jacques. I wanted us to go together.'

'Have things progressed that far? Tell me what's been happening! This is wonderful news!'

He listened to her telling him how the psychiatrist had been working with his mother and how his mother had opened up to the point where she was talking through her life. She was beginning to accept reality.

'She has done remarkably well in such a short space of time. The key seemed to be getting through to her that I know about you and am not ashamed of her.' Throughout her telling him this, his grandmother had held a pretty lace handkerchief, and now she dabbed her eyes with it. He felt his own eyes fill with tears at the sight, and crossed over between the opposite sofas they were sitting on and knelt by her, taking her hand. 'That must be wonderful for you to hear, Grandmama. I am so pleased. So, when can we go?'

'The psychiatrist wants us to wait a couple more days. Theresa is responding well, and talking in a coherent manner. She ... she has even spoken of her family – us ... me, I mean. Well, all of us. Her father, Terence, and ... you and ... well, there is something else. In order to help Theresa's recovery her doctor felt she should tell me about it. It is allowed apparently in those circumstances for a confidence to be broken. In this case the doctor felt that if I heard of it for the first time from Theresa, it might be too much of a shock. One that might make me cause a regression in Theresa if I reacted badly.'

'What is it, Grandmama?'

Her hand trembled in his. He waited.

'You have a sister.'

'What? Good God! A sister? Grandfather said nothing about another child.'

'He wouldn't have known. The shock was tremendous to me. It has taken me days to come to terms with it. The deceit... Oh, I don't mean Theresa. Well, not just her, but Terence, and my Charles.'

'You mean they all knew?'

'Yes, it seems it happened just as the war began. She went away. I knew nothing of it. I thought she was doing war work. Oh, dear...'

His concern for this woman who'd come to mean so much to him put his need to know more on hold for a moment. 'Don't fret yourself, Grandmama. You'll be ill. Tell me later. I can wait.' His words belied the truth. He wanted to know now. A sister? Just how incredible could his family's life be? A sister!

She leaned back and closed her eyes. All she'd gained in strength since the first time he'd seen her ebbed away from her. It seemed the knowing of it all hadn't been as bad as the telling of it as she said, 'Later or now, none of it is going to be less painful. She ... it seems she had an affair with a local. A man who...'

As the story unravelled, his own shock deepened. *What kind of person is my mother?*

With her frailty back, his grandmother now looked years older than when he'd arrived as she told him, 'And, darling, if that wasn't enough, she wrote it all down. In the years since, she has written her memoirs and ... and they are missing. They were in her bag – the one that was stolen. Oh God! The whole story could end up in one of those awful Sunday papers!'

It seemed this was more painful for her to take than all the deception and the loss of her grandchild. Sobs shook her body and she asked, 'What can we do? Dear God, what can we do?'

'Grandmama, don't. It will be okay. We'll go to a lawyer. We'll put an injunction on all the newspapers against the publication of any material to do with my mother.'

'This isn't America, dear. Whoever has the book may already have sold it to the *News of the World*. They only have to do a few checks as to its authenticity and they will go to press with it. It is a scandal and involves a family that is in the public eye, or used to be, and a war heroine. It will be considered as right that it is published. But, worse than that, what about the child – well, adult now, as she would be a couple of years older than you. She, like you, has been lost to me. If they had confided in me, I would have made sure she stayed with us. We could have found some story to cover up her true identity, though at that time she could have been passed off as the daughter of Theresa's ex-husband... Oh, you don't know about that.'

'I do, Grandmama.' As he told her how he'd researched the family and had read of his mother's very short marriage, he was relieved to feel his earlier thought of her only caring about the scandal dissipate.

'Oh, that's good, dear, as like me you have had enough shocks where your mother is concerned.'

'Well, I think we should both prepare ourselves for more. I think she is already showing she had a character you knew nothing about, and you are her own mother! Something bad must have happened to hurt Uncle Terence's wife, and I don't think it can be anything that we know already.'

'I know. I've been thinking about that. I can't ask

Louise, as it may be too painful for her. Perhaps Theresa knew something about Terence. She may even have the answer to what made him–'

'Don't think about it now. Yes, you have to accept that something more may be revealed, but none of this is your fault and you don't deserve this hurt.'

'Maybe it *is* my fault. I was very self-centred when they were younger. I left Theresa and Terence to their own devices. They were difficult to do anything else with. They were totally reliant on one another, and I accepted that. Twins are often like that to the exclusion of others, and they certainly were. I was too wrapped up in my grief for my sister and my insecurities where my husband was concerned to do anything about it. Silly, now I look back, but it was the done thing for husbands to have affairs. It was all around me, and I couldn't believe that Charles wouldn't do that to me. I became so that he had to give me his whole attention just to keep me happy. Those poor children! Even they had to tend to my every need, as I was considered frail. I deprived them of their father. I couldn't even share him with them. Oh, Jacques, I've been wicked ... wicked.'

'Grandmama, no! Don't do this to yourself.'

Her sobs were once more racking her body. He held her close, his confusion giving him more than he could cope with. He'd put this woman on a pedestal, and now she had fallen off, leaving him unsure of his judgement. But none of it mattered, did it? Surely all that mattered was the future and that they were all going to be united. One thing he did know: he would try to find his sister. That

358

might prove impossible if she was adopted, but he wouldn't give up trying. And what of her other family? They lived here in this very town, and they probably knew nothing about any of it!

Gradually, his grandmother became calm. 'I'm sorry, dear. I shouldn't have told you all of that. You will be sorry you ever found me.'

'Never, Grandmama. My grandfather had a saying: "Take as you find, son, but be prepared for what you think you have found turning out to be different than you thought." I did come over with this rosy picture of finding my wonderful family, and they would all be perfect and really happy to see me, and all the past would be forgotten, but somehow that would have been all false. Real people have failings and a past that has shaped them, and that's what you and Mother are: real people. But that doesn't make me love you less.'

'You have a lot of your grandfather on this side in you, darling. My Charles would have said something just like that in this situation. And at this moment I am very happy you are like him, as it means you won't run for the door.'

'That won't happen, I promise you. Now I have found you I am not going to lose you.'

She smiled at this and straightened her body, and all her dignity came back into her with the action. 'They say confession is good for the soul. Well, it is, but it gives you a thirst. Be a dear and pour me another cup of tea, darling. I really need one.'

It was with relief that he went to do the honours. As he picked up the milk, she said, 'Oh, you Americans! Tea first, dear. Tea first!'

She was back to her old self. 'That's more like it. I love it when you chastise me. Whether you'll succeed in Britainizing me, though, is another matter. Ha! You have some funny ways, you Brits.'

'Britainizing you! There's no such word!' She hit out at him in a playful way and giggled as she did so. It was a girlish sound that surprised him and made him wonder what she had been like when she was younger. A beauty, without doubt, but maybe a little bit of a tease. Definitely a woman who always got her own way with men, as she had him wrapped around her little finger. And even now that he knew she may have contributed to his mother's downfall with her self-centredness at a time when she should have been giving all her attention to her children, she was wrapped around his heart. If he'd had to pick his grandmother from a thousand women, he'd have chosen her.

They were both giggling now as he said to her, 'Here, ma'am, and I hope it's to your liking. If not, I'll see you outside and we'll do the ten-pace shoot-out.'

This had her putting her head back and laughing just as loudly as he had done. When she drew breath, she dabbed her eyes again, but this time it was in merriment. The time of shocking revelations and painful insights had lifted.

After taking a sip of her tea, she said, 'Enough of this fooling now. This is all a very serious matter and we have a lot to face, as has your mother.'

'Well, then, we will face it together. Poor Mother. She seems to have gone through hell. Even if a lot of it was of her own making, it has all brought her to a place where she can't cope alone.

But we'll make that right, Grandmama. Somehow, we'll put Mother together again and help her to enjoy life once more.'

'I hope so, dear. And I think you are just the person to do that.'

Twenty-six

Patsy – A Tangled Mind

Standing opposite the shop with its subtle night-lighting in the windows giving it a fairy-tale appearance, a moment of reality hit Patsy. *God! Am I mad? What am I doing?*

Her body began to shake. She tightened her grip on the cold metal of the can of lighter fuel, but didn't take it out of her pocket. If she did, that would be like she was really going to do it and she couldn't! Thoughts of Sarah and Richard, and yes, Ian, came to her. They'd be worried sick, and devastated if she carried out her plan. What if Harri was in the flat and she got hurt? But she couldn't be in there, could she? Ian hadn't said she would stay in Greg's flat. Run away with him to-morrow, yes, but if she knew Harri, Little Miss Prim and Proper who never let a man touch her, then tonight she'd be safe in a hotel somewhere and not even thinking of having sex until after the wedding.

A soft breeze flickered the net curtains of the flat above the shop. A shadow of a man silhouetted on them, elongated by the light behind him. It was him! Greg, that vile man who'd taken her sister away from her. Hate welled up and defeated the weakness she'd almost given into as a strength came back into her. *'You have to do this or you will never have Harri with you again!'*

Shut up! Shut up! Letting go of the can, her hands went to her ears in a desperate attempt to shut out the voice, but it persisted, telling her she needed to rid the world of the evil that was Greg King.

Feeling exhausted, she looked along the road. The bright light of the café she'd passed beckoned her. Maybe a hot drink would help. Her body was shivering uncontrollably. A tear ran down her cheek.

Once in the café, the cold of her still shivered her body and yet she was wet with sweat. Her chest hurt. Taking the bottle of respiratory drugs, she swallowed one, then thought about what she was doing. That had been her fourth or fifth dose. No wonder she was hallucinating! It must be that. She'd never heard voices before. But then, were they voices, or was it really just her talking to herself, urging herself to do something she really didn't want to do? She wished she could see Greg's flat from here. If those people would move from that table, she might be able to.

'Oh, Greg, where *is* she? I'm so worried about her. She's ill. Pneumonia doesn't just leave you; there's a recovery period where you are still in danger of a relapse.'

'Your parents seemed more worried about what

362

she might do than about her health, darling. Why was that? Is there something wrong with her? I mean, mentally? Is she capable of doing us harm?'

'No, she would never hurt me. I think like Ian: she is very cross at our plans and has decided to come to try to persuade us against running off to get married. Hopefully Ian will be here soon. He must be worried sick, but we have no news for him so can't ease his mind.'

'Yes, that's the most likely reason she is coming, and that makes me feel very guilty.'

'Don't, darling. Patsy knows how ill she is. She is almost a doctor, for heaven's sake! And she has no right to dictate to me what I do and what I don't do. She is obsessive sometimes, and very like...'

'What, or should I say, who?'

'Our dad. Well, what I've heard of him. Oh, Greg, you don't know anything about me, and yet we are marrying tomorrow! Doesn't that worry you?'

'Well, ditto, but it isn't stopping you!' He rose and came over to her, holding her to him. 'I know it is madness, but I love you. I would wait to marry you as long as you would stay with me, but I do want to marry you, and if that has to be at Gretna, then so be it.'

'I just couldn't settle unless we were married. And as I can't leave you, Gretna is the only answer. Our families have taken it well. It's just Patsy. Oh, I wish she'd just ring the bell!'

As if on cue, the bell did ring. Greg went to the window and looked out. 'It's Ian.'

Patsy had moved her seat. Now she could see the flat.

'Are you buying anything else, love, or are you just in here for a warm, 'cos we're not a charity, you know.'

'What? Oh, yes. I'll have another tea.' She had just about enough to pay for it. The man had taken her attention away, but when she looked back nothing seemed to have changed. Certain Harri wasn't there, she re-thought her original plan. If she went around the back of the shop she would find a door. There was always a back entrance to these shops. She could do what Lizzie had told her Rita had done and soak something – her cardigan, maybe – in the lighter fuel and then light it... No! My God! She couldn't do that! She wasn't an arsonist. She ... what was she? How could she hate someone so much, even though he'd saved her life and had risked his to do so? *What's wrong with me? I need help. But who can help me?*

''Ere, love, I don't know what's the matter with you and I'm sorry for your troubles, but my café ain't no place for sitting crying in. You're up-setting my customers.'

'But... Oh, I...' She hadn't realized she was cry-ing, but now she felt the wetness of her face and the desolation inside her. Getting up, she went to leave.

'Not without paying, you don't, miss. That's half a crown, ta very much.'

Giving the man the coin, she pushed by him. The night air had cooled and she shivered as she stepped outside. Pulling her short jacket around her, she walked back towards the shop on legs that would hardly hold her upright as they trembled under her. Sitting back down on the wall further chilled her as the coldness of the rounded concrete capping penetrated through her skirt. She felt so ill. Every breath was painful. Things around her took on shapes she couldn't make out. They blurred and stretched, faded, then became clear again. God! She was going to pass out!

A strong pair of arms held her. The familiar smell of a freshly washed shirt assailed her nostrils. She sank into it. She imagined it was Ian – strong, solid, Ian, who loved her... Whoever it was carried her up some steps and into a brightly lit room.

'Oh, Patsy. Patsy...'

'Harri?'

'Yes, love. You're alright, love. We've rung for an ambulance. Eeh, lass, what were you doing leaving the hospital? I'd have come and seen you in a couple of days.'

'I – I didn't want you ... to leave me. You ... left me for ... for someone you hardly know.'

'I haven't left you, you daft ha'p'orth! We'll see each other a lot. You could transfer to the same London hospital that I am hoping to. You could live nearby. There's all sorts as could happen. It'll sort out. Oh, Patsy. Look, love, you're not well. Let's get you to hospital.'

'You won't go tomorrow, will you?'

'Yes. I can't not go. Me and Greg love one another. I can't explain it; it just happened. I can't leave him and only see him every few weeks. I want to stay with him and for that we have to be married.'

'No. No! You're mine...'

'Patsy, don't. Harri has a life of her own and you have to let her live it. I'm here for you.'

'I don't want you, Ian. I want Harri!'

Greg stepped forward. 'Well, I think you're being very childish. For goodness' sake! I know it is sudden and you are looking at your sister moving away, but that is a natural process, and it's ridiculous for someone training to be a doctor to act in this manner!'

'Greg!'

'I *hate* you!'

'Patsy!'

'I *hate* him, Harri. He took you. He–'

'Patsy, stop this. You're ill and you'll make yourself worse. Harri, you and Greg leave me with her. Go on, she doesn't know what she is saying. This isn't Patsy. It's someone who is very sick and delirious.'

Without speaking they left the room. 'Now, Patsy–'

'I don't want you, Ian, I told you. Can't you get that through your thick skull? You're everything I don't like in a man; you're soft; you're a "yes" man; you do everything everyone wants you to even if you don't want to do it. You make me sick!'

'Well, at this moment, I'm all you have, so shut up and do as you're told. Because if you insulted me till kingdom come, I'd still love you. There, I've said it. I love you, Patsy Crompton, even though sometimes I don't like you. But all of that is by the by. If you don't calm down, you won't be here to hate anybody, because you'll bloody well die!'

Her sob tore at his heart. Sitting on his haunches next to where she sat on the sofa, he gently laid her down. She didn't resist. Her body trembled violently. Her breathing laboured and her eyes, her still bloodshot eyes, looked out at him, their expression pitiful. 'Help me, Ian. Help me...'

'I will, love. Lie still while I fetch a blanket.'

Going through to the kitchen he found Harri encased in Greg's arms. Her crying – a gentle sobbing. Greg stroked her hair. 'Come on, love. Everything will be alright. Like Ian says, she's ill and not in her right mind. She's probably hallucinating or something.'

'That's right, Harri. That's not the Patsy we know, now, is it? Look, I need a blanket or something. She's shivering, and it ain't a natural shiver. It's taking all her body.'

The Harri he was used to came back in an instant. 'It'll be the shock to her system. We need to get her warm. Greg, have you a hot-water bottle?' To his nod, Harri added, 'Right, you get it filled up. Ian, you come into our... I mean, Greg's bedroom with me.'

Within a few minutes they had Patsy warm and her shivering had stopped. She had no fight in her now. No insults to shout at him. She lay as if in a coma – still, and with her eyes closed. Her breathing came in short rasps, and her lips had a blueness about them.

'For God's sake, where's that damned ambulance?'

As Ian finished saying this they heard the tinny sound of a siren. 'Oh, thank God, Harri, they're here!'

Ian had stayed all night at the hospital, and it felt to him as if he'd lived in such places for the last couple of weeks. He'd rung home and assured them that everything was alright. He and Harri had decided they wouldn't tell Mam and Dad about the state Patsy was in or the full extent of her reactions, because both had seen something in Patsy that had frightened them, but both were worried they might be reading more into her delirium than was there. And so he'd only let his parents believe that it was as they'd surmised: that she'd made her way to London to try to stop Harri from making a rash decision. He'd explained that she was showing signs of delirium. He felt he had to do that much, but in this his dad had settled him somewhat, saying it was normal in someone with such a high fever and having been through the trauma Patsy had. Not to mention the side effects of the medication she'd taken.

His dad had promised to find out where her mother was now and to talk to her doctor about Patsy. It would be up to him or her if they would allow Patsy to visit, or at least to pave the way for her doing so.

This didn't sit easily on Ian's conscience. He'd have felt better telling his dad the whole truth about the extent of Patsy's actions and asking his advice as to whether they could all be put down to her being unwell, or whether there was a possibility of some other underlying mental health problem. *What if I say nothing and then she does harm someone? Harri, or her mother, even?*

It all weighed heavy in him. He'd never seen

Patsy like this. There had been something in her eyes, as if she was out of control. And with what he'd heard of her real dad and now her mother... *Is it possible there is something wrong with Patsy? Am I doing her any favours not confiding my fears?* These questions stayed with him as he sat at her bedside, and all of them had their root in him finding the lighter fuel. *Why would she have that on her? She doesn't smoke...* His mind would only give him one reason, and that shuddered a horror through him.

Patsy didn't stir for a long time, and when she did she had nothing more than fear in her eyes. Her whole demeanour was one of a fragile, hurt and scared child. She gave off an air of panic as she looked around her. This calmed when her eyes settled on him and then she'd closed them again and fallen back off to sleep. It was as if his presence was helping her. And though he ached from sitting on the hard chair and could have done with a cup of tea, he wouldn't leave her. Not even for a second. What if she woke while he was gone?

It took a lot for him not to read something into how she seemed to want to be assured he was with her, and he told himself that any one of them would have had the same effect. Just to see someone you knew was sitting with you when you were in a frightening place, as she must be, would be a comfort. But a little part of him hoped.

An hour later when she woke, it was as if nothing had happened, and he couldn't think why he'd had such thoughts about her as she smiled at him and said, 'Hello, you.'

'Hello, yourself. How're you feeling?'

'Better. Different. I – I did a silly thing, didn't I? I don't know why. It all seemed like my world had come to an end. Well, the world where I'd landed when I found Harri and all of you. I – I mean, the kidnap and ... and the rape, and then the... Oh, Ian, I'm sorry. It just ... I just couldn't bear to lose Harri on top of all of that.'

'It's alright, love. And you've not lost Harri. How can that happen? She's just moved on to another phase of her life. It could've been you doing that. But like you say, it happened at a bad time for you. It was just too much for you to cope with.'

'I didn't mean any of it. I don't hate Greg, nor you.'

'I know that, and so does Greg. You were delirious. Out of yourself. Everything will be alright, I promise. The doctor said you have been through what they call the crisis of the pneumonia. When they took your pulse and everything the last time, they said you would be on the mend from now on and probably able to recuperate at home. I'm just waiting for them to give me the say-so and I'll have you in me car before you can think about it.'

'Oh, Ian, that would be good. I can't wait to get back to normality. How's Lizzie coping?'

'Well, she hadn't had much time to settle when the worry of where you'd popped off to hit us all. I think she'll be alright. It must all be a bit strange for her. She'll settle, especially when you come home. You'll be company for each other.'

'I'm not stopping at home. Just as soon as I can get back to my studies I'm going to get Dad to fix it so that I can work as a student doctor in the same hospital as Harri.'

His heart sank at this, and it wasn't just because she would leave him behind, though that would hurt, but because he was afraid of how that would pan out for Harri and Greg. He decided he wouldn't say anything. Not now. He didn't want to upset her again. He wanted her well and at home where Mam could take care of her and Dad could work his magic on her and hopefully get her to change her mind.

'Di-did you find... I mean, was...'

'Aye, I've got it. What were you thinking to do with it, Patsy?'

'I don't know. I was, like you say, out of myself, but then I kept realizing what I was doing. It was very weird and a horrible feeling. One minute I... Oh, I can't believe it all now, but I do know that in my sane moments, I knew it was something I wouldn't ... couldn't do. The real me couldn't do it, only the demented me. You believe me, don't you, Ian? You know I wouldn't harm anybody. Don't you?'

He didn't know what to believe any more. He only hoped he'd never see the likes of the evil he'd seen in her again, but felt he could give her the reassurance she needed, with reservations. 'I do, but I'm worried, love. I think as you need help, just to make sure you're ... well, I mean, after all the trauma and that.'

'I know. I'll talk to Dad. I'll tell him everything and he'll sort it. He'll get me some counselling, but in a discreet way so that it isn't in my records, as that could affect my career. They won't allow someone who is unstable to work as a doctor.

And I'm not that. I just had a sort of breakdown due to what had happened, that's all.'

Ian felt better at this. Of course that was all. It would happen to anyone who'd experienced what she had. He couldn't give his mind to the horror of it, let alone think about what it would be like to actually go through it. 'I reckon as that's it. And your breakdown manifested itself in how possessive you are of Harri.' She looked cross at this. 'Now there's no use denying it. In fact, it would be harmful to your recovery to do so. You know you have become more and more attached to Harri. You seem to look on her as the only person who could make you happy.'

She was quiet for a long moment, then she said, 'You're right, of course you are. I know that. I just don't know why. Anyway, since when did you become the psychiatrist in the family? I thought you were only interested in farming?'

'I was. Well, that's not true, not really. I was just lazy and took a while to make me mind up what I really wanted to do.'

'Wow, this is a new Ian! What are you thinking of doing? Not medicine?'

'Yes, just that. I haven't spoken to Dad yet, but I will. I want to be a psychiatrist. I am fascinated with the workings of the mind, how it can play tricks, and how it can jumble up the memory ... oh, everything really. But I'll probably be a GP first.'

'Well, well. Good for you! I'm really glad to hear it. It annoyed me how you wasted your brains and education – things that came easy to you while I had to work after school and miss out on stuff my friends did, and then look for crappy work to do to pay my way through college. Not that it turned out that I had to in the end, as I found all of you, and your dad and mam saw to everything, but...'

'Aye, I know. I must have appeared such a wimp to you. I was, in a way. A lazy bloody wimp!'

She laughed and put out her hand to him. As he took hold of it, she smiled at him through a haze of tears. 'Help me to get better, Ian. I don't want to be like... Like me dad was.'

'I will, love. And you won't be like him. From what I've read about what ailed him, there's only scant evidence that a second generation can develop the disease, and you haven't shown any sign of a split personality. You're always the same. You have a jealous streak in you that has at times been obsessive, but that is due to your background, and you've had a bad episode due to trauma. But that is all, and both can be sorted with help. So forget all that. Just don't think of it, then it won't be another obsession. You will get well, I promise.'

'Oh, Ian ... I – I've not always been kind to you, have I? But then the old Ian drove me mad! I think I like this new Ian.'

'Only "like"?'

'We'll see.'

Her smile gave him hope and warmed him through, as had their little talk. It had erased his worries and he now saw that she could get better. He no longer thought, like he had feared, that there was anything wrong with her that couldn't respond to the proper care and help. His heart swelled as she continued to cling on to his hand.

Twenty-seven

Jacques – A Chance Meeting

Breckton 1963

What he'd seen so far of Breckton, Jacques liked. Even the row of old miner's cottages had a charm about them, and he loved the leafy lane that he now walked down that led to Hensal Grange. It all had a feel of what he'd imagined England would be like, and to think of his ancestors walking or riding their horses up and down this lane gave him a sense of nostalgia.

As he came up to two cottages on the right of the lane, a guy of about his own age came out of one of the gates. He was dressed in riding clothes and he doffed his cap in acknowledgement.

Jacques smiled to himself at this very British custom. 'Hello, I'm a visitor here.' Why had he said that, when it was obvious he was? He felt foolish now, but pressed on. 'I'm just on my way to look at the house at the bottom of the lane. My ancestors used to own it.'

'Well, you'll not find anyone in. The folk as own it now don't live in it. They come now and again to have a sort of holiday. They go shooting and fishing and horse-riding. I work there, like me granddad and me dad before me. I keep the garden done reet and see to the horses, exercise them

374

and that. I could let you have a look round, if you like. Not the house, though you'd do no harm looking through the windows.'

'Great, I'd like that. Thanks. Jacques Rueben.' He held out his hand as he said this. The guy took it saying, 'Ardbuckle. Benjamin Ardbuckle. What ancestors did you have live here, then? I reckon as Breckton is a long way from where you're from.'

'My grandmother and before her my great-aunt Laura, and before her, her husband's father.'

'You're talking about the Cromptons and the Harveys, I reckon. How come you being an American are related to them? Not that I knew them much, as they left when me dad worked there after... Well, there was an incident.'

'Yes, I know about that. Tragic. I'm...' He was about to say he was a grandson of Lady Daphne's, but they had reached the church. The building took his breath away, but not as much as the girl did. She was with a woman who he thought might be her mother. The woman was bending over a grave putting flowers in a vase. The girl's waiflike appearance gave him a sense of looking at someone not from this world. Her hair, fair and long, wisped out from around her face. The flowers she held added to her beauty, enhancing her fragility.

'Is she owt to do with you, as she's the second stranger round here today, and that don't happen often. Having one in our midst is a rare thing.'

'No, I don't know her.'

'I know the woman with her. That's Sarah Chesterton, as is now. The doctor's wife. Used to be Armitage before that, and Fellam before that. Not that that tells her story. She's had a rough time in the past and has a few to visit in the churchyard. The girl's a pretty thing. Pity about her being in a wheelchair.'

Somehow he hadn't registered the wheelchair, but the name Armitage struck a chord.

'Well, man, I can't stand here watching pretty girls, even if me boss ain't in residence. I haven't to be late back from having me breakfast. Them horses need their run out.'

It felt funny to be called 'man' by someone who was the same age. 'Oh, yes, sorry, I'll come with you.' As he said this the girl looked up and smiled. He smiled back. Her expression changed to one of ... shock or surprise, he couldn't tell, but he had the feeling that for a moment she thought she recognized him.

He wanted to go over to her and ... well, he didn't know what the 'and' was, but he did know something strange was happening to him. He waved and the girl waved back. Benjamin sighed. There was an amusement in his voice as he called out, 'Mornin', Mrs Chesterton. It looks like it's going to be a grand day. You got visitors?'

At this the woman stood up and looked at the girl and they both laughed. Benjamin just smiled and walked on, not at all offended by what looked to Jacques as if they were laughing at Benjamin.

'By, she smacked you where it's nice to be smacked, didn't she? Well, I know what that feels like. My girl did that to me the first time I looked at her. We're going to be wed this year. Eeh, I can't wait! "Nothing till the wedding night, Benjy," she says. It's a long wait, man.'

'Didn't you mind them laughing at you? I

thought it was a bit rude of them.'

'Naw, it's a standing joke round here, and one Mrs Chesterton must have told the girl. Every stranger seen in these parts becomes the subject of gossip and curiosity. You'll be one yourself. It'll be round afore we get to the grange that there's a new man in town. And with a new girl here as well, they'll have a field day. Brighten up their lives, it will, all the speculation!'

This made Jacques feel uncomfortable, but his grandmother must have known that would happen, surely? Maybe she thought it better over with, and that the sooner the people here got used to him being in existence the better. Though that didn't seem right, seeing as his presence could open up old wounds. Not as many as his sister could, though. God, when she was found it would stir something up! And for that lady they had just met, too – Mrs Chesterton, formerly Armitage – as she must be the wronged widow. A shudder went through him. He couldn't have said why.

By the time he and his new friend had looked around Hensal Grange – a place of beauty but a place whose secrets gave it a sinister air, making him not like it one bit – Benjamin was very behind with his chores. 'I'd be glad to give you a hand, Benjamin. I'm a dab hand with horses. We don't keep them at home, but I have a friend who does and spent a lot of my childhood around them and helping with them.'

'Aye, well, I'd be glad of it. There's them around here that would report me being late with me work soon as look at me if they get the chance, and I don't want any question over whether I slack when

377

the boss isn't around, but in them clothes?'

'Oh, these denims are my mucking-around gear. Don't worry about them.'

'Mucking around? Eeh, I'd love a pair of them for the barn dance, but can't run to them. You Yanks have allus had more than us lot. In the war we used to say of you, "overpaid and over here". They still do where you've got your military bases here.'

'Ha, yes, I've heard that. And I've heard as your men didn't like how our lot took all of your women!'

They both laughed at this. He liked this fellow. He was a good sort. 'Look, don't take this the wrong way, but you and me are about the same size and I have a pair of Wranglers that I haven't worn yet. I'd like to give them to you, as a sort of thank you for the welcome you've shown me.'

'Eeh, man. I'd not take that the wrong way! I'd be glad of them. By, I'd strut me stuff at the next dance. Me girl had better watch out for me an' all. Ha, ta very much.'

A warm feeling entered Jacques at this. He put his back into helping Benjamin with saddling the horse he was going to ride and reining the other one to it. They talked on during the process. Benjamin's questions weren't what you could call digging for information, just general and like-for-like, but he had given Jacques most of his life history by the time they parted, and Jacques knew a lot about his own family history in exchange. None of it he liked.

It appeared that Benjamin's grandfather, Gary Ardbuckle, had worked for Jacques's great-aunt

Laura. Gary Ardbuckle hadn't liked her and had seen the tricks she got up to to 'snare' (as Benjamin's grandfather had put it) the unassuming but very nice Jack Fellam. The rest of the story was horrific, with the only saving grace being that his great-aunt left a legacy to Jack, and he was now doing very well with his own farm. The stories went on, and some of what he heard was hard to take in. His own mother, who he hadn't identified to Benjamin, 'frolicking' as he put it with a Land Girl, and rumoured... God, he couldn't think of it! He felt physically sick! He managed not to show this, but the information gave him a possible reason for his uncle's suicide. His uncle must have come to a point where he couldn't put it behind him any longer, as according to Benjamin he was very much in love with his wife and loved his family, and had settled down to an idyllic family life working hard on his stud farm – the farm he'd procured from the unfortunate Jack Fellam, by all accounts. None of this endeared Jacques to his late uncle. And it was unforgivable what he'd done to his mother if the rumours were true. But it did give a reason behind the mystery. Thank God his grandmother didn't know of this! And judging by the blow it was to himself, he hoped she never did. No, whatever happened over the coming weeks, he would do his best to protect her from it. For the umpteenth time he asked himself, *What kind of a woman IS my mother?*

This thought mellowed as Benjamin carried on speaking with what Jacques could only describe as pride about his mother's war efforts. 'The town is reet proud to have her as one of us. There's one of the new streets named after her, on that posh estate on the perimeter of the town. Eeh, man, you don't look well. I haven't said owt... Eeh, me dad allus says as I let me tongue rule me brain. I'm sorry, man. I forgot these are your relatives.'

'No, it wouldn't make a difference, don't worry. I wouldn't like to hear of things going on like that no matter who the people were. I'm a bit of a softie. One of my tutors always said I'd end up being a do-gooder and waste all of my education if I wasn't careful.'

Benjamin laughed at this and the moment passed. But even though hearing of the street named after his mother pleased him, he couldn't get the thought of her and her own brother out of his head! Still, Benjamin had said it was just rumour, so more than likely there was no truth in it. Benjamin broke into his thoughts.

'Look, I've enjoyed your company, and I'm glad I haven't said owt out of turn, but I have to get going now.' He mounted the saddled horse and looking down from his elevated position said, 'Why don't you come at the same time tomorrow? There's some riding gear here. I'll contact me boss. He's a good sort, so I'm sure he won't mind you riding one of the horse to exercise them, 'specially when I tell him about you being related to them as used to live in the Grange.'

'Gee, that would be great! Thanks, I will, and I'll look forward to it. See you then. And don't worry about telling me about my family. It's fine. I asked the questions. My grandfather had a wise head on him, and he had many sayings. One was, "If you don't want to hear the truth, don't ask."

So, going by that, if anything upset me it is my fault for asking, not yours for telling.'

Benjamin's laugh rang out as he rode off.

Back at Tarrington House, he felt disappointed that the girl had gone by the time he walked back down the lane, as he'd made his mind up to talk to her. Now he'd have to find out where she lived and call on her, which would be a little embarrassing, to say the least.

His grandmother was pleased that he'd been to the Grange, 'Oh, how lovely, and did you like it? I was very happy there until Charles died. I moved out then, leaving it to Terence and his growing family, and came to live here. I always loved it, right from when Laura first took me there for a garden party with her then-boyfriend Jeremy. He was a really nice man. It was so sad when he was killed in the First World War. Poor Laura, her only child had died at his birth only two years before. She was very lonely after that. It was her loneliness that caused the scandal I told you of.'

She had said there had been a scandal, but hadn't told him what. Well, he knew now and he didn't think being lonely was enough of a reason to seduce another woman's husband. Nor, when thwarted, to take actions that would cause such devastation to innocent lives. He didn't say so. He just told her about the street named after his mother, which thrilled her, 'Oh, we'll have to drive down Theresa Street. That has a lovely ring to it, doesn't it? Theresa Street. What a lovely, fitting tribute. I'm so glad that what she did in the war hasn't gone unmarked. Oh, I know she was awarded a medal, and I'm very proud of that, but to have something here where she always loved being ... that is very special. I wonder if she knows?'

'Maybe. Wouldn't they have to get her permission? Anyway, Grandmama, I was wondering if you knew where the Chestertons live?'

'Chestertons? Oh, yes, that was the name of the young doctor who came to live and practice here. He was stepbrother to... Megan Armitage – oh, I mean Fellam.' She paused and looked troubled, no doubt remembering the sorry story he'd just heard, and the connection of his mother to the Armitages. After a couple of seconds she continued in a way that showed her pain at this: 'It was his marriage to Billy Armitage's widow that brought him to these parts. I – I told you about her yesterday. I know they did move into Hartington House quite a while before I left here, with their little girl…Well, not theirs. Billy Armitage's child.' Again she paused, but soon recovered and told him where the house was, finishing with, 'Oh, dear, such a lot of history and none of it really good. Even Hartington House is tied up with your Great-Aunt Laura's family.' She told him of the girl who'd lived there and how she came to marry Laura's father-in-law.

'Well! Will I have something to tell my friends at home about! I feel like I've landed in the middle of one of those Greek tragedies! I certainly wasn't born into a boring old, stuffy English family. Gee, I feel quite notorious.'

This made her laugh and he felt glad of that. She'd no need to carry all that had happened on

382

her shoulders as if it was somehow her fault, but he worried about whether it would be a good idea to call on the girl as he'd planned. But then, he didn't have much choice in that, as his heart compelled him to do so. He'd go later after lunch, but he wouldn't tell his grandmother. She hadn't asked him why he wanted to know – probably too wrapped up in her thoughts and memories to even wonder.

Lizzie sat in the garden after she and Sarah returned home. The sun was warm and Sarah had left the blanket around her that she'd put over her to take her for a walk. The stories Sarah had told of each of those whose graves she'd put flowers on were very sad. But overriding the thought of these were two emotions that vied for prominence in her.

One of these pressed heavily on her – the worry she'd had about having any independence whilst she was here. Just that one walk had shown her that this town, that seemed stuck back in another age compared to London, had too many pitfalls for her to even attempt to go out on her own. Many roads were still cobbled rather than tarmacked and the lanes held danger of her not being seen by oncoming traffic. Then there were hardly any dropped pavements, and even the pavements themselves were very narrow and often had a couple of wheels of a parked car on, which made it impossible for her to pass by. Even with Sarah's help it had been difficult. Her chair was heavy for anyone to push, which had had to happen on more than one occasion.

Then there were the strange emotions she had over seeing the young man. On the way back, Sarah had teased her about how he'd seemed taken with her. 'Eeh, lass, he couldn't take his eyes off you.' She'd laughed with her, saying she didn't think anything like that could happen to her, but at the same time hadn't been able to shake this feeling that he'd somehow taken a part of her. Oh, she couldn't explain it, but it disturbed her. Mostly in a nice way. And then, there was this other thing she couldn't get out of her head, that she had seen him somewhere before. Especially when he smiled. He had a rakish kind of smile... That was it! His smile and the way his dark hair flopped to one side... He was so much like Pierre! The image of him, in fact. But how could he be? It must just be a coincidence. Or, she'd just forgotten what the pictures looked like. But no, that wasn't possible; she'd looked at them so often, especially the one of Pierre! This thought made her blush as it came to her how she'd even fantasized over it, imagining that he was her lover and not Theresa's. The reddening of her deepened as she thought of the sexual feelings she'd had in these moments.

'Are you hot, dear? Oh, I didn't mean to make you jump!'

'No, I – I'm fine. Oh, thanks.' Sarah had brought her tea and biscuits on a tray that had little legs so it sat across her knee. 'I don't want to be a trouble to yer, Sarah, I will be able to do more when I'm feeling better.'

'Aye, I knows that, love. You don't have to keep saying it. But, it's a pleasure to do things for you till then. And it helps me an' all. Oh, by the way,

I rang Richard. He's going to try to get you a chair that will be more like what you need to get around the house. So that'd be good. We'll do our best to get everything reet for you, love. We love that you're here and know you hate having to be waited on.'

A lump came to her throat at this. She felt so helpless.

'There's sommat else, an' all, love. Richard has had some news. Look. Have a sip of your tea...'

'What is it, is it bad?'

'No, not bad, but upsetting for you. They think they've found your brother's body...'

Her breath caught in her lungs at this.

'I'm sorry, love. But in a way it's best. The police told Richard that they are taking your dad to identify him. They think it will be too much for you. Eeh, lass, you're shaking. Here, drink some tea. I've put a bit more sugar in it to help with the shock.'

The tea didn't steady her. It only made the turmoil in her stomach worse as she vomited, choking on the remnants of the bile left in her throat.

'Eeh, love. Come on, now. Let it all out. Don't worry about owt. Stuff can be cleaned up. You're the main thing. You've had a lot to contend with. Your life's changed in such a short span of time.'

After a moment she controlled the retching spasm. 'Thanks, Sarah, I'm sorry, it was such a shock even though I've been expecting it.'

'Aye, there was no easy way to tell you. Let me get this lot off you and I'll bring you some water to drink to clear the taste from your mouth. Then we'll see about cleaning you up, eh? Eeh, lass,

385

you've a lot coming at you, but we're with you every step of the way. I promise we'll be with you.'

This brought a comfort into her and as she had done before she thought, how was it that there were such people as Sarah and Richard in a world that mostly seemed to hold bad people? She'd never met anyone in her life like them before, but she was glad she had now, when she most needed them.

Twenty-eight

Lizzie and Theresa

1963 and 1944

Back out in the garden, where she'd asked Sarah to take her after she'd helped her to wash and change her clothes, Lizzie sat a moment thinking of Ken and Rita. She missed them, and yet in another way she felt a release from them, because between them they had shackled her – one with his obsession and the other with a weird kind of love. Rita's love for her was sometimes like that of a mother, but at other times it was conditional, and when those conditions weren't met, all hell would break loose. She was better off without them, and yet she felt so lost. Back then was familiar. They weren't good times, but they were *her* times, her surroundings, her way of life, her family…

386

Sarah had told her that Rita's body was to be released, and that they didn't think they would need to hold Ken's for long. An autopsy to determine that his death fitted with their stories would take place this afternoon, then they could have the body in a couple of days. Richard had already found an undertaker willing to fetch the bodies from the morgue and take them to the crematorium nearby. It was just a matter of when and if she wanted to attend and have a service for them. She didn't know if she did or not. In one way, she had already said her goodbyes, but in another, she felt as though something was missing from that, and maybe a service was what was needed. Not that she thought it would save either of their souls, though Rita had redeemed herself a little by trying to free Patsy. In a way she had saved Patsy's life.

Releasing the lever that kept the back of her chair upright, she leaned back until she was in a relaxing position. With the comfort of this she felt she could read a while and take her mind off things. When she'd last left off after reading about a couple more successful missions, Theresa and Pierre were about to be involved in resistance that would assist the planned D-Day landings. They had moved north with those men who could go with them, and had joined forces with other Resistance groups.

With so many now available to carry out the operations assigned to them by Command on or around the sixth of June, their own mission would be to sabotage the advance of any reinforcements that the Germans sent to the area once they knew an invasion had taken place.

Pierre was to head a group who were to sabotage German railcars just as soon as they knew which divisions were on the march and from where. The most likely one, and the one many spies were watching and gathering intelligence on, was the 2nd SS-Panzer Division, Das Reich, one of the most elite forces of the German army, at present stationed in the south of France following their campaign in Russia. The Resistance knew they had to do everything possible to delay their advance should they be deployed.

Theresa was also linked up with other SOEs, and between them they took responsibility for missions and intelligence-gathering. As her involvement was with Pierre's division and would take place immediately following the landing, she and Pierre could escape for a few days.

Both were beside themselves with joy at the prospect of seeing Jacques, now nearly nine months old. And Pierre was really looking forward to seeing his parents again.

Finding the page she'd marked with the photo of Pierre, Lizzie took a moment to look at him again. Shocked at just how much the young man she'd seen earlier really did look like Pierre, she stared at every detail. Even the dark shaven appearance was the same, and the smile had been identical – sort of lopsided, with an uplift of one eyebrow. It was uncanny. She had to force herself to tuck it into the front of the book and begin to read.

A Dangerous Mission of Extreme Importance – June 1944

It was a relief when they pulled up outside the farm. They had taken a great risk driving down, and it had taken them ten hours as against the normal six or seven. The couple of times they had been stopped by German road blocks, they had used their practised ploy: Theresa, with her dress stuffed with a cushion, had screamed in pain, and Pierre had begged that they let them pass and get on their way. Both were disguised – Pierre as a miner, his face, hands and nails pitted with soot, and wearing clothes of the type a workman wore. His hair was coloured ginger, while Theresa wore a wig, having refused to have her own hair dyed again. Her dress was that of a peasant, and her teeth looked as though they were rotting. Their van was old, and they said it had been lent to them.

The one time when they were miles from anywhere and not going in the direction of a city where there was a hospital, they had said they had been on their way to take Theresa to relatives for the birth when the pains had started. They now needed to get there as soon as possible, but if they didn't make it they would stop at a farm and beg for help.

The tension had been enormous, as more than once they had pulled off into a farmyard when they could see German vehicles in the distance. Only the last few miles had been without incident.

As Pierre hooted the horn, making a racket that

set her nerves even further on edge, Theresa said, 'We cannot take the chance of going back that way, Pierre. We won't be able to stay as long as we had hoped. We will have to set off back in a couple of days and return separately.'

'I have been thinking the same. You can return by train. I will do the first leg in this van as I will be safe for around two hundred and fifty kilometres. Then the next three hundred or so kilometres I will have to do cross-country, relying on farmers to take me short distances in tractors or concealed in amongst the vegetables if they are making any deliveries. I will get there. I did the same when I brought Jacques here, and I made it here and back in three days.'

All she could do was clutch his hand.

'Come, *ma chérie*. Let us not let the thought of that spoil the couple of days we do have. We can relax now. This place is very remote, and as long as Father has managed to keep up his quota of output, it is unlikely the Germans or the officials of the Free Government will bother to come anywhere near here. They would not waste their time.'

As he finished saying this, a fair-haired man of around fifty came out of the gate. His hand shielded his face as he peered at the van. Behind him was a woman with the same dark hair and eyes as Pierre had. Other than that, she bore little resemblance to Pierre, as her face was that of a Jewish lady with striking dark features and eyes. Both looked anxious.

'Ha! *Regardez, c'est ma mère et papa.*'

'Yes, I can see them, Pierre, but they cannot see

us. The sun is putting us in the shadow. They look so worried! We should get out and show ourselves.'

Pulling the cushion from under her clothes, Theresa opened the van door. Pierre called out to the couple in French as he opened his door, telling them it was him. This set up squeals of joy.

It was their last afternoon. They sat in a field alone. They hadn't been out much since getting here, as the time had been taken doing every little thing Jacques needed – playing with him and rocking him to sleep, then talking for long hours with Pierre's mother and father. She loved them both. They were such gentle people. Neither held any bitterness in them, when they would have been justified in doing so. Pierre's father had taken some pictures of them. 'I will keep them for you and you can have them when all this is over.'

The old farmer who had given Pierre's parents refuge had kept out of their way, giving them all the space they needed. There had been a moment of sadness when Pierre's mother had voiced her fears and had broken down. His father had comforted her, but had looked close to tears himself as he did so.

Now, Jacques was taking his afternoon nap, and they had needed to talk about things they couldn't discuss in front of anyone else.

'How will we contact each other if anything goes wrong? Oh, Pierre, with everything so vital to the Allied Forces' landing, and that only days away, we shouldn't have taken this chance!'

'It will work out, *ma chérie*, you have no need to worry. I have many contacts along the way. They helped me before, and they will do so again. And the train journey ... well, you have done those before, and have managed to get safely to your destination. That will be so again. You will wear your wig, and dress as a secretary. As that was successful for you once, you will be practised at it. Mother is the same size as you and always wore the most fashionable clothing. I am sure she has a suitable jacket in the wardrobe, and you have a skirt with you. We will make you look the part. We will rendezvous in Calvados on the border of Bessin and Caen. There is a flour mill there. Just say to the miller: *"Un kilo de farine."* Nothing else. Don't modify it to say you are here for a kilo of flour, or you want a kilo of flour. Just *"un kilo de farine"*. He will know from that that you are one of us and he will take care of you until I arrive. Now, as this is the last time we are to be together for days, are we going to waste it on talk?'

He gently laid her down. She looked up into his eyes. In them she read a deep love for her. Her lips accepted his, parted under the pressure he forced with his tongue, and then tasted the sweetness of him as he explored her mouth. She shivered as his head moved down to her neck, licking her, sucking her skin into his mouth, nibbling gently and releasing, saying as he did, *'Ma femme, ma femme adorée.'* Taking this as a proposal, she said, 'Yes, yes, yes, I am your wife for ever. I am yours.'

His tongue traced a path to her cleavage, where his hand kneaded her nipples until they pressed against the restriction of her blouse. 'Oh, Pierre, I want you. I want you inside me. Please...'

Her voice begged him, but he only made a sound

between a groan and a laugh. Undoing her buttons and helping her to wriggle out of her blouse, he let his tongue take the course down the centre of her stomach and around her belly button. Grabbing his hair, she begged once more, but with eyes full of desire and holding hers, he took her hands, and with a little pressure laid her back down. Lifting her skirt, he pulled aside her pants and with his tongue caressed the most sensitive part of her. Within seconds the sensation built to a crescendo that she could not bear. Raising the top half of her body, she grabbed his hair once more and pulled his head further towards her. She needed pressure whilst her orgasm pulsated through her. 'Hold still, Pierre.' The words gasped from her. 'Don't moo-o-ve. Oooh! Oh. Oh, my God!'

When the feeling subsided, it felt as though she would wane too – that she would be as if everything had been taken from her. Flopping back, she lay breathless and weak.

His voice hoarse and deep, he said, *'Maintenant, ma bien-aimée*. My beloved, now...'

Then he entered her with a thrust that put him deep into her. With it came his beautiful cry of joy and an exquisite moan, telling her that he too was draining himself of all that he was.

With his body flopped on hers, she knew a moment of feeling privileged to have shared this emptying of each other, this extreme giving and taking of love with Pierre, her soulmate and her life.

After a moment he lifted himself and smiled at her. 'So, you agree to be my wife? That makes me very happy. Thank you. As soon as this is over we will marry, *ma chérie*.'

She smiled back, but the troubled thoughts pressing to be unburdened shivered her body. 'I have something I want to share with you, Pierre.'

'But you are cold, no? And it is not always a good thing to empty your conscience. Nothing that has gone before matters...'

'This does. But, yes, I do want to dress first.' He only took a moment to pull up his trousers and button his flies. She took longer to adjust her clothing and put her bra and blouse back on. While he waited he lit two cigarettes. Taking hers, she inhaled deeply.

'I know you are troubled by something, *ma chérie*, but whatever it is it will not make a difference.'

'I had another child before I came here.'

'A child?' His face held shock, but after a moment he composed himself. 'A child born of love?'

'No. I – I...' She had come this far, and now only the truth would do. 'I seduced another woman's husband. He had a past. He was rough. Evil. He fascinated me. I – I had to give my baby away.' This came on a sob.

He was quiet for a long moment, then he said, 'Lust is a very powerful emotion, perhaps even stronger than love when it is at its height. You giving in to it I can understand, but not to care for your child ... this I find difficult. Why?'

'Many reasons, but none that soothes my pain at her loss. We had to keep it a secret from my mother, as she is mentally very frail. The scandal would have tipped her over the edge. The war was gaining momentum, and I wanted to do my bit. The man, he beat me after... This left me afraid of him. He released me from that fear when he committed suicide after murdering his poor mother, but by then I had gone too far down the line to change my mind, and my father had arranged everything. It seemed better to go through with it rather than cause hurt to my mother.'

She could not tell him of the other pull on her emotions that she had to escape: her sinful love for her twin brother. If she hadn't left, neither of them could have moved on from it. Both of their lives would have been left in tatters. No, she'd had to be strong and part of that was to continue with her plan in giving up her child.

Pierre wiped her tears, then kissed away the remnants of them. 'Will you be able to live with this when this is all over?' The gentle tone of this told that he understood.

'No. I want her back. I want to bring her here as part of our family. Could you accept her?'

'But of course! There is no question. She is part of you, so therefore part of me.'

This brought her tears flowing once more. 'Thank you, Pierre. Thank you. I love you.'

Parting with Jacques had fragmented her heart, but she was able to put all thoughts of the pain of it behind her as a few nights later, and after their meeting at the mill, she lay a few feet away from Pierre. Their mission was under way, their minds and bodies tuned into their task and that alone.

The darkness was cloying as they inched nearer

their target. Ahead there was light, and in its glow she could see the railcars. These were transporting thousands of the 2nd SS-Panzer Division, who had begun to march north towards the Normandy beaches, a trip that would normally take three days but because of measures of disruption caused by other factions of the Resistance, and excellent intelligence of their positions being relayed, they were already delayed by seven days. This was precious time the Allied troops needed to make a speedy advance, and precious information that the RAF needed to make air strikes to further disable them.

The mission tonight was to siphon off all the axle oil from the division's rail transport cars and replace it with abrasive grease. This act would make it impossible for the division to ship out tomorrow to continue their journey, and would render the railcars useless. She didn't know how long it would take for them to gather other means of transport for so many men. Her job was to kill on command – to remove the threat of discovery and of the escape of the guards, so they could not raise the alarm.

Along the track, she could see two guards patrolling the line. She watched them as they marched towards each other, turned when they met in the middle, and marched back the other way. The same was happening on the other side of the cars.

Pierre signalled to André. André could move like a shadow: noiseless and furtive. Dressed in black from head to toe, it was difficult to see him even when you knew he was on the move and where he was going. He was a deadly killer. Throats were cut in an instant, before an utter of protest could be made. He was a man you needed on your side, and there was no doubting his patriotism.

The patrolling soldiers met in the middle again. Complacent now, they stopped. One drew out a cigarette packet from his coat, offering it to the other one. A moment's glow told of the lighting up. A soft laugh told of them sharing a joke. *Smug bastards!*

The sound of a wood pigeon was the signal that told her she should halt her progress. Relief at this steadied her heartbeat just a little, but still terror ran through her veins. Now another coo. And then a noise generated by André which let them know he'd accomplished his mission and was causing a distraction. Not a loud enough one to wake the next shift of guards from their sleep, but enough to have those on duty now look in that direction, luring their attention and giving her and Pierre a chance to strike.

Knife at the ready, she was up in one movement. She advanced on her target from behind, kicked the back of his knee, bent over so that he fell backwards over her, she stood, and almost simultaneously felt the soft squelch of her blade digging deep into his heart. Her hand held his mouth, muffling his cry. His body lay sprawled next to his fellow soldier, who Pierre had killed at the same time.

The silence closed in on them, but they waited. Nothing stirred. Pierre lifted his hand. From out of the woods behind them came the mechanics. They would carry out the switching of the oil for the abrasive grease, while the rest of them would keep their eyes peeled for any Germans emerging from the railcars.

Theresa's terror gave way to the awareness of every movement, every sound. Her gun, cocked and ready, felt heavy in her hands. Sweat dampened her body. Tonight must go well. Please, God, they didn't have to open fire, as that would alert the troops who were garrisoned in the town.

With their mission accomplished, they made their way back to their nearest safe house. They would rest tomorrow and travel during the night back to Caen for their next assignment, leaving the German division in chaos. She, Pierre and André went first, hurrying along the side of the track and following it westward. Ahead of them were the garrison and more guards. The route was dangerous, but they were to make it safer for the others by killing the guards.

Pierre hadn't wanted her to go with him. He had wanted her to hang back while they made the way clear, but could not dissuade her. Her inner voice niggled away at her; her fear for Pierre's safety had increased. He was well known now, and anyone captured and tortured might give him away. She had to stay with him, trusting only herself to protect him. In this she knew she overstepped her remit many times over, as her job was often only to carry out the reconnaissance, report back to Command and to make sure she had supplies on their way in plenty of time and in the quantities they needed. But she was highly trained – much more so than most of the men she fought alongside. She had better hand-to-hand combat skills and stealth killing techniques, so she knew she was much more useful to Pierre in the field, fighting alongside him, than she would ever be by just doing her assigned duties. Besides, she could take the liberty of doing so under her remit to do whatever it took to help the success of planned missions.

The next night didn't see them travelling, but all huddled together in a bunker where their contacts had directed them. They were safe, but shattered mentally, and doing what they could to try to come to terms with the reprisals – men, women and children, herded into the church and burned alive! My God, the SS were animals! Killing was always an abhorrent but necessary evil of war, but to kill innocent civilians in such a cruel, calculated way? That was immoral and debauched.

Lizzie – 1963

As the thought of what it must have felt like to be burned alive, and the horror of such a thing really happening, sank into Lizzie, she let the book drop onto her knee. She thought of all those frightened people, like those who'd been forced into Monsieur Ponté's bakery. She imagined them and their wails of terror and their excruciating agony as their flesh melted from their bodies. As she did so, the sick feeling she'd had earlier came back to her, shaking her to the core and making her want to stop reading for now.

Rolling the book up and tucking it down the side of her, she remembered that it was the last but one book. What she'd do when she came to the end, she didn't like to think, because reading them had helped her get through everything. It was like leaving her life today and entering another world, because she could feel all that had happened in Theresa's life then as if she was there and as if it was happening to her.

What must it have been like for Theresa to have it actually happen to her? To feel the terror, experience the horror, and then to lose her son and the love of her life? A deep compassion settled in her. No matter what Theresa had done when she was younger, she didn't deserve to pay so heavily for it. If only Patsy could see that, but she wondered if she ever would, because now Patsy seemed to be going down the same path of mental illness that her father and her mother had, though it sounded as though Theresa was getting better now that they'd moved her to a convalescent home. She was glad of that. Really glad.

Twenty-nine

Lizzie and Jacques

1963

Feeling the chill of the sun having moved and left her in the shade, Lizzie decided to make her way nearer to the house and call out for Sarah to help her back indoors. As she turned her chair she looked into the face of the young man who'd been in the lane that morning. He was walking up the drive towards her. He halted his progress when she looked in his direction, and now he stood about ten feet from her. 'Oh, how long have yer been there?'

'I just came through the gates. You turned as I reached here.'

His face had an expression of someone who'd been caught out. He must have thought she was accusing him of watching her. 'Sorry, I didn't mean to be rude, but yer startled me! Did yer want to see Sarah? I mean, Mrs Chesterton?' Her heart raced, making it difficult for her to keep her voice steady. Her cheeks warmed under his gaze.

'No, I came to see you. I...'

'Me?'

'Yes. I ... well, I wanted to say hello, and thought I'd like to get to know you.'

'Oh!' She didn't know what to say. No one had ever said such a thing to her before. He'd probably had the usual feeling of pity when he'd seen her earlier, and wanted to make himself feel better by helping her. That bitter thought was born of years of seeing this reaction in people. Her condition made them feel guilty, and doing something for her replaced that with a good feeling, as if some-how they had lightened her burden and so they weren't bad people. Understanding this didn't make her like it. She hated being different and having to compensate for how others looked on themselves.

He had waited during her silence. With that heart-melting smile on his face and with his head held on one side, he conveyed a silent appeal. Saying something was even more difficult now, and it wasn't only because her throat had tightened and her stomach churned at the sight of him, but what could you say to someone who said they wanted to get to know you? It must be an American way of going on.

'I'm sorry if I'm intruding. Were you just going inside?'

At last her tongue unravelled: 'That or move into the sun. It left me stranded and feeling chilly.'

'Can I help you?'

'No! I – I mean... Well, I can manage, thanks.'

Again he stopped in his tracks. Now she had to move into the sun, because she couldn't get inside without help. *Trapped, always trapped... Stop it! Why am I like this? I'm not usually bitter and feeling sorry for meself.* But then, her disability had never been that much in focus before, as at home she'd had her ways of doing things. Or Ken and Rita had done things for her, but that had always been normal. Nothing was normal any more.

'Right. I'll do the introductions, then. My name's Jacques. Jacques Rueben, and–'

'Oh my God! You're *him!* You're Theresa's lost son!'

'You know my mother?'

'No. I...'

'How do you know I'm her son, lost, or not, then?'

Sarah's coming out of the house just as he asked this rescued the moment, as Lizzie had no idea how to tell him that she was reading about his mother's life, but that his mother didn't know,

402

or how to tell him that her brother was responsible for the state his mother was in now.

'Everything alright, Lizzie, love?'

'Yes, Sarah. This...'

'Oh, I can see who this is, and not unexpected, either. Can we help you, lad?'

This made the colour rise even more to her cheeks. Sarah was only teasing, but...

'I came to have a chat with ... well, Lizzie. She hadn't told me her name, though, ma'am...'

Lizzie jumped in. She had to protect Sarah from any further shocks, and Jacques from learning about his sister in the same way that she had blurted out about knowing who he was. She'd rather tell him everything first and let Richard give Sarah the news in his own gentle way that Patsy's brother had turned up. 'His name is Jacques. He came because we are both strangers in town.' She laughed as she said this. 'He's been told how we can expect to be gossiped about and thought we could gossip together instead.'

Sarah laughed too, and that eased the uncomfortable moment. 'Eeh, that sounds like a good idea. Well, I'll give you a hand by making a pot of tea for you.'

'He's American. I don't think they drink tea.'

'Oh, coffee, then?'

'Tea will be fine, ma'am. My grandmother has introduced me to it and I rather like it, thanks.'

Before Sarah could ask who his grandmother was, Lizzie said, 'Let's sit at the garden table over there, Jacques, shall we?'

'That'll be great. Shall I push you?'

'No, thanks. I can manage. Look, I need to ask

403

yer something before Sarah comes back. It's going to sound strange, but don't tell Sarah who your grandmother is. Not yet. I... Well, I have a lot to tell yer, and it's better we talk first.' Somehow she didn't feel embarrassed at talking to him like this. She had the strange feeling that she'd known him for ever and could say anything to him.

They had reached the table that stood at the end of the path on a rounded, crazy-paved area cut into the lawn. Jacques moved a chair out the way for her and she manoeuvred her wheelchair up to the table.

As he sat down, he said, 'Is it about my family and what has happened over the years? The scandals and everything? Are you worried that my presence will upset Mrs Chesterton?'

'Oh, you know about it, then? Well, that's something. At least you'll understand why I'm asking. I think she'll be okay once she knows, but I didn't want yer telling her out the blue who you were.'

'I don't like deceiving her. It doesn't seem right to take her hospitality...'

'Please, Jacques. I have a lot to tell yer of that I don't want Sarah to blurt out either. I know I'm not making sense, but I know she won't mind and will understand why I asked yer not to say anything. Yer see, me aunt was involved in... Well, she did something really bad to Sarah's dad, but it hasn't stopped Sarah taking me in.'

His expression now was one of bewilderment.

'I'm sorry. Yer must think you've come across an idiot.'

'No. No, I don't. I think I've come across the most beautiful girl in the world. And I like that you care enough for others to try to protect them, but I am a bit confused. First of all you know my mom and who I am, then you tell me that you have a past and you have something to tell me.'

This shocked her. No one had ever called her beautiful. Lost for words, she was glad to hear Sarah call out as she approached, 'Here you are! Eeh, it's getting a bit parky out here, Lizzie. Why don't you both come inside?'

'We're okay, thanks, Sarah.' A relief came with seeing Sarah had only brought out two cups. She'd worried that she might think to join them.

'Reet, that's grand then. Nice to meet you, Jacques. I'll leave you to it. Lizzie will tell me all about you and how you came to get all the way from America to our little town.'

As she left, Jacques said, 'I think fate had a hand in that.'

'You'll think that even more when yer hear me tale. And yer might not want to know me after it either.'

Again his lovely smile. 'I don't think that will happen, but I am intrigued.'

'And I don't know where to start. Look, I can only tell you how it is and say that I didn't want any of it to happen, but I couldn't stop it. But it will help me if you don't interrupt. I know you will have a lot of emotions at me telling you it all, but if you let me get it all out, then you might understand better by the time I get to the end.'

He nodded at this. 'Well, I'll pour the tea while you get started. I've been taught how to do it properly, so you needn't worry.'

She wished the little laugh he gave, which had

a carefree sound to it, would last even after he'd heard everything, but was really afraid that it wouldn't.

Taking a deep breath, she began by asking him as gently as she could if he knew he had a half-sister. His brows knotted in a deep frown as he said he did. He went to ask her something, but then must have remembered her request so just said, 'Go on. It'll wait.'

Jacques had wanted to cut in a dozen times during her story to demand this or question that. It all seemed unbelievable, and yet it tied up so many loose ends for him. To think that her brother and her aunt had been responsible for what had happened to his mother! And, his sister is here! My God, he thought he'd never meet his sister no matter how hard he tried, but he was now sitting in the garden of the very house she'd lived in for the last four years, and she had another half-sister, born on the same day as her!

Besides all that, Lizzie had his mother's memoirs and had nearly finished reading them. She knew everything about his mother, while he knew so little, but something in him didn't mind this part of her tale. Because if he wanted to share anything of himself, he'd want to share it with her. None of this had been her fault. From a young age, she'd lived a nightmare. He wanted to make up for that if he could.

His eyes stung with how he'd been staring at a rose tree swaying in the breeze – the same breeze that had begun to rustle everything around them. He moved his gaze to her, and saw that she had her head down. He saw a tear drop off the end of her chin and plop onto her blouse. The sight tore at his heart. 'Lizzie...' His voice would hardly squeeze through the tightness of his throat.

As she looked up, he felt as if her lovely blue eyes were pulling him into their depths. He wanted to put out his hand and stroke her long wispy hair, and catch strands of it as they blew about in the wind. He swallowed hard. 'It's alright. I don't blame you for any of it. Not even reading my mom's memoirs. You didn't know who they belonged to, and you said you hoped by reading them you would be able to find that out and return them. Then when you met my sister she gave you permission to carry on. Besides, you said there are parts of it that concerned your aunt? Well, whatever they are, it is incredible, isn't it? That we should meet like this, and yet my mom and your aunt knew each other?'

'It is. It's like you said, fate brought us together... I mean, made us meet.'

'I liked the first way you put it. Lizzie, I hope I'm not being too forward for what an English girl is used to, but I ... well, something happened to me the moment I set eyes on you.'

Her cheeks flushed with colour and her eyes twinkled through the as yet unshed tears left brimming in them. 'I – I felt the same. Only, well, this may sound daft, but yer were already in me heart.'

Once more she shocked him by telling him of the photos she had, and how attracted she had been to the one of his father. 'You're so like him, yer see. Look.'

From beside her she pulled out an old paper book, similar to those he'd written in back home when he first started school. She shook a photo from the inside of it, and the face looking back at him was very like his own. His dad. He had a similar one himself, but his didn't have the lovely inscription on the back. Reading the French was no problem, but seeing his dad's handwriting for the first time ever, was. His throat constricted. He swallowed again, but it didn't help. The tears that had gathered many times during Lizzie's telling now ran down his cheeks. Her hand reached out and touched his. The contact trembled through him. He knew it had through her, too.

'I'm sorry. I didn't mean to upset yer. I just...'

'No, it's alright. It just touched a chord. I cry a lot lately, especially since my grandfather died. He had a sad story. He was a wonderful man and he learned to cope with all he had to put up with, so I have determined that I shall. But it's just the little things that catch me out.'

'I know how that feels. It's the same for me. I can't say that those that I have lost were wonderful, nor have they left me many nice memories of them, but they were me family, and I did love them. And now I have to bury them. And same will go for me dad, only I'll know the minute he is to die, 'cos he will be...'

She couldn't go on. Like him, she was fighting for control and losing the battle.

'Lizzie, if you'll let me, I'll be with you on that day. I promise. And I'll be with you when you bury your aunt and brother. But only if...'

'Yes. Yes, I would let yer. And I know as I'll cope

better for yer being there. I know that sounds daft, as I've only just met yer, but it's how I feel, and knowing you any longer won't change that, I'm sure of it.'

'Oh, Lizzie.'

They sat for a moment, holding hands. Neither spoke, but it didn't seem to him as if there was anything they had to say.

The spell was broken by Sarah coming out again. He went to let go of Lizzie's hand, but she clasped his tighter. A tremor of trepidation went through him. Upsetting Mrs Chesterton was the last thing he wanted to do, but might be the first thing he did, because she wouldn't approve of him being so forward. Not if what he'd heard of the English way of doing things was right, she wouldn't.

As she came closer he could see she did have a look of concern on her face, and went to say something, but didn't. He wasn't sure what had stopped her, until she did speak: 'You both look very upset. Jacques, you're crying... Lizzie?'

He wiped his free hand over his face. He could feel Lizzie's eyes on him, willing him not to say anything, but he had to. 'It turns out, ma'am, that Lizzie and I have links in our lives that have their roots in some very sad times for us both.'

'Oh? Look, it's cold out here. By, it's turned with the sun going round. Why don't you come in and tell me about it, eh?'

'We can't, Sarah...'

'Why, love? There may be sommat as I can do to help you both.'

Again Lizzie looked at him, but though her look

held a warning, he had the sense that she trusted him. He only hoped that trust would stay intact when he went against what she'd asked of him. 'Mrs Chesterton, ma'am, there's things in my past that caused you hurt. I had no control over them, but I ... well, Lizzie and I, we don't want to upset you, and yet I don't know how not to. Am I making any sense, ma'am?'

'None at all. How can you, a young man from America, possibly hurt me? Well, whatever it is, it's sommat as is burdening you both more than you deserve, so I promise I'll cope with it. Come on in and tell me about it.'

'I'm sorry, Sarah. We didn't want ... well, we knew yer had to know, but...'

Lizzie had told Sarah whose son Jacques was, and she'd deduced that he was half-brother to Patsy. And now at the end of that Sarah just stood and stared at him.

'I didn't know, ma'am, I...'

'No, I know. I'll be reet. It's just so incredible, it's knocked me for six! Eeh, but none of it is down to you, neither of you. Aye, it's brought it all back. It does whenever any of those... I mean, your family are mentioned. But I'm not one to carry that forward down the generations. You should know that, Lizzie, with how I took Patsy in and then you.'

Her voice sounded hurt as she said this. Lizzie tried to put it right. 'I do know, Sarah. You're the kindest person I know, but I have seen yer upset and yer have so much to put up with at the moment. I didn't want us to add to that. I thought

I'd get Richard to tell yer...'

'Oh. I'm sorry, love. I misunderstood. Eeh, there's so much to keep coming back to me. But like Richard says, I won't get rid of any of it if I hang on to the hate. And of late, I've come to think that's reet an' all. I can't keep hating folk. They did what they did, but they've all paid in various ways.'

Jacques felt as though he could at this moment throttle his mother and his Uncle Terence as well, if he wasn't already dead. How could they have behaved as they did? Mother taking this lovely woman's husband within a week of her being married, and having a child by him! And according to what her aunt had told Lizzie, and his mother had concurred with in her memoirs, his Uncle Terence had tricked Lizzie's aunt into burning Sarah's father's stud farm down! And all so that he could step in and buy the business at a knock-down rate! Unbelievable! And then there was the other sickening behaviour that Benjamin had said was rumoured, about them having an incestuous relationship! God, he felt sick to be related to such people. He was beginning to think he no longer wanted to meet his mother.

'Ma'am, it has all shocked me. My family owes you an apology, and I hope you will accept that from me. I'm really sorry for what successive ancestors of mine have caused for you and your ancestors.'

'Thank you, that means a lot to me, Jacques. And I think as it will help me in me intention to stop thinking of you all as me enemies who are out to harm me and me family.'

'I hope so, because you already have one of us

in your home, and I would like to become the second one – to visit often, not to move in, of course.'

'Eeh, you're very welcome, Jacques. We'd be pleased to have you. That's if Lizzie and Patsy think so.'

He looked towards Lizzie. That lovely way he had noticed that she had of blushing at anything that involved the attention being on her happened again now, but with it she gave a shy smile, and his heart seemed to flip over. 'Well, there's no time like the present to find out, from one of them, at least. Lizzie, will you be okay with me visiting on a regular basis? And, while I'm asking, would you let me take you to dinner – when I can find some-where to go for dinner, that is?'

For a moment she looked as though she would say no, but being so tuned in to her in such a short time he realized she always had to consider her disability. She must wonder whether, if she said yes, she'd physically be able to get into where he chose.

'Not that I would book anywhere that didn't have your approval, of course. We could start with a drive out to find and inspect all likely venues. How about I pick you up tomorrow?'

'I'd like that, thanks.'

He winked at her, and once more was treated to her beautiful smile. She was so delicate and fragile-looking, and he wanted to take care of her and make sure she never suffered again.

Thirty

A Helping Hand for Recovery

Patsy and Ian

Patsy opened her eyes. 'What time is it, Ian?'

'It's seven-thirty. They'll be ringing the bell in half an hour for all visitors to depart. They've already warned me that they'll not let me stay the night now that you're on the mend.'

'But I thought we were waiting for them to come and say I could go home? Oh, Ian, I can't bear another night in here! I'm fine now.'

'They still might. The sister said they've had an emergency – a train crash. There are a lot injured and they are under pressure. If she can get a doctor to you she will, but she doesn't know if she can.'

'Bugger! That *would* happen.'

'Eeh, Patsy...'

'What?'

'Never mind. Look, I'll go and ring Dad. See if there's owt he can do. He might be able to pull some strings. I'll not be a mo.'

As he walked down the corridor to the public telephone, every part of him ached from the long hours he'd sat watching over Patsy. Not that he'd have had it any different. His stomach rumbled, reminding him that it had been hours since he'd

413

eaten. They'd brought a dinner for Patsy, but she'd refused it. He'd thought then that he could have snatched it out of their hands as they'd taken it away.

Walking back after talking to his dad, he felt a lightness in his step and couldn't wait to tell Patsy the news.

'You look pleased! Hope it means you've managed to get me out of here?'

'Not yet, though Dad said he would see what he could do. It might work if they know you're going home to a doctor, but he didn't hold a lot of hope as we're so far away from him. Anything could happen on the way – a relapse, for instance. He doesn't think they're likely to let you go without seeing a doctor.'

'So why the smiley face?'

'Eeh, Patsy, I've got some news as you're never going to believe. I think it'll lift you an' all.'

'Harri didn't go after all?'

'No, and that wouldn't be good news, 'cos she's very much in love with Greg and not going would make her unhappy. You shouldn't want that; I know I don't. Look, Patsy, love, you have to let go. I know as you're going to miss her – we all are – but it's a natural progression. What did you think, that you'd be together, side by side for ever, with no one else coming between you? That's silly and you know it.'

'You've taken on the role of "Me Who Knows It All" all of a sudden! Well, you don't know it all. Harri was like a prop to me. She gave me life purpose. These last four years she provided a hook for me to cling on to and to get away from me

414

past, and now that has all gone and I feel like I have been dumped for the second time in me life, and it hurts.'

'By, lass, if that is how you looked upon her, then of course it does. Eeh, Patsy, love, you were wrong to do that. Harri was allus going to fail in that role, 'cos she was allus going to move on in her life, as you should an' all. It doesn't mean she doesn't still love you. But, just as it will for you, she has found the kind of love that takes precedence over all others. There's a lot of different kinds of love, you know. And none of them diminish each other; they just demand different levels of standing in our lives.'

'Ian, you seem so different. When did you gain all this philosophy of life? I never noticed it before.'

'Aye, well, you never took the time to check what I was like. I've just been there in the background of what you think you want. This is me. Yes, I am what you said earlier, a bit of a lazy bugger and maybe a bit of a wimp an' all, though I'd say that was more me liking to keep other folk happy no matter how much it puts me out. But there is another side to me as you're now seeing.'

'I can only say sorry so many times, Ian. I ain't going to spend the rest of me life saying it.'

'Oh, so you see yourself spending the rest of your life with me, then?'

'I didn't say that. I – I don't know. But even if I don't do so in the way you want of me, you'll still always be there.'

'Aye, I will. Look, do you want this news or not?'

'Go on, then.'

'Your brother has turned up. He–'

'What? Oh, my God! When? Where? Oh, Ian...'

Her joy had her sitting up now. It shone from her face, radiating from it with all the beauty he'd ever want to see in his whole life. Taking her hands, all he could say was, 'Eeh, lass.'

She didn't take hers from his. 'Tell me, Ian. Where is he? Oh, God, this is wonderful! A brother! A real brother that's just mine!'

This statement worried him as he wondered how she'd take what he had to tell her. 'He turned up in Breckton yesterday. He ... well, he came across Mam and Lizzie in the churchyard and he ... it seems he was smitten with Lizzie.'

'Lizzie! Why?'

'What do you mean, why? Lizzie's a pretty girl. Delicate. The type a man wants to take care of. It'd be easy to be smitten by her. Anyroad, he called round later. It seems Lizzie had already thought she'd seen him somewhere before, and that was because he takes after his dad, whose pictures were in those things of your mam's. His name's–'

'Jacques Rueben. I know. Lizzie told me about him, but I can't get over him being attracted to Lizzie. How do you know that? Christ! I haven't even met him and someone's grabbed him...'

'Lizzie hasn't grabbed him. They are attracted to one another, that's all, and he came round to have a chat with her because of that. It was when she learned his name that she knew who he was. He's staying with his granny – well, your granny an' all, come to that.'

'How? God, this is all incredible. I've never met me granny, so how has he?'

'You never wanted to. You could have found her. He did.'

He told her what he knew about how Jacques had found his family and how Theresa, who was on the mend, told her doctor about her having a daughter. 'So your granny knows about you now as well. And listen to this: she is angry that she never knew about you before. It appears that your granddad and uncle were the only ones who knew, and that they sorted out you being given away. Your granny cried and said that if she had known she wouldn't have allowed it. You would have gone back to them and they would have passed you off as being the child of your mam's ex-husband. Jacques told them that she even said she would have taken care of you while your mam did her thing in the war. It all beggars belief how folk can change the course of a lifetime. Eeh, love...'

Silent tears had filled her eyes and wet her face as they ran down her cheeks. Her look was one of utter devastation. She crumpled in his arms.

Holding her and stroking her hair set up emotions in him, and he couldn't hold back from telling her, 'Don't cry, me little lass. I'm here for you. I love you. I love you with all that I am, and I'll never let you down. Everything's going to be reet, I promise you. You're going to get all your family back, and they all love you. I knows that. Me dad said as they do. Your mam's never forgot you, and says in them books how she was planning on getting you back after the war and

417

setting up a proper family with you and your brother and the man she fell in love with, but she lost them. She lost so much, her mind included, poor lass. But life's not over. If you can accept them, they are ready for you. Oh, Patsy, I love you, lass, I love you. So much, it hurts.'

Lifting her face she said, 'I know you do. And I'm grateful, but I have such a lot to come to terms with. Me life were hell, and for years I thought of me mam as the cause of that. I hated her. I didn't know all of this... Oh, Ian, what am I going to do? What if they don't like me and... Well, is me brother posh like them? I mean, will I fit in with them?'

'Course you will. By all accounts your brother's American, and he hasn't met your mam yet. Dad says he's a real likeable fellow and said, as Mam put it, "he has no side to him". He even apologized to her for all that his... I mean, your family, has done to her and hers over the years.'

'Why did he do that? I've never done that.'

'Well, he knows them. He's living with your granny at the moment. He probably feels because of that that Mam might think of him more as one of them. You're one of us and have been for four years. You've not and shouldn't feel any responsibility for anything they have done. Not that he should either, and Mam told him that. But it was a nice gesture and it pleased Mam no end.'

'Is he going to see our mother?'

'He's planning on going tomorrow. Dad asked me to ask you if you want him to tell your mam about him knowing where you are. Her doctor is telling her about him in the morning, and they are expecting it to be a big shock to her. She may not even be ready to see him. They don't know, but he has said that once she has met him and if that goes alright and she copes, he will tell her about finding you and then you can both go along together. But you have to agree with this too. Jacques doesn't want to do anything without your say-so, and will delay them telling his mother about him if that is what you want.'

'I – I don't know. I...'

'Look, love, think about it, eh? It's all been a shock to you.'

She laid her head back on his chest. His heart beat so strongly at this that he felt sure she could feel it as well as hear it. 'I love having you near like this, lass. I wish you could always be so and not in just a comforting way.'

'It's a start that you're the one who gives me the most comfort, Ian. Just let it be like that for now. I need time. I've so much to contend with.' She lifted her head again and looked up at him. 'I only know that how I feel about you has changed.'

They were quiet for a moment, and in this time he allowed himself to hope. Oh aye, he knew she was a handful, and would probably always be so, but he'd cope with that. He'd have to. He only wished he'd get the chance.

Still with no sign of coming out of his arms, she said, 'Would you phone Dad again and tell him to ask Jacques not to do anything yet? Ask him to delay things just for a little while, until I get used to it all and can make my mind up what I want. And ask Dad to tell him that I can't wait to meet him, will you?'

'Aye, I will, lass.' The bell ringing at that moment dampened his heart. He didn't want to leave her, but the way she clung on to him and what she said as she did, took away the sad feeling in him and lifted him higher in his spirits than he'd ever been.

'I don't want you to go. I feel so alone when you're not with me. Take me with you, Ian. Ask them to let me sign meself out.'

'Eeh, lass, I want to do that more than owt else at this moment, but because I love you I'm not going to. I'd never forgive meself if owt happened to you as a consequence. As soon as I book into a hotel, I'll ring here and give them a number for me. Then if the doctor does visit and releases you, then get them to contact me and I'll be here like a shot. I'll take you back to me hotel and then we'll set off in the morning. How's that for a deal, eh?'

'It'll do, but you needn't think you're getting me in your hotel room! I want a room of me own, so check they have vacancies before you book in.'

If she hadn't had a wry look on her face as she said this, he'd have been hurt at her thinking he would do such a thing, but as it was, he laughed at her. 'Who says I want you in me room? By, how the way you snore I'd never get any sleep. I used to hear you through me wall at night and I were across the landing!'

She laughed at this and gave him another hug. He hugged her back, not ever wanting to let her go. But if he didn't, he'd do as she asked and get her signed out and that wouldn't be the right thing to do, so he came out of her hold, told her to be a good girl until he saw her again, kissed her cheek and left before he changed his mind.

Thirty-one

Lizzie's Doubts, Theresa's Capture, Pierre's Death

1963 and 1945

Lizzie couldn't sleep. All kinds of emotions were assailing her, and her thoughts wouldn't rest. She went from thinking, what if Jacques didn't like her as much as she did him? And then to changing that to 'love her', as she knew she did him. And from asking herself, 'Is this how love feels?' to being sure that it did.

But then, if he did love her, would he be willing to take her on, because that's what it would be like: taking on a burden. Someone who couldn't do half the things he'd told her he did when they'd sat together after their talk with Sarah: surfing, water-skiing, dancing and, well, everything that required two working legs. And a life a million miles from the one she'd led.

There was a lot they could do together. He liked watching films, and had the same taste in these as she did: true-life dramas, Westerns and thrillers, as well as the classics. She'd been lucky in this at home, as the cinema had been close enough so that her wheelchair battery would last to take her there and back, and had been on ground level. The manager had helped her into the building and onto a seat. These times had been some of her best, when she could lose herself in what was happening on-screen.

Jacques also liked eating out, something he told her they did a lot in the States, whereas here it was just on special occasions and something she'd only experienced eating snacks in the café up the road when Rita couldn't get off the settee long enough to cook anything.

Thinking of this gave her another worry. She couldn't cook for Jacques, as she couldn't reach the stove. Not that she couldn't cook. If she'd managed to get Rita in the right mood, she'd often gone to the local shop and bought the ingredients for a recipe she fancied. Then, with Rita's help – chopping for her and passing her stuff she could manage, like beating eggs, that kind of thing, and then following her instructions on temperatures and taking things off the ring or out of the oven when she said – she'd achieved making some great meals. But it was this thing of always needing help... Surely that would put Jacques off? Oh, she hoped it wouldn't!

Then her thoughts turned to how Patsy had taken the news. It had sounded really positive when Ian had rung Richard back, and he never said anything about Patsy not liking the fact that Jacques had taken a fancy to her and had asked her out to dinner. Ian had said Patsy was recovering as well – really recovering. Lizzie felt so glad at this news, and couldn't wait for Patsy to come home. What they'd been through had brought them closer together, and she missed her.

Deciding that she wasn't going to sleep, she put

her hand under the pillow and took out the last of the books. She'd finished the other one when she'd first come to bed. Something in her didn't really want to finish them all, as she'd feel like she'd lost a big part of her that had almost been her. But despite that, she felt compelled to read on.

Theresa and Pierre had made another visit to Pierre's parents to be with Jacques at the end of August 1944. Many places in France were liberated by then, and his parents were talking of going back to Paris after the liberation of that city had taken place, but Pierre had counselled them not to. He'd told them to stay put until the whole of France was liberated, or even until the war ended, just in case. He was worried for his mother and grandmother, who would be singled out as Jews so easily. Again, Lizzie had read that they'd had a wonderful time, and she had found that the picture of Theresa and Jacques had come to life for her with reading about their time together that weekend.

Theresa and Pierre left with such hope of them all being together soon as a family. But they had to see the conflict through, and had now moved towards the east of the country to continue their missions to undermine the German defence.

Theresa – A Fateful Mission, January 1945

Theresa marched up and down, and for the umpteenth time the question that had been going through her mind posed itself again: *Where are you, Pierre? Please, please make contact...*

Pierre had left hours ago to meet a new agent. At

last it was time for her to go home and to be decommissioned. Pierre would go back to Paris and await her return from England. The new agent was to take over from her and continue operations that would take him and his group into Belgium, should the campaign being fiercely fought in this area succeed.

The German offensive had launched a massive counterattack that had already successfully regained the initiative in the Ardennes after being pushed back so far in November. But at that time the Americans had wavered in their support, and the French General de Lattre had been forced to pull back behind the French lines. The Germans had reacted swiftly and launched Operation North Wind.

Hers and Pierre's work had been difficult and extremely dangerous, as they had done what they could to hinder the Germans and to provide intelligence. Twice they had lost safe houses used by her to radio information and receive instructions, and although these raids had uncovered their activities, thank God they had escaped.

Now things were going well, as General de Lattre had made a move to liberate Colmar and reach the Rhine at Brisach, and she knew that very soon General Schlesser would lead a night attack that, if successful, would finally liberate France. How fitting that the French army should do this.

Command had said she was to be lifted out any day, and was to keep a low profile until that happened. She'd presumed it would be after the liberation. That must succeed!

Pierre was to pull out at the same time, but until then their position here was still precarious. The Germans would do anything to uncover their operation and capture them – the leaders and instigators of many of their frustrations. *Please God, let the end of the German occupation come soon!*

Once more her worry surfaced. Pierre had had to travel to Troyes to meet the agent, but should have been back by now. From the start something had worried her about the whole thing, although she couldn't put her finger on why. The message saying a new agent was to join them hadn't contained anything to cause her concern, but still, something didn't *feel* right. Why didn't Command drop the new agent in Belgium so he was on the ground ready to carry out his missions? Having to keep air time to the minimum, she hadn't questioned the orders.

As she thought of this, the smell of fresh bread permeated her room. This often happened at night, as she occupied the room above Monsieur Gaillard's bakery. He would be busy with his next day's batch. The aroma took her mind away from her concerns and brought the Pontés to her mind. A few weeks ago they'd heard that the Pontés had taken up their business again and were well. She was glad of this, but she thought it ironic that she was now working with another baker and his family, and that her role was once more that of an assistant, delivering bread and serving in the shop as a cover for her SOE work. She had come full circle.

Somehow she'd never tired of the missions – her and Pierre, side by side, and with a new band of men now, a group they'd had to gather together, organize and train – but she was ready to have an end to it all.

That end *was* in sight; she could feel it was so. Everyone she met had that hope – that feeling that soon the future would be bright. The Germans would be defeated, and then the task would be to put the world together again – mend the broken people, rebuild the buildings and sort out economies. That, she would leave to others. For her part, she just wanted to live a simple life with Pierre and their children, because Pierre now spoke of her little girl as his. Always they called her Olivia.

Their plan was to live in Paris, for Pierre to complete his studies. In this they were lucky, as Pierre's father would be able to access the money his own father had put into an American bank. From this he had promised to settle a generous amount on Pierre, as well as an allowance until he was working and earning enough for their needs. And she had money of her own: a legacy from her Aunt Laura, which she'd hardly touched, and a generous settlement from her ex-husband. This she had never dipped into. All of this meant they would be secure financially and would be able to buy a house. And then they would marry.

For a moment she forgot her worries as she imagined her gown, their honeymoon – Venice, as Pierre had never been to Venice. She would be able to show him everything, share a gondola with him, and he could feed her grapes as she lay with her head in his lap. Then St Mark's Square ... oh, and the Accademia Gallery, the art museum of Venice... There was so much beauty to share with him after all of this horror and fear.

Monsieur Gaillard's voice broke into her thoughts, bringing that fear crashing back into her. 'Olivia, there is a message for you from Pierre. You are to rendezvous on the outskirts of Wissembourg.'

'But why? I thought he was bringing the agent here! How did the message arrive? Was it in Pierre's handwriting? Was the proper code used?'

'Yes. It was a phone call. It was him. The code was correct. He has called in several of our group. I have relayed the message to all those he asked me to.'

'What is the mission?'

'To prepare a landing spot, guide in the plane and accept and store a drop from England.'

'I haven't radioed a request. Our job is done here.'

'The new agent came in with the details of the drop. It seems it is for his first mission across the border. You will leave through the shop. On the counter you will find a loaf of bread wrapped ready. To all intents and purposes, you are just delivering it to Monsieur Vailles, the neighbour of Monsieur Deprés et Madame. Monsieur Vailles expects you. When safely inside his home, he will show you a way through his cellar into the orchard of Monsieur Deprés. It is best that you make your way through this to the village. Your contact is Raphaël Blanc. He will be in the café and will take you to Pierre. Your code is *oeufs de canard*.'

'Why has Pierre not given me a guide that I know? This is not like Pierre. Something isn't right.'

427

'I do not know. Pierre wouldn't do anything he didn't think was right to do. He has recruited new men only last week, so maybe this is one of them.'

'Okay. Leave me to get ready. I'll get on my way in a few minutes.'

As she dressed in her usual trousers – green to blend in with the landscape – and a brown jumper topped with her thick black wool coat, her fear intensified. No matter how hard she tried, she just couldn't get it out of her head that this all felt wrong. Monsieur Gaillard sounded nervous. *What's going on?* But she was being silly. These people were loyal. They had never been under suspicion.

Setting out, she was horrified to find the light night provided her with no camouflage. Beads of sweat ran down her face despite the extreme cold. The saddle of her bike jolted her as though she was sitting on a rock as she manoeuvred her cycle over the rough terrain, but she arrived at Monsieur Deprés's without incident.

He took her through to the orchard. The trees, planted so close to each other, clawed at her as she tried to make her way between them, but the vines of the vineyard beyond were worse, scratching at her face as she bent low, dragging her bike beneath them to make her way to the road. Despite these hazards, she felt safer amongst them than when she stepped onto the road and climbed back onto her bike to cycle the last mile of her journey.

Tuned in to every sound, even a leaf blowing along the tarmac sent her heart plummeting. The

428

noise her wheels made was amplified in the silence. Why hadn't she had that squeak oiled? Her fear rendered her breathless and caused her nerves to jangle in her stomach until she thought she would vomit. The dread in her threatened to choke her when suddenly the sound of a heavy vehicle rumbled in the distance. Clambering off her bike, she threw it into the ditch, and was about to follow it when the lorry came into view. Its headlights blinded her. Within seconds she was surrounded by screaming German soldiers, and she knew it was over. Everything was gone: her dreams, her hopes and her life dried up like an empty, parched riverbed with a labyrinth of cracks shattering its surface, but for her those cracks would never be smoothed over and put back together again. For her there was no way back.

Her screams were stopped by a vicious swipe. The sockets of her arms burned as they wrenched her arms behind her and clamped them in cold steel. One of them hooked his leg around hers and brought her to the ground. Irons were locked around her ankles.

A soldier on each side of her hooked their arms through the crook of hers and dragged her towards the back of lorry. The pain of this seared through her as her shoulders threatened to dislocate and her knees scraped along the road. But she knew this to increase tenfold when from behind, her legs were lifted and she was thrown into the back.

Other soldiers inside lifted her and shoved her onto the bench. Her tears blinded her. Blinking sent them running down her cheeks, stinging her scratches and grazes, but clearing her vision. Opposite her sat Pierre.

Though she willed him to, he did not make eye contact with her. She knew this was procedure. If they showed signs of knowing one another, they would incriminate each other, so she looked away without speaking to him. Before she did, she drew strength from how he sat up straight, dignified and defiant. This stopped her tears and straightened her own body. If Pierre should look at her, he wouldn't see a broken woman but a brave one. One who could cope.

They hadn't gone far, no more than twenty miles, when the vehicle came to a halt. Pierre was dragged out through the already open canvas at the back of the lorry. Everything in her screamed against this. *What was happening? God help us!*

In French one of the Germans spat out all his hate and everything that his vile beliefs stood for: '*Sale Juif! Vous ne marcherez pas sur le sol Allemand et vous ne contaminerez pas notre pays de votre présence.*'

My God! No ... no! They know Pierre is a Jew. They are going to shoot him rather than let him set foot on German soil! Soil they say he will taint. Please God, no!

Time froze. The soldier raised his arm. Pierre stood tall. His eyes sent her a message of love. The crack of the shot ricocheted through her, blocking her ears and taking her into a world where all sound was like she was underwater. Pierre's beloved face disappeared. His body crumpled. There, on the border between the country he loved and the one he hated and feared, he died.

With his death everything that was her frag-
mented into a million pieces.

Miles and miles, they travelled. None of the
soldiers spoke to her. Though her soul wept, she
did not allow herself to cry outwardly. Her mind
screamed at her, *How did this happen? We were so
near to the end...* Then it dawned on her that besides herself there were no more captives in the
lorry – no new agent, no men that Gaillard had
said he was to contact. And how did the Germans
know that she was travelling along that road at
precisely that time? How did they know that Pierre
was a Jew? *Gaillard! He must be the traitor! My God,
I will kill him!* It was a silly thought, as she would
not live to take revenge on anyone. *But why? Why
did he do it?* Collaborators weren't always allowed
to survive. Despite the Germans saying they
would not carry out the threatened atrocity if information was given, they often did once they had
what they wanted. But it just didn't make sense in
this case. The Germans were all but defeated. *Oh
my God, if it was him, did he know about the planned
campaign? No, he couldn't.* She and Pierre had
never shared details with anybody – not specifics.
Only enough to encourage their group to carry out
the work needed.

One of the soldiers looked at his watch. What
she'd understood of what he said hardly affected
her, and yet, if she'd heard it before they'd killed
her darling Pierre her blood would have run cold,
as he confirmed with his fellow soldiers that they
would reach Dachau very soon.

Dachau. A place of evil. Intelligence had informed them of inhuman atrocities carried out in

the prison camp there on Jews, homosexuals, Jehovah's witnesses, gypsies, criminals and dissidents. The latter were tortured and then shot. She fell into this group. The former were sorted when they arrived, and those who were of no use in any way to the Germans – including infants and young children – were killed or experimented on, while the others were put to hard labour, starved and beaten until they too were of no use. Then they too were killed. It was a place feared by all agents, but at this moment she felt no fear. You couldn't frighten a dead person, and that was what she was: an emotionally dead person.

It began as soon as they arrived. A frump of a woman, her uniform fitted to every crease of her fat body in a way that looked as if she could hardly move against its restrictions, took charge of her. Dragging her to a room, bare but for a wooden bench, she removed the irons and ordered her to strip. Once she was naked, the woman tweaked her breasts and said, 'You've borne children – unusual for one of you pigs to have done that. Ruins your body. Look at how little life there is in your tits! They flop and droop. Pity, I like firm, pert breasts. The rest of you is good, though. Sad that it is to be wasted. I wouldn't have minded a chance to show you what real pleasure is.' Her laugh held an inhuman sound. Nothing more than a sick disgust settled in Theresa. She knew the pleasure of loving a woman, but this woman was party to the belief that homosexuals were the scum of the earth and party to the killing of those discovered, and yet she was of that persuasion herself.

The woman provided her with a coarse gown that chafed her skin. Her talk continued to be of a sexual and sadistic nature, telling her how her torturers would take pleasure in damaging her breasts. 'They will burn them with their cigarettes, cut them with their knives – ha, they may even take your nipples off! And your vagina won't escape their attention. They may fuck it first, but then they will put a hot poker up it and cut out your clitoris and make you eat it. Then if you haven't given them what they want, they will gouge your eyes out, pull your teeth or your fingernails, or both, with pliers. Stick wires into your ears until your eardrums burst. If still you refuse to talk, they may string you up by your feet and let you hang there until death stares you in the face, but they won't let it take you. They will cut you down, let the medical team make you well enough to take some more, and then dislocate your joints and break your bones, starting with your fingers. So, my beautiful one, tell them what you know. Save yourself all of this and come and work with my women. Eat three meals a day, then when we have triumphed over the world and are the master race, I will take care of you.'

Throughout all of this, Theresa felt nothing. She had no feelings. She was an empty shell.

This protection didn't stay with her long. It dropped away with the agonizing pain of the first cigarette burn on her breast.

In the room the woman had taken her to, a man sat behind a desk. His hair, black and greasy, was plastered to his head, and his face appeared skeletal in the way his skin stretched tightly over the bone structure of his cheeks, prominent fore-head and his chin. His eyes, so dark they appeared lifeless, were framed by the longest lashes she'd ever seen on a man. His body was small and thin, with a long neck protruding from a shirt collar that was too big. His Adam's apple stuck out as if he'd swallowed something of a triangular shape and it had got stuck. It danced up and down every time he spoke.

In his menacing voice, he'd asked her her name, her nationality and for her poem, the unique code that identified her when she radioed messages to Command. 'These things will be enough for today. Tell me them and you can go and have a bath and a meal.'

She didn't open her mouth. She just stared at him, letting her hatred for him burn through her eyes.

The slap he'd given her hardly penetrated the shield that had come down over her, even though it knocked her from her chair. At this he de-manded she get up and sit down in front of him again. When she did, she saw he'd placed her pill on the table within her reach. Her hand shot out towards it. When issued with it she'd found the idea of using it to take her life rather than be at risk of telling all she knew when tortured, abhorrent; now she saw it as her saviour. One bite and this would all be over, and she would be with Pierre. But as she almost reached it he stung her fingers with his cane. 'Ha, you missed your chance again. Weren't your instructions to take it the moment capture was imminent? You disobeyed, didn't you? Afraid of death, are we? Well, that will make the process even more enjoyable for me, because you will die if you don't tell me what I want to know.'

Theresa spat in his face.

His anger at this did not erupt. His controlled reaction was to call into the room two guards. These tied her to the chair with bonds so tight that she could hardly breathe as they wrapped them around her body. When done, they left. Her interrogator stood and walked slowly around his desk until he stood behind her. The smoke from his cigarette encircled her face as he leaned over her. Then with one hand he felt inside her gown, cupped her breast, pulled it out of the top of her gown and held the tip of his cigarette on her flesh. The pain had her drawing in a deep gasp of air between her gritted teeth. It went on and on as the pressure he applied wasn't quite enough to extinguish the cigarette. But then it stopped. Not because he'd withdrawn it, but because it had burned so deep it must have damaged the nerve, cutting off any sensation.

The release from the pain had her dropping her head forward. He yanked it back with her hair, pulling it until her neck was stretched as far as it would go and restricting her breathing even more.

'Tell me. Tell me your name. Your real name. I know your code name, Olivia Danchanté. I know your cover story, as we have it documented from soon after you landed in our midst, but somehow you escaped our net. Clever. But not clever enough, because we have you now and you are going to tell me all I want to know. Your real name, your nationality and your poem. And then you will reveal what you know of the French and American

435

positions and their plans for their next assault. All of this you will reveal in the next few hours, as I have decided not to give you a break after all.'

Still she did not speak.

He let go of her hair and walked around to the back of his desk, once more calling for the guard. One nod of his head and one of them swivelled her chair around. The other landed a blow to her stomach that billowed the vomit from her.

Choking on the remnants in her throat panicked her as the flow of air into her lungs was cut off completely. The room spun, and her eyes bulged out of their sockets. A darkness and a peace took her into its blessed depth.

The shock of cold water hitting her brought her out of it and back into reality. One guard stood in front of her with an empty bucket tilted her way. This he put down on the floor as he was commanded to loosen the ropes binding her and help her to breathe. 'I do not want her dead, not yet. She is too valuable.'

This gave her hope, because now she had decided she didn't want to die. Not yet. She wanted to live to see the destruction of this brutal regime. To see the world free and to bring Jacques and Olivia up in the world that Pierre and the millions of others had given their lives for, and to share that world and her memories of Pierre with them.

After enduring she didn't know how many hours of sexual, mental and physical abuse by a relay of different interrogators – some who treated her with kindness, others who raped her body with theirs and with hot pokers, causing her excruciating and unendurable pain – she'd lapsed into a kind of coma. The lack of sleep had disorientated her, so that now she was in a state of delirium – a wonderful place where all she heard was *you are the breath in my body, the blood that flows through my veins, and the life that is my heart.*

When she next woke to the real world, she was lying on a hospital-type bed. A man she assumed was a doctor stood over her. Her mouth tasted of blood and felt soft... *My God, I have no teeth!* Why hadn't she felt them extracting them? Had that made them decide to stop the torture? She tried to speak, but couldn't. The doctor leaned over her. His smile held something she could trust.

The injection stung. The smile went away from her. A voice, sounding like those of singers when the gramophone needed winding up again, came to her, but she could not understand the words. The black hole took her again, but before it did she wondered if this was it. Had they injected her with a lethal substance? Would she never see her children again? If not, may God grant them happy lives on which she and Pierre could look down.

When she woke again, she was still in the hospital bed. There seemed a peace around her, but that was soon shattered by the harsh voice of the fat woman. 'Get up! Get out of that bed!'

Where am I?

'Get up. Here, put these clothes on. Ha, you are no longer beautiful. Being toothless does not suit you. I will not want to play with you. You are ugly. Dress. You are coming out to the fields to work with my women.'

Memory slapped every part of her. The horror of the torture crawled back into her, but none of

437

it matched the pain of seeing Pierre standing in front of her, his eyes conveying love – until the arm had raised. Her body drooped... A hand grabbed her arm.

'Get off that bed. Do as you are told. Do it now!'

Though weak beyond belief, Theresa slid off the bed. Her legs gave way beneath her. The woman shouted and the doctor appeared.

From what she understood of the conversation, conducted in German, the doctor protested at her being moved, saying that she hadn't eaten or been taken out of the bed for four days. *Four days? Is that why they are not interrogating me any more? Was the French–American attack successful? Is France liberated? It must be so. It must be that they know I no longer have any information that would be useful to them, so they are going to make me useful in other ways. Put me to work. France is free! I'm going to live!* The next part of the conversation she heard dispelled this fresh hope.

The fat woman laughed and said in English, no doubt for her benefit, 'Ha! You need time to get her well for what? Her execution? The commandant is only awaiting orders from Herr Hitler. She is one of five on his request. All of them dissident scum who have hindered our progress, murdered our soldiers, and sent intelligence that gave our enemy the upper hand. She is scum, I tell you, and she is going to die! What is the use of making her well?'

Also in English, the doctor said, 'If she dies before the order of execution, it will be on your head. I need two more days to get her fit for work. She is of no use to you how she is, as she cannot stand. Her internal injuries are healing, but still prone to infection.' At his command, two nurses came forward and lifted her back onto the bed. The female officer huffed, turned, and left the room.

There was something indefinable about this doctor. Tall and blond – a typical Aryan – his exterior was as if made of steel. Very little expression, apart from the smile – the strange smile she'd seen as he'd injected her. Somehow she thought he had his own agenda. At this moment she could only be grateful to him, and tried to tell him so. Still she could not talk. And with this knowledge came awareness of the pain in her mouth. Letting her tongue travel tentatively over her gums, she felt what could only be stitches. Then she remembered they had pulled all her teeth. Why couldn't she remember the pain of that? Putting her hand to her mouth, she felt how swollen it was. Her lips felt like balloons.

Ugly. Well, what would it matter?

Thirty-two

A Reunion

Patsy and Jacques

'Patsy, love, it's so good to have you home. By, lass, you've been through sommat – stuff that isn't easy to live with, I know that from experience. But you know, the best thing you can do is to talk to someone. I am here for you, but I might not be the right one. Only you will know who that is. The thing is to be sure you don't bottle it all up. I know you're a strong person, but it can eat away at you and cause bitterness and even make you ill if you don't have that outlet of sharing it and getting it out of yourself.'

'Thanks, Mam. I've already made a start. On the way home I told Ian everything that happened on the boat – not just the facts, as he knew them, but all the details and how I felt and everything. Besides what was going on in me head when I left the Leeds hospital to set off for London. He has another side to him, Mam. It's one he hasn't shown before, not to me anyway, but he helps me.'

'Ian? Look, love, take care when you deal with him. He ... well, I think he has a bit of a thing for you and I don't want him hurt. Try not to give him hope that he may have a chance with you.'

'I know. I'm not without feeling for him, I'm just a little confused at the moment. I need to get well. I have a lot to deal with. I can't believe me brother has turned up. It's amazing.'

'It is. But he is so nice, you'll love him. Ha, that's a daft thing to say! Of course you will, he's your brother, but he could have turned out to be someone horrible. Lizzie's reet taken with him, and him with her. Anyroad, the lass hasn't got up yet, so if you feel up to it, how about you go in to her and I'll bring in a pot of tea for you both, eh?'

'Hey, you, lazybones. It's nearly lunchtime and you're still stinking in bed!'

'Patsy. Oh, Patsy, I'm so glad to see yer.'

'And me you, love. Hey, there's no need to cry at the sight of me... Lizzie...?'

'I'm alright. I... Oh, Patsy, it's all been so awful. I can't get things out of me mind. I keep reliving Rita's scream and seeing you go overboard and...'

'I know, I'm the same. Mam's been saying that we need to talk to someone, but I don't think each other is a good idea. We're both too close to it with it involving us both. We're bound to have different feelings about different parts of it. We'll upset each other and make things worse for ourselves. I used to have Harri, but she's run off just when I need her most.'

'I don't think she had a choice in that. Love is powerful; it consumes yer thoughts and yer just want to be with the person.'

'Oh, listen to the voice that knows!'

'I – I do, actually. I have fallen in love.'

'Crikey, mate, I knew you had an attraction for

me brother, but...'

'It's more than that, I feel like we are two halves of a whole.'

'Does he feel the same?'

'I think so. He has said things. Oh, I don't know, I know he likes me and wants to take me out, but...'

'What's he like?'

Listening to Lizzie set up a worry in Patsy, about how Lizzie was, with her not being able to walk and how delicate and vulnerable she was physically as well as mentally. She feared for her. What if Jacques didn't feel the same? The hurt to Lizzie would be much more than, say, to Ian if she found she couldn't return his feelings. As it was, Lizzie might think it was her condition that had put Jacques off, and that would add to the burden she already carried on that sensitive subject.

Suddenly it hit home to Patsy that what she'd been through wasn't worse than what others had. Yes, she'd been abandoned as a baby and never felt she belonged to anyone, but it hadn't been all bad. She hadn't lived in fear like Lizzie had, or been so badly injured by someone who should love her, like Lizzie had. She hadn't grown up with violence, or lived amongst criminally minded people and been totally reliant on them for her needs. *Christ! I've wallowed in self-pity all me life. And I've let that eat me up and guide me actions! I've blamed other people for it... Harri, oh, Harri, I must have made your life a misery at times. And me mother! God, how could I have wanted to hurt her?*

'Patsy, you're crying!'

'I'll be alright. I'm sorry, Lizzie, I'm so sorry. I

caused all of it to happen. I was so bitter and twisted. I should never have gone to Rita.'

'Don't be, Patsy. It wasn't a good thing to do, but good has come from it. My life has changed for the better since yer came into it. I was like a prisoner... I'm sorry that they're dead, and for all that happened, but a big part of me wouldn't want them back. You've done more for me than you'll ever know.'

'A bit of an unconventional way of doing it! And although I wouldn't like to go through it all again, or put you through it, I'm glad of the outcome. And I'll take care of you, Lizzie. You'll always have a friend in me.'

She'd sat on the bed when she'd first come in, but now she lay down next to Lizzie and put her arm around her. 'We can get strong from this, Lizzie. We both have a lot of healing to do, but we can do it.'

'We can, Patsy. And you'll always have a friend in me too. I promise yer that.'

They lay a minute in silence, and they were still lying together when Sarah came in. 'Eeh, it's good you lasses have each other. Here's your tea. I'll leave you to it.'

'Mam, it's even more good that we have someone like you in our lives. You needn't have taken us in. Especially me. I'm sorry, I must have caused you a lot of heartache turning up how I did, and ... well, me silly obsession with Harri. That must have worried you at times. It was just that I'd never had anyone of me own before. Not related to me. I'm over it now. I'm on the mend. I know I'm not like me real dad, like I feared.'

443

'Eeh, Patsy, love. Come here.'

It felt good to be in the arms of this woman she would always call 'Mam'. When she met her own mother, she wouldn't call her that. She only had one mam, and it was Sarah. Sarah, who'd opened up her home to her despite who she was. Sarah who she'd paid back by causing concern with her actions and was still causing concern over her son. Coming out of her arms, Patsy said, 'Don't worry about Ian, Mam. I'll take care with him. I love him very much, I just don't know if it is the kind of love he wants from me. But I will take care of him, I promise.'

'Oh, Patsy, I'm so glad to see you come out the other side of whatever held you in that place where you were so bitter about everything. You'll be alright, lass. You're amongst folk who love and care for you. And you have others who are waiting and wanting to love you, if you can just let them.'

With this Sarah kissed her on the cheek. 'Now, just take it easy. You're not well yet. We have to build you up. Don't be asking too much of your-self all in one go.' She went to leave, but before she did she said, 'Are you alright, Lizzie, love? You had a big day yesterday.'

'I've never been more alright in me life, Sarah. And I add me thanks to those of Patsy's. Because between yer, you've saved me life.'

Sarah picked up the bottom of her pinny and wiped her eyes. 'Go on with the pair of you. You're making me blab now.'

When she'd left, Patsy said, 'Why don't we sit in the window to have our tea. Get you out of this bed, eh?'

'Yes, I feel I can get up now. It's boosted me with you coming.'

'What made you feel so down, love? Oh, I know you've enough on your shoulders to put up with, but...?'

'It ... well, it was what I read in yer mother's books. I haven't been able to sleep.'

'Oh?'

'I'll tell yer about it, but it's not going to be easy for you, though some of it will make you happy. Patsy, yer know Jacques is going to see his – your mother today, don't yer?'

'No, he's not as it happens. He gave me a say in the matter through Dad. Ian has rung Jacques this morning and told him that I'd like to meet him first, and then go from there. And I want to meet our grandmother. I want us, Jacques and me especially, to know one another before seeing our mother. I think it will be easier for her. If we are not united first, it may all go wrong. My mother may feel too much strain from so many people coming back into her life. She may feel like she is in the middle of us all and besides that, each one of us is going to provoke different feelings in her. If we are already a family we can help her better than if we don't know each other. Does that make sense?'

'It does. And it's a measure of how well yer are. I worried about you, Patsy. You didn't seem to think right. But what you've just said is very different to how yer were. I think you're going to be alright, and that's what matters to me.'

'I know. I've been in a dark place. I even ... well, I won't talk about that. I need to think of what I just did, and had planned on doing, as me hallucinating and nothing more. If I let meself think that I am capable of such actions, I'd go down the road of thinking I am like me dad again, and I am not like him.'

'No, you're not. You're good and kind and care about people. You've cared for me and me feelings ever since I met yer. And not in the way most people do, with pity for me condition, and that has meant a lot to me.'

A knock on the door stopped Patsy answering her. It opening and Ian saying from behind it, 'Can I come in?' gave her a glad feeling she didn't expect. But she told herself to stop being daft. *It's only Ian!*

'Jacques has just phoned. Hi, Lizzie, you're looking better.'

'Thanks, but what did Jacques say?'

'Nice to see you, too, lass...'

'Oh, I'm sorry, Ian, it is nice to see yer. I didn't mean...'

'Only teasing you.'

'Well, don't tease her, Ian. Put the poor girl out of her misery.'

'The call was more about you, Patsy. He said if you are up to it, he'd like to come round to meet you. That he can't wait any longer, and that he has told your grandmother you want to meet her and she would love to meet you, if you are ready. He said to say that neither of them are going in today to see your mother, but your grandmother would like to go to see her tomorrow as she is asking for her. And not to worry, your mother doesn't know about either of you being found as

446

yet, but your grandmother would like to tell her tomorrow. Though they both agree with what you have said, that you should all meet before she is told and show her that there is nothing more to worry about where you are all concerned.'

'Oh, that's great news. Ring him back and tell him yes. I am ready to meet him and ... and my grandmother. Oh, Ian, I can't believe it all!'

Ian came over to her. He went down on his haunches and took her hand. 'I know, love. But are you sure as you'll be alright, lass? Do you want me to be with you? I'll even come to your grandmother's if you'd like me to?'

For a moment she didn't know what to say. Part of her wanted to do this alone, but to have Ian supporting her would make it easier. She looked down into his face, reading the love and concern there, and said, 'Yes. I would like that.' His expression showed she had done the right thing. But, more than that, she knew she had.

'D-did Jacques mention me, Ian? Only we are supposed to be going for a drive later.'

'He did, Lizzie, love. He opened the conversation with you, asking how you were and did I think it right he should take you for a drive. Eeh, lass, he's got it bad for you, I can tell. Then at the end of his conversation he said, "Give Lizzie my love and tell her it might be a bit later, but we will go hunting for that restaurant."'

'What's that all about, hunting for a restaurant?'

Lizzie explained that she thought Jacques was worried about her being able to get into it, 'though he didn't say that. He just said he wanted it to be my choice.'

'Aye, you're reet there, Lizzie, that is what he was concerned over, which shows he's an alright kind of person, not embarrassing you. Anyroad, when he told me this, I was able to help him out. There's a new place opened. It's on the outskirts of Leeds and used to be an old farmhouse. It's a grand place. It's all on one level, and there's no steps to get into it. Anyroad, Dad has a surprise for you that will help you access most places.'

'Oh, Lizzie. I can't believe it, you and me brother... You jumped in there quick!'

None of them took her up on this other than to laugh at what she'd said, and this pleased Patsy, as it meant they weren't looking for a double meaning in her. They both believed she'd changed, and with these two already on her side she could succeed in doing so.

'Anyway, me lasses, if you would be kind enough to make your way out into the lounge, Dad is waiting with his surprise. Oh, and by the way, Patsy, I surprised him as well. I told him and Mam that I want to go to medical school.'

'Oh, Ian...'

'What? You sound like I've done the wrong thing. They were really happy about it. Dad couldn't get over it and Mam cried. I'm really glad I told them, so stop worrying.'

'No, it's not... Oh, I don't know. Look, I'm really glad. Dad'll soon get you sorted. It'll be great, you'll love it. You'll find it easy, I'll bet, just like Harri.'

He left at this, telling them to hurry up and get sorted.

'Patsy?'

'What?'

'You know what. Yer don't want Ian to go, do yer?'

'I didn't know that I didn't. But now it looks like he might, it feels like a light would go out for me. I can't explain it. Oh, I'm being daft. Come on. Let me help you... Oh, I know. You can manage. Well, knowing you can doesn't mean you always have to. I can get you a bowl for your wash while you get out what you want to wear. Though you haven't got much, have you? How about I fetch a few things down that I've finished with, then before this dinner date, I'll take you shopping. Though Ian will have to drive us as I'm not up to that yet. I'm still a bit shaky.'

'But, I haven't any money.'

'It'll be my treat. No buts! I'd love to treat you. I owe you. You've brought something into me life you can't imagine and I can't put a name to, but it made me see meself and me life in a different light – and that's helped me more than you can know. Besides, we all need a helping hand sometimes. I know I did when I came into this family. And what they gave me is something else I can't put me finger on. Maybe it's called love, unconditional and generous love, and I just didn't know how to recognize it or how to handle it.'

'Okay, thanks, Patsy. See, I told yer it was a good day when I met yer. It can't have been a bad one if I'm to get a new frock out of it.'

They both giggled at this, then Patsy said, 'While we get you ready will you tell me about what it is you've read?'

Patsy found that her body was trembling by the time Lizzie had told her of what her mother had been through and the death of Pierre. Lizzie was ready now, but neither of them made a move to leave the room.

'It's not all bad, Patsy, love. I don't know how yet, but yer mother did escape, and it must be nice for yer to know she and Pierre were planning a family life that included you, and that Pierre was going to take yer on as his own.'

'It is, Lizzie, love, but at the same time it sort of twists the knife. I wish I'd have known this. I would have found my mother sooner, and all of me family. It couldn't have been that difficult to do. Jacques did it.'

'Yes, but he had someone who knew who he was and who his father and mother were. You had no idea, so where would yer have started?'

'That's right, but after I did know... Oh, Lizzie, they say that hate is destructive. It nearly destroyed me and it stopped me from moving on.'

Ian called out from behind the closed door at that moment. 'I'm coming in, ready or not! We're all bursting out here to show Lizzie what Dad has got. Anyway, if you don't hurry, Jacques will be here and then it will be too late for Dad to have his moment. So hurry up. Do you hear me, Patsy?'

In a low voice she said, 'Olivia. I'm not Patsy, I'm Olivia.'

Lizzie didn't comment.

The new wheelchair had them all laughing and the women shedding tears, but it was with joy more than sadness. Richard had, through his many contacts, located a chair that a family had had made for their daughter. Sadly the girl had since died, but the family had said it would make them happy to think of the chair being used and helping someone else to get around as it had done their daughter.

Lizzie was like a child with a new toy, Patsy thought, as she watched her. The tears, always ready to flow, were trickling down her cheeks.

The slimline chair was light and had large wheels at the back that enabled Lizzie to push herself around. It glided with very little effort, even with Lizzie's weak pushes. It folded small enough to go into the boot of a car, and it was on crossed bars that could be fixed into a high or low position. Much the same as you could a deck chair, but these enabled the seat to be set as high as she would need to sit up at a table. The leather of the seat and back was the softest Patsy had ever felt.

It was Lizzie's happiness that was getting to her. It was lovely to see her smiling and the look of sheer joy on her face. But when Sarah said, 'Eeh, love, we'll all be able to take you for walks in that, no problem,' Lizzie's expression changed. It was only for a moment, but Patsy saw it and knew all of the others had too.

Richard, as usual, saved the day. 'That will be nice sometimes, but I have something else I am looking into, something that will allow Lizzie to come and go as she pleases. Have you seen or heard about a three-wheeler invalid car, Lizzie?'

'Yes. Ken ... me brother Ken, he was trying to get me one.'

'Well, did he know that the government supply

them? Yes, it's a fact. I've found out all about it. And I have asked for an application form to be sent here. Once that goes in, someone comes out to assess you and then, if that goes okay, you get your car. I don't think they are driven like a normal car. They have a two-stroke engine and there's a rudder that steers it. The accelerator and brake are attached to the rudder, so you do everything with your hands. Don't look so worried, we'll get the hang of it between us. It just means you'll have to manage with our help for now. But it won't be long before you're nipping down to the shops on your own.'

Lizzie's face was a picture of happiness. Patsy couldn't help herself but to go over to her and give her a hug. This prompted them all to do the same. And set her and Mam and Lizzie herself off crying again.

'Eeh, you lasses. You can turn the taps on!'

This from Ian, Patsy knew, was just to cover his own feelings and stop himself from shedding a tear. She smiled over at him. His smile back warmed her heart.

The door opened and David came in saying, 'What's going on here, then? You all look like you're up to sommat.' When they told him, he said, 'By, it's not as if it's a new tractor or owt. I don't know what all the fuss is about.' They doubled over with laughter.

David smiled at his own joke and went over to Lizzie. 'I'm glad for you, lass. We haven't had much time to get to know one another, but it's a busy time on the fields and we're a man down with this brother of mine finding more important things to do. Not that our Patsy isn't important, but by, he don't need much of an excuse to skive! But once we've it all sorted, we'll have a chat. I'm not ignoring you.'

With this he went into the kitchen.

'Well, that was some speech for David, love. You're honoured! Reet, let's get some order in here. Ian, will you help Dad to get Lizzie's old chair into the garage till she needs it next. You won't need it in the house, will you, love?'

'No, Sarah, I won't need it, and I can't see me wanting to get out of this one much at all. I could even take it out in the garden. Oh, it's lovely, Richard. Thank you. Thank you so much.'

The doorbell ringing stopped them all in their tracks.

'Oh, God, that'll be Jacques!'

'It's alright, Patsy, love.' Sarah came over to her as she said this, a worried expression on her face.

'I'm okay, Mam. It's just excitement, not fear. Ooh, I don't know what to do or how to act.'

Ian winked at her as he said, 'It'll come natural, love.' Then taking charge, he asked his dad to get David's help with the wheelchair, telling him, 'I've promised to stay with Patsy while she meets her brother. Come on, Patsy, love, you go into the front room and I'll bring Jacques in there to you. Alright, love?'

She could only nod and do as he said. Her heart raced, thumping against her ribs making it hard for her to breathe. Her brother ... she was going to meet her own brother!

Jacques didn't look anything like her, but then she knew that by how Lizzie had described him.

453

But as he came through the door it was as if she'd known him all her life instead of not knowing of his existence until a few weeks ago. He stood a moment looking at her, then as if someone had given them a cue, they went into each other's arms.

Swinging her around then leaning back from her he said, 'Gee, my own big sis! And a pretty one at that. Boy, am I going to make them jealous back home when I show you off!'

She laughed. 'And a handsome little brother for me! That's something I never dreamed of having.' He hugged her again, but this time he made her wince. 'Oh, I'm sorry, Patsy, I forgot. You've been hurt. I – I...' His eyes filled with concern. 'Lizzie told me. And I'm so sorry. Not just for hurting you just now, but that it ever happened.'

'It's okay. I'm getting better. Just a bit sore. And as for healing from the experience, I know it will take time, but such a lot of good things have happened since then that it doesn't feel like it will take long. By the way, this is Ian. He is Sarah's eldest son.'

She watched Jacques as he greeted Ian. He was every bit as handsome as Lizzie had said, and nice too. She already knew she loved him, but she would have liked to have seen just a little of herself in him – something that tied her to him and to their mother. It seemed uncanny that she should look totally like her father's side and have nothing of her mother in her.

'Why don't you two sit down and have a good chat, eh? I'll leave you to get to know each other. You've a lot to catch up on.'

'Thanks, Ian.' Again that smile. What was different about it? Ian had always smiled at her. Maybe she'd never properly taken any notice before. *What's the matter with me? It's just Ian. Ian, for Christ's sake!*

'Hum, so big sis is in love, eh?'

'No! I mean...'

'It's none of my business? Well, you have to get used to it. As your brother, I am going to want to be the first to know what you're up to.'

This made her laugh, and with it came a feeling that relaxed everything inside her. It was going to be so easy to have Jacques in her life. She just hoped it would be this easy with her mother and her grandmother.

Thirty-three

Theresa's Liberation, 1945

MY LIBERATION. Theresa had headed most new chapters in the book, and under this one she had added: AND MY DESOLATION.

This seemed so sad to Lizzie. At a time when most were rejoicing, the woman who had done so much and had risked her life to save countless others felt nothing but desolation. Lizzie almost didn't want to read about it, and hesitated in doing so. But if she was to complete this journey with Theresa, she had to. And she had to do it as soon as she could, as the time was approaching when the books should be given back to their rightful owner.

It had felt strange for Lizzie to know that Jacques was in the house – to have him just the other side of a wall and not to be able to go to him. But she had to give him and Patsy time together, and she hoped with all her heart that they bonded. Ian had said their first meeting had gone really well and they'd greeted each other as if they'd known one another all their lives. She was glad about that.

Getting back to her own room had proved an easy task, and now she was in the garden with her book. No one could have walked easier than she had manoeuvred her new chair. It gave her a new sense of freedom that she loved.

As she opened the book, she couldn't believe that she would soon be meeting Theresa, as surely she must with her being Patsy's mum. With this thought she began to read.

April 1945

Rumours were rife around the women's quarters. 'The Americans are coming' was the one that excited Theresa. And then she heard that the SS Commandant, Martin Gottfried Weiss, had run off.

Fear entered her at this. What would happen? Would the Germans panic and start to shoot them all? But no, there was a kind of calm. The guards were all still armed, but they weren't showing signs of panic, only nerves. Their eyes often darted towards the gate. Cigarette smoke billowed like clouds from wherever they gathered. Them gathering at all was something she hadn't seen in such numbers. Odd groups, yes, as they went off duty, but not those on duty.

Her own jailer, Frau Hitler as they had nicknamed her, had left days ago. Since then, she and the other women had done their best to keep a low profile, thinking their best chance of surviving what must be the last days of the camp's existence would be not to be noticed. This was something they were adept at, as they were always trying to avoid the lustful eyes of the guards. Rape was rife. It had happened to her a dozen times. Always from the back. The Germans didn't have any taste for looking into their victim's eyes or toothless mouths, and nor did they want to see the gaunt look of starvation. They only wanted relief of their animal instincts. She had stopped fighting them, dutifully washing herself as they directed and bending over the table. There was always a table in the room that they took her to. Resisting only ended in a beating, and none of the women's bodies could take that. She knew hers couldn't. But worse than that, they faced being shot if they fought or complained.

Why this hadn't happened to her anyway, she had no idea. Had they forgotten her? The last couple of months she hadn't been returned to her original cell, but had slept in the long dormitory. Beds were narrow openings in what looked like shelves along both walls. She'd become used to the grime and the thin mattress, but never the cold. Nor the moaning of other women as they endured excruciating pain from torture or, their worst

457

enemy, starvation. When they had been fed it was usually only a bowl of gruel. Some days they'd had nothing. She could pull the empty skin away from her bones.

No one had put them to work for the last couple of days. They had sat around in huddles, trying to keep warm. They were in one now, but one of them was missing. Of no one in particular she asked, 'Where's Betty? Has anyone seen her?'

No one answered her. At times the women only cared about their own survival. She understood this and had experienced these times herself.

Betty was one that often looked out for her, but she'd feared for her lately. Her cough had worsened, and there had been blood around her mouth this morning. Getting up, she made her way back to the dormitory. Keeping her back close to the walls of the hut and not making any sudden movements enabled her to get there unnoticed. 'Betty. Betty, love, are you in here?'

The silence closed in on her, shuddering its implications through her and causing her blood to chill. When she came up to Betty's bed, her worst fears were confirmed. Stroking the hair of Betty's corpse, she said, 'Rest in peace, love. You are free now. The freedom we are all hoping for wouldn't have been what you would have wanted.'

Betty had nothing to live for. All her family had gone, taken one by one on the walk that was a daily occurrence, when people were taken from their beds or working party and never seen again. Betty had collaborated, allowing any German to fuck her when and where they wanted to. Whether this had saved her there was no knowing, but, God, she hoped that her tormentors had caught the syphilis she was sure had killed Betty.

Gunfire had her standing stiff and still. *Have they arrived?* Telling herself to keep calm, she walked out of the shed to what looked like a carnival. Prisoners were everywhere waving the flags she knew some had been secretly making. They were on rooftops, up trees, and dancing around wherever there was a spare space.

More gunfire. Peeping around the corner, carnage met her eyes. Germans were being gunned down by American soldiers. They weren't fighting back, just dying – their bodies falling like skittles hit by a ball. Bile came into her throat as she saw some of the more able-bodied prisoners rush at the unarmed soldiers and begin to slay them with their bare hands, or slashing at them with shovels. Some had even got hold of the Germans' weapons and were helping the Americans to shoot them! God! This wasn't right! Yes, she felt like killing the soldiers herself, but they had laid down their arms. They had surrendered!

Turning her head away, she pressed her body even closer to the wall, but her legs wouldn't hold her. She slid to the ground. Tears wet her face. Her parched throat rasped with every sob that racked her body. Then the shooting stopped and the Americans began to round everybody up. 'Okay, we want y'all to settle down. Sit where you are and don't move.' The voice boomed through a megaphone, 'Y'are all safe now. Keep still and let us do our job. Once we have all the Germans in custody, we'll do everything we can for you.'

Machine-gun fire drowned him out. It went on

and on. Theresa covered her ears. Madness came to her in the shape of the end of the world. Bodies twisted and still, mouths gaping, eyes staring. She couldn't stand it. This thought triggered a scream that she had no control over. It started somewhere deep inside her. Her own ears rejected the awful sound as it came out of her mouth. Hands grabbing her arms and shaking her brought it to a stop, and in nothing more than a whisper, she said, '14609, Theresa Laura Crompton, Officer. Special Operations Executive.'

A woman's voice, low and incredulous, said, 'My God, I thought you were all dead. I'm a reporter. I've been following our soldiers as they advanced. Come with me. I'll take you to Brigadier General Henning Linden. He'll know what to do.'

As she walked across the compound and through the inner gate, the full horror of what had been happening hit her. Against what she knew to be the execution wall, hundreds of bodies of German soldiers were lying dead. The sound of a single shot took her eyes further along the heap of bodies. American soldiers were walking along the bodies and systematically shooting those that were dying.

The woman looked at her and shook her head. 'Best to forget what you see here. Come on.'

In the brigadier's office, they sat her down. When told who she was, the brigadier checked a list in front of him. 'Yes, ma'am, your name appears on here as "whereabouts unknown", suspected executed at Dachau. Well, how did you get lucky, ma'am?'

Lucky! 'Sir, I didn't get lucky.'

Now he'd noticed that she had no teeth. Now he looked at her emaciated body. He soon lowered his eyes. When he did look up, he stood and saluted her. 'Ma'am, the world owes you a debt of gratitude. From what I have glanced at here, just a fraction of what you have been accredited with, I am honoured to be in your presence. Are there any more SOE survivors here?'

'I do not know. I have kept a low profile, afraid every day that they would come and take me for execution. I did not make any enquiry or tell anybody who I was. I do know there is a wing of political prisoners and French Resistance, but I have not made contact.'

'Okay.' Turning to the woman reporter he said, 'Miss Garrivon, I know you're here to report, but there are some bathrooms through there. Would you give this lady a hand and maybe provide her with some clean clothes?' and then to her, 'Or would you like to eat first, ma'am?'

She shook her head. She had become used to the pain of starvation, but the matting of her hair and the filth of her body and the vile things that had been done to it? Never! She needed that bath.

'We'll get you out of here and back to France, ma'am. I'll contact the British Division there and get them to arrange to have you lifted out.'

Lifted out... Oh, thank God! I'm saved. For my children I am saved.

The September sun beamed down on her windscreen. Parking her car outside the farm gates, Theresa's heart pounded. None of the warmth of the day reached her. She shivered with cold. It all looked deserted!

Feeling stronger in body if not in her real self, after her month in hospital and three weeks in convalescence, her heart had sung at the prospect of travelling to France to pick up Jacques. She hadn't been home. Nor had she allowed her family to visit her. She couldn't face seeing how normal everything had remained for them, or having to look into the cowardly face of her brother. Because comparing him to Pierre and all of the men she had fought beside, that was what she now knew him to be: a coward.

Maybe one day things would change, but in the meantime she would find a place in Paris to rent and then she would hire someone to find Olivia and bring her to them. They wouldn't be the family that she and Pierre had planned, but Pierre would always be with them, looking over them and protecting them.

She would never be able to tell her family about Jacques, and her mother would never know about either of her children. The shame would kill her, and Pater would never forgive her for that. Not after the first time, not after he'd done all he could to protect her. Well, that's what he had told himself, but if the truth was known, he had needed to protect her mother more. Always, Mater had to be protected.

This thought didn't come with bitterness, because her mother was beautiful, kind and caring, but fragile – though sometimes it was clear to her that the fragility was a weapon. But at others, when Mater had cried or she'd caught her sitting in a window staring out, her hands in her lap, her face anxiously watching for Pater to come home, her whole body trembling, then her heart had gone out to her and she'd have done anything to make her happy and strong.

Taking her mind off these thoughts, she allowed her own anxiety to creep into her once more. Pierre had told his mother and father to stay put until they arrived. It had been one year and one month since they'd last seen them. Pierre had never contacted them after that. He hadn't been able to.

The moment she was freed she'd written to tell them she would come for them, and then again from her hospital bed, giving them the address there to write to, but they hadn't replied. Because of this she had travelled to Paris first, visiting their old home and making enquiries. She hadn't found them, and no one could help her as none of the people around had been there long enough to have even known them. Now, as she walked up the weed-infested, gravelled drive towards the small gate in the fence that enclosed the farmhouse, her mind begged, *Please, please, let them have waited!*

The gate creaked as it swung back on its hinges, and the window of the bedroom she and Pierre had slept in banged open and then shut and then opened again as the wind blew it on the one hinge that still held it to the window frame. The sound was like a death knell on all of her hopes. No one answered the door. Seeing in through the windows was almost impossible, as filth from many rainstorms had left them all but blanked out. Round the back of the house the door was open. Going inside confirmed what she already knew: the farm really was deserted. Running back round to her car she frantically drove to the village to make enquiries.

Monsieur Becke had passed away, they told her. His son, as far as they knew, had moved out, but they did not know where to. He had left before the old man died, probably causing his death by doing so, some said. The old man wasn't found for weeks after his death, and was only discovered because some boys had cycled up to the farm and had spotted starved, rotting animals and this had prompted an investigation.

Stopping at the shop as she went, Theresa bought a posy of flowers. Finding Monsieur Becke's grave, she placed them on it. As she did so, her knees gave way. Everything that was her folded in on itself. Tears streamed down her face, wetting her cheeks and her blouse and aching in her chest as it heaved with sobs that came from her weeping heart. And just as that emptied itself, so did her soul. *Help me, Pierre, help me.*

It seemed she'd slept for ever. The whitewashed walls around her and the distinct smell of hospital told her where she was, but in France? Or England?

'Theresa?'

Looking towards the voice, once so beloved to her, she wanted to spit into the face it belonged to.

'Don't look at me like that, old thing. I'm sorry. I – I, oh, Theresa, my darling, forgive me.'

She knew she never would. This brother of hers had taken so much from her. He wasn't all to blame, but his early games had led to awakening something in her she'd not been able to deny. He'd taken away her childhood. No, she hadn't to think like that, because she had given it up willingly to him and with him. Left to their own devices, they had invented a world, a grown-up world, fuelled first by his over-awareness of his sexuality and then by hers.

But she did not want to be reminded of that. She didn't want those thoughts to taint what she had had since. She wanted him to go away.

The scream started in her soul. His look of horror turned it to laughter. *Ha, even a scream scares him!* She laughed in the face of this coward. This spoiler of women; this monster! But even though he'd gone, she couldn't stop. A sharp pain in her thigh halted it to a giggle as she went into the kind of sleep that is almost oblivion.

When next she woke – really woke: woke to the world – and became aware of her surroundings, they told her the war had been over for five years. In the mirror a person looked out at her that wasn't her. Eyes that were drugged and dead stared back out of a creature she'd never met, but had no inclination to reject.

Terence was there. For a moment she'd thought he hadn't left when she'd screamed, but knew that wasn't right.

She no longer wanted him to leave – knew she hadn't for a long time.

'Darling, do you know who I am?'

'Of course. Why?'

It had shocked her to hear that he had visited every week for years, as had her mother and father, and she'd shown no signs of recognizing them. She thought she'd been with Pierre and Olivia and Jacques, but then at other times on missions, and at others the dark, dank cell had claimed her and she'd been through the torture all over again...

1963

This was where the structured writing ended. From here the notes were scrappy, and Lizzie imagined them to be written in times when Theresa's mind had cleared. From them she deduced that once well enough to leave the institution she had not been able to face living at home. She had bought a house in London.

The next thing she wrote was: 'Those bastards in that bloody hospital kept me drugged for all those years. It seems they thought me a danger to myself until my father had insisted they try the electric shock treatment he had read about. Once I showed signs of responding, they let me come round. Now it is too late to find my children. I am not well enough.'

As Lizzie read through the notes it appeared that Theresa's existence from then on had been between reality and madness. Her thoughts at times were harrowing. At others she had written about the loss of her father and her scant visits home. Then one entry told of Rita coming back into her life, of her loving her and how she remembered the phone having rung whilst Rita was there and how what was said had sent Theresa's life reeling backwards, landing her once more in an institution. Her brother, her darling Terence, as she put it, had taken his own life and Rita had gone and it was all Theresa's own fault. All of it.

A later entry told of how Theresa couldn't face her mother again, and how she felt her wickedness had destroyed everybody she'd ever loved. And that she deserved to rot in hell. But a bit after this she wrote that she knew that if she was ever to get out of the institution she'd have to cooperate, so she'd begun to allow her mother to visit.

Then another entry written after she was back home again read simply, 'Rita is back.' And then, 'Today, Rita loved me and I am happy.' And yet another: 'Today, Rita was drunk and demanded money. If I don't pay she will go to my mother. *Help me!*'

And the last entry, Theresa wrote: 'Nothing seems real. I am cocooned in a net that tangles my mind. The Germans are within miles of me. The radio said they are escaping over the wall... They are coming for me. I must build a barricade. Rita will help me...'

'Lizzie? Lizzie, darling.'

His voice and the endearment had her closing the now finished book. What happened to Theresa after that, she already knew. Poor Theresa. What a life. Thank God she was about to know the happiness she deserved.

'What has upset you, Lizzie, my love?'

Jacques was on his haunches beside her chair. His eyes looking up at her held concern, and all she ever wanted and needed: love.

She wiped her tears. 'I've just finished yer mother's book. You and Patsy should read it. It is a pity there isn't time before yer meet her. It would help yer to understand her and to know her.'

'I know. I wish I'd had that privilege. But a part of me wants her permission to read it.'

'Oh? Jacques, do yer think I have been wrong to read it? I only–'

'No. You didn't know who she was, and like you say, there was a connection with your aunt. And from what Patsy has told me, it has been the things that you have told her that have changed her thinking on our mom. So, I think you have done the right thing.'

'When yer see yer mother, treat her gently. Forget the bad things you've heard. She couldn't undo them, but she more than atoned for them.'

'I know. I've had my moments of anger towards her since I arrived here and met you all and heard such things, but if Patsy can put them to one side after all she has been through, then so can I. I will give my mother nothing but love and respect.'

'I'm so glad.'

'Lizzie, I'm not sure I can make our drive out. I'm so sorry. I need to take Patsy to meet our grandmother. If that goes well and I can leave them, I'll come straight back for you, but if they have difficulties with each other, then I'd feel obliged to stay with them.'

'I understand.' She didn't really. Inside she felt

a disappointment gnawing at her.

His smile undid this feeling as the promise in it told her there would be many more times. The feel of his kiss on her hand sealed that. She lifted his to her lips, giving him the same promise.

'Gee, Lizzie, you've gotten to me in a big way.'

This whisper brushed the hairs on her arms. 'And you have to me.'

'I'm acting out of character. Back home I'm known as a slowcoach where the girls are concerned. They'll never believe this. I can't believe it myself, but I can't deny it either. I love you, Lizzie.'

It came easy to her to tell him, 'I love you, too, Jacques. I love yer more than I thought it possible.'

'I want to kiss you.'

With this simple statement, the right of all lovers, the difficulties her condition posed opened up a barrier between them. A physical barrier. She wasn't like other girls: he couldn't just take her in his arms and pull her close to him and kiss her.

This thought had hardly settled in her when Jacques surprised her by standing up, releasing the brake on her chair and running with her to the bottom of the garden. There, out of sight of the house, he bent over her and hooked her arms around his neck and lifted her out. Holding her with her face next to his, he said, 'Oh, Lizzie, my Lizzie...'

The kiss was something she couldn't have imagined. No one had ever kissed her lips before, but even if they had, she knew it wouldn't have felt like this. This kiss fed her soul with love. It took her whole being from her and replaced it with his. It planted a joy inside her and gave her back the life she'd lost when just a child. She *was* somebody. Somebody *did* love her.

Thirty-four

Theresa's Fragility Destroys the Dream

When they alighted from the car, her grandmother took her hand and held it as they walked along the corridor. The gesture sealed the love Patsy had found for this beautiful woman whose heart could open to her and who had spent the first few minutes of them being together apologizing for the selfishness she'd displayed when her children were young. This, her grandmother had thought, had caused it all.

This explanation had given Patsy feelings of anger, but they had only lasted for a moment. Then in a gesture that showed a spontaneity she never knew she possessed, she'd taken her grandmother in her arms. And they had hugged. In that moment it came to her that no one was to blame. It was a set of circumstances that had happened, and none of it mattered. If she let it, it would spoil what really did matter and all that was to come in her future life.

Her grandmother hadn't known that her way of conducting herself to keep her husband close had affected her children. They had always seemed happy and carefree to her, and she hadn't ever

470

thought there would be decisions her husband would think he had to shield her from. The fact that what happened to Patsy was a consequence of this was what now tore at her grandmother's heart. Putting that to rest had been difficult, but in achieving it Patsy had opened a path for them, and she and Grandmama had run down it towards each other.

Now, after only spending a short time with her grandmother, it felt as though she had known her all her life. Today it felt to Patsy as if there was no 'other' life. Everything began from this moment that was upon her.

The plan was that as long as her mother coped with meeting her and Jacques, they could take her home for the afternoon. If that went well, there would be more visits until the time came when their mother could come home for good. Then, Grandmama had said that she would go back to York and leave the house to them. Patsy would move in with her mother. A live-in nurse would be engaged to take the strain of everyday care and companionship whilst Patsy was at work.

As for Jacques, he would return to America to continue his studies and to sort out some friends from Poland, whose story he'd told them about the evening before when he'd brought Lizzie back from their drive. It had been wonderful to see the happiness on Lizzie's face, and on Jacques's – and how their grandmother had taken to Lizzie.

As they had talked, the idea had come to Patsy that if Lizzie didn't go with Jacques to America this time, then she would ask her to come and live with her and her mother. Lizzie would be just the person to help her mother. She already loved her from reading her memoirs, and she knew everything there was to know about her.

Everything would work out. Harri and Greg had phoned when she'd arrived home. They were coming home in a couple of weeks. Poor Mam and Dad, they had gone into a frenzy of *What should we do about this* and *What should we do about that?* Harri and Greg wanted a 'do', and Mam and Dad needed it, so that they could give their daughter a proper send-off.

She and Ian had giggled at them, and then had gone for a walk to leave them to it and for her to tell Ian everything that had happened. The walk had ended in a kiss. She didn't know how, nor did she know how she felt about it. The kiss had been nice. It had been the best kiss she had ever had, and she hadn't wanted to come out of it. But something in her wasn't ready. Ian had respected that, and this had deepened the feeling she had for him. She'd left him with a promise. One day. One day...

Theresa had watched the group get out of the car from her window. She'd gone to wave, but had stopped herself when she'd seen her mother take hold of the young girl's hand. *I should be the one doing that. She is my Olivia!*

Her eyes fixed on the girl's red hair. *My God!* No. She couldn't do it. She couldn't live with that reminder every day. *Oh, but look at my Jacques. My Pierre. Jacques is Pierre reborn. Oh God, Pierre, where are you?*

Her hand groped for her pocket. Her fingers

gathered the pills together that she had been saving. Reaching for her glass of water, she swallowed them down. Mother would look after her children. She herself couldn't. They would know from the note that she loved them. Now she had seen them she would go to Pierre.

Picking up the note she sat down in a chair facing the door and reread it:

My darlings,

I am your mother and I am found wanting. I have not led all of my life in the way I should have and for that there is bound to be recriminations or answers sought by you.

I am frail; my mind goes to other places without me wanting it to and without me having control of it doing so. I know that you know my story, telling it was my need. In reading it, I hope you understand; I am a different person now.

My story isn't always good, but I tried to make amends for all the bad I had done. And I did that because of and for, you, Olivia – that is the name I have always called you and it is fitting that I use it here.

Because of a sin I committed, I was given you, my beautiful baby girl, only to have my soul ripped from me by having to give you up.

And for you, Jacques. Jacques, you sealed a love that was my whole reason for being. That love was my prop. My barrier to my past – your father – my Pierre. When I couldn't find you after the war ended, Jacques, it broke my heart and my spirit.

You are both the future, but that future cannot have me in it. Your constant need to ask questions will destroy us all. Go forward together knowing my last act

473

was an act of pure and unselfish love, the greatest legacy I can give to you – to leave you in peace.

Be happy, love one another and let the deep love I have for you be your bond. Make a life that is good. Let go of the past and go forward.

I love you with a love that is so intense it gives you your freedom from me, to soar high without the bondage of my past. What I will have done by the time you read this will also free my troubled spirit and let me go to my beloved Pierre. He will be waiting for me. His love will manifest once more.

Know that all that is me is nothing without him, and be happy for me. Look after your Grandmama, the three of you are very precious to me. I love you, Mama. xxx

When the door opened and they stood there smiling through their tears, Theresa knew a moment of regret. But she knew too that she had done the right thing, taken the right action for them. They would not think it for a long time, but she hoped they would come to know it.

'Mam!'

Mustn't give in to the tears. Go away! Tears weaken resolve. They went, and in their place a huge smile came from deep within her. It reached out to these children of hers.

'Mom. Oh, Mom, it is sure good to find you.'

Their different worlds showed in their voices. Patsy, she knew, had grown up in the East End of London and Jacques in America – so far apart, but now they had found each other. They came towards her, they had no reason to halt their tears – theirs wet their cheeks, but she was rewarded to see their smiles and the love they had for her glistened through them.

'Oh, Mam, everything'll be alright now. We have plans. We'll look after you.'

'It will, Mom. We are a family once more, Mom. We have so much to tell you.'

The love that shone from them both was a love she had yearned for – the love of her children. They were close now. She could smell the delicate perfume Patsy – her Olivia – wore, and feel the rough feel of Jacques's jacket. As their arms enclosed her, her world completed a circle and smoothed the jagged edges that had marred it.

The sleeping pills she had swallowed chose that moment to haze her brain; her head slumped onto her children. The note fluttered to the floor.

'Mom, are you alright, did we hurt you... Mom?'

'Mam ... Mam, what is it? Are you not well?'

'Theresa? Theresa, my darling daughter, what is wrong?'

The concerned faces of her mother and her children, the only loves she had in this world swam around her. She wanted to hold on to the image of them, but couldn't. A creeping, swirling darkness cloyed at her.

Where is the light? So many have spoken of the light? Pierre, where are you? No answer. No let up to the blackness. *Oh, but what is that in the distance? Yes, it is there. I can feel its warmth.*

A voice echoed from the light, *'Theresa, Tu es le souffle de mon corps. Le sang qui coule dans mes veines et la vie dans mon coeur.'*

'I hear you, Pierre.' As her spirit left her body in the arms of her children and floated towards the voice, she said his words over and over: 'You are the breath in my body. The blood that courses through my veins and the life inside my heart.' To this she added, 'We will be together for eternity...'

As his mother's body slumped back into the chair, shock held Jacques and Patsy silent, only Grandmama could be heard, gently sobbing, 'Theresa, my baby, no ... no...'

Bending, Jacques picked up the note. Taking a deep breath he read it out loud. When he'd finished he looked at Patsy. Tears matching his own ran down her cheeks. Her distress creased her face, but she nodded and a little quivering smile played around her lips. He nodded back, and he knew, the understanding he had in him was in Patsy and they would do as their mother had asked. They would leave her to eternal peace with her Pierre and they would go forward in life, united as brother and sister.

Acknowledgements

Heartfelt thanks to my children, Christine, Julie, Rachel and James, for their unstinting love and support. They are always there for me, as are my wonderful grandchildren and great-grandchildren and 'Olley' and 'Wood' family. I could not have completed this journey without you all.

To those who have helped me along the way, editing, proofreading and book-cover designing during my self-publishing days, thank you, especially Rebecca Keys, Julie Hitchin, Patrick Fox, Stan Livingstone and Zoe Rigley, besides many more too numerous to mention. I hope you know how grateful I am to you all.

Thanks, too, to all at Pan Macmillan, especially my lovely editor, Louise Buckley, to whom I owe so much. Her faith in me and her guidance has made all of this possible.

Grateful thanks, also, to my agent Judith Murdoch. To have you by my side has helped me tremendously. As I stepped into an unknown world, you eased the way for me – thank you.

Finally, no author can be successful without the most special people of all – readers. I am blessed to have a community of wonderful followers on my Facebook page, 'Books by Mary Wood', who support and encourage me every step of the way – they have been on my journey with me and I thank them from the bottom of my heart.

The publishers hope that this book has given you enjoyable reading. Large Print Books are especially designed to be as easy to see and hold as possible. If you wish a complete list of our books please ask at your local library or write directly to:

Magna Large Print Books
Magna House, Long Preston,
Skipton, North Yorkshire.
BD23 4ND

This Large Print Book for the partially sighted, who cannot read normal print, is published under the auspices of

THE ULVERSCROFT FOUNDATION